THE TIGER'S FURY

THE TIGER'S FURY

JOSEPH P. CODY

A Thriller

Autotech Industries

St. Paul, Minnesota

This is a work of fiction. Any resemblance to persons living or dead is purely coincidental. Names, characters, places and events, except where noted, are products of the author's imagination and are fictional. The views expressed herein are solely those of the author and do not necessarily represent the position of Autotech Industries.

The author wishes to thank members of the National Guard for their help in answering his many questions about M1 tanks. Any errors in describing the tanks, or their use, are entirely the author's.

Copyright © 2006 by Joseph P. Cody

This book is written, printed, and bound in the United States of America

First edition: December 2006

ISBN-13: 978-0-9791167-2-8
ISBN-10: 0-9791167-2-4

A Publication of:

Autotech Industries
688 – 11th Avenue NW
St. Paul, Minnesota 55112

Autotech Industries is a publisher; it does not sell books. This and other books by Joseph P. Cody may be ordered from Amazon.com or any book store.

To Andy . . . thanks for being a friend

— 1 —

Oklahoma

Ed Breckon was jarred out of his concentration by a deep rumbling. His first thought was to curse his misfortune for what seemed to be the complaint of a tire going flat on his rental car. He took his hands off the steering wheel briefly to see if the car would pull to one side, only to discover that the car handled perfectly even as the sound increased to a pulsing throb he could feel deep in his chest. The appearance of a great gray ghost moving into his view in the upper right of the windshield snapped his mind into the correct space-time continuum. The miles west along Highway 62 had slipped by more quickly than he realized, and he was approaching Altus, Oklahoma. The "ghost" was a mighty C-5B global transport that screamed and growled as it passed over the highway in front of Breckon. It seemed to be howling in indignation, straining at the bonds of gravity, as it tore the atmosphere on its climb into the cloudless June sky.

Altus Air Force Base lay beyond the fence that ran parallel to the north side of the highway. Having flown out of Minneapolis the evening before, Breckon had arrived in Oklahoma City late and spent a short night there. That morning he made the two-hour drive from Oklahoma City. Watching the aircraft disappear in the distance, he remembered what a thrill it had been to see and hear those beasts take off and land during his first visit to the base. However, he would've happily forgone the sight today if he had been spared this trip. There was nothing about it he liked.

Breckon slowed as he entered the city of Altus which, though in a farming area, was primarily a military town. He passed the static display of the B-47 bomber mounted on concrete pylons making a pretense of flying up into the sky, its actual flying days long past. At the center of town, he turned north on Main Street and proceeded a dozen blocks to Falcon Road, where he turned and headed east a couple of miles to the main gate of the base. He knew there was a shorter route, but took the route he knew. In his haste to leave home, he had forgotten his maps of the area.

The red brick guardhouse at the entrance to the base formed an island in the middle of the road between the in-bound and out-bound traffic lanes. As Breckon stopped and lowered his window, the uniformed guard stepped out of the building. Breckon said, "Edmund Breckon to see Mr. Kester at the C-17 Corrosion Control Facility."

"Oh, yes, Mr. Breckon, they're expecting you. Just a moment." The guard disappeared into the guardhouse, returning a few moments later. "They pre-registered you. Here's your badge to be worn visibly on you shirt at all times, and this is the sticker for your car. Do you know where to go?"

"Yes, sir, I do," Breckon said with a bit of an edge to his voice. With a crisp wave of his hand, the MP motioned Breckon to proceed.

Breckon was an electrical engineer, though he was equally at home working as a mechanical engineer. In his mid-twenties, he had a solid build, and exercised to keep trim. He stood six feet even, one-eighty pounds, with black hair, blue eyes, and well-balanced facial features, except for a square jaw. Six months earlier Breckon had finished supervising the installation and start-up of the three tele-platforms in the hangar called the C-17 Corrosion Control Facility. The tele-platforms were used to suspend and maneuver an operator and his equipment around C-17 and C-5 global transports to wash them. Periodic washing of the skin and control surfaces with the proper solvents reduced corrosion and increased the time between overhauls of the aircraft. The day before, TAC Corp., where Breckon worked, had received an urgent call from Altus that something was seriously wrong with the controls of one of the tele-platforms TAC had supplied.

It had looked like a beautiful summer weekend in Minnesota, and Breckon had made plans to enjoy it outside. Then came the call. Because he was single, it seemed, he always got picked for jobs like this. There were certainly other qualified engineers. Everybody always had such good excuses. "I'm going to a wedding." "I've got plans for this or that."

Ten minutes later Breckon arrived at his destination after having encountered the frustrating maze of streets on the base. He parked his car on the west side of the hangar as he had done before. The runways and tarmacs ran parallel to the east side. The size of these buildings always left him somewhat awed. However, those were some big toys the Air Force used to haul cargo and troops around the world. They had facilities to care for and pamper the big transports too. Breckon heard a heavy roar as another C-5B thundered down the runway. The ground trembled.

Besides being a tough job to check out the machinery, the problem had occurred on a weekend. His mind returned to the persistent refrain: Why was it always him? He had plans, too. George Ratling, his boss, had called him into his office and said, "You go." He should have said no. It was time for someone else to take a turn at the rotten duty. However, he hadn't, so here he was. Breckon resolved for the hundredth time that things were going to change.

Breckon removed his backpack with laptop, test equipment, drawings, and manuals from the trunk of the car and went into the building. As he walked down the hall toward Bert Kester's office, he heard voices drifting out of Kester's open door. He knocked on the doorframe and entered.

"Hi, Bert, what's this I hear about a runaway tele-platform?" Breckon asked with a hint of annoyance in his voice. Kester looked up. He was average in height, fifty, with a dark complexion. He had one of those faces where the skin seemed to hang loose, making him look tired, even a little depressed most of the time.

"Hey, Ed, how's it going?" This was Kester's standard greeting, something he said to absolutely everyone he met, inserting the shortest version of the person's name he could. Kester, seated behind a desk with one of his feet propped up on it, had been chatting with two other men sitting on chairs in front of the desk. Ray Aldrich, in his late forties and fighting an expanding waistline, occupied one chair. Ron Gooder sat in the other chair. Gooder, in his late twenties and of slender build, had sandy hair that hung in his eyes at times, causing him to toss it back with quick swipes of his hand. Breckon had worked with all three men during the installation.

"Here, take a load off," Kester said as he dropped his foot from the desk and lifted a disorderly pile of papers from a nearby chair. Laying the papers on another pile, making a precarious mound, he pushed the chair in Breckon's direction with his foot.

"Yeah, for a few seconds we had some scared operators out there. That platform seemed to get a life of its own. Talking to them afterward, I found that the controls have been acting up lately."

"Acting up how?" Breckon asked.

"When the operator pushed the button to stop the motion of the bridge beam traveling north, it didn't stop. Even when the operator pushed the emergency stop button, it didn't stop. After a few seconds, it finally stopped by itself. That's an intolerable situation with a plane in the hangar. Another couple of feet, and it would've crushed the tail."

"Any other clues or information?" Breckon was hoping to figure out the problem quickly and be on his way.

"Well, a couple of times when the start button was pushed, it didn't move. Then, there were times when commanded to stop it stopped, but not right away. It went another six inches or so. These incidents weren't mentioned until yesterday when it went several feet before it stopped."

Breckon was getting a picture of the problem. "Let's take a look at the ailing platform and get to the bottom of its problem. Did you get the man-lift I asked for?"

"Should be here at noon. That okay?"

"Guess it'll have to be. There are several things to check before I'll need the lift anyway."

"Yeah, and we've been running behind schedule, so we need this thing fixed fast!" Kester appeared to have a laid-back attitude from the untidy state of his office, and even his manor of speaking seemed to portray this. However, Breckon knew he could be a demanding man under pressure.

As they walked into the big hangar, the humidity and smell took Breckon by surprise. Washing airplanes all day meant spraying a lot of water, and the solvent they used had a funny, sweet-sour smell. When he finished the commissioning, he had left before they started washing airplanes. Also, it had been winter when he had installed the machines. He could imagine how hot it would be up on the man-lift today.

The operator's platform of the tele-platform attached to a telescoping mast for vertical movement. The mast in turn attached to a trolley that rode on a bridge to give the fore and aft movement. The bridge was constructed of heavy beams that spanned part of the hangar. End trucks attached to both ends of the bridge and ran on rails suspended from the underside of the roof trusses. There were a total of three. One tele-platform was on either side for the forward part of the fuselage and wings. The third one, the one with the problem, was used to wash the rear fuselage and the tail surfaces.

To Breckon, the problem sounded like a malfunctioning switch at the operator's station, but the emergency stop should have overridden that. This could be easy or hard to solve. As Breckon had learned in the past, luck would play a big part. He set to work and, after the first hour and a half, had eliminated the obvious stuff like faulty switches. Intermittent problems were the worst. They appeared one time, caused all sorts of trouble, and then disappeared, only to appear again when least expected.

As Breckon worked, the man-lift arrived. "Dump it off anyplace," said Aldrich. "We'll call you when we're finished with it."

The lift was on a tipping bed truck, and the driver tipped the bed and drove it off.

"Hey, let's get some food." Gooder said when the delivery truck had gone. "If we have to work on Saturday, at least we should eat. Maybe if we get Bert to come along the 'gommn't' will pay."

It took awhile to get Kester off the phone, and when they got to the restaurant the service was bad. This was all irritating Breckon. He wanted to get the job done and return home. When they finally got back to the base, it was two o'clock and fifty degrees hotter in the hangar. He managed to get the large hangar door open to circulate some air, but even then, it was still hot enough to fry a man's brains.

Breckon said, "Ray, do you still have those radios? They'll save a lot of hollering."

"Yeah, they're in the office, I'll get 'em."

Aldrich returned a few minutes latter with some well-used hand-held radios. He handed one to Breckon. "The transmit button is a little slow sometimes, so you have to press it harder than normal, but they carry good."

Breckon pressed the transmit key extra hard and said, "Testing one, two," nodded in approval and headed for the man-lift. There he put down his tools and instruments as he put on a harness of web straps that looked much like a parachute harness. This was his fall arrester.

The main electrical enclosure for the malfunctioning tele-platform was welded to the north side of the bridge. It was out in the open for easy serviceability by means of a man-lift. The trolley supporting the mast had been moved all the way to the end of the bridge to get it out of the way. The two parallel beams of the bridge were each five feet high with flanges top and bottom. Between the two beams sat the drive motor and gearbox that moved the bridge. The trolley supporting the telescoping mast ran between the beams also.

The man-lift, a four-wheeled contraption six feet wide and eight feet long, had a bucket on the end of a jointed boom. With the controls inside the bucket, the operator could drive it around on the floor as well as lift it to the height that he needed.

Breckon climbed into the bucket, maneuvered the man-lift to the correct place on the hangar floor under the electrical enclosure on the bridge, and lifted himself the eighty feet to the bridge. After minor ad-justments of his position, he was a little to the east of the electrical panel attached to the bridge beam. He secured the clip on the lanyard of his fall arrester to an eye welded to the bridge for that purpose. He frowned as he saw once again that the eye had been welded much too far from the en-closure. During installation, he had intended to have it moved, but in the rush to meet the start-up schedule, it had been overlooked.

Though this made things uncomfortable, he still used his fall arrester. If he fell from this height, it was good-bye Breckon. When he started working for TAC, he made a deal with himself that he would always use it. That some guys wouldn't use them seemed nuts to him.

Normally, when the handle of an electrical panel door was turned to open it, power to the panel was disconnected for safety. Breckon used a large screwdriver to turn a recessed screw in the door handle, bypassing the interlock mechanism. This procedure was used so electrically com-petent people could open the panel for troubleshooting without inter-rupting the operation of the machinery controlled by the panel.

Breckon opened the door of the enclosure, which hinged on the right. The sweat was starting to drip off him already. This sort of rubbish was going to stop! What did they say about this job, the three D's—dull, dirty, and dangerous? He flipped the switch, and the fluorescent light inside the box blinked on. He began a quick visual once over of the inte-rior of the panel. To anyone not proficient in electrical wiring and control systems, it was a maze of wires, circuit breakers, contactors, and assorted electrical components. To Breckon, it was like reading a newspaper. He assumed the problem had to be with the control components in the motor starting circuit. He pulled two relays out of their sockets and reinserted them to make sure the pins made good electrical contact. He tugged on all of the wires to be sure they were tight under the screw terminals. He flipped off and then on each circuit breaker in turn to be sure it operated properly, and listened for the characteristic snap from each.

Then he noticed something odd. Near the top of the panel was a line reactor. Made from an iron core with copper wire wound around it, this was used to stop voltage spikes made when starting contactors connected power to motors. Unabated, these spikes disrupted sensitive electrical devices like phone systems and personal computers. This particular re-actor had been coated with an epoxy-type insulating material. But the coating had obviously not been mixed or applied correctly because it was dripping off.

"Hey, Ray," he said into his radio, being careful to press the transmit key with extra force.

"Yeah. What ya got?" came back in Breckon's radio. Aldrich was sitting at the central control panel at floor level across the hangar from Breckon. From that location, all three tele-platforms could be maneuvered as needed without having anyone on the platforms.

"There seems to be a gooey coating dripping off a line reactor. Has anybody been messing around in this enclosure with solvents or something?"

"As far as I know it hasn't been opened since the installation. You were probably the last one to be in there."

"Okay that." Breckon raised the bucket so he could get closer to the line reactor. He touched a drop of the gooey stuff. It was really sticky. As a kid, Breckon had built model airplanes and used two-part epoxy a lot. He knew what happened when the two parts weren't mixed in the right proportions—they did not cure and remained sticky.

He noticed that the defective epoxy material had been dripping onto the contactor that operated the bridge motor, located immediately beneath it. It hit him that, with the start of hot weather, this partially cured coating material on the reactor had started to run and drip into the contactor used to drive the bridge to the north side of the hangar. That's what was causing the intermittent problem. He was pleased that he had identified it so quickly.

Contactors, special relays that used small electrical control signals, connected large amounts of electrical power to devices like motors. Their moving iron core was magnetically pulled into the stationary iron block surrounding it. The motion was only a quarter inch, but it closed the contacts and sent power to the motor's windings. This was a reversing contactor. It had two cores and sets of contacts, one for each direction of rotation of the motor.

A chill suddenly went through Breckon in spite of the heat. He realized that if the bridge were started in the northerly direction, it would probably not stop when ordered and would push over the man-lift. Before coming up, he should have had a strategy talk with Aldrich to decide what he could and could not do with the man-lift next to the bridge. Because of the late lunch, he had been in a hurry to get the job done and had not planned properly. There was apparently a lot more goo in the contactor now than earlier in the day. The operation of the tele-platform in the morning had heated up the interior of the enclosure. During the long lunch break, it had gotten hotter still. Now it was all messed up, and he was in danger.

Pressing the transmit key on the radio, he said, "Don't push the button for 'bridge north'!" But, in his sudden concern about his vulnerability, he failed to press extra hard on the transmit button.

Aldrich heard, " . . . t push the button for 'bridge north'" and assumed the " . . . t" was a little static.

"Roger, bridge north," he replied.

In alarm, Breckon saw the contactor pull in after a hesitation, and the bridge started moving. "No!" Breckon bellowed so loudly that Aldrich heard it even though Breckon had not used the radio. "Stop! Stop! All stop!" Pigeons, startled by his shouts, flew up from the wall toward which the bridge was headed.

Breckon heard the snap as Aldrich slapped his hand on the emergency stop button. Nothing happened. Breckon's fears were instantly realized. The contactor had pulled in and had stuck there. The bridge continued to move and was already pushing the man-lift over. He grabbed the lanyard of his fall arrester near where it was clipped onto the bridge beam. Quickly he pulled himself up onto the beam, putting his feet on the lower flange as the man-lift toppled over and crashed to the floor in twisted wreckage. More pigeons flew. Frantically Breckon lunged for the panel disconnect lever, but it was too far away. As he reached, one foot slipped off the beam's lower flange. This unbalanced him. He spun half around, and the second foot came off. Now he hung with his chest at the height of the lower flange. Scraping the skin off every limb, he managed to pull himself up so he was crouching on the lower flange of the bridge beam, lanyard over his shoulder, facing the wall.

Breckon was a foot taller than the height of the bridge beam. As he started to straighten up, he saw a crossbeam from the roof trusses pass over him. He had a new problem. It had been a real engineering nightmare meeting the full-travel envelope of this particular tele-platform. Since the platform had to pass over the tail of a C-5B, the bridge had been placed as high as possible, meaning that the top of the bridge passed only a few inches beneath the roof trusses. If he tried to stand up or get on top of the bridge, he would be cut in half.

He looked at the north wall. A three-inch pipe ran horizontally along the wall at knee level as he now stood. Even if he managed to heave himself up and lay on it at the last minute, there still wouldn't be room for him. The tele-platform was headed to the hard stops. At that point, Breckon would be reduced to a few inches thick.

To jump and let the fall arrester support him was not a good bet as he had just seen. He wouldn't clear the bottom flange on which he was standing, so he'd be crushed as the bridge hit the end of travel. He looked frantically at the wall bearing down on him.

He could see he was going to die. He thought of how someone would have to tell his mother that he had been killed in a freak accident. He said in his mind, "Well, God, here I come. Didn't think it would be so soon." A dozen things came to mind that he had intended to do but, for one reason or another, had not, and now never would. He had regrets. Maybe this was his life flashing before him. He saw that fateful, final accounting coming, but . . . he wasn't dead yet.

His mind raced. He considered and discarded possibilities. Nothing would work. Suddenly, hardly aware of what he was doing, he slipped into a state where calculating stopped and intuition took over. No solution was perfect, but several merged until a possibility became apparent. If he were five feet further to the right, there was a place where the inner corrugated metal skin of the wall and the insulation had been removed. If he could lie down on his side on the top of the pipe at that place, he might fit between the bridge beam and the outer skin of the wall. But to get into that space, he would have to detach his fall arrester at the last instant. He would have at most two seconds after he detached the lanyard before the bridge beam closed the remaining few feet to the wall.

If he made it into the cavity in the wall, the space still wouldn't be wide enough for him to lie without falling off, the bridge itself would have to keep him in place. If the bridge were to reverse, he would fall to the floor, careening off pipes and other protrusions on the way.

At the right moment, he grabbed the lanyard, pulling himself up close to the web of the bridge beam while keeping his head bent down, and unsnapped the lanyard of his fall arrester. He lunged out and put his hands on the pipe with his feet still on the bottom flange of the moving bridge beam. He shuffled to his right and lunged onto the pipe on his left side. The large bridge beam closed in on him like a wall, and the building shuddered as the massive tele-platform hit the hard stops. The noise in the constrained space hurt his ears, and a foul-smelling dust threatened to gag him with every breath.

A sharp pain shot through his left leg. He had not gotten that leg up in time. It was pinched between the vertical web of the bridge and the pipe. He cried out in pain.

"Ed!" Aldrich cried in anguish, thinking Breckon had been crushed.

The thermal overloads in the motor contactor weren't releasing as the stalled motor continued to growl. The gooey material still held the contactor and fed live power to the motor regardless of the action of the control circuit. It occurred to Breckon that during assembly, some dip in the electrical shop probably had not had the right overloads and put in some rated for a larger motor. Whatever the reason, Breckon was afraid of the motor catching fire.

"Don't reverse the bridge!" Breckon shouted. "Don't reverse it."

Aldrich shouted back. "No reverse. Got it!"

"Hit the main breakers, now!" Breckon yelled. After a moment he heard a loud *whomp*! The motor went quiet, and the brake set. After the echoes died away, the hangar was very still, in a sort of twilight as most of the lights had also gone out. Summoned by the shock that shook the entire building, others began to appear in the bay.

Immediately Aldrich yelled up from under the bridge again. "How are you? Are you hurt? Can you live where you are?"

Breckon said, "I can breathe. My ankle or foot . . . maybe it's broken or crushed. I don't know. My leg's numb. I guess the rest of me's okay for now. Ray, listen, there's only one way to get me out of this alive without dropping me to my death." Breckon's voice had started to rasp. He was trying not to panic, as he fought claustrophobia. He felt he was in a heavy, steel coffin. And it was hot. He was drenched in sweat, and the air stank. "Get some ladders. No . . . call a fire truck. They have long ladders. Find . . . find a cutting torch with . . . hoses long enough to reach up on the bridge. Can you hear that?" He could hardly talk.

"Ron's calling a fire truck, and two other guys are getting a torch."

"Get a pipe wrench. Hold the input shaft to the gear box from turning while you burn off the coupling between the motor and the gear box." He was panting, and his chest could not expand enough to breathe deeply. "Ow," he moaned, "my foot really hurts! Don't try to dismantle the motor brake . . . takes too long. You hear that?"

"Yes, Ed. Slow down. We'll get ya out. Don't panic."

"Be careful backing off the bridge. I'll slip out . . . fall. I had to detach my fall arrester."

"Yeah, Ed, okay. You sure you're not hurt somewhere else?"

"Don't know. My foot's killing me." And what was that terrible smell? He suddenly realized his head was resting on a pile of pigeon droppings. "Know what else?" Breckon rasped.

"No, what?" Aldrich's voice was strained.

"Pigeon poop stinks!"

He heard Aldrich chuckle. "Yeah, hang in there, buddy. We'll have you out in no time."

This is it! This is it! Breckon bellowed to himself. When he got home, *if* he got home, the resume was going out. He'd call that headhunter who had contacted him several times. He liked his life nice and regular. People often told him to get out and have some excitement. This was a tad too much.

The way his foot throbbed, he thought he might be bleeding to death. Sweat ran into his eyes. He couldn't shut out the thought that he was in a burning, hot, steel oven. He fought the urge to go berserk.

Then Breckon could hear the harsh honking of the fire engine. The hangar vibrated as the huge machine rolled in. That's one serious diesel, Breckon thought. He could smell the acrid fumes. In minutes, someone was up on the bridge. The beam shook slightly, and Breckon could hear two men talking.

"Here's how we'll do this. First. . . ."

"Wait a minute," Aldrich shouted. "The guy you're rescuing designed these tele-platforms. He knows every bolt. Before you do something you'll regret . . . he'll regret . . . you'd better talk to him. Ed, can you hear me?"

"Yeah, I heard ya. Careful backing this thing off," Breckon said hoarsely and as loudly as he could. "I don't want some numb nuts dropping me to my death. Do as I say!"

"Don't worry," said the first man. "Here's the guy with the cutting torch. Let's get it up there."

"Back off the bridge four . . . five inches by turning the input shaft to the gear box with the pipe wrench. I'll try to get my hand on my lanyard. Then pass a line down to me, and maybe I'll be able to connect to it . . . my foot really hurts. . . ." Breckon's voice trailed off.

Breckon could feel himself drifting into unconsciousness. He fought it but to no avail. He was next aware of being in a tunnel, but he was encouraged when he saw a light ahead. He was walking toward it with discouragingly slow progress. Now, what's this? Water started dripping on him from the roof of the tunnel as the light neared. Then the light went out, and it hit him what was happening. Someone was pouring water between the bridge beam and the wall to revive him. The mumbling in the distance came closer and became more coherent.

"Can you hear me? Answer me. Breckon, come on. We can't help you, if you can't help us."

"Okay, okay," Breckon replied, weakly at first. He swallowed and struggled for a full breath. "Stop nagging. Where's that rope?" Breckon could hear himself talking but wasn't sure others could, even though the noise of his voice was loud in his ears. Everything was spinning. His thoughts were disjointed.

"I hate this pigeon. . . . What's taking the rope so long? Now what's crawling on me?" He felt something sliding on his neck like a snake. He could barely get his right hand up to his neck and tried to brush it off, but it seemed to be piling up. He clawed at it and felt it tug back. Thirst was suddenly over-powering him. "Where's the water I asked for? Can't anybody get anything . . . ?"

"Ed! That's the rope. The rope! Do you understand?" someone called from above him.

Breckon looked around. He was on a long foot bridge with mist around it. There was the light ahead of him again, closer this time. He wondered why it attracted him so strongly. Heading toward it, he felt powerless to do otherwise. This time he was intent on getting to it, but then he felt the water again. Suddenly his thrust overpowered his yearning for the light. He turned his head and tried to get some water in his mouth. A few drops were all he managed. Mostly it went in his eyes. He coughed.

"Ed! The rope! Can you grab the rope?"

"Stop yelling. I'm not deaf! Yeah, I got the rope."

"Find the end. Can you find the end?"

"No! Pour down more water. I keep passing out. I'm dying of the heat." Breckon could hear voices in the distance, and he could feel the bridge beam shake. Something was going on. Then it came, torrents of water, splashing and falling in rivers. It felt cold at first, but it revived him. Breckon even managed to get a little into his mouth. Dirty and foul tasting though it was, it was great. He was soaked. Then the fire hose was turned off. It was steamy but definitely cooler in his steel chamber.

A voice from above called, "That better? Are you with us now? Find the clip on the end of the rope."

"Yeah, that helped. Rope? Yeah, here. Pull it up slowly." Breckon felt it slip through his hand as it was pulled up. "Stop! I've got the end."

"Try to snap the clip on any part of the web harness of your fall arrester. Can you do that?"

Breckon moved the little he could but it was not enough. "No. Back off the bridge a few inches, but slowly!"

After thirty seconds, which seemed much longer, Breckon felt the pressure on his pinched leg release as the huge beam moved away. The throbbing stepped up a notch or two. One inch, two inches, and still more. "Stop!" Breckon could feel himself slipping off the pipe. The water had made the pigeon droppings slippery, and Breckon couldn't help shifting until his left side was wedged in the opening between the bridge beam and the pipe. He tried to roll a little onto his back and get his left arm out from under him. Failing this, he pressed his right knee against the bridge beam to hold himself back. "Now, a few more inches. Slowly!" The beam started to move again. He slipped further into the opening. "Stop!"

Now he could maneuver his right arm and hand. He struggled to attach the clip to the strap around his waist. With each movement, he could feel himself slipping further into the gap. Finally, it seemed he had it. "Okay, I have the clip on my waist strap. Back it off more." The beam started to move again. "Tighten the rope!" he yelled. The rope instantly pulled taut. Breckon held the rope as close to him as possible by hooking the inside of his right elbow around it. Then he slipped off the pipe.

He scraped the skin on the back of his head as he fell free and stopped with a jerk. He cried out briefly as everything twisted and pinched at the same time. The gap was now two feet wide as he dangled in space with his head at the level of the lower flange of the bridge beam. Water was still dripping from him and everything else.

"You're killing me! Let me down!" With that, the line was played out, jerk, jerk, jerk. At the same time, the tele-platform continued to back away so he could clear the equipment attached to the wall as he made his way to the floor. Breckon looked to the left in the direction of a strange noise. The frightened pigeons were fluttering about ten feet away at eye level.

Finally, on the floor there were many hands to help as he was laid on a gurney. In seconds he was in the back of the base meat wagon and on his way to the local hospital.

— 2 —

1996, Baghdad, Iraq

The August wind blowing through the window was hot and dry. Hashim Zahir, the president of Iraq, liked the heat and the wind. It had the unique smell of the desert in it. He tilted his head back from the report he was reading and turned his olive-brown face toward the window as he flicked a fly from the back of his head where his jet black hair was thinning. When streaks of gray had appeared at his temples some years earlier, they were instantly submerged with dye, never to be seen again.

The curtains on the window flapped in the breeze, sending a dancing pattern of shadow and light to the floor. Zahir's wider-than-average nostrils above his black mustache flared as he took a deep breath. The shirt stretched over his stout frame was becoming wet with sweat. The sand would start lifting off the scorched Iraqi landscape in an hour as the hot, dry northwest summer winds, the *shamal*, picked up speed. Yet, even that did not bother him. He liked the arid climate. It was part of the only world he had ever known.

Zahir was holding his meetings that afternoon in a suite of rooms at the top of an apartment building. Each day he operated out of one of a collection of randomly selected sites. He knew this was the surest way of staying alive. He did not fear his own people. He held them in check with tyrannical cruelty, but many foreign countries would like to see him replaced. He, on the other hand, dearly wanted to get the UN inspectors out of the country and the trade embargo lifted.

The war with Kuwait had been ridiculous from the start. What had been meant to be a two-week incursion into that tiny country to resolve a border dispute had gotten out of control by the totally unexpected and disproportionate reaction of the United States. Kuwait had been slant drilling under the border and pumping out Iraqi oil. Iraq simply intended to remedy the situation. The Arab countries had been forced to go along with the Western coalition so as not to give away to the greater world the unity that had developed among Islamic countries around the world. This unity had resulted in the formation of the Inner Council of Islam.

The Inner Council was a secret department of the Organization of Islamic Conference, or OIC, founded on September 25, 1969, and currently made up of fifty-seven nations with Islamic governments. The OIC was well funded, and whose organization chart was available to anyone on the Internet. Its workings, while not publicized, weren't secret. The Inner Council, however, *was* secret, so secret that its existence was not even known by the leaders of most of the member nations. The OIC provided a convenient way to transfer money to the Inner Council, as well as giving an easy explanation for otherwise unexplainable meetings of heads of state and other key figures.

Zahir was feeling pleased with himself. The Inner Council, of which he was a member, had charged him with an important task, and he meant to succeed. It was part of a new offensive, called Jihad Sting, in the centuries-old war against the infidel. His meeting to begin work on a new project did not start for a few minutes. He had things to do, but his mind wandered over the historical events that had brought his people to this point.

September 11 was the day that marked the high point for Islam, the last of its glory—so near, yet so far. If only one could go back . . . . On September 11, 1683, Grand Vizier Kara Mustafa had stood before Vienna, Austria, with his Turkish and Tartar army of a quarter million. He had held the city under siege since July, and the city was poised to fall, but he held off on the final assault. His reason was tied up with Islamic law, a special law that held that a city fallen in battle was given over to the soldiers for three days and three nights for plunder before authority was established. If, on the other hand, the city surrendered, all the spoils went to the Islamic rulers. It turned out that all Islam would regret his fateful delay. As a general, Mustafa failed to give proper attention to the strategic value of the heights to the north of the city and the German armies accumulating there.

On the morning of September twelfth, the Germans attacked with the Danube on their left. The Turks fought with their backs to the wall of the city that they had faced with eager anticipation the day before. The king of Poland, John Sobieski, had also answered the plea of some weeks earlier to assist the beleaguered inhabitants of Vienna. His army appeared shortly after noon of the twelfth on the right flank of the Germans. He doggedly forged ahead against the fierce resistance of the Ottomans and by late afternoon had turned the battle, routing the Turks. Not since Queen Isabella of Spain ejected the last of the Moors from her lands in 1491 had Islam suffered such a resounding defeat, this time to end their advance against the infidel Europe, and the West, forever.

Things really looked grim after the Second World War. The population of the United States, the strongest nation on earth, surged in population in what became known as the baby-boom. The leaders of Islam saw this as a fearful thing: the strongest, wealthiest nation on earth also having an exploding population.

Then a series of things occurred that changed the picture. Oil was discovered in great quantities in many of the lands controlled by Moslems just as the West developed an insatiable appetite for it. At the same time, the leadership of the U.S. was more afraid of its rapidly expanding population than of the old enemy of the West, Islam. A huge propaganda campaign was launched by the Western governments stressing the finite resources of the planet. Finally, the U.S. Supreme Court in 1973 made abortion legal. From the point of view of Islam, that was a gift straight from Allah. In the twenty-three years since that decision, Americans killed nearly fifty million of their own people, something that could not have been done in a hundred years on the battlefield. In the late seventies as it became apparent what was happening, the Inner Council of the OIC was formed to plan the march of Islam across the earth.

As the West wallowed in its hedonistic materialism, its birth rate fell sharply, much more than the planners had thought possible. All the while, Moslem populations around the world were on the rise. They were on their way to conquering the earth by the simple fact of having large families. The population of Saudi Arabia doubled since 1970, and many other countries showed similar growth. Moslems were being allowed to immigrate to all Western nations in large numbers to make up for the shortage of workers left by low birth rates. Everywhere churches were being purchased at bargain prices and converted into mosques.

Things were progressing nicely until the U.S.S.R. fell apart and the United Nations with the help of the U.S. began the end-game in the drive to see who would control the world. It was called the "New World Order," which was to be nothing less than one-world government. In the six years since the end of the Cold War, the one-worlders had made gigantic strides in their quest for world domination. It was clear there would be no room for Islam in that world. And, there was no longer time to let demographics take their course. Islam had to act. Jihad Sting was born.

Zahir's thoughts were broken by two knocks on the door. He looked up. The door opened immediately, and a guard in desert camouflage fatigues stepped into the room. "Mr. Mirza Rahman is here as well as Alwan Najafi."

"Send Mr. Rahman in, and tell Najafi I will see him in a short time."

As the door closed behind Mirza Rahman, he took a few steps toward the desk where he, the president of Iraq, sat. Zahir said, "Be seated, Mirza," as he motioned to a chair by the side of his desk. Zahir had found a Western-style desk and chair the most efficient way to conduct business in the modern world. With so many documents, the traditional carpet and cushions were not practical.

Mirza Rahman, the Director of Intelligence, had fine facial features and deep-set brown eyes. The eyes were dark ringed and covered by metal rimmed glasses. He had the look of one with a great responsibility who frequently lost sleep worrying about not meeting the demands of his boss. At fifty-eight his flabby condition was particularly noticeable in the flesh hanging on his jowls.

Rahman sat under the steely eyes of the president. "Any more information on the Israeli agent you identified last week? It seems he operated in our midst for some time before you detected him."

Director Rahman felt the displeasure in Zahir's voice. He replied, "Nothing of note has happened since we spoke yesterday morning. We continue to shadow him and know that in time he will lead us to others."

Changing the subject, Zahir said, "We are here to discuss Jihad Sting. It must be made to appear as solely an Iraqi operation to all who have any knowledge of it."

Rahman knew the type of terrorism Jihad Sting would inflict on the West. "The West suspects we are doing things like this anyway, so if by chance it is discovered no one would draw wider implications."

Zahir nodded. "We must do our part, on schedule with no mistakes." After a pause, he continued, "How well do you really know this Alwan Najafi you propose to start the project? You recommended him highly."

Mizra hated these spots Zahir put him in. If he had not given Najafi a glowing recommendation, Zahir would have asked why he had chosen him at all. In fact, Mizra did not entirely trust Najafi. In a land ruled by fear, nobody trusted anybody. "I have used him before. He has been the mastermind behind several terrorist acts against the Western countries.

He is an ambitious and clever man. He has also been pivotal in our ac-
quiring prohibited arms and other equipment since the war with Kuwait."

Looking directly into the president's eyes, Mizra continued, "Those
few times I had Najafi followed, he was always doing what he said he
would be doing. There was no fault I could find, especially since his missions have always been successful."

Zahir was sitting with his elbows on his desk and his hands together
below his chin as he observed Mizra. "Let us see what he has to say for
himself. Then I will see if I agree with your assessment."

Mizra went to the door, opened it, and nodded to the man in the outer
room. Alwan Najafi appeared in the doorway and followed Mizra into
the room. "Mr. President, this is Alwan Najafi."

Najafi bowed as Zahir motioned him to a chair in front of the desk.

In his late thirties, Najafi had a slight build. Though in superb physical condition, he was shorter than the average Arab. His eyes were light,
tending to gray, indicating his ancestry might have been from the northern Kurdish stock. But, in fact, he was born in the southern deserts of
Libya. As a youth, he had entered Iraq with his parents, who were part of
an underground movement. When he was nine, he was orphaned when
his parents were discovered and executed as traitors. He was brought up
as an Iraqi by distant relatives. Years later, Najafi learned that his parents' movement had been infiltrated by the CIA, and his parents were
exposed as scapegoats to protect an American operative. This left him
with a burning hatred for Americans.

Zahir addressed Najafi. "You have had a chance to study the proposal
Mizra sent you three days ago. I would like your opinion of this plan.
Will it produce the results intended?"

"It will work, I am sure of that." Najafi assumed, nearly correctly, that
the plan was to get the United States and its allies to lift the trade embargo from Iraq.

"What makes you so sure of this?" asked Zahir.

"The key is not to think about how the leadership of countries will
react but how the people in those countries will react. Take the Gulf War,
for example. The American people thought that the price of oil would go
up if Iraqi forces were not driven out of Kuwait, so they favored the war.
The average American knew he would not have to fight. The U.S. military is all volunteer. They were willing to let others fight. That is what
they signed up for, that is what they were paid for, was the attitude.

"This program will produce terror because it is aimed at the people, not the military or the leaders. Every citizen of a targeted country will be directly affected. People living in small rural towns will be as much at risk at those in large cities. They will not tolerate their life style being attacked in this way. When that happens, the people will tell the leaders what to do or they will replace them."

Zahir gave a nod and said, "Continue."

Najafi picked up his line of reasoning. "Westerners live in their materialism. It is the only thing they know. It is their 'religion.' This brilliant plan of terror is an attack on their religion. It is something that is never discussed, even their most bizarre movies do not touch on it. I lived in the U.S. for nearly a year, making connections for arms deals. In addition, I travel there occasionally for operations to which I am assigned. With my knowledge of the Americans I could offer some suggestions."

Rahman was slowly shaking his head as he looked directly at Najafi. Not wanting Najafi to displease the president by talking too much, he interjected. "Your role will be to take the steps necessary to procure equipment that can do what is described in the plan you have been given."

Not taking the hint, Najafi pushed on, hoping to work his way into the planning of the project. "Did you see the magazine story I sent to you?" he said looking at Mizra.

Mizra nodded.

"It is the story of the Tylenol poisoning in the U.S. in 1982. In that incident someone bought several bottles of the headache medicine Tylenol and replaced one or two capsules in each bottle with capsules filled with cyanide. The bottles with cyanide capsules were then surreptitiously replaced on the shelves of stores. Seven people died out of a population of 230 million, but the U.S. has spent billions of dollars to put tamper-proof covers on every container that contains something that could be ingested. The poisoning was a very simple thing to do. Anyone from a well organized terrorist group, or a crazy person, could have done it. The American people went wild, and they never caught the one who did it."

"How are you sure they did not catch him?" Zahir's voice had an unpleasant hardness to it. "Maybe the government caught him but did not want the people to know because they wanted to keep the people guessing. Or maybe it was a prank by the child of a very influential person, or any number of reasons. You do not know."

"Yes, Mr. President, I *do* know. They did not catch the person who did it because, if they had caught him, I would not be here now. I would have been executed. I assure you that it was very easy to do."

"You did it?" asked Zahir, a bit surprised. The man before him had made world headlines with his mischief. "Not that I mind seeing a few of the infidel dead, but why?"

"That was during the time I lived in the United States. I had been cheated by some of those money-grabbing demons, and I was angry. I also had a score to settle for my parents' death. But, rather than kill people where the deed might be traced to me, I decided on a more general revenge. I was also curious to see how the Americans would react. They did as I predicted. That is why I am sure this plan will work."

"Your past antics aside," said Zahir seeming to warm ever so slightly to the man before him, "how much money would it cost and how soon could we complete the project as outlined to you?"

"In the short time I had to evaluate the proposal, I estimate twenty months, maybe two years and thirty to forty million U.S. dollars for the plant and equipment." Najafi immediately saw disappointed looks on the faces of both men.

Zahir spoke after a pause, "The money can be made available. That is not a problem. But the time is longer than we require. We thought this could easily be done in eighteen months."

Najafi, hoping not to lose the project, responded, "It is possible the time could be less. But as I see it, we need sophisticated automatic equipment that can turn out a large variety of models in a short time. The needs will change rapidly, so this is important."

Zahir wished he could tell Najafi more of Jihad Sting so he didn't go off on a tangent. Still, Zahir was beginning to grasp the significance of being able to change production runs quickly. It would give flexibility to Jihad Sting, and maybe some types could be put to uses of his own devising.

Mizra Rahman was stern as he spoke. "Modern automatic assembly equipment would, of course, be desirable. But, this requires highly trained operators, which we do not have. And it requires very reliable equipment that would operate unsupervised in a contaminated work room for extended periods of time and not break down. That is something that does not exist."

"What you say is mostly true," Najafi said. "But, the state of automatic equipment is improving dramatically each year. There is a big robotics show in Chicago in a week. I plan to be there if you, Mr. President, approve. I will also visit other equipment suppliers. If we cannot find a way to get the equipment I propose, we must take a different approach to the project."

"All right," Zahir said firmly, "I will give you twenty-two months, no longer, and you will do all you can to make it less. Report back with a detailed outline and schedule that shows how you intend to meet that time frame. If you have an acceptable plan developed in one month, we will start then."

Najafi got up to leave as he said, "That will be enough time. I will not fail."

After Najafi left, Zahir managed a thin smile as he said, "I see why you wanted him for the project, Mizra. It will take some stern direction to keep him on the path we intend, but he will do nicely. And now, Mizra, I have other business." As Mizra stood up to leave, Zahir added, "I want to be kept closely informed on all aspects of this project."

When Zahir was alone, Jihad Sting continued to occupy his thoughts. From his point of view, the crumbling of the Western economies would affect his impoverished nation very little. An old adage came to mind to the effect that, if you have a person with nothing to lose, you have a dangerous person. The same could be said for countries. And, Iraq had little to lose.

"If it isn't the great Edmund Breckon, or is it James Bond these days? Sounds like you tried to make a pâté out of yourself. Not a good career path, I'd say."

Breckon recognized the voice as that of Cindy Thomas from the purchasing department. He looked up from some electrical schematics lying in a wrinkled pile beside his computer monitor. A new addition to his cubicle was a pair of crutches leaning against the wall.

"Hi, Cindy. How's my favorite person in the whole company," Ed said in a cheerful voice. He knew there was some measure of hyperbole in the comment. Cindy had joined Purchasing a few months ago. She was quite attractive, or so it seemed to him. In her mid-twenties, she had shiny brown hair, and deep-blue eyes that unnerved him when they were smiling, which was not always the case. In her drive to be professional, she could be demanding about the accuracy of specifications for the things he ordered, to a point of being annoying. He had wondered a time or two what she was like in real life, not that he was that interested. He didn't even know if she was married. Then he noticed her right hand. No ring. Darn it. Is it the left hand or right hand where they wear those rings.

In a more serious tone she continued, "I hear you escaped death by a breath . . . . "

"Less than a breath, I assure you."

"You're starting to worry me. If it was so close, how *did* you manage to stay alive?"

He thought a few seconds. "You know something, I don't know. It's very strange, I should be dead, but I'm not. In another sense it wasn't a close call at all."

"What are you saying? You just said you came closer than a single breath from getting killed."

"That's true. But in the last few seconds before I was to be crushed to death, time seemed to nearly stop. In a few seconds, all the details of what I had to do to stay alive came together. I remember going through several alternatives and discarding them. Then I hit on the one that would work. At the time, I was hardly aware I was doing it."

She squinted her eyes and tipped her head to one side. "But, people can't change the flow of time."

Breckon raised his eyebrows. "Don't be so sure. It depends on what you think people really are. Most people think humans evolved from some monkey and before the monkey came from a lower form and so on back to a microorganism. In that view, you're probably right. What happened to me couldn't happen because we're nothing more than what we see every day. But, if you believe, as I do, in the idea that humans were created as higher beings, and due to sin we can't use all of the powers we were created with, then there could be times when some of these other powers peek through. Extreme stress could be such an event. That's what I think happened."

Somewhat absentmindedly, she replied, "Well, all's well that ends well."

"I'd never say that. It's not only my leg that was injured. That'll heal. It's what goes on in my head. Oh, listen to me get carried away. What I can do for you?"

"Oh, yes, I almost forgot. Brian from the Electrical Sales Company called. He asked if you wanted the serial interface option with this one-hundred-horse-power, variable-speed drive you requisitioned." Then she snipped, "If you were more complete with the specifications, it'd save us all time."

Breckon let out a slow breath hoping his irritation didn't show. "Brian's forgetting that at one-hundred-horse-power and above, the serial communication option is standard. We rarely use motors that big, and he probably overlooked it. Call him back. He'll realize it as soon as you mention it."

When Thomas had gone, Breckon sat staring into space thinking how silly he must have sounded when telling about the accident. Yet, when he was pinched in that confined space between the beam and the wall, he had had two near-death experiences. Having checked on the web, he knew that was what it was called. And even now the whole episode of his figuring out what to do, and the subsequent experiences were merging into one. He had a strange feeling that something about him had changed, like he'd have more control over events next time. But, that would never happen again, so what did it mean? He shook it off, and got back to work.

"Ed!"

"The wild cry of the water buffalo," Breckon said under his breath. It was George Ratling calling. He had returned from lunch and probably had a "good" idea, as usual. Ratling made a habit of networking with managers from other companies, to a fault. He had lunch with them, played golf with them, went fishing with them. It was a wonder his wife ever saw him. From what Breckon figured, these guys would deliberately give Ratling crazy ideas as a practical joke, and he would latch onto them. Then when he got back from lunch or a game of golf, Breckon would try as tactfully as possible to burst his bubble.

But the idea for the gantry robots was different. It would combine complex automation with unheard of ease of use, thereby opening up the market to small, less sophisticated companies. It would be much like the computer industry. In the early days, computers were very expensive and took many trained technicians to use and maintain. Then the personal computers, the PCs, came along, and anyone could use them.

Ratling and Breckon had worked out the concepts in some detail. Breckon had spent a lot of his own time putting it together. There was one big difference of opinion between the two men. Ratling wanted some get-rich-quick product while Breckon wanted to revolutionize an industry. They compromised many times, but Breckon thought the design was more to his way of thinking than to Ratling's.

Breckon had gotten literature from many suppliers of servomotor controls, specialized optics, and software packages. He had really enjoyed developing the concept, especially since he had been getting bored with the tele-platforms. He had thought of quitting the company, but had not done so because of this project. After the incident at Altus, he figured he'd never be at TAC long enough to see the project launched, yet he was torn. What if he left shortly before Ratling got funding and some other engineer was hired to do the project.

In Breckon's opinion, Ratling was a rat wannabe who hadn't met enough bad companions to make the grade. The talk around the office was that he was having an affair. This did not sit well with Breckon, but in this society, there wasn't much he could do. And maybe the rumors weren't true. One thing he knew. Ratling was one crazy salesman. If it were possible to find funding for this project, Ratling would get it.

"Ed, where are you?"

"Coming!" then under his breath, "Dear." He added, "I'm a little slow getting around on these crutches."

Breckon hobbled to Ratling's office, carrying a pad of paper between two fingers as he worked the crutches. As soon as Breckon was through the door, Ratling began. "There's a board of directors meeting this evening. They want me to give the sales projections for the coming year. I'm also going to make a presentation on the gantry robot idea we have."

"We're not ready," insisted Breckon.

"We don't have the time or money to do much more than we've already done. We need funding. In the meantime, someone else might put together many of our ideas, and we'll be out of luck." Breckon had to admit Ratling had a point and said so.

"I've prepared some Power Point slides I want to review with you so we get the best presentation possible." The two of them spent the next two hours revising the presentation. Breckon frequently pressed Ratling not to make too many outlandish statements. At times, Breckon would use graphics programs on his computer to make adjustments to the slides. By four o'clock, they thought they had it as good as they could make it. It presented the case with only a few uncertainties.

— 3 —

Chicago

"What's the new idea you have here?" asked one of the many people who stopped by the TAC booth at the robotics show. George Ratling had heard it a dozen times already this first morning.

"We're developing a new line of gantry robots for automatic assembly that'll be easier to use and cost less than what's currently available. Here are some pictures that show how it works," said Ratling as he opened a three-ring binder with color prints of the slides he had used for the presentation to the board of directors the previous week.

Before he was halfway through the slides, he was stopped. "Bring an operational unit to the show next year, and we'll talk." That was the usual response. Ratling could not get anyone interested in discussing the idea, to say nothing of getting a commitment of up-front money. To Ratling's chagrin, the board had refused to fund the project unless he could get a partner company to share in the development costs. This, from his point of view, was the same as publishing the idea in a trade journal.

The robotics show got bigger each year. Suppliers were all putting on the best display their advertising budgets would allow. The big companies had entire systems in operation assembling real products. Interspersed with the large players were many smaller companies selling components or services to manufacturers of robots or those companies that used robots. There was a constant chatter, and the high-pitched whine of servo-motors being put through their paces for the edification of the attendees.

Joe Cabot, the other salesman for TAC, was at the booth with George. They took turns at the booth giving the other time to see the rest of the show. As George was returning to spell Joe, he saw him talking to a man who appeared to be of Mideastern extraction. Joe said, "Here's the man who can give you the details on the new system TAC is developing."

The man introduced himself as Hon Robbie with a clearly Mideastern accent. He was smaller than average with quick, sure movements but definitely not someone who would stand out in a crowd. His visitor badge listed Alcem International as his company.

Robbie said to Ratling, "Mr. Cabot has been telling me about a rather clever concept you have. Could we perhaps discuss it in more detail?"

"With pleasure," Ratling said as he placed the three-ring binder on the table in their booth.

George opened the binder to the first page that showed a gantry robot and began his pitch. "There have been advances in several areas of technology which if brought together in a unique way could revolutionize robotics. This would open up applications that have never used automation before. First, let me define a few terms. Gantry robots are gantry cranes with the same precision and programmability as the familiar pedestal robots, but with an arbitrarily large work area. There are any number of tools that can be put on the bottom of the mast called end-effectors. In fact, the end-effector is frequently as capable as a pedestal robot by itself. We have worked out many of the details and have come up with a system to make precision "smart" gantry robots much easier to use than any on the market today."

Robbie nodded at times as he paid rapt attention.

George continued. "Present-day robots of any type have two problems that this system would overcome. The first is that the robots must be taught in precise detail every move they are to make in order to do a certain operation. This is the tool path. As long as everything is always in exactly the same place as it was when the teaching was done, the assembly will work. The new system eliminates the need to teach tool paths or calibrate the system.

"The second problem the new system solves is that it doesn't bump into things as it does its job, because it maps all objects in the work cell. In present systems, operators must be careful not to put anything in the work cell that was not there when the tool paths were taught.

"The mechanism to solve these two problems is to have electronically aimable lasers mounted at up to twelve locations around the outside of the work envelope. There are sensors located on the end of the vertical mast and at the tool tip. These sensors detect the location of at least three of the laser transmitters like a Global Positioning System sensor locates three or more of the satellites in the GPS constellation to determine its location on the earth. This gives the location of the tool tip in the work envelope at all times to within one-thousandth of an inch.

"The same laser transmitters and sensors are used in a second system. The entire workspace is divided up into one-centimeter cubes. The lasers systematically scan the entire workspace and map it. Then using artificial intelligence based on fuzzy logic, the tool path is calculated from part pick-up to its destination. If there are new objects in the work envelope, the machine calculates a path around them. This is particularly helpful for the safety of personnel. While the whole system is computationally intensive, it's not beyond the capacity of several late-model personal computers networked together. Communications among the various elements of the system, computers, sensors, etc. are with fiber optics."

Robbie interjected, "It seems like looking at all the one-centimeter cubes in the work space fast enough so the machine can avoid hitting new things is too hard to do with personal computers."

The astuteness of the comment took George by surprise, but he was ready with the answer. "There are some sophisticated programs on the market that make it unnecessary to look at all the points. For example, if you put a box three feet on a side in the space, an algorithm similar to those used for CAD, that's Computer Aided Design, solid modeling would determine the shape of the box. Then the sensors wouldn't have to look for the points inside the box. Similarly, it would know never to look inside an electric motor once identified. Also, the shape and anatomical movements of an average person would be in the computer."

Robbie nodded thoughtfully. "These are some good ideas. I must put together a business plan for a new undertaking. This could be a part. First, I must locate other machinery for my project. Perhaps, I'll see you again."

Ratling could hardly believe what he was hearing. "May I ask you for your business card, and contact information?"

"Unfortunately, I seem to have left my business cards in my hotel room. I have your card and company literature. I'll contact you. Thank you for your fine explanation." With that he shook George's hand and sauntered away.

Ratling couldn't help thinking Robbie was spying for a competing company. That naturally was the danger of this type of selling.

Three days later, the show was all but over, and Ratling had not gotten a single, solid lead for a partner to develop the new gantry robot. Mentally he had written off Robbie from the first day as someone out to steal ideas. Now, he considered his options. To quit his job at TAC and start his own company was a possibility, but he would have to put up nearly all his savings and home equity as part of the deal. In addition, Breckon would probably not go along with starting a new company, and he needed Breckon. Things looked pretty bleak.

"Think I'll take a break and get a cup of coffee before we start packing up," said Joe Cabot.

Just then, Ratling saw Hon Robbie making his way down the aisle. When Cabot left, Robbie walked right over and shook Ratling's hand. "We meet again. Having any luck selling your idea?"

"Honestly, no. It's pretty hard to sell an idea with no working hardware at a trade show. Still, since it makes use of existing technology with no breakthroughs needed to make it work, I would've thought there'd be more interest."

Robbie listened intently then said, "At a show like this, people are interested in things that are ready to go. However, the people I represent are interested in cutting-edge ideas like yours. In fact, this is a more mature idea than I had expected to find."

Ratling's instincts to close the deal were shifted into gear. "You're looking for new ideas to invest in then?"

"Not for the sake for investing, but for a fairly specific marketing strategy. My client in Eastern Europe needs equipment like you describe. Furthermore, we don't even want the competition to know we're looking for this type of machinery. That's one reason why I'm shopping in the United States rather than Europe. After you pack up, could we have dinner together? Maybe we could put together a mutually beneficial business plan."

"I had planned to go back to Minneapolis later tonight, but I could easily make other arrangements. Could you give me a general idea of what you have in mind?"

"Under the proper arrangements, I could probably come up with the money to develop your new robotic system. But don't tell anyone about this until you have heard the offer. No one!"

"I'm at your command, as they say. I'll say I'm staying in Chicago to have dinner with a friend. And because tomorrow is Saturday, nobody'll question it."

"Fine. I'll meet you in the lobby of your hotel at seven o'clock. Oh, by the way, bring along that three-ring binder of slides you used here at the show to make your pitch. Is that okay?"

"That'll be fine. At seven then."

Mr. Robbie turned and drifted away in the diminishing crowd. When Cabot returned, Ratling casually mentioned, "An old friend of mine stopped by a couple of days ago. We made arrangements to have dinner tonight. He wasn't sure he could make it, but he called, so it's on. I'll change my flight and come back tomorrow." They packed up the display items, extra literature, and all the paraphernalia used in the booth during the show. Ratling let Cabot make arrangements with the movers to get the boxes shipped back and then said good-bye.

As he walked the few blocks back to his hotel, Ratling hardly noticed the other pedestrians. At six o'clock, the warm, humid day was drawing to a close. Pondering his dinner meeting, he wondered how Robbie knew the hotel where he was staying. The thought occurred to him that maybe Robbie had had him followed. He decided to forget it and make the deal.

Ratling was in the lobby a little before seven. A few minutes after seven, Hon Robbie walked through the door from the street. "Hello, George."

"Hello, Mr. Robbie."

"By all means call me Hon."

"All right then, Hon, where would you like to go for dinner?"

"There's a nice Lebanese place down the street, if you don't mind a few steps in the evening air. Have you ever had Arab food?"

"No, I can't say I have, but it sounds good to me. I take it you're familiar with this cuisine."

"Yes, in Eastern Europe, there are many Arabs, and, of course, they bring their way of eating with them." When they arrived at the restaurant Ratling found that Robbie had made reservations. They were seated immediately in a booth with high backed seats near the rear of the restaurant. It was almost a private room. They ordered drinks, and Ratling noticed Robbie ordered a nonalcoholic cocktail. After the waiter left, Robbie began his presentation.

"As I mentioned earlier, the people I represent need some general-purpose, automatic assembly equipment. Your situation fits perfectly for several reasons. Because we don't have a skilled labor pool to draw from, the relative ease with which your gantry robots can be programmed and operated is very appealing. Not requiring precision alignment of the various parts is another. In short, it looks like a high-tech robotic system for a low-tech user."

"Exactly," replied Ratling, very pleased Robbie had grasped his idea so quickly.

"Another reason I am interested in your company, and your robotics, is the fact that you have never made something like this before."

"Well, that's true," Ratling said a little defensively, "but before coming to TAC I had many years experience designing and selling gantry robots."

"Yes, yes, that's not what I meant. Please let me continue."

Ratling caught himself. He had to be careful not to get too eager

"In some ways we would like to have a company with a long, unbroken history in this business. But I am hoping your past experience will compensate for that. But, there is another consideration," Robbie continued. "Now, this is rather delicate, and I am not sure how you'll react."

Ratling's antennas were fully deployed.

"My clients are in Bulgaria. The present U.S. policies would never let a sophisticated robotic system be exported to that country. But since you have never made one, you could export it as a common variety cable-hoist crane, and nobody would question it. With some help along the way, it could be exported with no problems."

Ratling could tell Robbie was watching him as intently as possible without being obvious. After a moment Ratling said, "We'd have to somehow tie the sale to the department that makes the cable-hoist cranes. I'd have to make arrangements with management so I'd get this sale to count in my bonus plan. I think that could be arranged, though."

Robbie was relieved and somewhat surprised that the thought of an illegal sale to a foreign country had not caused Ratling a second's hesitation. "I'm glad you see it that way. To make this idea work, the development will have to be very secretive. Any inquiries you get as a result of this trade show or any other way will have to be put off so others won't know you are working on this system. We don't want anyone getting suspicious that we intend to become competitors of certain companies."

Ratling had expected that a confidentially agreement would be a condition of any company putting money into the development. "We'll have to see the contract you have in mind for all the details, but what you suggest should be acceptable to my management. Are there any other items we should discuss? For example, who will own the design?"

"You will, of course, as long as the units you deliver to us work as you have shown in the presentation you gave me at the show."

"Units! How many do you want? I was assuming that you only wanted one for evaluation."

"This is another thing that's a little different. We want two gantry robots consisting of bridge with end trucks, trolleys, and telescoping masts to run on one set of rails. The dimensions we'll discuss later, but the robots aren't for evaluation. These must work when they're put in. The contract my clients want is basically this. The technical specifications will be based on the slides you showed me with the exception that there will be two robots instead of one. I see you brought the three-ring binder with you. May I have it? I assume you can make another set for yourself."

Ratling handed over the binder without a word. He knew the man across from him could be working for a competitor, but he saw no alternative. If he lost this great idea, the board of directors would have only themselves to blame.

"I'll select an engineering firm to conduct two tests to insure that the specifications are met. The first will be for the prototype. You'll be able to keep this machine. Then the two deliverable units will go through a final test before shipment."

"That makes sense. I see no problem with that." Ratling's mind was racing. *What was in those slides anyway!* He had never intended them to be the basis for a contract. After all, he was a salesman who always exaggerated a little, and at times a lot.

"There is one more thing. We want the prototype test in eleven months after signing the contract, and the two deliverable units are to ship ten months after that. Assuming no more than a month to get this started leaves twenty-two months from today to ship."

"Wow, that's a fast-track program!"

"Can you do it?"

"I'm not sure. We'd have to do concurrent engineering and fabrication, which means we must start ordering long-lead-time items almost the first day. Some of the stuff we order will be unusable if the design changes. In short, we'd lose money."

"Money won't be the biggest problem. Performance and delivery will be the most important."

Ratling shook his head as he spoke, "I'm not going to say we can make that delivery. There's some pretty tricky matching up of software packages to be done, difficulties will likely come up."

"Let's look at it another way," Robbie said leaning forward. Ratling noticed a hardness in his expression. "You and your wife make good money, well into six figures of combined income. But the two of you are spending more than you make, and you are the bigger spender. A good portion of your share is spent on Andrea, your mistress. I doubt your wife knows about her, to say nothing of how much she's costing you."

This hit Ratling like a wet towel across the face. He flushed with anger. Just as quickly it switched to fear, then to the realization that this was exactly what the scoundrel had expected. This man had connections and money to have done so much investigating in the few days since the start of the show. This went through Ratling's mind in a flash. He had been taken off guard in negotiations before and prided himself on being able to land on his feet.

"It sounds," said Ratling slowly, "like you've been doing some homework. I gather you're implying that there would be enough, shall we say, 'compensation' in this to be worth my while."

Robbie smiled evilly and sat back. "You understand correctly. What do you say?"

"I think we can do business."

At that moment the waiter returned to take their order. Robbie said, "Do you mind if I order for both of us?"

"No, not at all. I wouldn't know what to order anyway."

"Fine, I'll order a sampler tray so you can try several of the foods of the desert people."

When the waiter left, Robbie reached into the breast pocket of his suit coat and pulled out a fat envelope. "Here's the contract we have in mind. It's not such a long contract as it might appear from the size of the envelope. Put it in you suit coat pocket and review it when you get back to your room. Give me a call next week. All the information you need is in the envelope."

From that point, Robbie changed the conversation to other topics. They finished the meal pleasantly discussing such things as baseball and fishing. Robbie insisted on paying for the meal. After they shook hands in front of Ratling's hotel, Robbie continued on down the street.

It had come together better than Robbie had ever hoped. Here was an American firm that could make automatic assembly equipment that did not need experienced or highly trained operators. And due to the type of company TAC was, there would be little difficulty getting these things exported.

When Robbie got to his hotel, he did something he rarely did. He went to the lounge and ordered a double Scotch on the rocks. This was one vice he had learned during his time in this decadent land. The fact that the whisky was not made in the U.S. helped to alleviate the tinge of guilt he felt.

When Ratling was finally alone in his room, he allowed expression to the anger he felt and tossed the envelope onto the bed. "That snake! Digging into my life that way! How dare he do that!" Ratling seethed through clenched teeth. He threw off his suit coat, and snapped off his tie. After splashing some cold water on his face, he returned to the room. "Not a long contract," he said aloud looking at the envelope on the bed. "It must be and inch thick. From the looks of it, they, whoever they are, have every contingency from killer molds to the end of the world covered." He brushed his teeth, hung up his suit, and got out a clean shirt for the next day.

Having calmed down somewhat, he picked up the envelope and slit it open. The contents were wrapped in a sheet of paper with a typed note on it. "If you are not agreeable to the contract, mail the entire contents of this envelope to the following address, and we will part friends. If you accept the terms, call me at the number provided, and we will expect performance as stated." Following this was an address consisting of a post office box number in New York City, a zip code, and a phone number.

He was getting tense. Unwrapping the contents he saw a few sheets of paper along with a large bundle of cash, U.S. currency, some fifties, but mostly hundreds. His eyes opened wide. There were clearly thousands of dollars, all in well-circulated bills. Oh, this *was* the big time. He knew what the note meant. If you accepted a bribe, you *must* perform. Failure was not something you even considered.

Breathing heavily, his heart pounding, he sat on the edge of the bed with his fist full of money. "Good thing I didn't open the envelope in the restaurant." But the way it was handled, he hadn't had a chance. He could see Robbie knew he'd find this hard to take so he let him lose his composure when he was alone.

"That piece of low life is playing me like a fiddle. He knows how I'll react, knows my whole life, and I know nothing about him." For the first time in his life, Ratling was being used like he had always used others. It left him decidedly unsettled.

The last page of the contract really nagged at him. That page was an addendum not referenced any place else in the main body of the contract, so if he chose not to show it to anyone it would remain unknown. It required

TAC to supply a fully competent engineer to supervise installation, and start-up of the system at the site. That would be tough. Breckon wouldn't do it, but there would be other engineers hired for this project. There had to be a soldier of fortune out there some place.

But then his mind went back to the timetable. It was too short! If Breckon didn't buy into it, there was no chance. He knew better than to think of bribing Breckon. He had almost decided to turn the deal down unless he could get an extension on the time . . . but, that money looked so good. And, then there was Andrea. If he refused to cooperate, that guy would make sure Claudia found out about Andrea!

All through breakfast the next morning and the flight home, Ratling thought of the money, how much he wanted it, and how he did not want to get into something like this. He couldn't see a way to get off the horns of the dilemma. What to do?

When Ratling paid the taxi driver in front of his house in Plymouth, Minnesota, he was no closer to a solution. As he entered his house with its three stories, grand entry, turrets, dormers, nooks and crannies, he found Claudia sitting in the living room reading a magazine. She was in her stocking feet as usual while in this room. The carpet was the only thing he genuinely didn't like about the decorating scheme. It was nearly white and showed even the smallest amount of dirt. Other than that, it was a pleasant room. George thought Claudia had spent too much furnishing it, but he was always proud to bring home business associates from out of town.

Claudia had a beautiful clear complexion and a striking face. Her blue eyes were set off by reddish brown hair, which she wore longer than shoulder length. With frequent trips to the beauty shop, it always had loose curls in it. The good life was starting to show on her hips and thighs where a few nasty little pounds had crept up on her. Several times, she had mentioned going to some exclusive weight-loss place, if there were ever enough money.

"Well the world traveler returns," was Claudia's greeting. George noticed the sarcasm in her voice. "I suppose you're home to start spending some of our hard earned money, or should I say *all* our hard earned money?" George sat down on the sofa and said, "We both have a way of getting rid of money."

"We!" Claudia almost screamed. "I was reconciling the bank account this week, and you've been taking money out of the automatic teller machine like it was water out of a faucet!"

"Wait a minute, I'm not the only one who uses that little machine." His voice was raising, as was Claudia's. They had had this argument many times before, but there seemed to be a special barb to her tone today.

"You've been getting home late a lot of nights. You say you're out with some of your friends or going to a movie. Something's going on. Are you cheating on me?"

The muscles in the back of his neck tightened, and a chill went down his back. She knew! She had found out about Andrea. "What can I say?" He was sitting on the edge of the sofa resting his forearms on his knees and looking down at his hands, picking at his thumbnail with his index finger. Why hadn't he broken that thing off with Andrea? He didn't even like the woman. What had started out as little more than a dare from his buddies would ruin his life.

"It would certainly explain where the money's going."

Then it hit him. She really didn't know! She was guessing. But, the interrogation had to stop or sure as God made little green apples he'd slip and reveal something. He'd been ambushed again. Think man! Land on your feet. Where has the money been going?

Ignoring the accusation, he said, "I'm afraid I *have* been spending a lot of time at night walking around trying to figure out what to do. Things haven't been going well at work. Profits are way down. There are too many small start-up companies that have almost no overhead, and we have to keep cutting our margins to get orders. I'll have to come up with a new market niche at TAC or find a new job."

Claudia was partially appeased but the story still wasn't satisfying her. "That explains the time, but what's been happening to the money? Walking around at night doesn't cost much." Her tone was less harsh than before.

"Okay, okay, I'll tell you where the money's been going. You know how we, or should I say, *I*," he said as contritely as he could muster, "seem to go through the money until it's all gone? I've discovered I can't stay away from that ATM, so each time I've been taking some of the money and putting it aside. I'm addicted to the fool machine, can you believe it? Here, I'll show you. Wait right there."

Ratling casually picked up his suitcase and briefcase and went up to the master bedroom. He took a gob of the cash from the fat envelope, all of the fifties and a nice wad of hundreds, enough to make at least three thousand dollars, stuffed it in another used envelope from his briefcase and went downstairs.

"Here, this is what I've put aside so far. It's not too much but it's a start." He handed Claudia the envelope.

She took the envelope and took out the contents. Her mouth dropped open. "There must be thousands here. You keep this in the house? Somebody might have broken in and stolen it." It's always amazing what a wad of cash would do to people. This represented only a fraction of the money that George had gone through in recent months, mostly on Andrea. Yet, it completely changed Claudia's attitude on the subject. He was left awed by how dumb the ATM story was. It had worked because of how desperately Claudia wanted to believe any explanation but the true one.

"Yes, I think it's close to three thousand dollars by now," George said casually.

She looked at him intently. "This is a side of you I've never seen."

"It's been hard sometimes, but it's working. From now on, I'll take less from the ATM. I think my spending habits have changed enough for me to handle that now."

George sat down on the sofa again and leaned back. Claudia had a pleasant smile and a far away look in her eyes as she was thinking of the ways she could spend the money. He was wondering if Hon Robbie and whomever he was working for knew this was the weekend he would need some ready cash. Well then, this was how it happened. Now there was no turning back. Not one big decision, but one dumped on him by hundreds of shady little decisions over the years. One step always led to another.

It was good his wife was absorbed in her own thoughts because for a few moments George's face was a mask of horror. Something he had heard when he was quite young came to mind. "Nobody goes to hell by accident, nor goes there in a day, but souls are lost by a lifetime of small nasty unrepented acts. The day comes when a final step is taken, possibly almost unnoticed, that leads over a precipice from which the return is nearly impossible. So it was with Judas." He physically shuddered.

Claudia's attention was drawn to him, and she asked, "Are you all right?"

"Oh, it's nothing," he replied. "I'm okay. How about going to lunch?"

She accepted. Oh, the warming effect of cold cash.

— 4 —

"Ed!"

"Oh, boy, back from the trade show are we?" muttered Breckon. "Coming." Breckon had gotten rid of his crutches and only had a little limp left. As Breckon entered Ratling's office, he saw a very serious man. Something was different. "How'd things go at the show?"

Ratling ran his hand through the hair on his left temple, and then nervously rubbed his hands together. He didn't make eye contact with Breckon as he said, "As the saying goes, I have good news and bad news."

"What's the bad news?"

Ratling screwed up his face. "Twenty-two months."

"Can I assume that the bad news is in some way connected to the good news?"

"Yes, you can. You remember that I mentioned the board said I was to look for a partner to put up some of the development money for the gantry robot project. The good news is I found a company to completely fund the development . . . . "

Breckon blinked. "But, we must have a working prototype in twenty-two months, is that it?"

"No," Ratling said, taking his time, "That is not it. We must complete the prototype, and then manufacture two fully functional production units in twenty-two months."

Breckon gaped. "That's not bad news, that's stupid, irrational news!"

Ratling spread his hands wide. "Maybe it isn't as bad as it sounds. Now, listen. They're willing to fund concurrent engineering. These guys seem to have lots of money. We could put together the hardware design in a few months, and, if it appeared to work well enough, we would order long lead-time items for the production units right then. In effect, the electrical and mechanical parts of the production machines would be done, say, two months after the prototype. The biggest part of this project is the software."

"Yeah, and that's where the risk is."

"Stay with me on this, Ed. I'll see that you get a substantial pay raise at the start and a nice bonus on successful completion."

"How likely is it we'll get the contract?"

"Unless there's a snag with the company lawyers, it seems to be in the bag. The client wants tight security. We'll rent space in a different building and hire contract people, as many as needed. I'll manage the project with half of my time, and you'll be *completely* in charge of the actual implementation with an almost unlimited budget. What do you say?"

This was the most tempting offer Breckon had ever heard. With enough money, there were always ways to get things done. "I'll think about it for a day or two. What do you know about the company funding the project?"

Ignoring that question Ratling said, "I must have your answer in less than two days because without you I wouldn't want to tackle this thing. Concerning the company, there isn't much to say."

As they discussed the contract, Breckon noticed that Ratling was being evasive when it came to the source of the funds. Breckon would have to decide if he could live with that.

As soon as Breckon got to his apartment after work, he picked up the phone and punched in the number of his old friend. "Darin, what're ya doing tonight? I need to talk. Ratling came up with a wild one this time,"

"Sure. Why don't ya come over, and I'll fry some burgers."

"See ya in a half hour." Darin Harris and Breckon had been friends since they met in the fourth grade. It grew into a camaraderie that lasted through high school and into their adult lives.

Harris, an outgoing person, was more willing to try new things than Breckon. In that way, they complemented each other. Harris's flair expressed itself in writing, drawing, and photography. Building on these skills, he had gotten some articles published while he was working other jobs. These had come to the attention of a New York publisher, and soon he was doing well as a self-employed, free-lance writer and photographer. He even managed to make enough to keep up his private pilot's license he had started working on in high school. He was a member of a flying club that owned three planes, which permitted him to keep current in different airplane types.

———————————

"Hi, Ed. Sit down, and I'll get some food going." Harris was a little less than six feet, had dark-brown hair and blue eyes. He had a rather long face with pronounced cheek bones. With his quick wit, he was easy to like and he got along well with everyone.

"Sounds good," replied Ed.

"So what's up?"

"It's George. He never stops. He found some financial backers for the automatic gantry robot project I've mentioned to you. Only problem is he has promised to deliver two production models in twenty-two months. I don't know if it's possible. This is supposed to be very hush, hush, so don't mention it to anyone."

"What happens if you go into this and can't deliver?"

"I don't know. Ratling seemed rather evasive on this and several other issues."

"Sounds like you'll be putting in some long hours. In that case, you'd better get paid up front, no promises of bonuses and stuff like that."

"Yeah, I think I'll ask for a big raise or get overtime pay. How are the burgers coming . . . and let's do some planning for that trip out west to the mountains we've missed the last couple of years."

———————————

Within a week, the contract was signed and a letter of credit for $2.4 million was in the bank. Breckon agreed to be part of the project, and they started. Cindy Thomas was assigned to work on the project because of her past experience with contact personnel, and renting equipment. The building Ratling rented, called Plant 2, had a high-bay, meaning it had a two-story-high shop with a crane to assemble tall machines. Breckon started interviewing engineers and programmers. He knew he would need to lease several workstations for programming, CAD modeling, and simulation.

Breckon was acquainted with Joe Rogers, who ran a company called Professional Computing, Inc. that dealt in computationally intensive workstations and computers customized for professional users. Breckon had told Rogers what he wanted, and they set up a time to meet. When

Breckon arrived, they discussed the number of machines, length of the lease, and maintenance support.

Breckon had the project buy the best laptop he could find for himself. He had the responsibility of insuring security of all data files on this project, and his laptop would be the master computer containing the encrypting codes, and other information needed to access the master data storage.

Something had been nagging Breckon since the start of the project. With Ratling being so secretive about the customer and the installation location, he feared that one day Ratling would say he had to go to some rotten hole on the other side of the planet for installation and start-up support. Breckon decided that, if he could manage to make it so that the best arrangement was for him to stay at the plant supporting someone else on the site, he'd solve this problem. That could only be accomplished if he could assure communications with whomever did the traveling.

Breckon hoped Rogers might have some ideas. "Joe, I'd like to find a way to put a universal communicating device into my laptop. Something like an Inmarsat (International Maritime Satellite) phone, but from what I've learned they're much too large." Breckon took this approach because he didn't want to give away what he was doing in case the issue ever came up.

Rogers thought for a minute. "You're right. The Inmarsat wouldn't work. There's one possibility I can think of, though. The Iridium phone system being built by Motorola. It's a direct-to-satellite system that'll use a constellation of satellites in low earth orbit for direct calling to and from any point on earth."

"Oh, yeah, they started it five or six years ago, didn't they? It's not operational for what, another two?"

"Something less than that, I think. A year ago." Rogers continued, "the Iridium Corporation managed to get the FCC to set aside a portion of the L-band of radio frequencies for that system."

"Can you get your hands on one of the Iridium phones? I'd sure like you to build one into my new laptop, if it's possible."

"I doubt they'll be on the market for quite a while. But, ya know, one of my school buddies is working on that project. I'll track him down and see if there are any prototypes they'd let me have."

Rogers went to where he had a laptop computer taken apart on the workbench. "I wonder if they've ever thought of building these things into laptop computers. Maybe I could get into the laptop part of the market and make some money. I could experiment on your computer. Then when the system's ready for initial testing, maybe you could be a trial user, and then finally a regular subscriber, and we'd see how well the laptop idea works."

Breckon knew the time to do this was right then, at the start of the project, when there was still plenty of money. "How much do you think this'll cost?"

"Assuming I can get some prototype parts, I'd charge you, say, two thousand to put it in you computer. I'll put in more time than that would cover since I can see some benefit for me in this. When the Iridium system gets up and running, we can discuss the method of paying for the service if you want it. You could take delivery of your computer in a few days and then, with any luck, bring it back if I get the Iridium parts. I'd bury the antenna in the cover. That'll be the hardest part."

Six weeks later, Harris and Breckon got together at Harris's apartment. "How's the project going?" Harris asked.

"So far, so good. We've been hiring people, ordering long-lead-time parts and equipment, and designing the mechanical structures. We have general specifications such as the load that must be carried and the overall dimensions of the gantry robot. We, or rather I, don't know what they're going to do with these things, and I doubt Ratling does either."

Changing the subject, Darin asked, "How's your data-encoding scheme coming? You mentioned it would use the one-time-pad system. Tell me again how that system's supposed to work."

"Making it work is mainly a matter of getting random numbers. The experts say the only way to get genuinely random numbers is from quantum-mechanical events, like the ticks on a Geiger counter measuring radioactive decay. Machine generated random numbers aren't random enough. Atmospheric static is a second best, and was as good as I could do. That Iridium phone Joe Rogers built into my computer is perfect. There's no traffic on the part of the L-band set aside for Iridium with no phones in use yet. That means I get great static. Using a program I found in a computer magazine, I extract random numbers from it, and store them on a CD ROM disk. I make a master and one copy as a backup in case the original gets damaged.

"The letters, numbers, punctuation marks, and nonprinting characters all have a standard eight-bit number assigned to them. To encode text, the program computes the bit-wise exclusive-or of the binary number representing a character and a random number from the code disc. The result is another random number, the encoded character. The only way to get the original character back is to reverse the process used for encoding. The code disc is separated into sectors of ten thousand random numbers. At the start of the encoded data, the number of the code disc and the identifier of the code sector are given. By the way, is it okay if from time to time I send you a brown envelope with some CDs in it?"

"I don't see why not, but why?"

"I need an off-site place to store a copy of my encoded project data. What I think I'll do is send some encoded data and some random-number encoding disks, but not the disks to decode that data in the same envelope. The code disks will be for the encoded file disks in the previous envelope. I don't care what you do with them but don't lose them."

"Don't worry, I'll think of something."

"Hey, old buddy, I've got to be shoving off. Take it easy and stay out of trouble."

"Keep in touch."

The following July, the customer had a local testing company come to TAC to perform the interim test of the prototype machine. Breckon was not completely ready with programming, but Ratling wouldn't delay the test lest the "off-the-books" money he was receiving stopped coming. Ratling, being the salesman he was, managed to convince the testers that a slightly revised test plan was as good as the one the specification required. After the testers had gone, Breckon started to protest what Ratling had done, but was cut off.

"We got the test off our back. Now, you can concentrate on the programming. How are you doing against the schedule?"

"Terrible. As a matter of fact, I'm falling further and further behind. The problem is this, George. I've been spending too much of my time with administrative things that you should be doing. That puts me behind on my work."

"You'll have to work harder. There's no other way."

Breckon shook his head in resignation.

— 5 —

February 1998, Baghdad, Iraq

Alwan Najafi handed his credentials to one of the two armed guards. At times, he felt a tinge of schizophrenia as he shifted from his Hon Robbie persona of western society to Alwan Najafi, the name of his birth. A minute earlier he had entered a small woodworking factory with the smell of fresh sawdust in the air and the sound of power saws in the next room cutting into lumber. The old wooden floor had creaked as he approached a man at a desk and asked to see the director. The man's hand motioned to his left. "Through two doors," was all he had said.

Najafi first went through a wooden door and then a metal door. Beyond the second door was a different world. Everything was concrete and steel. Here he encountered two guards. As one checked Najafi's papers, the other searched him for concealed weapons. They both looked at his picture ID and carefully regarded him. Finally, the one with the superior rank said, pointing to yet another steel door, "Though there and down the stairs to the bottom. Third door on the right."

This guardroom was the entrance to one of forty deep, concrete bunkers constructed in Iraq in the 1980s. More importantly, it was one of several that had not sustained much damage during the war with Kuwait and had been put back into use. Each bunker had been designed to hold a maximum of one thousand elite Republican Guard troops during times of extreme danger. They could withstand shocks up to eight on the Richter scale—safe shelter from a close nuclear explosion. A stairway descended fifty feet underground to a tubular main corridor. Branching off at right angles from this central tube were seven larger concrete tubes on each side. Each branch tube was large enough to bunk up to 100 men. In addition, there were rooms for a headquarters, kitchen and eating area, sick bay, and utilities. The only things penetrating to the surface were ventilation shafts from the various rooms. These ventilation shafts had been targets for many of the laser-guided "smart" bombs used by the coalition planes during Desert Storm.

When Najafi reached the correct door, he saw it standing open. Only the flat floor set a fourth of the way up from the bottom of the curvature broke the tubular outline. The air was not musty as one might expect so far underground, but it had a faint chemical aroma. The air filtration system was designed to protect from chemical and biological as well as nuclear weapons.

Sitting in one of the chairs around a rectangular table was a solitary man in uniform. From the insignia on his shoulder boards—crossed scimitars with an eagle above them—Najafi knew he was a major general.

Najafi nodded to the man and said, "Good morning."

The general got up and stretched out his right hand to Najafi. "Good morning. I see we are the early ones," he said in a somewhat stiff voice as if making light conversation were an effort. "I am Major General Raja Majeed."

"I am Alwan Najafi. You must be the commander of the armored forces. I asked that you be here," said Najafi pleasantly. "What is the state of readiness of your armored vehicles and the training level of your officers and men?"

"I have enough vehicles to outfit one complete division and a good part of another. The men are willing enough, but we cannot conduct proper training. We have to be careful not to wear out our vehicles because we have very few replacement parts. I make an exception, though, for four elite battalions. They make up a full regiment. We keep these at peak readiness."

"I see. Are you expecting border problems with any of our neighbors?"

"With the no-fly zones imposed by the UN in the north and south, armor is the only way we can effectively maintain order in our own country should trouble break out. Ostensibly, this is the most important reason. From my point of view, there is another. I want to be ready should I get another crack at an American armored unit. They cut us to shreds in the Gulf War only because they had overwhelming superiority in numbers and air cover. Our elite units were ordered to the rear so all the Americans met were the oldest tanks with crews that had little training. Sometime there will be an opportunity to take them on when we are matched—and I want to be ready." The general was becoming more animated as he spoke. He leaned toward Najafi and continued. "Then they will see the real meaning of Arabs at war. They are not born to the desert like we are. They do not have sand in their blood. We will leave their bones to be bleached by the sun and ground to dust by the blowing sand."

Suddenly becoming self-conscious, the general stopped talking, and his exuberance vanished. His face fell, and he looked almost pleadingly at Najafi. "I did not mean in any way to imply that I would ever be insubordinate. You have to believe that." In this land of absolute tyrannical rule, it was never good to express a personal opinion to anyone, especially a complete stranger.

"General, I would not believe that. But enough. I hear others coming." The general immediately changed his expression to attentive passivity.

In walked a middle-aged man with a trace of gray at the temples and with a stern, lined face. He had square shoulders and wore a military uniform. His jaw was set and gave the appearance of being all business. Najafi knew him to be General Ejaz Ahmed, the Minister of Defense.

Mirza Rahman, the Director of Intelligence, followed him close behind. Najafi knew him better than the Minister of Defense, and had seen him twice since the meeting on the top floor of the apartment building more than a year before.

Following these two men by a few seconds, was a younger man in his late twenties. With his black hair, brown eyes, and black mustache he looked quite average for the Middle East.

General Majeed snapped a salute as they walked into the chamber. General Ahmed returned the salute and said, "Be seated, and we will start. General Majeed, this is Alwan Najafi. He is one of our international agents looking after the interests of Iraq beyond our borders. He is in charge of most aspects of the activity we will discuss. This is Arzika," he said nodding to the average man. "He will lead a small team that is to see to all aspects of security."

Najafi had never seen this man before. He looked like he worked-out regularly. His movements were smooth and conservative. Najafi thought his eyes looked intense, too intense. There was a hardness in them like a wolf that had missed too many meals. The fact that the general had not even given his full name during introductions meant more than what was said. It implied that this man was in charge of more than normal security. He would be watching them all. Najafi knew the type. With a word, he could sever a man from his job, if not his life.

General Ahmed began. "The purpose of this meeting is to discuss the progress of a project of utmost importance. General Majeed, you have been asked to attend because the plan now is at a point where we require the assistance of some of your armored units. I cannot stress enough the secrecy or the importance of this project."

Mirza Rahman opened the folder he had placed in front of him on the table. He looked at General Majeed. "The site of the project is in a remote part of our country to keep it away from the prying eyes of the UN and especially the U.S. The site is located at Nukhayb. There is, as you probably know, a military airfield there. Actually it's a highway airstrip with a few buildings, including a hardened aircraft bunker."

They all knew a "hardened aircraft bunker" was a hangar with room for up to four fighter planes that had an arched, steel roof covered with several feet of reinforced concrete. This hangar was then covered with many feet of sand. It had a two-foot-thick door that opened by rolling to the side into a concrete cavity. In front of the door was a reinforced concrete blast wall to protect the door from missile attack. The door was set back far enough to let a fighter plane pass out by making a ninety degree turn after leaving the bunker.

"The hangar at Nukhayb was chosen because it is one of the few that has underground quarters similar to this one. The hangar and bunker were damaged by laser-guided bombs during the Gulf War, but the entire complex is quite usable if we make a few allowances. However, we do not want it to appear to the western intelligence satellites that we are refurbishing that complex.

"Now we are at a point where we must do some serious remodeling of the underground chambers to accommodate this project. This will require removal of concrete and earth and the installation of new reinforced concrete. To mask these operations we want you, General Majeed, to start some armor maneuvers in that part of the desert. A portion of the vehicles supplying your units will actually be supplying this remodeling operation. You will pick base camp locations that vary from time to time, and when we need major movements of material, you will set up near Nukhayb. These are to look like routine armored training exercises."

"Thank you," said General Ahmed, nodding to Rahman.

"General Majeed, one week from today you will have for my review operational plans for an extensive training exercise. Plan to have them last eight months. Are there any questions?"

"No sir, you will have my plan in a week."

"Good. You are excused. We must now discuss other details of the project."

After saluting, General Majeed left the room. General Ahmed thought he noticed a little more spring in Majeed's step than this assignment should have warranted but dismissed it as his imagination.

Najafi then explained the detailed design of the site. He showed the modifications that would be necessary to make the kitchen and eating room into a space big enough to house the gantry robots and the other machinery needed in the automated work cell. The main effort was to make the gantry bay high enough. This meant lowering the floor two meters as well as making additional tunnels between tubes.

"And how is the acquisition of the specialized equipment coming?"

Najafi reported that he was able to get all of the specialized equipment ordered. "All of these machines will come in a single forty-foot shipping container. The gantry robots and a motor-generator will all fit in a second forty-foot container so all outside shipments would come in only two containers. This is safer than using many small shipments. I can report that full scale production of the automatic gantry robots is on schedule."

"Machinery of any kind showing up at the borders of Iraq will be questioned."

"I have thought of this. The robots will come in as lumber. It will work."

June 25, 1998, Plant 2

Ratling entered the high bay where the robots were set up for final testing. Breckon had one of them operating with a simple single jointed arm and gripper for the end effector. It was picking up small bricks from a random pile and piling them neatly on a table.

"Ed, those things look great."

"They may look great, but the programming isn't completed yet. We're close, I think, but nothing is certain until it works. It's *not* working now."

"It looks fine to me. You'll make it."

"The thing neither of us counted on was having two bridges on the same rails working simultaneously. The robot arms attached to the bottom

ends of the masts can interfere with each other, and this adds a programming problem."

"I don't get it. What's so hard about making the two arms avoid one
another?"

"Have you ever been walking down a hall and met someone who
moved to the same side as you to avoid a collision? The way you manage to resolve the conflict is that there's a different sense of courtesy in
the two individuals. With these robots, the identical programming is present in both machines and it's running on separate but identical computers. They could spend all day trying to resolve the conflict. At this point
I simply don't have a solution."

Ratling slowly asked. "Ed, are you saying you may not have all of the
programming done for the final test?"

Breckon turned and squarely faced Ratling. "Finally, do I have your
attention? I've been trying to tell you this for months. Yes, it's almost
certain it won't be done. Where have you been? I've been putting in all
the time I possibly can, weekends, long days—but there's no more. It's
not getting done!"

"You should have been more forceful before."

"What more could I do? I have given you three memos stating this.
On the rare occasions you've been here, I've always mentioned it. I
would've sent letters to the president and the board of directors. But no,
this is too secret for anything to get out. Now we're on the edge of a real
disaster."

Ratling had that hangdog look he had whenever things weren't going
right on the project.

"After you pulled off that prototype test with your tricks," Breckon
continued, "You seemed to write off this project like it was done. Well
tricks won't save us this time. Either the schedule slips or the customer
doesn't get what he thinks he's getting."

"That . . . that . . . that," Ratling stammered, "That's just not an option."

"I'm sorry it took so long for you to grasp this," Breckon continued.
"If there's nothing else for now, I have a lot of work to do. I want to get
this thing shipped on schedule as badly as you do. I need a vacation."

Ratling returned to his office at the main plant and sat for some minutes
thinking. Then he got up, closed the door, returned to his desk, and punched

a number into his phone. From time to time he had sent contributions to his local congressman in Washington. Now, it was time to call in a favor.

After waiting several minutes, he finally got Congressman Bentner on the line. It took some coaxing, but he got him to commit to sending him anything he could find that would make exporting machinery to Eastern Europe harder after the first of August.

In the following days, Ratling showed up at his Plant 2 office for at least part of the day. He had gotten an envelope of information from Congressman Bentner. There were a few insignificant changes, such as the way packing lists were handled. Then he saw one rule change that would cause commodity codes, numbers that describe all goods bought and sold, to be more carefully scrutinized. For example, there are separate codes for each type of bearing. Frequently the most obvious code for a ball bearing might be used all the time. Under loose rules, if the bearing really was a spherical roller bearing it would be passed through, but with strict rules it would be stopped until it was described properly and then checked against lists of restricted items.

It had been Ratling's hope to export the gantry robots using some general "industrial machinery" commodity code. This regulation change was a genuine reason to ship before August first. In fact, the robots had to be out of the country before that date.

July 1, 1998, Plant 2

Breckon was at his desk concentrating on a print-out of computer codes. He was completely engrossed in his work when Ratling's overly loud voice broke through his concentration. "I don't care about the rules. You must meet me, here, tonight, while you're in town. Wait a minute." Ratling got up and closed his office door. That was all Breckon heard.

Breckon wondered what would be happening tonight. Later in the afternoon, he saw Ratling and said, "I must leave at a regular hour today. I have to go to the bank and get something straightened out."

"Oh," Ratling seemed almost relieved, "that should be all right. You've been putting in some long days anyway. Any progress on the programming?"

"You know, three steps forward, and two backward. Yes there's progress, but it's slow."

"Yes, I understand," said Ratling apprehensively.

After stopping at the bank Breckon called Harris and asked him to come over with his best camera and a telephoto lens.

When Harris arrived, Breckon was pulling a frozen pizza out of the oven. "This afternoon I overheard Ratling arrange a meeting at Plant 2 with someone. I don't know who it was because he closed his door after the first few seconds. He seemed very emphatic that this meeting had to take place tonight before this person left town. There's so much mystery surrounding this job that I thought we might be able to get a picture of somebody or something. Maybe it's dumb, but I feel any clue would help."

"When do you think this meeting will take place?"

"I had to leave earlier than normal today to go to the bank, which seemed like a relief to Ratling, so I'd guess any time. Let's grab a couple cans of soda and take the pizza with us. Can we take your truck? He'd instantly recognize mine."

They found a place to park across the street from Plant 2. There were some shrubs that partially hid Harris's truck but still gave them a good view of the plant. Ratling's car was still there but otherwise the parking lot was empty. At six-thirty a car drove up and parked beside Ratling's. Harris took several pictures as the man got out of his car and headed to the building.

"This guy looks sort of Mideastern or something like that," said Harris. "Now what?"

"I don't know. Wait, I guess. If it's an emergency meeting, there usually aren't too many options, so it's a matter of making one decision or another. It shouldn't take long."

Inside the building, Ratling and Robbie were in the break room where Ratling was making a new pot of coffee. "I tell you, Mr. Robbie, it looks like it'd be a good idea to ship the gantry robots before August 1. Starting on the first, the U.S. will be much more careful in checking the commodity codes on export papers. And we don't want any unnecessary poking around the container with these things in it." They went into Ratling's office, and George pulled the information from Congressmen Bentner out of the envelope.

Robbie looked at the regulations that had some lines, dates, and paragraphs highlighted in yellow. After several minutes he said, "Yes, I see what you mean. When do you think we should ship?"

Ratling, feeling relieved, replied, "It would appear the middle of July at the latest to be sure the container clears the U.S. port before the first."

"Are you ready to conduct the final test early as well?"

"That's the hard part. We won't be ready for the final acceptance test that soon. It's a matter of some of the parts not coming when we were told they would." This was a lie, but Ratling was pretty sure he would get away with it. "The rest of the system has come together very nicely."

Robbie said, "I too am in favor of shipping before the end of the month to avoid any customs complications. We aren't as concerned with the final test as having your best engineer come to the site and supervise installation and start-up."

George was thinking that Breckon was his best *and* his only engineer. "We could find a good, competent engineer who does installation supervision as his job. I'd guess there would be five or six weeks from the time of shipment to arrival at the site. That would be enough time to find someone and train him."

"No!" said Robbie emphatically. "We want *your* best engineer. Some general engineer won't understand the fine points of the system. It's too complicated. You'll recall that having this engineer for start-up is specifically part of the contract, and you have been paid to deliver on that contract." This was an obvious reference to the bribe money.

In a deadpan voice, Ratling said, "The bottom line is my best engineer won't go."

"You Americans are so soft. If you fail in this, you'll lose your job, and all the rest of your comfortable life will go too. When Claudia finds out about Andrea, things will change fast."

Ratling was trapped. A few days before, he had tried to break it off with Andrea, but she had asked for a lot of money or she'd tell everyone. "Well, what do you have in mind?"

"It's simple. Your engineer goes. We'll fly him to the site in the client's private business jet."

"That'll take some real arm twisting. What's in it for me?"

"Now we're doing business again. There will be plenty in it for you. Here's how it's handled." Robbie then went over the plan in detail.

July 6, 1998, Plant 2

When Breckon got to work the Monday after the Fourth of July holiday, Ratling was waiting for him. Breckon had worked Friday, the holiday, and Saturday, but took Sunday off for a change. Ratling immediately said. "Ed, will you come into my office? There's something we
need to discuss."

Because Breckon had never heard Ratling use such a mild tone of
voice with him, he was immediately suspicious. "Sure, what's on your
mind?"

"I've received a directive from the customer that we must ship by
July fifteenth. I gather that it has something to do with the customer's
financing. The hardware's all done, isn't it?"

"Yeah. There's some tidying up to do, but it's done."

"Good. This is July sixth, so take, say, two days to finish up. Take
pictures of everything, every screw. Then tag each part that must be removed. We want to make it so someone can put it back together in his
sleep. We'll get a container in here with some riggers and load it all for
shipment on the fifteenth."

"And the final performance test?"

"There won't be one. After the gantry robots have shipped, you'll
continue working on the software using the original prototype. Then
we'll down-load the final software to the site by modem."

Breckon was dumbfounded, "But there's only one prototype, and we
haven't kept it up to the latest configuration as we made changes to the
design of the units for shipment. The prototype is hardly representative
of what we'll ship."

"We'll use parts from the spare parts set they've ordered and backor-
der parts we use. That's the way it has to be. Do the best you can."

— 6 —

The White House, Washington, D.C.

The president of the United States was seated behind his desk in the Oval Office for his regular Monday morning briefing. Across the desk from him sat his national security advisor, the Secretary of Defense, and the DCI (Director of Central Intelligence). Since the president took office, he had tried several approaches to keeping abreast of world events and had finally settled on this format. This was not an official meeting since it left out several important agencies, but he had found these were people he could work with and get the results he wanted.

Jason Hughs, the DCI, fiddled with his tie, feeling the knot with his fingers to be sure it was exactly centered between the points of his shirt collar. He was always meticulously dressed. Secretary of Defense Vince Packard, came out of industry. With a good senior executive salary and stock options, he had done well. He could have easily taken the cabinet position at no pay. The president's national security advisor, Carl Winton, came out of academia. He was on sabbatical from a professorship at Harvard where he taught political science. He looked the part of a professor with a ready pipe in his hand whenever he could get away with it, and a well-worn sport coat with leather patches on the elbows.

They were discussing North Korea. "Jason, is there any indication they'll do anything other than make threats?" the president asked the DCI.

"Not really, they've been down this road before, so at this time I don't think it's worthy of an official response."

"Fine, is there anything new in the Middle East?"

Secretary of Defense Packard leaned forward. "On routine flights over the no-fly zone in the southern part of Iraq we have been seeing an increase in armor maneuvers. Nothing on a large scale, just a couple of battalions more or less."

"Are they threatening Kuwait again?"

"No, these are much further to the west, out in the desert away from everything. One thing is peculiar, though. On two occasions, pilots saw them some miles south of the border into Saudi Arabia. This shouldn't cause any alarm. It's just different. After all, the border there's just a line on the maps since there's nothing in that area that anybody wants."

Carl Winton broke in. "There's a road, the Tap Line Road, that follows a pipeline running parallel to the Iraqi border and twenty miles south of it. It runs all the way from the Persian Gulf coast to the Mediterranean Sea. Could they be trying to make it look like they're threatening a pumping station or something to get everyone's attention off the UN inspection team searching for WMDs?"

The president broke in, "Jason, here we are again. Can't we get someone into that country to find out what's going on? We're just blind. Even with the UN inspection team digging around in there, we get nothing of any value."

"Mr. President, that's a UN team not a U.S. team, which makes a difference. In addition, because of the Gulf War, the sadistic leader of that beleaguered country killed ten innocent people for every spy, but he pretty well got all the spies, including ours. But, I'll see if we can step up some activity and learn about the armor movements."

"Good, and, Vince, make a few more flights in that area and report on all tank movements. But make sure it's not obvious we're taking any interest in this activity."

The president stood. "Gentlemen, I have another meeting in a few minutes, so that'll be it for today."

After some long days, the container containing the gantry robots had shipped the week before on July fifteenth, the day specified. Breckon still had that nagging feeling that something was wrong. There was a requirement to leave the rear eight feet of the container empty. That was not hard to accommodate since they had received a full forty-foot container. Someone obviously wanted to put a last piece of machinery in the container at the freight forwarder's warehouse.

The software was workable but not complete. Breckon's first priority was solving the problem of the two robots sharing the same workspace. It was also important to complete the documentation. Cindy Thomas had experience with the vendors, many of whom still owed them manuals and drawings, so she was still part of the team.

He noticed that Cindy looked particularly appealing as she came to work this day. Over the months as they had been pushing to get the project done on time, they had gotten to know one another quite well. Through the times of disappointments and setbacks, the characters of each had come out. Being able to anticipate pending disharmony, they learned to work around it. For the past few months, Ed had been wanting to ask Cindy out on a date, but he couldn't work up the nerve. Now with the project nearing its end, she would go back to the main plant, and their close working relationship would end.

At mid-morning Ed came up to Cindy's work area and asked, "Have you seen the manual on the scanning lasers around here? I thought they were here yesterday."

"I thought you took them to your desk to check the schematic against the point-to-point wiring diagrams," she responded.

"Well, I'll have to dig around in my office again." As he was about to leave it occurred to him her dress was extra nice today, almost like it was a special occasion. He wasn't given to complementing women on their clothes, but he thought the situation required a response. "Cindy, that's a very attractive dress."

Cindy smiled and said, "Thank you." *Attractive dress!* This is not attractive. It's a beautiful, simply stunning, too revealing, paid-blood-for, weapon-of-last-resort dress! But . . . attractive's a start.

Cindy had been in love with Ed for months. She longed for an excuse for them to get together socially, though she hated the thought of her having to ask him. She had hoped that with the shipment of the equipment, things would slow down, and he'd notice her. The compliment on her dress was a first.

Long after twelve, she was still at her desk as Ed walked into the reception area where she worked. She was full of anticipation. She could see him swallow hard as he forced some words to come out.

"Look at this, it's twelve forty-five already. Say, Cindy, would you like to go get something to eat?"

I can't believe it, he asked me! "Oh, it's nice of you to ask. Yeah, I'd like that."

As they walked to Ed's truck, he asked, "Where'd you like to go?"

"Wherever you'd like," she said demurely.

"The crowd should be thinning out at Mulligans about this time. How'd that be?"

"Sounds good to me."

When they walked into the restaurant, they were seated immediately in a nice booth next to a window. "You certainly look radiant today," Ed said. "Maybe you look like this all the time, and I just didn't notice. I've been going nuts getting those darned machines done."

The waiter walked up. "Good afternoon, my name is Sherwood. Could I get you something from the bar?"

Ed looked at Cindy and asked, "Cindy, anything?"

"I'd like a diet cola."

"Are you sure?" Ed coaxed. "Couldn't I interest you in a glass of wine, maybe a Chardonnay?"

"Oh, I don't think I should." She was thinking about how little she had eaten that day. She didn't want to screw it up by sliding under the table now that she had gotten this far.

"Come on, be adventurous," Ed continued.

"Okay, just a small one."

When the waiter had gone, Cindy said, "You're being awfully nice to me today. How come?" She could see the question made him uncomfortable, and she wished she hadn't asked it.

"Well, ah . . . you see . . . ah, well, I've wanted to get to know you . . . ah . . . but that job was so demanding, and I didn't know how to ask. I wasn't even sure you liked me. Now that the job has shipped, things can slow down a little."

"Well, you asked me today, and it was just perfect."

"I guess I'm sort of a klutz when it comes to women. You're very nice to say that, though."

The wine arrived, and they ordered the fillet mignon that was on special.

After the first swallow of wine, Cindy felt warm and good all over. She began eating bread sticks, crackers, anything to allay the effects of the wine. When the steaks finally arrived, sizzling on hot metal plates, she was not sure she could handle the sharp knife without cutting herself, not that she'd feel it if she did. The food tasted good. Nothing had ever tasted so good. The steaks were done just perfectly—slightly crisp on the outside and juicy on the inside. There were some mushrooms on the side and a separate plate of hash browns.

About the time they were finishing their meal, they ordered another glass of wine. When it arrived, Cindy was smiling at Ed as he was explaining something or other about programming the controls. She dipped her finger into the wine, stirred it around absentmindedly a few times, and then stuck the end of her finger into her mouth. "Yep, that's a good one too."

Ed stopped talking and smiled. He leaned over the table and whispered, "Can I have a taste too?" She started to slide the glass toward him. "No, no, the way you did it."

Taking the hint, she sensuously stirred her fingertip around in the wine and slowly held the finger out toward him. He stuck out his tongue and gently licked the drop of wine off the under side of her finger. Then he lurched forward a couple of inches and grabbed the tip of her finger in his lips. Startled, she jerked her hand back and giggled.

She held her hand close to her, and looked at her finger as she slowly bent the tip back and forth. Then she peered out from under dark lashes at Ed, her eyes sparkling. Ed laughed lightly. Looking down again, she said, "You'd better be careful little finger, that might be the big bad wolf."

They both laughed. It seemed they were laughing and giggling a lot.

Finally it was time to go. Cindy took his arm as they were walking out. She was feeling the wine and did not want to stumble. How could it have hit her so hard?

As they drove back, Cindy was sitting right next to Ed. She had lifted up the center armrest and used the center seat belt. They didn't talk much. Ed pulled into the plant parking lot and parked in his usual place.

As they walked to the front door, Ed said, "There'll probably be a reception committee to meet us. You know how nosy Brad is."

Cindy looked at her watch. They had been gone two hours.

As they walked in, Brad just happened to meet them. Just happened, ha! "Well, did you kiddies have a good time at the swing set?"

Ed looked awkward, but Cindy stuck out her chin and in a perky voice said, "For your information . . . yes!" She then headed for the ladies room. Once inside, she giggled as she splashed cold water on her face and neck, in between scooping water into her mouth. Wow, thirsty, an ocean of wine! She felt great.

The president opened the regular Monday morning security briefing. They rather hurriedly went through the dozen items on the agenda. When they finished, the president said, "Gentleman, last Monday Vince mentioned that the Iraqis were engaged in some tank maneuvers in their desert and were crossing the border and marauding the pipeline in Saudi Arabia."

Secretary of Defense Packard replied, "Excuse me, Mr. President. I believe I meant that they were crossing the border in the *neighborhood* of the pipeline."

"Well, anyway I had the Secretary of State mention this to the Saudis. They weren't too concerned, but, when pressed, they agreed to let us conduct some maneuvers in the same area south of the border. Mind you, just a few tanks with no big show of it."

Packard could sense the president had one or his "wonder" plans stuck in his head. He felt he had to do what he could to head it off. "Why would we press the Saudis to put in some U.S. tanks? By the time you get all of the supporting units, those few tanks turn into a contingent of two hundred men and woman. That size of force isn't easy to hide. You don't just deploy tanks. There are also Bradley fighting vehicles, probably artillery support, Apache and Blackhawk helicopters, maintenance units, fuel, water, and supply trucks, supporting staff. And, what's the mission, anyway?"

"Take it easy, Vince. Your concerns are noted. The mission is to get the Iraqis to fire on U.S. forces. We want them to appear vulnerable. There will be some risk, but a manageable one. I want a reason to take out the president of Iraq. That part of the world will never settle down until that guy's gone. It's as simple as that.

"I propose putting in a minimal force—some Abrams tanks, some Bradleys if you want, and a few maintenance and supply personnel. We'll try to get the Saudis to help behind the scenes with logistics. Then when they fire on our forces, we ratchet up the stakes as events develop. Eventually we straighten out that mess. Jason, have you had any success in getting any more information on what's going on?"

"Only a start. But, we're looking under every rock. We have a very good man who works in Kuwait and eastern Saudi Arabia. He's developing new contacts as we speak."

"Vince, by Wednesday I want you to give me a couple of plans of how we can inconspicuously get some tanks into that part of Saudi Arabia. Make use of as much equipment already there as possible. There must be some stuff that we left there after the Gulf War that nobody uses. I'm pressed for time today, so that'll be all. Good day, gentlemen."

On Wednesday morning Vince Packard and the others from the Monday morning meeting were in the Oval Office with the president at the unheard of hour of seven-thirty, unheard of, that is, from the president's normal schedule. "As you requested on Monday, I've come up with some assets and ideas for putting some tanks into northern Saudi Arabia," Pakard began. "There are some forty early model Abrams M1 tanks in storage near KKMC, that's King Kalid Military City, a large military complex in northern Saudi Arabia. It's north-northwest of Riyadh, and eighty miles south of the Iraqi border. It's equivalent to the Pentagon, plus having many operational units in its environs.

"These tanks were left after the Gulf War and have had minimal maintenance since. We could conduct a sort of readiness test to see how the tanks survived seven years of storage. This would be an endurance test, so we would plan to put on miles and in the process get out to the area where the Iraqis are having their maneuvers."

"That's a pretty thin excuse for starting a war," Hughs said. "Anybody seeing that plan would say you should drive the tanks around a test track if you want to put on miles. There're bound to be break-downs, a lot of them. Why have your dead tanks spread over hundreds of square miles?"

Packard, irritated by the whole plan, responded. "I know that, and if you have a better idea, I'm listening. This is as inconspicuously as this type of operation can be handled. This way we only have to fly some crews over there on temporary duty. Otherwise we have to call up units for overseas deployment, and the press will start a feeding frenzy. One way or another we'll have to get at least two M88s in there so . . . . "

The president broke in, "What are M88s? And how much stuff do we really need? We don't want it to look like we're actually starting a war."

"Mr. President," Packard spoke again, "M88s are tank recovery vehicles. They are themselves large tracked vehicles used to tow disabled armored vehicles back to base. As Jason just noted, there will be break-downs, especially with these old tanks."

"All right," the president conceded. "Say we try to get five or six of the forty tanks running, use only the best ones."

Packard begrudgingly nodded his approval.

The president brightened up. "That sounds like a plan. Vince, I want you to set this all up. After we get a half dozen running and tested, I want the CIA to take charge of the operation. Take the tanks, crews, and a minimum support structure and make a base near the area where we can make contact with the Iraqi tanks. Keep in mind we need maximum

security on this until the shooting starts. Let me know when the operation is ready to go."

The president got up and was walking toward his reading room when
he added, "Oh, by the way, Vince, take care who you pick to lead this
operation. He must be good in making the tanks work, but bad in using
them. We don't want to get a budding Patton, or a fledgling Rommel out
there."

"Yes, sir, we'll search our personnel records for just the right man."

Four days later, Fort Hood, Texas

"That's Bravo Company, Rebic's outfit, coming in now," said Master
Sergeant Hendric to the corporal beside him. A formation of M1A1
Abrams main battle tanks had begun to appear over the rise a half-mile
away. The sergeant took the cigar out of his mouth and spat a bit of to-
bacco on the ground as he counted the tanks. "Ha! He's managed to collect them all again. That Rebic's a wild man with his tactics. The senior
brass hates the way he splits his force and does such erratic stuff. The
platoon leaders love it though, always seem to know what's going on."
Pausing to take a draw in the cigar, he continued. "He drives my staff
like he owns battalion maintenance. His crews go nuts keeping their
tanks in top shape. Pays off though. Not many of his tanks get towed in."

Corporal Stevens, driver for Colonel Marston, the brigade commander, took it all in without comment. He'd heard about Captain Rebic
a few times too. Both men stood beside the HMMWV (High Mobility
Multipurpose Wheeled Vehicle), Humvee, or Hummer, Stevens had
driven to the motor pool. The ground shook and the air pulsed as a total
of nine hundred tons of steel propelled by an accumulation of twenty-
one-thousand horsepower surged past them with an ear-splitting clanking
roar. As he saw the tank with the light blue flag embossed with "B6"
flying from the radio antenna come past him, he waved and pointed to
the HMMWV. Captain Rebic nodded. On the battalion radio net, Rebic
had been told to report to brigade headquarters immediately upon his
return to garrison.

Fifteen minutes later Captain Rebic walked to the waiting HMMWV.
A hard-set jaw set off his lean deeply tanned features. In his olive-drab,
nomex flight suit, he appeared out of place in the sandy landscape,
though this was the standard tanker uniform. He returned Stevens's salute

and got into the right front seat of the vehicle. They rode in silence to the headquarters building.

Captain Tom Rebic was still lost in his own thoughts as Stevens stopped in front of the Second Brigade headquarters building. The single-story, red-brick building was typical of the newer ones on military posts. Though nothing to tweak one's artistic senses, they were functional. Rebic got out without a word and started toward the door. He was apprehensive as he walked through the large open foyer and down the hall to the left toward the brigade commander's office. His normally quick pace came a little slower as he approached the unknown.

He was at a loss as to what to make of Colonel Marston's summons. Rebic had completed his ARTEP (Army Training Evaluation Program) a week before, and the dust still hadn't settled. The ARTEP was an exercise that all army units underwent each year to see how well they were prepared to perform their mission. This determined the level of training of the men as well as the readiness of their equipment, and, above all, it tested the competency of the commander.

Rebic's ARTEP had gone smoothly in most respects. The readiness of his vehicles and training of his men had rated top scores. But, his big worry was the highly critical assessment of him as a battle commander. In his engagement of the opposing force, referred to as the Op Force, he had repeatedly used unexpected maneuvers that left the enemy off balance. In fact, on one occasion, his OCs (Observer Controllers) even lost track of him.

The last straw came on the final action where he divided his force and sent one platoon on a twenty-five-kilometer flanking attack. As he engaged the main force from the front, Charlie platoon, as if by magic, appeared on the enemy's right flank, catching them totally by surprise. Their "whoopee lights" flashed on like a swarm of fireflies on a warm June evening. Rebic's company destroyed most of the Op Force.

For training, each tank was equipped with a MILES (Multiple Integrated Laser Engagement System) which shot a laser pulse where the main gun was pointed when the gunner triggered a simulation round. Each tank was also equipped with a vehicle harness containing laser receptors and a post with a light on it, the whoopee light. The light flashed a few times for a near miss and continuously to indicate the tank was destroyed.

Rebic was expecting to see a couple of the OCs at this meeting to give him a good berating. Taking a deep breath, he walked into the colonel's outer office.

"Captain Rebic to see Colonel Marston."

"The Colonel is ready for you. Go right in," the brigade adjutant said.

He knocked twice on the door, and a voice from within said, "Come."

As he entered, he was surprised to see only Lieutenant Colonel Lanham, his battalion commander, in the office with Colonel Marston. Marston was sitting behind a large, oak desk with assorted memorabilia on it. Hanging on the wall behind the colonel was a painting of an Indian brave on the back of a wild mustang. The horse and rider were engaged in battle, and their muscles stood out in stark relief. The Indian was madly grasping the horse's mane with one hand while the other was flung above his head. The horse's nostrils were flared, his head down, and his hind legs thrust out. Clods of dirt were suspended in the air having been thrown up by the pounding hooves. On a plaque beneath it was the title, *TEST OF WILLS*. Rebic wondered if the tense expression on the Indian's face was something of a reflection of his own.

"Captain Rebic reporting as ordered, sir," he said as he snapped a salute.

Colonel Marston returned the salute. "At ease, Captain. Have a chair. Colonel Lanham and I have been looking at the results of your ARTEP. For my part, I think that was a pretty gutsy thing you did with the flanking maneuver. If that platoon hadn't covered those twenty-five kilometers around that mountain in time, you would not only have been unable to out flank your opponent but would've been under gunned to meet the head on attack. But, as usual, you had the highest availability of equipment of any company in the brigade. At least you can get 'em to work even if you can't get the hang of how to use 'em."

Captain Rebic had a stoic expression as he thought how relieved he'd be when this meeting was over. His flanking platoon did not arrive *just* in time. They slowed down near the end of the twenty-five klick drive to be sure they arrived at exactly the *right* time, but, what was the point?

"That aside, let's get down to why I called you in here."

"I don't understand, sir."

"Of course you don't. It's top secret," was the terse reply.

Rebic blinked hard, as his heart started to beat faster.

Marston looked at the expression on Rebic's face and said, "If you're bewildered, so are we. You've been selected to lead a special mission in

Saudi Arabia. The Pentagon picked you for reasons we can't imagine. We agree—neither of us would've chosen you."

That burned.

"Your top secret clearance came through a few months ago," said Lanham, "in time for this assignment, and, as I hear, just as you've decided to leave us."

That statement was more patronizing than it sounded. Rebic was leaving the army soon, one way or the other. Marston and Lanham knew that his review for promotion to major was coming up in a few months, and he would not be promoted. The army's policy at the time was that if you weren't good enough to promote after the standard time in rank, you weren't good enough to keep.

"Here's the story," Marston began. "Before the Gulf War in the early summer of 1990, when Iraq began massing its forces in the Kuwaiti border, someone got the bright idea that we should quietly get some war materiel on the way over there just in case. There happened to be a battalion of fifty-eight M1 tanks being prepared for movement from the active Army to a reserve unit. These tanks were from the first two years of production. Since they were being loaded on a ship on the East Coast for shipment to the West Coast, it was decided to divert the ship to the Persian Gulf. If they weren't needed, the ship would turn around and take them to the West Coast as planned.

"As it turned out, the ship arrived a day or two after Iraq invaded Kuwait. It may have given the Iraqis pause to realize the United States had reacted so fast. We immediately flew over some crews. The tanks were moved from place to place at night so it looked like we had many more than there actually were. They did a good job of the mission assigned to them. After the war, they were left in Saudi Arabia as prepositioned equipment in case anything flared up. But really, there was no reason to bring them back. They were worn out, and, of course, obsolete.

"Now someone wants to activate as many of those tanks as possible as soon as possible for an 'extended field test.' Ostensibly they want to put a lot of miles on them and see how well they perform after extended storage."

"So, what gives?" asked Rebic. "If the tanks are worn out, why would anyone want to know if they perform like they're not worn out?"

Marston continued. "It doesn't take a genius to figure out that a simple exercise like that would never be classified top secret. So, expect some surprises. In any case, when you arrive, you'll get your orders from the commander in the region who is located in KKMC."

"Will I be free to select the men I'll take?" Rebic asked.

Marston and Lanham knew the meaning of the request. Marston responded, "Yes, you will."

The two senior officers knew Rebic would select only men to accompany him. It was his strident disapproval of women in the military that would be the cause of his leaving the service, not his use of unconventional tactics, though the latter would be the stated reason. The issue of women was so sensitive, neither one wanted to even mention it in an official document like a promotion review.

The highly classified nature of the mission meant Rebic's force would be operating independently in some isolated area. Marston and Lanham both knew that an all-male force gave Rebic an edge on being successful, to say nothing of surviving, if it came to that. But, if there were complaints about his choice in personnel, they'd dump on Rebic.

Lanham said, "The first contingent to go with you will be part of the battalion maintenance platoon, and a couple of tank crews. You have the whole battalion to choose from."

As Rebic recovered from the shock, he tried to approach the problem professionally. "So there are some old model M1s there. What else will I have? If they're worn out, they'll break down a lot. I'll need a couple of M-88 retrievers. Where do we get our food, fuel, and other supplies?"

"You'll have to take that up with the folks in KKMC when you get there. It only says you're to exercise the tanks."

"How soon will this happen?"

"Plan to load on a C-17 six days from now."

— 7 —

The sky was clear and the sun warm. Overhead was a dome of the most beautiful blue there ever was. On the top of the load of hay bales there was a breeze, and it felt good to Keith as it evaporated some of the sweat. He was fourteen, and with him on the load were his brothers John, fifteen, and Terry, ten. All wore straw hats. Their dad drove the 1953 Ford tractor as they wound their way down the field road toward the barn. The smell of the fresh hay was everywhere and was just part of life on the small farm.

Nine high! Normally they only piled the bales eight high. During loading, Terry drove—at ten he was old enough for that. Dad picked the bales from the ground, and then Keith had carefully placed them on the wagon so that the pile would have a good foundation and not tip over as the wagon creaked and rocked as it moved along. It was a simple wagon with planks on it so the load was only two bales wide. When the load got high enough, the second one on the wagon would take the bales from the one below and work on the higher layers. The bales thus were moved from one boy to the other to the top using a lot of manpower, or boy power as the case was. Bale handling machines were several years away. For this first load of the day Keith was the "upper story man." When he had a good start on the eighth layer there was a pause as they turned at the end of the field, it was then that he had puffed and snorted and gotten a bale on top of the eighth layer, a sort of trophy. It was no small feat to work standing up on a swaying wagon, lifting bales that weighed half as much as the slim, lanky boys.

His father looked up at it and shook his head a little. Keith knew his dad thought it was stupid; the load might fall over because of that. But, what do you say to young men testing themselves? Let it go, they'll learn.

It was hard work but it gave a sense of self-worth beyond compare. Even Terry knew he had an important part in earning his keep. The family lived entirely from the profits of the farm. Life was so positive in those times. It was hard to imagine they were ever so young, so eager for the future to arrive . . . . Ring!

"Why did we ever invent phones!" thought Keith Gibbon, "interrupted a perfectly good daydream."

This was not rural Minnesota in the mid 1950s, it was Saudi Arabia in the late 1990s, and Gibbon was not the young man he had been then; he was nearly sixty and feeling every year of it.

"Yeah, Keith here," he said into the phone that was used only as an intercom since the only outside line was in the general's trailer. "General" had no reference to military, but was short for general contractor.

"Someone is here from the U.S. Department of the Army and wants to talk to an American. Can you come?" said a voice with a distinct Japanese accent.

Wondering what this could be about Gibbon answered, "Okay, I'll come." He lifted his slender six-foot-two frame from the swivel chair and grabbed a hard hat. He was in the back row of a dozen construction trailers placed in a three-by-four grid. The first trailer one encountered was the general's trailer belonging to Mitsubishi Heavy Industries.

Gibbon had come to Saudi Arabia to supervise the installation of ArmCon's part of the 1.2 billion-dollar expansion of a petro plant. It was a few miles north along the coast from Al Jubayl on the Persian Gulf. He had been in the Mideast several times in the last eight years and had decided this would be the last time, but that's what he decided every time. He was getting too old for it—he said that every time too. If all went well he would be going home in six weeks.

He felt the heat as he stepped out of the air-conditioned trailer. The sun was nearly at its zenith, and the temperature was probably nearing a hundred and twenty already. He had been here a week and was becoming acclimated to it. It was dry desert heat, so if a guy kept his head covered and drank plenty of water, he could survive.

As Gibbon entered the general's trailer, he saw a man looking a little lost standing to the side, and assumed this was the man he had come to see. "Hello, I'm Keith Gibbon. Are you the Department of the Army?" Gibbon asked as he smiled and extended his right hand.

The stranger, six feet tall, a little overweight and balding, extended his hand. "Not the whole Department of the Army. Just one member. I'm Craig Kardell. Could I have some of your time, perhaps in your office?"

"I guess you could. Come with me, and we shall retreat to my spacious, comfortable, elegantly appointed office," he said in his customary light-hearted way.

After they were out of the "front" trailer Kardell said, "Actually I'd prefer if we could walk outside so we could speak in private. What I have to ask you is a little embarrassing, and I hope we can keep our conservation confidential, at least at first."

"Okay, but I think we should stay inside. There are only two other guys in my trailer at the present, and they're at the other end."

When they were in the relative comfort of the trailer, Kardell explained his predicament. Kardell had been selected to replace an ill member of the United Nations team in Iraq looking for WMDs. He had been in Iraq for three weeks and this was his first break. The head of the United Nations WMD team had sent him with several others for a four day rest in Saudi Arabia. In real life, Kardell had a degree in chemical engineering and was employed by the U.S. Army in Arlington, Virginia, where his job was developing doctrine for fighting on a battlefield where the enemy used chemical weapons. His problem was he did not know how chemical weapons were actually made.

Gibbon thought a moment and said, "The plant expansion we're installing here wouldn't be much help. This is a PET plant—very special purpose and not designed for anything else."

"By PET you mean polyethylene-terephthalate, I assume."

"Yeah. The only purpose of this entire expansion is to crystallize the amorphous PET so it can be molded into the clear plastic beverage containers. But you may be in luck. I was here four years ago for the installation and startup of a plant in Kuwait. That plant is of a different construction so it can make a variety of chemicals. People there might give you some help."

"It must be very discrete. I don't want any of the Arabs knowing my purpose."

Gibbon chuckled. "In this part of the world that may be a tad difficult." Gibbon dug through some papers in his desk drawer. "Here we go. This is the guy to call. I assume you have a car, so let's go down the road a couple of miles and find a public phone."

After arriving at a general merchandise store, they found a phone booth. "Pick up the phone and tell them you want this number," Gibbon said, handing a slip of paper to Kardell. "They place the call, and when you're done you pay the store. Ask for Ali Taryam. Make up any excuse you want. I know him, and I'll go with you, but don't tell him that. I want it to be a surprise. Make the appointment for tomorrow morning, around nine o'clock."

With the appointment made, Kardell dropped Gibbon off at the plant after agreeing to pick him up at his apartment in Al Jubayl at six the next morning.

It was a three hour drive up to the plant. Kardell borrowed one of the inspection team cars after explaining what he wanted to do. At the Kuwaiti border, Kardell showed his UN credentials, and they were waved through. "That's the way to travel," said Gibbon.

When they arrived at the petro plant, they went into a modern, immaculately clean front office. The floors and walls were white and gray marble, and there were several potted palms setting off a graceful entry. As they walked in, the woman at the front desk looked up. She was strikingly beautiful. She paused a moment and said in a heavy accent, "OG, we thought we might never see you again. How nice of you to come." She pushed a key for an extension on the telephone panel and said, "Abu, come quickly. See who is here!"

A minute later, a middle-aged Arab came into the lobby. When he saw Gibbon, he smiled broadly and held out his hand. "Welcome, OG. What can I do for you? So nice of you to stop by to see us."

"I'm here with Mr. Craig Kardell. Craig, Mr. Abu Iqbal. We have an appointment with Ali."

"Please, come to my office. I will find Ali. I think he is out in the plant."

As they followed Abu to his office, Kardell whispered to Gibbon. "Why are these people so glad to see you?"

"It's a long story. I'll tell you on the way back."

When they had taken seats Abu picked up his phone and told someone, "Tell Ali to come to my office at once. He has a visitor."

Presently an Arab man in his late twenties, five-foot-five and of slight build, walked through the door, stopped a moment and then smiled broadly. "Oh, it is you! How nice of you to come." He warmly shook Gibbon's hand. "How is the side. Did it finally heal?"

Gibbon responded, "Yes, thank you, it did. It's good to see you. You look well, in fact disgustingly fit and *young*."

They both laughed. "OG, you could always make me laugh. Father and I spoke of you last week. We must spend a few minutes and get caught up on what has been happening. Is there anything I can do for you?"

"Well, not for me, but let me introduce you to Craig Kardell. He called yesterday with a request, and I sort of tagged along."

"Very sneaky of you OG. I might have expected something like this. Please come with me, and we'll see what we can do to help."

In Taryam's office, definitely elegant and well appointed, Kardell began his story. "I'm a chemical engineer who works for the Department of the Army, U.S. Army that is. When the U.S. chemical weapons expert on the UN Inspection team in Iraq took ill, I was chosen to replace him. I know how chemical weapons are used in combat. My specialty is protective gear for soldiers. But, I'm not knowledgeable in how these chemicals are manufactured. Keith thought you could show me some of the workings of your plant that would help."

Taryam nodded. "We're concerned with our neighbor to the north, having recently experienced considerable unpleasantness at its hands. I'll call one of our chemical engineers who determines how the plant is configured to make a range of products. You two can discuss chemistry while OG and I visit. After lunch we can tour the plant if that suits you."

"That sounds great."

A few minutes later, an Arab man entered. In his forties, the man's skin was very dark. He was introduced as Abdul, after which, Kardell and the engineer left. As Taryam and Gibbon chatted, the conversation turned to the UN inspectors.

"Ali, what do you hear about what's happening in Iraq these days, especially with the UN inspectors?"

Taryam shifted uncomfortably in his chair. "They find what the Iraqis want them to find. But on the other hand, having to move their labs and facilities around all the time means the Iraqis aren't getting much done. So, the UN is indirectly accomplishing its mission. From what I know, things are under control. You must know that even though we don't agree with the present leader's heavy-handed methods, he will pass away, and the Iraqis will still be our neighbors."

Gibbon looked surprised. "Is anything happening that might mean the leadership could change?"

Taryam fell silent again for a few seconds. "The only change we've seen is some military maneuvers in the far southwestern desert, mostly armor units. That's a mystery for now. Maybe he's becoming paranoid because of the incessant bombing by the U.S. There are many rumors. Everyone watches everyone else around here."

"You mean spies, double agents, listening devices, and stuff like that?"

Taryam nodded. "It's so pervasive that I'm somewhat concerned for you. You may have quite honestly tried to help this guy, one of your countrymen, but I'm afraid you've acted naively. This is one of the most heavily spy-infested areas of the world. Nothing happens that's not relayed to someone. Sometimes quite innocent things are reported, something gets lost in the translation, and you're in trouble."

"You mean even when a pipe doesn't fit at the plant and it has to be cut and rewelded, the information ends up in an intelligence agency some place?"

Taryam replied. "Almost that bad. As you have noticed, we have many guest workers in Kuwait and Saudi Arabia. They come from all over—India, the Philippines, Indonesia, some from Puerto Rico, and other countries. Most of them have low-paying service jobs. If someone comes along and offers them a day's pay for some information, they will gladly supply it if they can. The politics mean nothing to them."

There was a knock on the door, and the chemical engineer entered with Kardell in tow. The four of them had lunch in the executive dining room. Some people find it hard becoming accustomed to Arab food. With the right chefs, and they had the right chefs here, it was delicious. After the meal, they went out to tour the plant. Gibbon remembered much of it, and at times mentioned changes that had been made since the installation. As they walked, Ali said, "By the way, I spoke to Father briefly before lunch, and he insisted I extend an invitation to you to come visit us while you are here. He told me to be very insistent. He will send a car to get you."

"I appreciate that very much, and I intend to accept his kind invitation. But things will get very busy in a day or two. The plant will be ready for my equipment to be installed, and we'll work long days. After that, I'll have slack time until start-up. Maybe in four weeks or so. Let me know what works for you and your father."

After the tour, Ali walked out to the car with Craig and Keith, who both expressed their gratitude for the help, said good-bye, and drove off. Kardell said, "Thanks for helping me. You didn't have to, but it was invaluable to me. Now please tell me why those people are such good friends of yours. It can't be simply because you make Ali laugh."

"No, there's a lot more to it than that. Since we have three hours of driving, I'll tell ya the story. In 1994, I was here for the installation of part of the plant we visited. Ali had, six months before, returned from the U.S. where he had gotten his chemical engineering degree, as well as a minor in international trade. We hit it off from the start. I think he missed the American life, and I reminded him if it. We'd kid around, and I'd call him the young snip, and he'd call me the old guy. I knew he was connected but not how."

"That's where the name OG comes from?"

"Yes, but that came later. One day he came into the construction trailer . . . . "

"Hey there, old guy, your bolt-turning wrench monkeys installed a valve backward in the nitrogen feed line under the fourth floor. Better get it changed before more equipment gets put in and you can't get at it."

"That's valve 3324-LV4. It's in correctly. That's a left-hand model with the actuator on the opposite side from the normal ones."

"Not so. I saw the arrow molded in the housing, and it was pointed the wrong way."

"You must be blind," Gibbon retorted. "Are you sure you don't need a cup of coffee?"

"I'll bet you a cup of coffee it's wrong, but you'll have to trust me unless you can get your old bones up to the third floor." There was a taunting grin on his face.

"You're on, you young snip."

"Follow me."

The valve could only be seen looking up from the third floor. Since much of the equipment was several floors high, the floors were put in after the equipment was in place. In many places the floors gave way to nothing more than steel-plate platforms connected by catwalks. In the area under the valve in question, a platform was in the process of being built and did not yet have handrails. Some temporary posts had been welded to the sides of the beams supporting the decking. The construction crew had left for the lunch break before attaching chains to the posts.

When they arrived on the third floor, Taryam led the way across a catwalk to the platform under the valve. Gibbon looked at it carefully and said, "Okay, I see the valve. It looks fine to me."

Taryam craned his neck. "The light's not the same as before. Earlier in the day the sun was shining in here and the arrow was clearly visible." In his eagerness to prove his point, Taryam walked around on the platform trying to see the valve from different angles. As he was intently looking at the valve, he put his foot down so it was partly off the platform. He lost his balance and gave a short cry.

Gibbon looked over and saw him waving his arms trying to regain his balance. Gibbon was near one of the posts. In an instant, he saw he could not reach Taryam to stop his fall. He turned, dropped to a sitting position beside the post with his arm around it, and stuck his leg straight out toward Ali, and yelled, "Grab my leg!"

Taryam saw the foot and at the last second caught it. The weight of Taryam falling while grasping Gibbon's foot pulled Gibbon off the platform, scraping his ribs unmercifully as he went over the side. Gibbon was grasping the post for dear life as he felt his joints jerk as if he were being pulled apart. He now swung in free space below the platform with Taryam dangling from his foot. Managing to maintain his hold on the post at the level of the platform decking, he gasped in short words, "Climb up me, I can't pull us up."

At that moment Taryam yelled, "Help" in two languages. Two floors below, the last of the crew leaving for lunch looked up and saw the two men swinging from the platform. The men turned at once and started running back up. Both Gibbon and Taryam knew it was not a good option to let go and fall. Forty feet below them lay partially complete concrete work with re-bar sticking straight up.

Taryam grabbed the bottom of Gibbon's pant leg in his fist and started to climb, grabbing some of the fabric a little higher with each pull. The weight on his pants made Gibbon's belt dig into his hips. Blood from Gibbon's side dripped in Ali's face whenever he looked up. "Hurry up, and don't jerk or swing . . . can't hold much longer." Ali finally managed to get Gibbon's foot between his knees. As he grabbed some of his shirt in his fist some buttons on the front tore off, and he almost fell.

Gibbon could feel the vibration as the men came running across the platform. The first man knelt down with his shoulder braced against the post and reached down. He grabbed Taryam's left hand, but Gibbon's blood and Taryam's sweat made his hand slick, and he slipped free. The man fell to his stomach, reached further, and they clasped each other's wrists. He gasped something in Arabic to another man. As the second man lifted the first man up off the deck, a third man grasped Taryam's right hand, and with a heave, he was lifted onto the platform.

The removal of Taryam's weight came just in time for Gibbon as one of his hands became too weak to hold and slipped off. At the last instant, a strong hand grasped the wrist of the remaining hand. Gibbon looked up and saw his savior with his shoulder braced against the post, straining as though the blood vessels in his neck would burst. Kieth now hung by his hand from the mighty grip of the workman, too weak to help himself. Gibbon saw the post against which the man braced himself start to bend, and he imagined them both falling to their deaths in the next second.

The man managed to hiss something through his clenched teeth, and the other two men clasped his free arm. They weren't moving up, but the post stopped bending. The first man managed to pull Gibbon up a few inches, and one of the others pulled on Gibbon's armpit until Gibbon got his arm above the deck. Then they pulled on his clothing and skin and managed to work him up onto the platform. Kieth growled through clenched teeth as they dragged his injured side across the edge of the decking.

Gibbon lay on his good side and saw Taryam sitting on the deck leaning against an air duct. Taryam was pale and shaking. "That was close my friend," Gibbon said in a short, halting breath.

"O . . . G . . . , you saved me from death." Taryam moved to get up, but one of the men motioned him to stay.

"We made it though." Gibbon closed his eyes, laid his head on his arm, and remembered nothing more.

Gibbon awoke in a bed in the home of Ali's father, Sheikh Ahmad Bin Khalid Al-Taryam, an extremely wealthy and influential man. They got to know each other, and in the days that followed, they spoke many times. Sometimes Ali joined them, as did others of Sheikh Ahmad's household and staff. The house was impressive. It had been thoroughly trashed by the Iraqis during the occupation in 1990, but restoration was nearly complete except for the gardens. There were many desert plants that grew slowly and would take a generation to return to what they were.

To help pass the time, Ali, who had recently taken up sport flying, took Gibbon out to see his airplanes. Ali had a Stearman in perfect condition. As Gibbon watched, he took it up and did some loops and rolls.

Ali appeared to be a good pilot from the way he handled the plane. Gibbon could not help worrying because light plane accidents were seldom the result of mechanical failure or inability of the pilot to control it. Usually they were due to errors in judgement.

After Ali landed the plane, they were sitting on a bench beside the hangar, and Gibbon told him what worried him. "You know, Ali, several years ago, I met another young pilot quite by accident. He had recently gotten his license. I live in a suburb some distance north of St. Paul, Minnesota, and the land west of my house had not yet been developed. The engine in his Cessna 150 stopped, yet he managed quite skillfully to get the plane down safely. I saw him land because, while a person normally ignores the sounds of planes overhead, the engine of this one suddenly stopped. That caught my attention so I went outside.

"As I approached the plane, I saw the pilot empty the gascolator, then get in and start the engine. He was ready to take off again when I waved at him to stop. With the engine off, I asked him what made him think it wouldn't stop again. He replied that the gascolator was full of water so he emptied it, and the engine ran fine now.

"I then asked him what he'd do if it stalled again at 500 feet over a densely populated area. He shrugged and, looking sheepish, said nothing. I told him to start the engine, and I'd grab a wing strut and rock the plane, so if there were more water in the fuel tanks, it'd run into the fuel line and get trapped in the gascolator. The engine ran a few minutes and sputtered to a stop. Bad judgment nearly killed him."

Taryam was thoughtful for a few minutes and said, "What you're saying is there are many areas other than the obvious ones like weather and maintenance where good judgment is important. I'll have to remember that."

Gibbon leaned back against the side of the building and stared at the sky. "Ya know, there's a saying, 'Gold and silver make one's way secure, but better than either, sound judgment.'"

The monotonous towns on the coastal highway slipped past. Gibbon said, "Ali mentioned he was still flying, and as you could see, he's still alive. That's always a good sign."

After a pause Kardell asked, "What brings you to Saudi Arabia? I know you work for ArmCon, but this is a hard life. By now I'd think you'd have a more secure position where you wouldn't have to do this sort of thing."

"I agree, but life isn't always as we'd like it to be. Early in my career, I worked for an electronics firm. Through a merger, my position was eliminated. During the Reagan years, I worked on some military projects. I worked on the M1 Abrams tank during the early production years, then on instrumentation for an aircraft program. After the fall of the Berlin Wall, a surprising amount of military work stopped, and I looked for anything I could find. The people with a lot of years in the petrochemical industry are the ones back in the office. I'm here simply because I need the money."

They rode in silence for some time. Keith could see there was something on Kardell's mind. Finally Craig let out a long sigh and said, "I can't put this together. On the one hand Arabs are trying to kill us every chance they can, bombing this, blowing up that. And, then this today. Those couldn't be nicer people, just like you and me . . . doesn't figure."

Gibbon chuckled. "Remember, the people we talked to are at the top of the food chain in this part of the world. They can afford to be nice."

"You lived in the man's house. Even if he is rich, you must have learned something that would indicate how they think."

"Yeah I did. And since then I've given it a lot of thought. There're two sides to this, them and us. First of all, take them. It's not Arabs as such, but Moslems that concern us. But if you mention this to someone, you'll get a response just like you made. You have to think of Islam. Ninety-nine percent of the Moslems are generally nice people leading ordinary lives. It's the jihad fanatics like those from the Wahhabi and similar sects that are the problem. But, here's the main point. Not a few of that ninety-nine percent send money to support Moslems around the world. Some of this money goes to support the Wahhabi type schools and training camps. Also remember, there are a billion Moslems in the world, so that little one percent of crazies amounts to ten million. In the end, though, they know they're going to win."

Keith could see the look of disbelief mixed with shock in Craig's face. "How so?"

"To answer your question, we have to take a good look at us. I once worked for a guy who had a saying 'There're things you know but you don't know.' What he meant was we're all aware of certain facts, but have never made the logical conclusion they demand. When you point out the conclusion, people will say 'Of course' like everybody knows that, but in fact, nobody does. The answer to your question is something like that.

"Our government is on this kick pushing the New World Order, which means one world government. It goes without saying that if they ever succeeded in making world government happen they would force the western life style on the rest of the world. Now, all western societies—North America, Europe, including Russia and Japan—have birth rates that are well below replacement. The thing that you 'know but don't know' is that if we did manage to force our life style on the whole world, the human race would die out. It's so obvious it's hard to grasp. The Moslems around the world are having lots of babies. Why does it come as such a surprise that there are still people in the world who think the human race should continue? As for terrorism, look at it as they're giving the demographics a push. If we don't change, and it's unlikely we can, it's a certainty they *will* win—end of story, end of us."

"But, that doesn't give them the right to go around killing anybody that's not one of them?"

"Good point. But look at the history of Islam. It's militaristic and vicious. In the past decade, as an example, at any time you could look at all the armed conflicts in the world where people were killing one another on a regular basis, and nineteen out of twenty of them were Moslems beating the snot out of their neighbors. Jihad is a part of Islam. Period.

"I'll put it another way, if the Marxists had gotten us to call Communism a religion, we'd all be speaking Russian now. Because we classify Islam as a religion, our politically correct society is compelled to overlook those parts of it that could kill us."

They bantered the idea around for a while. An afternoon dust storm was picking up, so they retreated to the safety of a neutral topic, the weather. After the long ride, Kardell pulled the car to a stop by Gibbon's apartment building.

— 8 —

King Kalid Military City, Saudi Arabia

The C-17 touched down on the southern runway at late dusk. Stars already graced the clear desert sky. The plane had taken off from Ft. Hood, Texas, the evening before. With midair refueling, they had flown straight through.

As the ramp in the rear lowered, a blast of hot air, exhaust fumes, and engine noise hit the men. Having come from Texas, the heat was no surprise. The men were tired and stiff after the long hours of sitting. Moving around felt good. The truck crews vigorously attacked the tie downs. The aircraft load-master directed deplaning the vehicles. Most of the equipment was loaded on the two trucks they had brought along.

The men were clear of the plane with all of their gear in eight minutes. The aircraft load-master plugged his head set into a jack near the rear ramp. He said something into his mike, and the ramp started to lift as the C-17 started to roll. The men stood and watched the plane taxi to the southeast end of the runway and swing onto the long strip of concrete. The harsh roar of the engines reached them as it accelerated, rotated, and lifted. Soon it was lost in the black to the northwest.

"I wonder why they were in such an all-fired hurry to get out of here," one of the soldiers said to no one in particular. Almost immediately two five-ton trucks pulled up. They were driven by Arabs in Saudi uniforms. It was a tight fit but everyone was loaded and accounted for. They headed south on a paved road that soon turned to gravel, and then to little more than a track. Rebic rode beside Sergeant Rodriguez in the communications/electrical repair truck. After several miles, they pulled to a stop with buildings in the headlights.

As soon as they had unloaded, the Saudi trucks departed. Captain Rebic yelled out, "Muster formation!" There was a lot of milling around in the dark for a few minutes. His next command was, "Report."

"All present," came the reply from WO Charles Boyd.

Captain Rebic was relieved. It was easy to lose someone in the dark in a strange place. "Everybody stay in the area. No snooping around. Nobody goes in the buildings until morning. Sergeant Hendric, find places for the men to bed down for the night in squads, then locate two guard positions and post guards on two-hour shifts. It'll be a tactical night. Everybody sleeps with a loaded weapon, full light and sound discipline." Captain Rebic was taking no chances. It was black as pitch, and they knew nothing of the area they occupied. They had eaten MREs (Meals Ready to Eat) on the plane an hour before they landed. The water in their canteens would have to do until morning.

Captain Rebic located Sergeant Rodriguez, the electrical-systems sergeant. "Don't we have some night vision goggles?"

"Yes, sir, we drew six from supply before we left."

"Good, get out two. No, make it four, and put fresh batteries in them. I want each guard to have a set as well as the sergeant of the guard and one for Sergeant Hendric. The men are tired. Having something to occupy them will help keep them awake on guard duty. It'll also give us the edge in the unlikely event we're probed." He remembered the attack on the Air Force barracks at Al Kahobar in June of 1996.

Private First Class Sean O'Brien had started his shift at guard duty twenty minutes before, at midnight. He was tired but determined to stay awake. Twenty years old, he hailed from Wyoming. He had entered the army immediately after high school. Good-looking, muscular, 175 pounds and five-foot-ten, he had strong features with a nose a tad oversized. He had always been active and exercised regularly. As the loader on one of the two tank crews, he would not likely have much to do the first few days. He assumed this was the reason he had been chosen for this job.

The night-vision goggles were neat. He had joined the army to see the world, and there it was, all green. Looking up, the stars were dark spots on a green background. As he looked around, the entire scene was in shades of green, the result of the starlight amplifiers and artificial display in his head set. For the first time, he had a chance to see the area. There was a rectangular building with two rows of windows which appeared to be a barracks. The other three buildings were Quonset huts probably for shop space or storage. He stood on the shoulder of a sand dune but saw that, in the dark, they had picked a poor guard post. He was unable to see more than a short distance except for up and down the valley through which they had driven. This valley, more like a shallow ravine, continued past him to the south. There were some bushes similar to sagebrush on the side slopes . . . .

What was that! He heard a clank of metal to the south. Or had he? It seemed pretty close. He began to wonder if he had imagined it. In the haste and confusion of setting up the guard detail in the dark, it had not been established how he would warn the others. He didn't even have a radio.

There, another noise. Sort of a creak. If someone were planning to attack, they weren't doing a very good job with noise discipline. Should he go back? No sign . . . there something moved, a small thing, an animal like a rabbit dashed for cover on the far side of the ravine a hundred yards away.

Sean had been raised on a ranch and had grown up with a rifle in his hands. Hunting was a way of life. That animal was not foraging. It had been startled. Someone or something was behind the ridge. As quietly as he could, he jacked a round into the chamber of his M16. Safety on? Yes. He could feel sweat starting to run down his back.

He looked all around quickly. Nothing. Was the whole camp surrounded? He could see others of his group sleeping seventy yards away. It occurred to him he could not see the other guard from his position. He must be in another less-than-perfect location . . . or had he been dragged away by the attackers? He looked back at where the small animal had come over the ridge and saw that a rider on a horse had appeared. He slowly dropped to one knee and raised his weapon.

The rider was further away than the startled animal, and his horse looked funny. He knew horses, and this wasn't right. Then another appeared. He could faintly hear the clicking of the rider's tongue as he directed the animal. Should he sound the alarm, shoot a warning shot? But . . . they didn't appear aggressive. The animal turned so it was broadside to him. Camels! Look at the way they walk, I'll be darned.

Most people wouldn't have noticed the gait of the camels with such interest. But O'Brian had seen horses walk from his earliest memories. They walked by supporting their weight on diagonally opposite corners while the other legs advanced. Camels walked by supporting their weight on the two legs on one side while both legs on the opposite side advanced.

Four more camels appeared. They all meandered down the slope to the draw and turned to the south. *Bedouin* is what the briefing had called the nomads of the desert, passing through, probably like their ancestors had been doing for thousands of years. They continued on their way, oblivious to the fact that they had almost been blown to blazes by one scared American soldier. He was shaking a little as he wiped the sweat from his forehead with his sleeve. Sean O'Brian was now on both knees in the sand. He sat back on his heels. His fatigue shirt was wet with sweat.

The unsuspecting soldiers slept as the stars wheeled overhead. The night passed uneventfully for all. All, except for one young man far from home.

Dawn. Clear. Sleepy eyes opened. All were tired but curious to know where they were and what they'd find. With first light, a guard was posted on the highest point of land, an up-thrust chunk of rock that rose twenty feet above the area occupied by the platoon. At sunrise, the lookout signaled that vehicles were approaching, led by a HMMWV.

When the vehicles arrived a lieutenant colonel in desert cammies got out of the right side of the HMMWV. Captain Rebic went out to meet him with a salute. "Captain Rebic, sir. I'm in charge of this detachment."

The colonel was in his fifties and a bit overweight. It was obvious from his light skin and the shine on his boots that he spent little time in the field. The senior officer returned the salute. "I'm Colonel Liston. Welcome to Saudi Arabia, Captain." He extended his right hand. "If you'll direct the trucks to where you'd like your mess tent, I've brought a field kitchen for you and a crew of Filipinos to staff it."

"The men'll be glad to see that. The last food they had was on the plane yesterday. What will we do for water, electricity, and fuel?"

"All in good time. There's a well here, I'm told, and it has an electric pump. There are underground electrical cables coming from KKMC. The power will be turned on after the transformers and local service is checked out. I've brought along people for that. We'll also see to getting a couple of phones connected for you. There's an underground fuel tank, and two fueling trucks will be at your disposal. They'll get here in a couple of days along with two M-88s. The two five-ton trucks and the water tanker I brought with me are also yours for the duration of your deployment. Let's go someplace we can sit down and have you sign the property transfer forms." Some things never changed. Always plenty of paper work and always accountability for equipment.

After the "signing ceremony" Colonel Liston leaned back in his chair and lit a cigarette. "During your deployment here, you'll report to me. The specifics are on the orders that got you here." He then gave Captain Rebic the phone number of his station as well as the procedure for after-hour emergencies. They were authorized to use a dispensary and hospital at KKMC.

Captain Rebic asked, "Do you know any more about this deployment? What are we supposed to accomplish?"

"You're to get some of these Abrams tanks into first-class running condition as soon as you can. That's on your orders, too. When you get at least six tanks checked out and 'good for a thousand miles,' I believe is what the orders say, you're to contact me. Then I'll call my contact. Any further orders will come from him."

"The tanks are supposed to run a thousand miles? That's new information to me. My orders only mentioned running. Are they supposed to be in fighting condition?"

"I don't know what to say. What would you suggest?"

"We need ammunition, of course. Say, five hundred 105 training rounds, and at least some service 105s, both HEAT and sabots. Also, try to find some fifty-cal and 7.62 mm machine-gun ammo. We'll also need permission from the Saudis to use a firing range, I'd presume."

"That's all noted. I'll hang around for awhile to let you get your staff together and make a list of what you need. I'll see what I can do."

"Fair enough, thank you, sir."

An hour later, the lists had been prepared, and the colonel left.

Warrant Officer Boyd was the battalion maintenance officer on whom Tom Rebic had relied for nearly two years. He had a knack for the job that few had. He knew every part of the M1 tank, what made it work and what made it fail. A stout, good-natured man, he ran a tight ship keeping an upbeat attitude among his crew. As the men took shelter in the shade for a mid-morning break, Rebic walked over to him. "Well, Charles, what do we have?"

"Fifty-two Abrams M1s and twelve Bradleys. The missing six M1s, assuming it was a full battalion, must have been hauled out after the Gulf

War. Based on their serial numbers, the M1s are from the first year's production."

So far, things were developing exactly as Rebic had expected except for the Bradley Fighting Vehicles. "I didn't expect the Bradleys. They could be helpful if we can get 'em going. Is there anyone here who knows Bradley maintenance?"

"Not really. But if the engines run, we should be able to handle the rest. There's not much similarity between turbines and diesels. Why not tell headquarters to send along a couple of Bradley mechanics when the tank crews come over?"

"Worth a try. How do the tanks look?"

"Half buried in sand. The log books the colonel brought along don't show a pretty picture." Every military vehicle had a logbook in which gripes or problems were recorded after each use, and the maintenance record showed how those deficiencies were remedied. Boyd proceeded to show Rebic that few of the gripes had been repaired, and those that had were poorly done. "From what we've seen on the couple we looked at, the operators didn't bother entering the defects toward the end. In other words, the machines are a mess. They haven't moved for at least six years, so now what we need most of all is a bunch of brooms. Boy, they need some cleaning up. By the end of the day we'll know if we can get any to run."

They used a concrete slab in front to one of the Quanset huts as a washing stand. After a tank was checked for "basic bodily fluids" it was started, assuming it would start, moved into the shop area, and washed down.

It was up to 120° Fahrenheit by mid-afternoon, and all work stopped. Even with periodic soaking of their clothing, it was too hot to work, and it was time for a siesta. WO Charles Boyd was sitting in the blast of a fan in the Quanset hut located furthest to the south. He chewed on a piece of beef jerky with a liter bottle of water in one hand. Rebic sat down beside him. "Well, Charles, tell me some good news. What did you find with the first tank you pulled apart? I see there are parts all over the place."

"Tom, the news sucks. That tank literally had the wheels run off it. Somebody's smoking something if they think that it'll ever be fit for anything other than a museum. You said our mission was to see how well they held up in desert storage for several years. Storage has nothing to do with what's wrong with these machines. They were worn out before storage. The tracks, road wheels, drive sprockets, and shock absorbers show heavy wear. Engines and transmissions may be in a little better condition, though most of them have a lot of hours on them. Too many. Here, have a piece of beef jerky, not bad."

Rebic took a piece of the dark leathery meat from the package offered to him as Boyd continued. "I thought it got hot in Texas, but this is like I've never seen."

Rebic was thinking, the wear was in keeping with what he had been led to expect. So why the story about desert storage effects? Rebic took a long drink from his water bottle. "Drinking gallons of water in a day is hard to get used to. I was told they had been driven hard to show up at different places each day, so the Iraqis would think there were many more than there actually were. They even stenciled different unit markings on them each night."

Boyd nodded. "That'd explain the good condition of the Cadillacs and all the rest of the turret hardware. It was never used." The Cadillacs were the controls the gunner used to control the turret traverse, gun elevation, laser range-finder, and firing controls. The name came from the Cadillac Gauge Company in Michigan that manufactured them.

In his upbeat manner, Boyd had the mission figured out. "So, what do we do? Dig them out, wash them, change fluids, drive them a few miles, do some firing, write a report and go home. That's how I see it."

"Well, that's not quite the way others may see it," Rebic said in a hushed voice even though the sound of the fan made eavesdropping impossible. "Keep this to yourself because I don't know what's classified for sure, but that colonel this morning told me to get at least six of them ready for a thousand-mile, cross-country march. When they're ready, I call him for further orders."

"What's this," Boyd said in surprise. "Do they want to drive these junk tanks all the way to the Mediterranean? Give me another day, and we'll inspect a good sample. If they're all like this one, we'll need a trainload of drive parts to have any hope of making a thousand miles."

"Okay, get started, and remember, not a word beyond a maintenance test."

"Gotcha, Captain."

The next morning work started at sun-up to beat the heat, so lunch was at ten-thirty. "Well, Tom, we found out what we needed to know this morning." Boyd sat down by Captain Rebic with a tray of food and a cup of tea without ice. "We sure could use an ice machine, couldn't we?"

"Yeah, we could. So what'd you find?"

"For the most part they're all the same. A few of them completely wore out and had some major repairs, but the parts weren't properly installed. It was like truck mechanics fixed 'em. It looks like they did the best they could, but they didn't have the proper tools or training."

"Can you make a few good ones by using controlled exchange?" Controlled exchange was an Army euphemism for cannibalizing parts.

"We could get lucky, but I doubt we'd get any good for a thousand-mile march. One more thing, Captain. We inspected the electronics on a half dozen of them. As far as we can tell without actually firing the 105, most of the fire control system components seem to be okay except for the cross wind sensors." The gun aiming system was referred to as the "fire control system" as opposed to the system that automatically detected and extinguished fires in the engine compartment, which was called the fire suppression system. "The fire suppression system in the engine bay is shot on most of them, too."

"Okay, let's make up a shopping list, and then I'll call Colonel Liston and tell him to shag a few tons of parts over here."

Boyd shook his head. "*Several tons* of parts for *each* tank. There's no other way."

After siesta, Captain Rebic found Sergeant Rodriguez sitting at a wooden table in the back of the middle Quanset hut. There were a half dozen identical electronic modules on the tabletop in a neat row. He had a cable from a testing device connected to one of them. With a reflective expression on his face, he was turning knobs on the tester as he watched the needles on a pair of gauges move under their little widows. "Sergeant Rodriguez, sorry to break your concentration, but I need to know what's wrong with the cross wind sensors."

Sergeant Miguel Rodriguez had Spanish features as his sir name implied, and he spoke with a noticeable accent. "Captain, they were removed and stored inside the turrets along with the radio antennas, and other sensors that could be damaged or stolen. So, that isn't the problem. We've taken the top off two, and they're different from the ones I've worked with. I've heard of these but never seen one. During the first few years of M1 production, they used some sorta ion-flow technology. The manuals we have describe them. Then they switched to a hot film type— different suppliers, different principle of operation. We've tried all of the fixes the manual suggests, and no improvement."

"Okay, we'll order replacements. Thanks, Miguel."

On the morning of the fifth day, Warrant Officer Boyd sat with Captain Rebic in Charles's cramped office. "Okay, Tom, we've gone through the used tank lot and took a reasonably good look at each tank. We got all but three to start, and we've rated each tank from best to worst on two categories, drive system and turret. Many of the electronic modules can be swapped and only the best ones used when we decide which tanks have the best chance of lasting."

Rebic smiled and said, "Maybe your assessment will change when you hear the news I received a few minutes ago. Two, count 'em, two, C-17s will be arriving at KKMC at dusk with parts. They're to be unloaded immediately, and the tarmac cleared before dawn. So, after the ten-thirty lunch break, give the crew the rest of the day off. We have a long night ahead of us."

Boyd blinked his eyes. "What's going on? That should have taken six weeks, and this has only been a few days. If I were a worrying man, this could get me kinda worked up. Somebody has something in mind. You might want to say something to the men. They're not stupid."

Rebic thought a minute. "You're right. After lunch we'll have a meeting in the mess tent, but I can't say much because of the classified nature of all this. By the way, Lieutenant Denton and his four tank crews, along with two Bradley crews and two Bradley mechanics are coming too. That 'somebody' seems to be in a hurry."

At dusk they set off with the two five-ton trucks and one M-88 traveling the six miles to meet the C-17s at KKMC. M-88s were heavy tracked vehicles and were the only vehicles in the U.S. Army inventory with enough power and bulk to tow M1 tanks. In addition to being the wrecker to tow M1s, they had a boom for heavy lifting. Most commonly, they were used to remove major parts of tanks like turrets and engine packs, but were used for other lifting as well. For this operation, the boom would be used to load pallets onto the five-ton trucks. The second one would be used to unload the trucks at the maintenance base.

Through the night the men worked, truckload after truckload. Rebic was in charge at the airport, and Boyd handled the unloading end. By three in the morning, the job was done. Rebic got out of the cab of the last truck. In the headlights, he saw crates and pallets stacked everywhere. Boyd came over as soon as he saw Rebic arrive. He looked tired but was beaming. Rebic could imagine this was maintenance officer heaven.

Rebic's foot hadn't hit the ground before Boyd started. "Captain, we hit the jack pot. I can't believe it. See those crates stacked there. Six FUPPs, and they're not rebuilt. They're new!" Rebic knew the term well enough. A FUPP was a dream come true. It stood for Full-Up-Power-Pack. Only in time of war were FUPPs seen as spare parts. They consisted of the fifteen-hundred-horse-power turbine engine, the four-speed automatic transmission, the drive differential, the massive multi-disk brake system, the solid nickel heat exchanger, engine controls, and a complete fill of all fluids in a single compact package. It was the entire drive system for an M1 tank. A competent crew could change out a FUPP in an hour.

"And the rest of the stuff—complete track sets, shock absorbers, road wheels, even tools found only at depot maintenance." His face suddenly became more serious, like a dark shadow had crossed his mind. In a subdued voice, he said, "Captain, these are going to be new tanks when we get done. This isn't a test of tanks left in storage. We're getting ready for something serious."

They both knew that, except for a few electrical connectors, any FUPP would fit in any M1 tank ever built. These could have come right off the production line at the General Dynamics, Land Systems Division, plant in Lima, Ohio. This was big. "Yeah, Charles. As soon as I heard the two C-17s were coming, I had the same feeling. All I can say is, let's get six working and then we'll find out what we find out."

―――――――――

Three days later, Lieutenant Art Denton stepped down from his tank near the headquarters Quanset. His tank and the three following it continued on to the staging area with the characteristic grinding sound of tracked vehicles. They had used the new parts and had six M1s in good shape. Rebic was waiting. "How'd the firing go?" This had been the first chance to live fire the main guns. Captain Rebic was keenly interested in the results because of the gnawing uncertainty surrounding the mission.

"Well, Captain, everything's in pretty good shape. We were surprised. The laser range finders worked fine. The MRDs are good too. By swapping electronic modules, we're getting good sets."

The MRD, Muzzle Reference Device, was one of the many innovations that went into the M1 Abrams. It shot a small laser beam out to a reflector on the end of the gun barrel. By sensing the returned beam, the MRD corrected for misalignments that occurred in sighting systems. For example, the top of the barrel expanded more than the bottom as the sun shone on it, and it bent a small amount. If correction were not made for this, the first round would miss the target. Before the M1 tank, crews had to bore sight the main gun several times a day.

"I'd say we're ready for whatever comes next, except for the cross wind sensors. The self-check functions give them a clean bill of health, but they don't measure properly. In case you haven't noticed, the wind is often above twenty miles per hour. We'd never hit anything under those conditions."

Rebic looked worried. "We requested wind sensors with the drive parts, but none came. Still, we got drive parts and tools we didn't even ask for."

"Colonel Liston, this is Captain Rebic. I'm calling as ordered. We have six Abrams tanks ready for a thousand miles, except they're not battle ready."

"What's that mean? They're either ready or they're not."

"I'm saying the drive trains on these tanks are good. But, the fire control system is less that a hundred-percent. The cross wind sensors are all bad. Replacements were ordered but didn't come."

"Why's that wind sensor so important?"

Rebic remembered that Colonel Liston was from the infantry and was not familiar with tanks. He tried to explain the role of the cross wind sensor. This was a rugged sensor that sat on the back of the turret. It measured the speed of the wind blowing across the path the projectile would travel. The 105 mm shell traveled more than a mile a second, so a head or tail wind of, say, thirty miles an hour was not significant. However, a cross-wind could throw off a projectile enough to make the difference between a kill and a miss. And it was not as if one could get a hit on the next shot. The system was automatic and would miss every time.

"We'll order them again. Maybe they were overlooked. Meanwhile, I'll notify my contact that six tanks are ready to travel."

Keith Gibbon was thinking how he didn't like this place nor this job as he got off the elevator and walked down the hall to his small apartment. But, it wouldn't be long, and he'd be leaving for good. He put down his case, dug out his keys, and opened the door in anticipation of a shower followed by a good meal.

As Gibbon straightened up, he saw a stranger sitting on one of the chairs by the small dining table. "What's this? Who are you? I know this is my apartment. The key worked. Wait, let me guess, you must be a CIA dork, right?"

The smug expression on the face of the ordinary looking Arab man switched instantly to a look of shock. "How did you know who I am? We've never met."

"It wasn't too hard to guess."

"But how?"

Gibbon could see the man was angered. "Oh, for crying out loud, how stupid do you think people are? First of all, who bribes someone to get into an apartment for a private conversation? You have to be a spook. But whose, I had to ask myself? Had to be U.S. because you showed little inventiveness. So, you see it was elementary." Gibbon remembered that Ali had said his visit to Kuwait would be noticed. "I suppose you have identification."

"Yes," his guest said cautiously. "My name is Yousuf Hamoud. Here." He held out his folded ID case, which held the CIA shield on one side and his picture on the other.

"Hmmm. I suppose I won't get your carcass off my chair until I hear why you're here, so go ahead. I'm tired."

"Okay, I'll get right to the point. We, your government, need information, and I think you could get some for us. You know a certain Sheikh Ahmad Bin Khalid Al-Taryam, do you not?"

"Yes, I know him."

"In fact, you more than know him. You were a guest at his home for some weeks a few years ago while recovering from an accident in which you saved his son's life. You visited with his son recently and perhaps you were invited to dinner in Kuwait or something."

Now it was Gibbon's turn to be surprised, and his face showed it. He was not surprised that the CIA knew about his trip to Kuwait, but surprised at how quickly they had capitalized on it. "That's mostly true, but it doesn't show we're friends. Remember, he was understandably grateful at the time and probably still is. It doesn't mean I can ask him questions, and expect him to spill his guts."

Hamoud shook his head. "You really have a low opinion of what the CIA does and our prowess in the art of intelligence gathering. I assure you I had nothing of the sort in mind. Let me put a very sharp point on it. If you for some reason happen to meet or speak with the sheik while you are here, let me know beforehand, and then afterwards let me ask you some questions. It would surprise even you how important the slightest comment could be."

Gibbon saw he'd have to humor this guy, or he'd never get dinner. "Okay, give me the information I'll need to contact you and, let me see the badge again." Gibbon took a good look at it as Hamoud wrote down a phone number. As he handed the badge back, Gibbon said, "Now, if you don't mind, I'd like to get cleaned up and get something to eat. If you feel more comfortable leaving by the window, I don't mind. This is the second floor, but I suppose that lump under your pants leg near your ankle is a repelling rope."

"You don't miss much, do you? I'll leave by the door, thank you."

As Hamoud walked down the hall to the stairwell he was beginning to wonder if contacting an engineer was such a good idea. He had been told scientists were usually easy to recruit and gave reliable information since they were generally politically liberal. However, engineers were practical people. They were in the business of making things work, hence were detail oriented. This guy was obviously pretty smart and quick to figure things out. He'd even noticed his back-up piece. That man could be trouble, but managing risks was what "spooking," now he had him doing it, was all about.

— 9 —

25 August, Saudi Arabia

This was an odd day in a mission that was odd from the beginning. Captain Thomas Rebic paid the taxi driver when he arrived at the U.S. Consulate in Dhahran on the Persian Gulf coast. He hoped he'd get some answers here. It seemed like KKMC or Riyadh would have made more sense for this meeting. And it was strange that Colonel Liston wasn't attending, though he had arranged for a jet to pick him up at KKMC and fly him to the military air base to the north of Dhahran.

Inside the building, he walked up to the desk. "My name is Captain Rebic, I was told to report here at ten hundred hours to meet with a Mr. Stanus."

"Certainly, Captain. I'll call upstairs." The man behind the desk wore half spectacles on the end of his very tan nose.

After a brief exchange, the man looked up and said, "Someone will be down to take you up to the CIA offices in a moment."

Rebic's muscles tensed at the mention of the CIA. How on earth had he managed to get into this? Why him!

Rebic tried not to look disturbed as he casually looked at the pictures on the wall. There was a copy of *Washington Crossing the Delaware*, and a framed Declaration of Independence. He was moving on to a third when a woman's voice behind him said, "Captain Rebic?"

Rebic spun around a little too fast.

Satisfied she had the right man, she said, "Please follow me." The woman, a Caucasian, about thirty, was attractive in an ankle-length, black skirt and a long-sleeved white blouse buttoned to the chin. She led him to the elevator and pressed the button for the third floor. As the door opened she said, "You'll be meeting with Mr. Stanus, who is in from

Washington, and a special officer stationed in the area." She led the way down the hall and indicated a closed door.

He knocked, opened the door, and saw two men, one sitting on either side of a conference table. "I'm Captain Rebic, I was told to meet with Mr. Stanus." Stanus was in his thirties with wavy blond hair. He wore a sport coat and wash pants. The other man was Arabic, average height, with a singularly unremarkable appearance. His clothing, hair cut, even the way he sat in his chair made him look like the most average Arab Rebic had ever seen.

"You're at the right place. I see you're prompt. This is Special Agent Yousuf Hamoud, and I am Special Agent Harold Stanus. Both of us work for the CIA. Yousuf works out of this office. I'm from Washington."

Rebic tried to keep a placid expression on his face as he asked. "And what did I do to deserve this honor?"

Stanus replied. "We were given a mission. The Pentagon searched its personnel files, and you were chosen. You must be good at something, that's all I can say. But don't worry, this is a fairly open-and-shut operation. Sit down and we'll discuss it. Yousuf knows the background, so he'll go first. Then I'll tell you what we want."

Hamoud unfolded a map of the region and laid it on the table. "Recently the Iraqis have been conducting armored operations in this region." He indicated a large portion of southwestern Iraq. "Sometimes they dash across the border as far as this pipeline in Saudi Arabia," indicating a line on the map twenty miles south of the border and running straight as an arrow parallel to it. "We want to find out their intentions."

Hamoud stopped talking as if to elicit a response from Rebic. He unconsciously took the prompting and asked, "Why don't you take an A10 and shoot a few rounds across their bow, so to speak, to remind them they're on someone else's territory?"

Having gotten Rebic feeling he was part of the discussion, Hamoud continued. "Saudi Arabia and the U.S. know of this from pilots that enforce the southern no-fly zone. And, to answer you question, we don't want to start shooting for nothing."

Stanus rolled the combination dials on a leather briefcase. He took out an envelope marked "Top Secret." "These are your orders. They're not that complicated, I assure you. You're to take as many M1 tanks as you can get into good condition, at least six, and a minimum number of support vehicles, across the desert to the area south of Ar'Ar and set up an operations base. You're not to use the Tap Line Road because we don't want anyone thinking there's a military deployment in the works."

Rebic thought a moment. Not wanting to say something on which he would be unable to deliver, he replied. "Yes. We have six tanks in pretty good shape. That's because we received all new drive components for that many. Any more will have to came out of the scrap heap, which doesn't look promising at this point." Looking at the map he continued, "That looks like a 300-mile cross-country trek. How can we refuel? My fuel trucks would have to operate half loaded not to get bogged down in loose sand."

Stanus replied, "The trip is more like 400-miles following the route you'll have to take. We've thought of the logistics. You'll have two Blackhawk helicopters assigned to you that have been modified to act as tankers. Between your tank trucks and the Blackhawks, you'll have to work it out. Now, back to your orders. You are to operate in groups of two, three, or four tanks and try to intercept the Iraqis. When you do intercept them, note the number, location, and time. Beyond that, watch and note what they do. If they fire on you and you can avoid firing back, do so. We don't want a pitched battle started for one obvious reason. There's little backup support for you.

"You'll continue to rely on Colonel Liston at KKMC for logistical support," Stanus continued. "But, for operational matters, you'll call Yousuf. We have some communications devices that use the Inmarsat direct-to-satellite phone system." Called sat-phones, they were the size of an old-fashioned laptop computer but were reliable and rugged. "You'll be given two. That way you can communicate the 300 miles from the forward base to your maintenance base. Colonel Liston will have one, and Yousuf will have one. These are special models that have a scramble mode."

Hamoud leaned forward, "See, we'll take care of you. Periodically, perhaps weekly, I'll call you to set up a meeting to get a first-hand report."

They spent another hour or so going over the rules of engagement, call signs, and other matters. Each time the rules of engagement were brought up, the response varied from the time before, which was causing no little consternation for Rebic. Finally, he could resist no longer. "There's a major deficiency in the M1 tanks we have. The cross wind sensors don't work."

Both of the CIA men looked at him. Hamoud then asked. "What is the importance of the, what did you say, the wind sniffer?"

"The cross wind sensor. It's used to correct for windage when the main gun is fired. Without it, our ability to hit targets when the wind is blowing is substantially degraded. And, as you know, the wind blows nearly all the time in the desert."

Rebic was looking at Stanus and saw he was looking intently at Hamoud with a strangely pleasant expression. In an instant Rebic turned his head and looked at Hamoud. He saw him very slightly nodding his head as he returned the look at Stanus. There was a fleeting moment when Rebic thought this information pleased them. Then immediately Stanus replied a little sternly, "Your mission is one of reconnaissance, not battle. I don't see that the problem you describe should in any way affect your mission. The speed and maneuverability of the M1s, if you're properly trained, should be plenty to keep you out of trouble."

Rebic was taken aback by the crack about his training. And what was the meaning of the look they had given each other at his mention of the wind sensor? From scuttlebutt, he had heard what it was like working for the CIA. Was it true? These guys really did look at the people they used as expendable.

By eleven-twenty, they were finished. As Captain Rebic got up to leave, he looked at Stanus. "Is there some place around here I could get a bite to eat?"

Stanus smiled, appearing pleased to be able to offer something to Rebic. "Yes, we have a hospitality room on the first floor. Here's a pass. The gal who brought you up here will take you there," he said as he held out a card with that day's date stamped on it. "Have a beer and a burger on the CIA."

Prompted by his suspicions, Keith Gibbon decided to borrow a car and drive to the U.S. Consulate in Dhahran to check on one Yousuf Hamoud. He arrived in the city at ten forty-five. The State Department information sheet said the consulate general was located between the Aramco Headquarters and the Dhahran International Airport. Spotting Aramco, he knew he was going in the right direction as the consulate came into view. It had no parking lot as usual. It seemed to Gibbon that this country hadn't invented them yet.

Gibbon drove past, circled a block across the street, and parked out of sight of the Consulate. He figured they would be photographing every car that parked near the place. He wouldn't make it easy for them. Everything to do with government made him uneasy.

He showed his Minnesota driver's license at the desk as he entered. The general contractor for the petro plant project had his passport which was required procedure for foreigners working in Saudi Arabia.

"And what is your business at the consulate today?" asked the man behind the desk with half spectacles on his nose.

"I'd like to be directed to the CIA office. It regards some work they've asked me to do."

"Are they expecting you?"

"No, but that's the way I want it." Gibbon replied.

It took a few minutes on the phone and some indecision on the part of someone on the other end of the line until Gibbon finally said, "If they don't want the information, that's fine with me. I'll leave."

After relaying that comment, the man said, "Someone will be down to escort you up in a minute. Please have a seat," the clerk said pointing to a row of chairs against the wall.

A woman arrived after ten minutes and looking at Gibbon, the only Caucasian in the entry area, asked, "Mr. Gibbon?"

"Yes, that's right."

"Please follow me." He was led to an elevator, taken to the third floor, and then into an outer office at the end of the hall. His guide left him by a desk with a man behind it.

"Mr. Keith Gibbon, I presume."

"You presume correctly."

"What can we do for you?"

"I want to speak to whomever is in charge here."

"That would be Mr. Atwood. He's very busy. Can I ask the nature of your business?"

"Someone from this organization has asked me for something, and that's all I'll say. Is Mr. Atwood available?"

The man sat there for a few moments in indecision. Finally, he punched a button. "Mr. Atwood, there's a gentleman here, a Mr. Keith Gibbon, who says the CIA has asked him for something and insists on speaking only to you."

The man's expression did not change as he waited. Finally, a voice from the intercom said, "Fine. Send him in. I'll see him."

"That office," the man said pointing. "Mr. Atwood will see you."

Gibbon opened the door and saw a pudgy man in his forties, pulling his tie tight. His government-issue desk was moderately neat with several piles of papers, not too high, not too low, a very moderate bureaucrat.

The man got part way up from his seat and extended his hand across the desk. "Mr. Gibbon, I don't believe we've met. What can I do for you?"

"I'm here to verify the identity of one of your officers. When I arrived at my apartment a few days ago, he was sitting on one of my dinette chairs. Yes, I had locked the door when I left. He had bribed someone to be let in. He asked me to collect some information for him, for the CIA. He could be anyone, so I came to check him out."

Atwood seem puzzled. "This is very unusual. People rarely check out our agents. Didn't he show you his CIA picture identification?"

"Of course. But, come on! Any group of intelligence gathers, GRU, Mossad, anybody, could have produced that badge. Besides, I've never seen a CIA badge before so I wouldn't know if it was real or a bad imitation."

"Very perceptive. What line of work are you in, Mr. Gibbon?"

"I'm an engineer working for ArmCon, one of the major subcontractors for the petro plant expansion north of Jubayl. I'm here for several weeks to supervise the installation of ArmCon's equipment."

Atwood got a scrunched up look on his face as though something Gibbon said was displeasing to him. "What's the officer's name? Maybe I can put your mind at ease."

"He gave it as Yousuf Hamoud, and that was the name on the ID."

"Ah, yes, just a moment." As he got up from the chair, Gibbon could see he was badly out of shape. He went into the next room. Gibbon heard file drawers open and close. Finally, Atwood reappeared with a file folder in his hand. He took a picture out of the folder and held it up for Gibbon to see. "Here we are. Is this the man who approached you?"

Gibbon took the picture and looked at it closely. "Yes . . . that's him."

"That's Yousuf Hamoud, as his ID said."

"Yes, that's the man I met all right. You've been very helpful. I have what I came for. There's one piece of intelligence information I'd like from you, though."

Leaning forward in his chair, with a perplexed and almost defiant tone of voice, Atwood asked "And what might that be?"

"I haven't eaten since early morning. Is there a restaurant near here you'd recommend?"

Atwood chuckled and said, "The consulate has a hospitality room that might interest you. This compound is American territory as you probably know. American customs prevail. If you'd like a beer and a cheese-burger, you're welcome. Ask the gal at the desk, and she'll give you a pass and take you there."

"Thanks, the beer sounds good, I'll take you up on it."

Keith Gibbon was escorted to the dining room at the rear of the building on the first floor. A few tables had people sitting at them eating an early lunch. They all wore badges clipped to a pocket or hanging on a bead chain around their neck. It gave him the willies being around so many government types.

To his left was a counter. As he approached it he was asked, "What'll it be today?" The man behind the counter had a white apron tied around his waist and a white cap on his head partially hiding black, curly hair.

"I was told I could get a beer and a hamburger here," Gibbon said as he laid his pass on the counter. "Do I give this to you?"

"Yeah, that'll be fine. We serve the best beer in Saudi Arabia," he said with a chuckle, "Good hamburgers too."

"The beer sounds good, and could I get a cheeseburger and some fries?"

"Funny thing, that's my most popular order." He reached into a cooler, took out a cold beer, and set it and a glass on the counter. "Take a seat. I'll call you when the food's ready."

Gibbon looked around the room. There was a serviceman wearing desert cammies sitting at a table alone. He walked in that direction. "Would you mind if I sat with you? I hate to eat alone."

The man looked up as if startled. "Oh, sure, I guess so."

"I hope I'm not intruding, but those government bureaucrats at the other tables make my skin crawl." Gibbon saw the man was a captain in the armor corps. Having served in the army, Gibbon was familiar with most insignia. "Captain, I'm Keith Gibbon," he said, extending his hand.

"I'm Tom Rebic. Please sit. Some conversation might do me good."

"From your insignia I see you're in armor. Is it Abrams, Bradleys?"

"Mostly Abrams tanks."

"Since the start of the M1 production, I've been interested in the Abrams," Kieth said, as he sipped his beer. "I was involved on a part for it from the late development through pre-production and into the first few years of production. That was in the early eighties. You know, I've never seen an M1. That must be some formidable battle machine."

Rebic responded off handedly, "It is, assuming all the systems are working. Where do you work, ah, Mr. Gibbon, was it?"

"Call me Keith. I work for a company called ArmCon. I'm here as the installation supervisor for ArmCon's equipment at a petro plant expansion north of Jubayl."

Captain Rebic tipped up his beer glass and emptied it. Gibbon could see he wasn't too interested in all of this when Rebic casually mentioned, "What part of the Abrams did you work on?"

"Most people don't know what I'm talking about when I mention it, but you will. The cross wind sensor. We supplied them for the first three production years, then the contract changed hands, and the army went to another technology." Gibbon saw a sudden interest in the captain's expression.

"Tell me about those things." He said it quietly, but there was an intensity in his voice Gibbon found odd.

Gibbon lowered his voice also. "Well, they use the ion-flow technology. I've often wondered if any were still in use. I sort of assumed they'd all been replaced by the second version. After the loss of the contract, I was out looking for another job and lost contact with the M1 program. The reason for the change of contractors is quite a story."

"Back to the ion-flow. How does it work, and what would make it *not* work?"

"Cheeseburger and fries are up," said the cook.

"That must be mine." Gibbon went and got his food. When he returned he took a bite of the burger. "Now, that tastes like home cooking."

"The ion-flow."

The man's insistence was beginning to disturb Gibbon. "The wind is ported through what amounts to a little cave in the head of the sensor. The roof of the cave has an ion-sensing array on it. Below a hole in the cave floor is a very sharp needle with 4,000 volts on it. This needle produces ions. They migrate through the hole in the floor of the cave up to the roof, crossing the wind stream as they do. The faster the wind's blowing the more the ions drift down stream before they land on the sensor array. The sensor detects where the ions land, and this is the measure of the wind velocity. It has no moving parts, is rugged, and reliable. Could I ask what brings you to Saudi Arabia?"

There was reticence in Rebic's voice as he replied, "Oh, nothing very exciting. I'm here with a couple of platoons to do a maintenance test of some old M1s left after Desert Storm. They were in bad shape where we found them, but we've gotten a few of them more or less working except for some of the electronics. We've managed to get some spares like engine parts, tracks, and stuff like that, but not electronic modules, especially for the fire control system. One of the problem modules is the cross wind sensor. They appear to be this ion-flow type, and none of them work."

Gibbon was enjoying his cheeseburger. In between bites he said, "If you're not deployed too far from here, maybe I could come and look at them. I remember the problems we had with them and the way we fixed 'em. There are some things definitely not to do to them or you'll destroy them. The fixes are generally simple but not obvious."

"Unfortunately we're not very close. Have you ever heard of KKMC? We're near there."

"That's something like a hundred miles to the west, isn't it?"

"More like two hundred fifty miles."

"That's farther than I thought. You wouldn't have anything to do with those Iraqi tanks that are marauding the Saudi pipe line out west, would you?"

The captain's eyes were like bullets looking at Gibbon. "Who are you?"

Gibbon was taken aback by the severity in the voice of the man across the table. "I am who I say I am," Gibbon said in a somewhat startled tone. Then returning to Rebic's concern, "If you're going to *need* those wind sensors to work," Gibbon said, "I have information you need to know, but not here. When do you have to go back to your station?"

"I'll call a taxi when I'm ready to leave." Captain Rebic's eyes looked a little wild. Gibbon sensed something was wrong.

"I have a green Nissan that I borrowed for the day parked on the street near the consulate. As you leave the main entrance, go left to the corner. Turn to the right and cross the street. Fifty yards past the corner is the car."

Gibbon gulped down his cheeseburger and finished his fries and beer. "Give me a five minute head start and then leave. I think it's best if we don't look like we're together." Gibbon got up and casually walked toward the door.

––––––––––––––

Gibbon could see Captain Rebic crossing the street by looking in the rear view mirror. Rebic was taller than the average Arab. He stood out like a sore thumb in the camouflage clothes as he made his way along the busy street. He noted how, among the Arab townspeople, the clothing designed to hide him on the desert made him stand out. As he walked up, Gibbon leaned over and opened the passenger side door.

"I don't know why I'm doing this," said Rebic. "You could be anybody."

"Well, look at it this way. I'm old and crotchety, and you're young and strong. If I try anything, you can pummel me."

A thin smile came to the captain's mouth. Once the car was moving, he said. "How do you know there are Iraqi tanks out there?"

Gibbon decided not to mention Ali. "A few days ago an Arab engineer I'm acquainted with mentioned them. There's a road that goes along the pipeline, and there are people around here who drive trucks up that road. People trade stories here like anyplace else."

They drove to the outskirts of the city. Gibbon pulled off the road in an open space, and they sat there letting the engine run for the air conditioner. Gibbon continued. "This Arab also said there are a lot of spies in this area. The guest workers are frequently used to collect information. If there are any Puerto Rican, Filipino, Indian, or other guest workers near you, be on guard. If the wind sensors don't work, anyone who wants to know stuff like that now knows they don't work." From the look on Captain Rebic's face, Gibbon guessed there were some guest workers involved.

Rebic was staring into the distance as he said, "Who can you trust?"

"I don't trust anyone. I assume when I call home or even discuss my work at the plant, others are listening. When people around you insist they only speak Arabic, you can't be sure they don't understand English."

Captain Rebic was silent for some time. Gibbon assumed he was turning his mission over in his mind against what he had just been told. Then he said, "Can you give me information on how to fix the wind sensors?"

"I think I can. The most likely problem is that the tip of the needle is full of gunk. If the tanks were driven a lot with the wind sensor powered-up, the needle would have ionized pollutants like diesel exhaust and gotten a glob of matter on them. With no maintenance, they would eventually stop ionizing. Squirt rubbing alcohol into the holes at the base of the head that angle up and are aligned with the tip of the needle. Don't touch the tip of the needle with a solid object or you'll damage it."

"I guess we damaged some then. We took the tops off a couple and there was a small bit of stuff on the tip of the needle. We knocked it off with a small screw driver."

"Then how did it work. Anything at all?"

"Nothing, no change."

"Generally when you touch the needle you bend the tip. It still works, but it's out of calibration. The damage is microscopic so you won't see it."

"Well, there was no change on either one."

Gibbon readjusted his position in the seat so he could look at Rebic without turning his head so far. "This is a long shot but it might be the problem. The tanks were made radiation hardened so if there were a nuclear explosion nearby, the electromagnetic pulse, the EMP, wouldn't damage the electronics. There're some small components on the circuit board inside the wind sensor. These are fast-acting diodes the size of a half-Watt resistor. They're there to shunt the current generated by the EMP to ground. We found that some of these were leaking and were going to issue a recall and replace all of these components when the contract changed hands, and the army went to the other technology. Perhaps with time they all failed."

"Can we fix them? I wish you could come to our base and show us how to do it."

"Well, try this. Use one of the units you've damaged already to practice on." Gibbon proceeded to describe in detail the procedure.

Rebic listened intently to what Gibbon said. "I'm still skeptical as to who you are, but if this information is correct, I guess I don't care. We really need these things to work."

"My advice is this. If you do get them to work, don't let anyone know. Especially not the guest workers. Keep the enemy, whoever he may be, in the dark."

Sounding uncertain, Rebic asked, "Is there any way I can contact you if we need more help?"

"Best way is to call me in the evening at my apartment in Jubayl. Call yourself Fred Jones. Don't mention tanks or wind sensors. Talk about tubes, or as much indirect stuff as possible. Assume my phone is bugged. How can I contact you?"

"Pretty hard, but call Colonel Liston at KKMC." They traded phone numbers. "You can be Captain Adrian Jackson from Fort Hood. I can't say if it'll get relayed to me or not. I'm having a hard time believing this code-name stuff is necessary, but why not."

At two o'clock Gibbon let Captain Rebic off a couple of blocks away from the consulate and headed back to the job site.

———————————

Shortly after Captain Rebic left the consulate to meet with Gibbon, another man left by a rear entrance. It was Yousuf Hamoud. He walked to his dark-red Toyota parked in the walled-in compound that would keep it from prying eyes. He headed back to Jubayl where he had his apartment.

For years, he had cultivated contacts with people in several of the countries that adjoined Saudi Arabia in hopes he would find a situation like this. If the people he had met with earlier today knew of some of these contacts, and the kind of relationship he had with them, it would earn him a firing squad. Hamoud had no meaningful notion of patriotism. His only motivation was doing what profited him. What did it matter if he took a little money from time to time for passing along information to contacts in Iran or Iraq?

This opportunity had fallen into his lap, and he was not going to let it pass. It was a perfect setup to net him a good sum of money. Playing both sides of the fence always had risks, but the players recognized this and paid handsomely if the man were in the right place.

During the Iraq-Iran war, Hamoud had worked with an up-and-coming Iraqi colonel. Since then, the colonel had received a couple of promotions. Now he would contact Major General Raja Majeed with an interesting proposal.

— 10 —

26 August, Plymouth, Minnesota

As Ratling walked up to his workstation Breckon casually mentioned, "I wonder where the robots are now?" He was using a yellow legal pad beside the computer terminal with notes scribbled on it to guide his work. "It's been five weeks since we shipped them."

Ratling had the morning mail in his hand and shuffled through it as he spoke. "They were to leave an East Coast port and sail to the Mediterranean. I'd guess they should be at their destination port by now. It'll be a week or two before they're delivered to the site. Say, you wouldn't reconsider going to the site to supervise installation, would you? You're so good at that."

Breckon shook his head. "You've had my answer on that from the beginning. It hasn't changed."

"I'd hate to see something happen that we'd both be sorry for." Ratling abruptly stopped speaking and Breckon could see Ratling wished he hadn't said that.

"What could happen to make us both sorry? I've done the best I could in view of the fact that I've never talked to an engineer from the company that will be using those things."

Ratling hesitated nervously and said, "What I meant is this. It's always good to have someone from the project on site to look after the company's interests. If things go wrong and there are back charges, we'd only have their word for it if we weren't represented. I've discussed this with the customer, and I'm authorized to offer you a good bonus if you go to the site. A half year's salary for a month of work in addition to your pay. What do you say?"

Breckon looked at Ratling in disbelief and said. "Now, I know I don't know what's going on. That's too much for a normal job. The answer is no." Ratling walked away. The old confident salesman was gone. Something was very wrong

Ed was glad he and Darin had decided that Friday, two days from now, they would leave for a vacation in the mountains. They had been planning it for three years. He would be happy to get away from this place—and Ratling.

28 August, Plymouth, Minnesota

Ratling sat in his office rationalizing. He had tried everything, and Breckon wouldn't cooperate. He told that infernal Arab that Breckon would never buy the bonus thing. If he went on vacation, it would mean Ratling had failed to deliver, and he'd pay dearly. There was no other choice. He reached over and punched a number into the phone.

"Hello, is the driver there?" asked Ratling. This was the code he was to use when he called the number Hon Robbie had given him.

"Just a minute. I think he's out back." That was the counter sign. After a few seconds, a voice returned to the phone. "Do you have a pick-up for me?"

"Yes, a parcel at the apartment today between four and five."

"All right. At the apartment today between four and five. Good-bye."

Ratling knew Breckon would never leave early. He was too conscientious for that. Nevertheless, Ratling planned to leave before four, afraid that if he hung around, Breckon might stay even later. He would watch the plant so he knew when Breckon did leave. If Breckon left before four or after five Ratling would call the "driver" again.

Breckon was excited that they were finally going on vacation. Harris had wanted to start early Saturday morning and miss the traffic, but Breckon had insisted on leaving Friday afternoon. Even though the traffic would be heavy on Interstate 94 on the way to Fargo, Breckon was afraid something would happen and they wouldn't be able to go. Breckon would leave work at four o'clock and stop by his apartment for a few minutes to pick up some food from the refrigerator. Harris would meet him there. They'd take Breckon's truck, which had a topper. He had all of his gear in the back already.

He made a last encoded copy of the programs and put it in his computer bag. Then, he put a second copy in a brown envelope along with the random number disks from the previous batch of disks. He addressed the envelope to Harris. He would drop it in a mailbox on the way to his apartment. Since Harris had stopped his mail delivery for the vacation, it would sit in the post office until they got back—what safer place. He put an envelope on Ratling's desk with a vacation slip in it requesting four weeks of vacation.

Shortly after four, noticing that everyone else was gone, Breckon picked up his computer bag, set the alarm system in the front entry, got in his truck, and drove away. It felt good.

He drove into the apartment parking lot and parked in front of his garage. This would be safe from the complainers. There weren't enough parking spaces, and the people without garages got mad if people with a garage used a space outside. He didn't want any grief today even if it made a longer walk. His garage was the second from the end. He had pulled up beside a conversion van parked in front of the end garage. Though he hadn't seen it there before, he thought nothing of it.

He got out of his truck, then turned to walk between the two vehicles to the rear. As he did, a large man appeared from behind the van and rushed menacingly toward Breckon. As Breckon stopped and started to turn, both of his arms were grabbed from behind by a second man. He was immediately forced against the side of the van. The first man said, "Don't fight it, bud. Ya can't get away." The first man rifled through his pockets, taking everything out as Breckon twisted and turned, trying to get free. At first, he thought they were common thugs robbing him. "Found 'em. Here they are," the first man said as Breckon heard the jingle of his keys. Why the keys? If they wanted his truck, there were easier ways.

Suddenly Breckon, with all his strength, twisted sideways, thrust his foot at the knee of the man with the keys, hitting it a glancing blow, and then collapsed his legs. As Breckon fell, he felt the grasp loosen on his arms, and he moved as fast as he could. He was on the ground and crawling under the van. "Help me grab him!" said the second man. The first man dropped the contents of Breckon's pockets. Breckon heard the jingle of his keys on the pavement. Two hands grabbed his leg and tried to pull him out from under the van. Breckon tried to shout, but he was using all of his strength to free himself.

In the shuffle, Breckon's wallet was kicked under the van, tumbling near his elbow. The van was parked over a storm sewer and Breckon had a grip on its grating. He tried to kick at the men, but now each of them had a leg, and his grip was slipping. As his right hand lost its grasp, he swatted at his wallet, intending to shove it further out of view. The two men made a mighty pull on his legs. Breckon lost his grip, and his swipe at the wallet nearly missed. It only went as far as the sewer grating. Despair gripped him as he saw it slide onto the grate, slip through a slot and disappear. There had gone his chance to leave behind a mark of what had happened to him.

They pulled him out on his stomach. One man knelt on his legs and grabbed Breckon's wrists, and bound them with a plastic cable tie. At the same time, the other man grasped the back of Breckon's neck, rotated his head to the side, and stuffed a rag in his mouth. In a moment, the abductors had the sliding door on the side of the van open, and they forced Breckon in between the front and second seats on the floor, and he felt a second band pulled tight around his ankles.

Lying on the floor Breckon turned his head and saw the back doors of the van open and his camping gear casually being loaded from his truck. Breckon realized this looked exactly like what Harris and he had planned to be doing a few minutes from now. The rear doors of the van slammed shut. Breckon heard the engine of his truck start, and his garage door open. They put his truck in the garage. The garage door closed, and the two front doors of the van opened. Once inside the driver said, "You got his computer bag?"

"Yeah, yeah, you think I'm dumb? The guy specifically told us not to show up without it." As the van started to move, the man in the passenger seat reached back and grabbed Breckon's upper arm. "You can get up on the seat if you behave. We ain't going far." Breckon wrenched is arm out of the man's grasp. "Have it your way," was the response.

Breckon saw red as he glared at the man. He had never in his life had such a wish to kill, and it was several seconds before his stopped straining against his restraints, his muscles quivering with exhaustion. He had considered managing things so he wouldn't have to go back to his apartment after work, but that had seemed too paranoid. Although Ratling was a low life, he never thought he'd stoop to a trick like this. *That rat of a Ratling did it to me again!*

Slowly his anger changed to apprehension and then to fear. This was serious. Kidnapping was a felony. More importantly, it indicated that

Ratling was truly desperate. Even worse, Breckon had turned in his vacation slip, so Ratling had a good excuse why Breckon was not at work.

Although these soft-headed asses who had grabbed him were serious, he could tell from the way they operated they weren't professionals. That meant this was probably not something conducted by the FBI, CIA, KGB, or anything like that. He knew he had to stay calm, if that were possible. He'd wait for a chance. Nobody was perfect. Everyone made mistakes. These guys would make one soon enough, he hoped.

As Harris turned into the parking lot of Breckon's apartment building, he noticed a van at the far end of the lot near Breckon's garage. He scanned the parking lot for Breckon's truck parked among the other vehicles. Once again his eyes fell on the van. Two men were getting in. The van backed away and drove toward him. As they passed by him, Harris thought nothing more of it. The important thing was that he didn't see Breckon's truck. Harris was a little late, and he thought Breckon would be there waiting for him.

Harris parked near the apartment building entrance and waited. After fifteen minutes, he grabbed his cell phone and called Breckon's apartment. No answer. He called him at work. No answer. This was very strange. Harris had a key to Breckon's apartment and went in. The perishable food they intended to take along was still in the refrigerator, so Breckon hadn't been there. Maybe he had stopped and bought some last minute item, but he was now close to thirty minutes late.

Harris looked around the apartment. There was no sign Breckon had been there since breakfast. He knew where Breckon kept a spare garage key. On a hunch, he decided to see if Breckon's truck was in the garage. To his astonishment, he found the truck. He even made sure it was Breckon's truck. There was the small scratch on the right rear fender from when Breckon had slid up against a guardrail last winter. As he was about to close the garage door, he stopped and tried the door on the truck. It was unlocked, and Breckon always locked his doors. He got into the driver's seat and looked around. Nothing appeared amiss. He looked into the rear of the truck, where the light was shining through the rear window of the topper. The camping equipment was all gone!

He sat in the front seat of the truck feeling sick as realization dawned. What had he seen as he was driving into the parking lot? There were the two men getting into that van. What if Ed and all of his gear had been taken in that van? It could only be the installation of the gantry robots. Ed had mentioned several times how Ratling was pressuring him to go to the site for start-up.

Harris berated himself for not realizing what he had seen. He could have followed them. That was too far fetched, though. Nobody got kidnapped in broad daylight in the parking lot of his apartment building. But, if they *were* taking him out of the country, they couldn't use a commercial flight, and the closest general aviation airport was Crystal. Harris closed and locked the garage, ran to his truck and was off to the Crystal Airport as fast as he could.

Breckon was familiar with every street in this part of town. He figured they were taking him to an airport to fly him to the job site. His captors were familiar with the roads too. He lived near the intersection of Interstate 494 and Rockford Road. They took Rockford Road east, then went north to Bass Lake Road, then east always staying on city streets. This would take them to the Crystal Airport. Crystal was a general aviation airport with no scheduled airline flights, and if he guessed right, he would be flown out on a private plane with no flight plan.

They rode in silence. His captors didn't talk, and he had a rag in his mouth. Breckon had kicked around so the man not driving had forced him up in a seat and put a seat belt around him. With his hands and feet tied, he was now completely immobilized. As he suspected, they drove into the Crystal Airport, went down a service road, and drove up to a hangar. After the driver beeped the horn twice, the hangar door opened to reveal a twin-engined business jet. If Breckon could remember his planes right it was a Cessna Citation. They drove in, and the door closed. Breckon's gear was removed from the van and stowed on the airplane. The two men opened the sliding door and pulled him out. With his feet bound Breckon couldn't stand by himself. He was met by a man of slight build and olive complexion. He looked familiar, but from where?

"Here's your package," said the driver of the van.

"Was all of this necessary?" the man asked, looking at the firm hold one of the men had on Breckon's arm, the gag and the hand and leg restraints. The accent said the man was from the Mideast.

"He fought hard."

"I thought you were better than that. Looks like a clumsy job to me."

He looked at Breckon, pulled the rag out of his mouth, and said, "You will be under my charge from now until you reach your destination. I hope the rest of your trip would be more comfortable than it has been up until now. But make no mistake, I always deliver my man. You can make it as easy or as hard for yourself as you wish."

Turning to the driver he asked, "Where are his personal effects?" He was handed a set of keys, a small pocketknife, a ballpoint pen, a few coins, and a handkerchief.

"Where is his wallet with his identification, money, credit cards?"

"Come to think of it, I had a wallet," the man said. "But he tried to get away, and I had to drop all this stuff to grab him."

"There couldn't have been," the driver said. "As we drove away I looked all around the area, and there was nothing on the pavement. It's got to be in the van." They went and searched in the back of the van.

"They're obviously holding out on you," said Breckon while they searched. "Deal with scum bags, and you might as well expect that." Breckon realized that with no identification they did not know if they had the right man.

"Enough of that," the small man said to Breckon. Then to the two abductors "Well, have you found it?"

"It's not here, that's for sure."

"You guys are real pros," Breckon interjected, "You commit a felony by kidnapping someone, and then you have no way of knowing if you've got the right man."

"Shut up," snapped the small man. "Get him in the plane, and we'll get out of here. Where's the pilot?"

"Right here." An overweight man of thirty-five was walking toward them. He was the most untidy person Breckon could ever remember seeing. He needed a shave, and had food spilled on his dirty, mostly unbuttoned shirt. His overhanging stomach was met by his underwear, which stuck up over his trousers. Breckon hoped he took better care of the planes he flew than he did his personal appearance. His leg restraint was cut, and the two men forced him up the steps into the plane. In his seat, Breckon could hear the pilot talking to the small man through the open door.

"I've finished the preflight and everything that was working during the flight into here is still working, but that ain't saying a whole lot. I think I found what was making the autopilot kick out. By the way, those crates you loaded into the plane must contain solid steel or something.

They're not all that big, but by the way this old bus is hanging on its shock absorbers, I'd guess we're overloaded."

"There's nothing you can do about it. The freight goes, that's final."

"If we lose an engine we're going down. Thought you'd like to know."

"Then don't lose an engine."

"With this old crate, that ain't funny. Tell your gorillas to push the plane out of the hangar. It should be easy for them, and it'll save time not having to call for a tractor."

The small man nodded to the two men. One opened the hangar door, and they slowly pushed the plane out of the hangar onto the tarmac, turning it ninety degrees so the jet exhaust wouldn't hit the building.

Breckon watched out of a window as the small man handed something to the van driver, probably his pay. The small man gestured emphatically as he spoke, perhaps expressed his displeasure at the missing wallet. Breckon's hands were still tied, and one of his ankles had been bound to a leg of his seat.

The pilot entered the cabin and looked at Breckon. "I'm only the pilot. I fly the plane for them and don't ask any questions about the cargo. Can't afford to. By the way, my name's Rollins."

"Rollins something or something Rollins?" asked Breckon.

"Just Rollins. What's your name?"

"Call me CJ," said Breckon. It was the first thing that popped into his head. No use giving them the satisfaction of knowing they had gotten the right man.

"CJ something or something CJ?" asked Rollins.

"Just CJ," said Breckon. He gave the man a sarcastic grin.

Rollins gave him a wry smile and said, "Now, let's see if I can get this piece of junk to go." He turned and settled into the pilot's seat.

From what Breckon could see, Rollins's description fit pretty well. He had never given it any thought, but what did happen to those beautiful corporate jets in the magazines? The first owners traded them in when something better and faster came on the market. Because they're still in good shape, some smaller company buys the used ones. The process ends with a final trip to the junk pile, and that's where someone must have intercepted this one.

Most of the seats had been taken out to make room for freight. Those left had threadbare, torn upholstery that was unspeakably dirty. The carpet had long ago worn through, and what was left torn out. Small swatches of carpet could still be seen under some of the legs of the seats. As he looked around, he could see past the crates Rollins had mentioned. In the rear was a five-gallon can of hydraulic oil strapped down with an old seat belt.

The plane smelled funny too, a mixture of oil, fuel, and urine. Something like a shower curtain hung across the rear of the cabin. Nearby were some jugs and a pail. These utensils had a web strap running through their handles to keep them from flying around the cabin during turbulence. That was probably the in-flight rest room.

Breckon could hear Rollins flipping switches and talking on the radio to the tower. The door to the cockpit was tied open so Breckon could see and hear most of what went on up there. The first engine started to spool up and then dropped in speed only to get another spin up to a faster speed. Again, it started to drop. Breckon could tell as the pitch of the whine increased and decreased in a sort of random fashion that this engine was not eager to start. Finally it got to a fairly high pitch and held steady. Breckon began to feel apprehension at flying in such a plane to say nothing of having been kidnapped and spirited off to who knew where. The second engine started in what seemed like a normal sequence.

The small man came up the steps and pulled at a cable to help the worn-out mechanism lift the steps and seal the door. With the door latched, the man came up to Breckon. "I'll take the plastic band off your wrists now. Don't try any heroics. Even though I'm small, I can handle you. I want you to be in good condition when we get to our destination. But I'll get you there in any way that's necessary. Fasten your seat belt. We're ready to take off." Breckon latched his seat belt and inspected his wrists. They had been bruised and scraped as he was pulled loose from his grip on the sewer grating.

The plane taxied out from between two rows of hangars and onto the main taxiway. Since it was Friday afternoon most of the planes were leaving and there were few landings. At the end of the runway, it was only a five minute wait before they turned onto the runway and soon became airborne.

The small man then said, "Permit me to introduce myself. I am Alwan Najafi and you, I presume, are Ed Breckon."

"You can presume anything you like, but they call me CJ."

Najafi had a sour expression on his face. "Oh, don't do that. You might as well be mature and make the best of a bad situation. If you don't cooperate, it will go harder and harder on you until you do."

Breckon was still defiant. "I don't understand what you expect to gain by this. What you're doing is downright stupid."

"Have it your way."
Once again, Breckon was trying to remember where he'd seen him.

By noting the position of the sun relative to their direction of flight, Breckon knew they were headed in an easterly direction. How they would get across the Atlantic Ocean he was not sure. These business jets had a two-thousand mile range as he remembered. As he was growing up, he had been fascinated with airplanes and read books showing all the types, listing their statistics. Yet, he could not remember his geography well enough to have a good idea of how to get across the Atlantic in two-thousand-mile steps.

Thinking of regular maps would be deceiving, since they would be flying great circle routes. A globe would be needed. He remembered that Charles Lindbergh flew over St. John's Newfoundland and then the North Atlantic to get to Ireland. From there, he flew down to France. Probably St. John's would be their first stop.

As the time passed, Breckon worked on his situation. It made no sense to try to take control of the airplane while in the air. Even if he could overcome the Arab guy, there was Rollins. He was needed to fly the plane. So, he'd have to wait it out and look for an opportunity on the ground.

Breckon sat on the right side of the plane and Najafi was one seat behind him on the left side. There were only two seats on each side. He glanced back at Najafi, who had laid back in his seat with his eyes closed. He wasn't sure when the idea first took root in his mind, but he was now thinking fixedly about how familiar he looked. Then it hit him. That was the man Darin had photographed at the plant with Ratling.

Though Breckon was tired, he couldn't sleep. Anger, fear, and worry alternately weighed on him. He thought about everybody back in Minneapolis going about their lives as before. Especially Cindy came to mind. They had gone out together several times, and it had been wonderful. Would he ever see her again? He pushed her out of his mind and tried to concentrate on his predicament.

They flew until he thought they must be nearly out of fuel. Finally, he heard Rollins speak into the microphone, but was unable to make out the words. The response from the cockpit speaker was clear.

"Citation, 47250 Bravo, this is St. John's Center, you're cleared to land on runway zero three left. Winds north by northeast at twelve knots.

Breckon's wrists were swollen by now and turning black and blue, while the lacerations were becoming increasingly uncomfortable. When they touched down, the shock absorbers bottomed out, then slowly lifted. The plane yawed from side to side since the wind was not head-on. Breckon had flown enough in small planes to know the plane was sluggish, which meant it was overloaded. They taxied to some fuel pumps, and Rollins cut the engines.

Najafi was up as soon as the plane stopped and was talking with Rollins. "Fuel up. Check and fix anything you must. Be ready to go in half an hour. He pulled out a large, plastic cable tie from his bag and bound Breckon's ankle to the leg of his seat.

"Hey, while you're out, get some antiseptic and bandages for my wrists!" Breckon held up his arms to show the lacerations and bruises. Najafi looked, then turned and left.

An hour later, with no food, or bandages, and nothing fixed, they were airborne again.

Breckon struggled to awaken from a deep sleep as he heard a ringing like an old, mechanical alarm clock. He shook his head as he opened his eyes. The ringing was coming from the cockpit. There was a growl and some bumping around until finally the ringing stopped. After a few minutes there was the standard radio talk as Rollins got landing instructions for Sao Miguel in the Azores. Once on the ground, Rollins again pulled up to some gas pumps and cut the engines. Breckon was bound to the seat again. After telling Rollins to fuel as fast as possible, Najafi was gone.

As Rollins came past, Breckon asked, "What was the ringing?"

"My alarm clock."

"You were asleep?"

"Of course, you don't see a copilot do you? I put it on autopilot and set the alarm clock for ninety percent of the time I figure it'll take to get to the next destination. When the alarm goes off, my GPS gadget tells me the direction and distance to go."

"That's unbelievably risky. There are a hundred things that could go wrong."

"Hey, I'm getting paid to break the rules. Gotta go juice up."

The number one engine was not mentioned. Instead, they were off again in twenty minuets.

"Citation 47250 Bravo, this is Rabat Control. Proceed on bearing one-zero-five thirty kilometers and come right to two-seven-five." Breckon had no idea where in the world Rabat was. After the engines were shut down, Rollins stuck his head around the corner of the cockpit door and yelled back at Najafi. "Get food and water! We're getting hungry."

Alone again, Breckon watched a business jet taxi to the southeast end of the runway and begin its take off to the northwest. A change in the sound of the jet caused him to look again. He saw it had its spoilers up, flaps down, and was breaking. Then it was lost from view. A few minutes later it came into the ramp area two hundred yards away following a small truck with flashing lights on top.

Breckon's plane was getting very hot inside, and the smell was worsening by the minute. At last, he heard the sound of the door being opened. It was Rollins.

"No luck for the engine. I found a mechanic, but all he could offer was to remove it and send it to Casablanca for repair. Take at least a week. So pray if you do. Has Najafi been back?"

"No," replied Breckon. "But leave the door open. The smell's getting bad in here."

The sound of an engine without a muffler could be heard approaching. "Rollins, give me a hand!" Outside the door was a pickup truck in as bad a shape as the Citation. Several boxes and brown bags of supplies were hastily dumped into the plane. Najafi handed money to the driver and in a low voice said to Rollins, "Get going fast. You have drawn attention to us. You were looking for a mechanic, weren't you? There are people headed this way, and they don't look like mechanics, unless mechanics wear guns."

Number one was starting unwillingly while number two started to spin up. As soon as number two had enough thrust to move them, they were rolling toward the southeast end of the runway. Najafi was in the copilot seat. They were still only a little over half way to the end of the runway when Breckon heard the control tower operator say. "Citation 47250 Bravo, hold your position. Wait for the guide truck and follow it back to the ramp area."

Both engines were running okay now. Najafi yelled, "Now, fly into the air. We must not be stopped. Turn onto the runway here and go! Do you want to rot in a Moroccan prison? Go, now!"

The engines spooled up, and they turned onto the runway. "We only have half a runway. We can't make it," yelled Rollins. "Look, they're going to pull a truck onto the runway!"

"More power! All power! Now!"

With the engines screaming like never before, the acceleration pushed Breckon into his seat. The plane rotated and lifted. Breckon could see the end of a truck as it passed beneath the leading edge of the wing. Men were running and rolling in the dirt beside the runway attempting to avoid what was sure to be a crash. The Citation narrowly missed the truck and struggled to fly but settled back on the runway. They were still accelerating at full throttle. They rotated again at the end of the runway. There was a bump, and Breckon saw a vibrating chain link fence as it appeared behind the wing, but they were flying.

"Citation 47250 Bravo, land at once. You may have gotten contaminated fuel," said the cockpit speaker.

Najafi was almost shouting, "Don't answer. Swing wide over the ocean to the left and head southeast. We cannot allow them to see our cargo or our passenger. Go to the eastern border of Morocco by the shortest route. Don't fly over cities."

After ten minutes, Najafi came back into the cabin and went to work securing the supplies. He slit the restraint on Breckon's ankle, and dropped a bag on his lap. It contained a good-sized first-aid kit. He noticed that while his watch read 7:45, it was early afternoon where they were. Only fourteen hours since he had been taken, but it seemed like a lifetime.

Then they ate. Rollins ate his meal as he sat in the pilot's seat so he could keep an eye on the engine instruments. The air in the cabin was breathable again, Breckon's wrists didn't hurt as much, and he had finished his first meal in a long while. He slept in his seat and did not dream. Rollins's yelling shattered his comfortable oblivion.

"Najafi, big trouble!"

There was a scurry of movement as Najafi plunked into the copilot seat. "Number one has finally had it. That stress we put on it at take-off was too much. I've been throttling it back, but it's still in the red zone and I'm shutting it down to prevent a fire. We're too heavy to fly on one engine. We'll continue to lose altitude, but we should be able to go some distance. Even though we're in Libyan air space we gotta find a place to set her down."

The number two engine was making more noise from having its power set at maximum. There was tense conversation in the cockpit.

Rollins was fumbling with a map and trying to fly the crippled airplane. "Here, Alwan, take the map. I've got all I can do to fly the plane. All I have is the million-to-one sectional charts of this part of the world. I didn't plan to land here. We're on chart ONC H-3. Find twenty-nine degrees north and fourteen east. My GPS says that's where we are. Each large square on the chart is a hundred kilometers on a side. We can fly two or three squares yet. The open circles are unpaved strips. Find the one closest to the coast and a large airport. Airports with paved runways are closed circles with heavy, solid lines through them. "

After a pause, Najafi said. "Where's the chart next in our direction? We're at the end of this one."

"In my case, ONC H-4."

More fumbling around and a long pause. "Okay, the best airfield noted on map H-3 is two and a half squares away from the coordinates you gave me. It has the best roads going to the Mediterranean coast where there are paved airports. It doesn't seem to be shown on H-4. The charts seem to overlap in this area, but I can't be sure."

"What are the coordinates of the strip in degrees and minutes?" Rollins was flying with one hand and had the GPS in the other.

"Okay . . . , 29:45 north, and say, 17:35 east."

Rollins was pressing in the numbers with his thumb as they were read off. "The GPS says seventy miles to go. That's one square. We should make it but without much to spare. The charts for places like this aren't too accurate. I hope there's a strip there."

"On H-4 it shows a different thing there."

"Hold your finger on the chart and show me."

Najafi held the crumpled map up in front of Rollins's face with his slender finger pressed against it. "That's a tower of some kind. It'll be a landmark."

Najafi continued to look at the chart. "There are other airfields east or south of our track. They all appear to be associated with the main oil field in Libya. But none of them are paved so this one's our best choice. Will there be police or soldiers at that airfield?"

"Doubt it. Probably that's an oil field strip, put in while they were drilling the wells and laying the pipeline." After a pause, "At our present rate of sink, we'll make it with a thousand feet to spare, if number two engine lasts. I'll have to line up and land regardless of wind direction."

The remaining few minutes seemed to move like a miser's hand at a charity auction. The howl of the number two engine wore on everyone's nerves. Breckon watched the terrain below. It become increasingly rugged as it came up to meet them. If they came up short of the desert strip there was little chance of surviving a landing in the gullies, sand dunes, and rocks below.

"There, there, to the left is a tower. Is that it? Will we get there?" Najafi's hand shook as he pointed at a radio tower held up by guy wires.

"It'll be close. I see the strip. Gear down." After a pause, "The left wheel won't lock down, we must've hit something as we took off. Wheels up. We go in on the belly. Engine off. Fuel off. Strap in. CRASH POSITION!"

"This cursed heat," muttered Hans Mueller flopped in the hammock like a pile of discarded rags. His place of repose was under the awning he had rigged up to extend from the east side of the building. High paying jobs in Switzerland were hard to find, so he, like many of his countrymen, took jobs in other countries. This really was nowhere, out in the Libyan desert doing maintenance on oil well pumps. There was nothing to do, not even anybody to talk to. His two Arab helpers at least had each other for company.

He had his schedule. At first light, he started out with his crew driving the boom truck, while he drove the Land Rover. Most of the work was hand work, changing oil in the gear boxes and replacing seals on the drive system and well-head valves, or similar repairs and maintenance. At times, a gearbox required a new set of bearings or gears. This required the boom truck. They worked from dawn to ten, and from five until a little before dark.

He raised his head at the sound of an airplane. It sounded funny. He got out of his hammock and looked to the west, shielding his eyes with his hand. It was a business jet and really low. When it was overhead, he saw the wheels come down and then go up again. Then no sound. With no engines, it was going to land, but certainly not at *that* airstrip. It had been abandoned for years. The plane was out of sight now. Mueller figured the rate it was coming down and thought that it must have landed by now. There was no explosion, so they must have made it.

He got back in his hammock and drank some water. He tried to get interested in the book he was reading for the second time. A while later there was a rumble from the east. At first, he saw nothing, and then a low, dark cloud. He decided that when they finished the afternoon shift, he'd go take a look. It wouldn't be wise to go now for fear that his Land Rover would break down in the heat.

The sudden stillness, as the number two engine stopped, made Breckon catch his breath. He thought there was a hint of exhilaration in Rollins's voice. The only sound now was the slipstream of air past the sides of the airplane. The plane tipped to one side and then the other as Rollins side-slipped off excess altitude. He appeared to actually be a good pilot.

"Ready or not, here it comes," yelled Rollins. They were level as the belly made contact. One second it was still, and the next an incredible screeching, roaring sound erupted as the packed gravel runway tore into aluminum. Then a hiss as they went across sand, followed by quiet as they were thrown into the air, nose up. Rollins corrected and the nose started to come down. Seconds later they felt a hard jolt as the tail hit the ground, the nose pitched down, and the plane slammed into the packed earth. Now they were skidding to the right. Rollins cursed as he fought to keep the plane straight. It was coming back to center, but because he didn't stop correcting soon enough, it skidded to the left. They were in the sand to the side of the runway as the left wing dug in, spinning them completely around. They slid backwards for a few seconds and stopped. They were down, more or less in one piece. It was silent, three, four, five seconds.

"Everybody out, grab what you can!" Najafi yelled.

Breckon had his seat belt off and was unlatching the door in a second. With Rollins at his side, he pushed harder. It gave and fell open. They all tumbled out. After the cool air in the plane, the desert heat was crushing. Combined with the sudden exertion, the sun and hot air made Breckon and Rollins bend over and put their hands on their thighs. They squinted their eyes at the blazing, white-hot sand. It was between four or five in the afternoon and the sun was a shaft of searing pain on the men.

Najafi smirked. "Welcome to the desert, gentlemen."

Rollins started walking around the plane. "Look for fuel leaks."

None were obvious.

Najafi snapped. "We need our possessions. Only one in the plane at a time. If a fire starts, run fast, far. Rollins, you first, get your charts and bag." Using this procedure they managed to rescue all their belongings as well as the food and water.

Looking at the horizon, Breckon could see the heat waves coming off the sand. Two dark objects, shimmering some distance from the airstrip, caught his eye. If they were buildings, they'd offer shade. It was obvious as they stood in the sun that neither Rollins nor Breckon would last long in this sea of fiery heat.

"You two wrap something around your heads. Something white or light. Do it now!" Najafi ordered.

Breckon took off his shirt and T-shirt and wrapped his T-shirt around his head. He quickly put his shirt back on. It felt as though his exposed skin would be sunburned in minutes. Rollins dug in his bag and found a dirty light colored shirt. Breckon strapped on his frame pack and picked up his hiking boots and computer bag. He wondered whether the laptop would survive.

The dark objects turned into real buildings as they approached. They covered the distance in fifteen minutes, dumped their bags in the shade, which was on the side roughly perpendicular to the runway, and went back for another load. Back at the plane, they all drank from the bottled water and headed back with the remaining food, water, and miscellaneous items. It was not until they got to the building that Breckon and Rollins noticed that Najafi had stayed behind.

Rollins dumped his load and took another drink of water. "Wonder what happened to him?"

Breckon took the bottle and drank too. "Don't worry, he's up to some low down, stinking thing. By the way, did I sense that you were enjoying that crash landing?"

Rollins chuckled. "Ya noticed, huh? Yeah, I guess I did. I've gone through a belly landing a thousand times in my mind, and finally I had a chance to do it. It was lucky I came in on the belly, though, because with that sand drifted onto the strip the wheels would've caught and twisted us around. I would've had no chance of control after that, and we would've broken up and probably burned."

They saw a figure approaching through the heat waves like someone appearing from another dimension in a sci-fi movie. When Najafi approached, he was watching his wristwatch rather intently. Suddenly there was a flash of light in the mirage as the airplane exploded. A smile of satisfaction came to Najafi's face. The first flash was followed by secondary flashes. Najafi looked at them, then started giving the building a close inspection.

The building they were using for shade was in surprisingly good shape. Gray, sandblasted boards covered the sides in a patchwork of sizes, probably from shipping crates the oil well equipment came in. The large vehicle door was locked from the inside and the small door had a padlock on it. Breckon watched as Najafi picked the lock like a pro.

As always, Najafi had the lead. "Rollins, you can pass off as some sort of Arab mix with your black hair and brown eyes. When we meet people I was the pilot of the airplane. Let me do all the talking. Your clothes fit in well with the image of a slave. You don't speak. If they ask you something, point to your throat, and shake your head for no. I'll tell them you lost your voice. However, you are a problem," he said looking at Breckon. "Black hair is good, your height and build are good, but your eyes are so very blue and your skin is so white. Don't you ever see the sun?"

"No. I have spent the last two years literally day and night designing and building those robots for you, and look where it got me." Najafi could see the anger rising in Breckon.

"Enough! We'll improvise. We flew over oil wells before we landed, and the air sectional map shows a camp a few kilometers to the west. If the camp is inhabited, someone will come to investigate the plane fire. You must stay out of sight in the building," he said looking at Breckon. "I'll try to get us transport to the coast tonight, and if you can stay out of direct light maybe it will work. Into the building now. Take food and water. Stay quiet. If you have any old clothes in that pack, put them on. Figure out a way to carry your clothes and computer in a less western way. This is serious. People would kill you for the clothes you're wearing. And with no identification you could get us all killed."

Breckon had no choice but to go into the building where it was even hotter. After the door shut, he listened to the padlock close with a sinking feeling. He had slept a few hours before the landing but now, with the added stress of the heat, the fatigue returned and was almost overpowering. But first things first. He had to see if the computer worked and try to send a message. He found a place to sit where some wooden boxes hid him from direct view of the door.

The computer came on. He put together the best message he could but was not sure how coherent it was. He encoded it, connected it to the modem, and then to the Iridium phone. He was unbearably hot, and was using the T-shirt to mop his face and keep the sweat out of his eyes. After ten tries in five minutes, he had a satellite acquired. At the slow transmission rate of the Iridium system, 9600 baud (9600 bits per second) it took ten seconds to send the message to Harris's AOL mailbox.

He drank again, put the computer back in the case, and looked around the building. The sun was getting lower and the temperature was falling, but the fatigue was still there. He needed different clothes. He had been captured while wearing his work clothes. No wonder the Arab thought they were too good for a situation like this. His camping clothes were junk. They were something he didn't mind losing if he burned a hole in them or tore them on a rock. He dug them out of the small gym tote he had taken for the change of clothes before they hit the trail. He also put on his hiking boots and wide-brimmed trail hat. That should help in the sun.

Breckon found a large, battered canvas bag something like a sea bag. He shook the dirt out and transferred the contents of his frame pack to it as well as the clothes and shoes he had just taken off. Half way up in the bag he put in his computer case followed by more clothing and a light parka he had packed for the mountains. Even in late August, a cloudy, windy day at ten thousand feet could be cold. He had heard how cool it could get in the desert at night. Right now he doubted he'd have that problem.

There was a can of brown oil in the back of the building. He tried rubbing some of it on his arms. It was so dusty in the old building that his clothes already looked like he had been in them for days. A plan was forming in his mind. He could not possibly pass himself off as an Arab so why not some Caucasian, like a German or Czech, there to repair oil well equipment?

The temperature was falling. "It must be under a hundred degrees by now," he said under his breath. He sat down and dosed off in the heat.

— 11 —

Harris's mind was one confused mess. He could not deny what he had seen at Breckon's apartment and garage the previous afternoon, nor that Ed had disappeared. It was very strange behavior for one of the most reliable people Harris had ever known. But the idea that he had been kidnapped was too crazy. Harris had raced to the Crystal airport, as fast as rush-hour traffic on Friday afternoon allowed. He had driven slowly down the service road and looked up each taxiway between the rows of general aviation hangars. He had not seen the conversion van or anything suspicious.

It was now nine-forty-five, and he had gotten back from a few errands. On the way back, he had stopped by the post office to pick up his mail. He had left it held for the vacation, thinking Breckon would show up with some weird excuse.

He turned on his computer as he did every Saturday morning. To his surprise and relief, he had an e-mail from Breckon. He opened it only to find it was all gibberish. Then he noticed at the top of the page a line of regular text almost unnoticed next to the full screen of random characters. It was coded. He realized that during encoding the whole message was encoded as a string, even characters that didn't print.

The line of clear text read:

Insert CD as indicated, type in sector(s) shown, press Ctrl Alt Y keys at the same time. Disk and sectors: F4-22.

It was a coded message using one of his coding disks! F4 had to mean the number of the CD and 22 was the sector to use.

Harris ran to his bedroom, threw the mattress off his bed, and lifted up the box spring. He tore off the bottom fabric. He had taped the coded CDs to the inside of the box frame. Grabbing the first batch of CDs, he flipped through them as if he was dealing cards. There were six of them and the numbers all started with "D." He grabbed another pack. There were four and all started with "B." He got through all of them and discovered the packs starting with "A" through "E."

To his dismay, he realized Breckon had not sent the "F" batch! He couldn't decode the message. Harris sank down into his only easy chair, a cloud of despair hanging over him. After a minute, he got up and grabbed the E4 CD. He tried it hoping there was a mistake.

After he loaded the CD, he could hear the computer accessing the disk. It paused a few seconds and a different set of random characters appeared. It appeared to be decoding but he was using the wrong CD of random numbers. He needed the "F" CD. Why hadn't Ed mailed them to him? Then it hit him. The brown envelope in the mail he had picked up that morning.

Ripping open the envelope, he found the F4 CD and put it into his computer with the following results:

Darin,

Sorry I missed our trip. Was taken by force in my apartment parking lot, put on biz jet at Crystal, Cessna Citation, I think, old, real junk. My handler is Arab guy we photographed with George so real connection with the project. I feel this is meant as a one way trip. NO POLICE. I'm out of U.S. anyway, and no CIA, FBI! If time for them I say, not before. They may be involved. Many strange happenings. No hero stuff. Must find my destination.

Flew from Crystal to St. John's, Newfoundland, then Azores, then N Africa, Rabat, where's that? Pretty sure of this, saw signs, heard talk. Then east 3 hr. over desert, lost engine, plane overloaded, forced to land at desert airstrip, belly landing, N Africa, Libya. Handler, called Alwan Najafi, very worried.

Am locked in wooden warehouse. If he returns, I'll transmit where I am. If you get, send short message soonest, coded, use F4. Never use sectors second time, keep track, there are plenty. Messages short, must be clear, hope this is.

In struggle to get free in parking lot, my wallet went down storm drain near my garage. They don't know, so have no ID at all, may be good or bad. Don't try for wallet. Stay out of sight until we figure this out.

Been thinking NSA will see our messages and unbreakable code, will flag them, especially from N Africa. They might be watching Iridium traffic. Remember we're on vacation, keep it that way. They won't like unbreakable code, so go to my apartment and toss it, wear gloves, idea is "bad guys" are looking for password to my AOL acct. and yours as well. They monitored our traffic and know we're on vacation. Plan to use our accounts while we're gone. Then toss your apartment and leave. If you have better idea try me.

Must warn Cindy. She's closest to project after me. She's in the phone book. George is dangerous, will probably kill if he thinks needed. Tell Cindy as much or little as you want. She'll want it all, maybe best, but she MUST NOT tell another living soul. Could be fatal. Must act like she knows nothing. When you contact her don't use your phone, use pay phones, then meet. Be inventive.

Must go, message too long but necessary. Ed

"Oh boy, if that doesn't cork it!" Harris said aloud. "But, what can I do?" He read the message again. "First send a message that I got his message, of course."

Ed, got your message and decoded it. Play it cool, don't antagonize them. Play along like you think you're coming home. That's all I can offer. If you can, send short message so I know if I'm doing it right. Darin

After taking twenty minutes to get everything right, it seemed the message went correctly.

Next, he had to warn Cindy. He and Ed had double dated once, so they were at least acquainted. Finding her phone number, he walked down the street to a pay phone, called, and set up a meeting at a park.

1750 hours local, Libya

Having slept for an hour in the shade of the second building, Najafi walked to the larger building. He had been in tough spots before, but this was bad. His success had always been in having things under control. As soon as an operation gave signs of coming apart, he had managed to slow things down and gets it back on track. This time it was different. First, he had been unable to steal a decent airplane because of the urgency of getting those spent uranium 120 mm tank rounds out of the United States. Then the botched job of capturing Breckon followed by nearly getting arrested in Morocco. Now a crash landing in the desert. It just kept happening! They had to get another airplane, but in all places, Colonel Ghadhafi's Libya. The biggest worry right now was some military patrol finding them.

Then there was his captive. He wasn't even positive he had the right man. He was pretty sure, but the guy wasn't being cooperative at all. It was inconceivable to him that Breckon had passed up that big bonus Ratling has offered him. He knew Americans. They all responded to money. It all seemed wrong. He thought it might go better if he humored the man a little.

As he approached, he saw Rollins slouching in the shade of the first building. Rollins sat up and said, "Hey, know why this runway's so bad? On air chart H-3 in fine print it says 'NOT USABLE.' Well, we used it," he said with his characteristic chuckle.

Breckon was awakened by the sound of voices followed by Najafi working on the lock. Najafi opened the door asked, "CJ, are you okay?"

Breckon gave him a blank stare still not fully awake. "What are you talking about? I'm Ed Breckon." The sum total of the shocks he had been exposed to followed by the extreme heat of the building were having their effect. His speech was even slurred.

Najafi was taken aback by the change in attitude. "Come out. We have some planning to do." The man who stepped out of the building was a different man. His clothes were different. His walk was different, well, unsteady. His voice even sounded different. His skin was different. What had happened?

"Boy, it actually feels cool out here," Breckon said as he staggered to the side of the building and slumped down.

Najafi could see that he should not have put Breckon in the building. It could have killed him. He had forgotten these guys weren't acclimated to the desert heat. He watched as Breckon rubbed his face trying to regain full consciousness. He leaned his head back against the building and took deep breaths. He got up on his knees and stood up steadying himself with his hand on the building.

"What happened in there? You don't look like the same person," Najafi said as he felt panic for the first time in years.

"It was too hot in there. I'm almost dead from the heat. I drank water but it didn't seem to help toward the end. I don't feel like eating and I'm dog tired."

"But your appearance. You hardly look like the same man."

"You told me to put on different clothes so I did. When I joined your stinking band of outlaws, I was wearing my office clothes. I put on some of the clothing I would've used for backpacking in the wilderness. There was some oil in there so I rubbed some on my white skin. A different look. Big surprise."

Najafi knew this didn't look right. His mind was telling him this was a trap, but he couldn't see what it was, or by whom.

"You said we had some planning to do." Breckon drank some water and, taking off his hat, poured some on his head. Shaking his head, he continued. "I agree, and I have some suggestions." Breckon sat down a few feet from Rollins, rubbing his face from time to time. "It makes more sense if Rollins remains the pilot. Sooner or later, flying and piloting questions will come up, and you're not the one to answer them. Try this. I'm some European injured in the eye at some mining operation or oil field or something to the west or southwest of here. You called in a jet to take me to, say Rome, to a good hospital. You're the boss of the job site. This way we can wrap some of the cotton gauze from the first aid kit around my head and I can groan a lot. No one will expect me to talk and won't see my blue eyes. And . . . . "

"Not bad, if a vehicle shows up it will add urgency to get us to the coast tonight. We put you in the back seat and I give you a pill every now and then. There must be something in the kit."

"Yeah, there are some headache pills. You say they're strong pain pills, and I can only take them for a few more hours before they'll harm me."

Najafi interrupted, "You got stung in the eye by a scorpion. You were careless, and didn't check your bed before you went to sleep."

"Does that make sense? Will people believe that?"

"Yes, easily. There are many kinds of scorpions in the desert and some are extremely poisonous."

"Bandage me up. We've got to be ready if anyone comes. It's getting cool enough to travel."

Najafi was becoming convinced this was a different man. He was full of good ideas and so helpful, almost like it was scripted. As he worked the problem, he ambled off around the corner of the building opposite the runway, mumbling to himself. The thought came over Najafi like a dark cloud before a thunderstorm. Was it possible Rollins was a CIA agent and *caused* the airplane to crash land right here? It certainly didn't look like there was anything wrong with the number one engine. And what if a CIA replacement, this guy, was in the building waiting to switch with the engineer? Not having a picture ID made it impossible to be sure who he was. Somehow, the loss of the wallet must have been planned. He changed clothes in the building and said the heat had harmed him so that a change in his voice could happen. He smeared oil on himself so if the skin color didn't match, who'd be able to tell? But, with my remark about his white skin, and his out-of-place clothes, what Breckon did was reasonable. It meant one other thing, though. If there was a switch in the building, the first man was still in there. While it was still light enough he'd have a look.

Rollins was taking all of this in with no comment. As Najafi disappeared from sight, he said to Breckon, "I've worked with this guy a couple of other times, and he's a cool customer. But, you got him talking to himself. CJ, or Breckon, or whoever you are, you're some piece of work. You surely are."

Najafi appeared with a determined look as he stalked to the door. At the moment he grabbed the padlock to begin working the tumblers, he was stopped.

"Najafi," yelled Rollins. "You were right. Here comes a vehicle."

Najafi hesitated. This was his chance to expose the plot. But he couldn't make it seem obvious that he was wise to their scheme.

Breckon walked to Najafi. "You must be sure that the vehicle comes here and doesn't go to the plane. It's possible that some of the bombs you were carrying didn't explode. If it's a military vehicle and some soldiers find unexploded ordinance, it'll go hard on all of us. Go out, shout, and wave at him to get him to come here. I'll do my act."

The timing of the vehicle's arrival was too much to be a coincidence. It would cause Najafi to lose his chance to search the building! But he had no choice but to play dumb or he could end up dead. Forced to submit to the situation, Najafi yelled, "Rollins, yell and wave, get him to come here, and not to the plane!"

The vehicle changed course at their display and came toward them.

Much to his relief, Najafi saw that the driver was not an Arab. "Do you speak English?" asked Najafi.

"Pretty good. I work with English and Americans sometimes, so I learn. I am Hans Mueller."

"Good to meet you Hans, I am Alwan Najafi. I am in charge of a new mine to the southwest. We need help very much. That man," he said pointing to Breckon, "has been stung in the eye by a scorpion. He needs a good doctor very soon. Our plane had bad fuel and the engines stopped. This is a very bad airstrip but we had no choice. We almost died when we landed."

Mueller interrupted, "I saw your plane come over in afternoon. Bad place to have engine stop."

"He will die anyway if we do not get medical care for that sting."

"Many kinds of scorpions in the desert. Most do not sting, only few kinds, fat-tailed scorpion, Mediterranean yellow, African gold, and few others. All rest no problem. Fat-tailed worst. Does not run away. Real mean. Most of poison not go in that man or he dead already."

"Yes, yes. How far to the coast and an airport, and can you please take us there? I will pay you well."

"It takes four hour to get to Matratin. Airport there. Better airport east on coast, another hour. Sometimes Canadian Occidental has jet airplane at one of those airports. Maybe they help."

Najafi took out a wad of U.S. money and flipped out five one hundred-dollar bills. "Here, I pay this much if you drive us. If you drive us to the coast tonight, I pay this much again when we get there. But we must leave now. Is there enough fuel in the truck to get there?"

"Yes. That is much money. Why so much?"

"This man may die. I gave him pills for pain. With no pills, he is crazy like madman, yelling and jumping around. These pills are bad, dangerous, so sting might kill him, or pills might kill him. Very hard to get good, technical guest workers here, like you, Hans. If word goes back men die in the desert, they will not come. Must go now, please."

That was good money. U.S. dollars were good almost anyplace. Hans was strictly forbidden to use the Land Rover for personal use, but this was an emergency. He could be back in eight hours if he drove faster than normal. He also had an idea from what he had heard from others.

And, as he figured it, there would be enough time. He certainly had the inclination, and most of all he had the money.

"We go to coast now. Must be back by dawn. No jumping and shouting, give pills, okay?"

"Yeah, yeah. We go."

Rollins and Najafi got Breckon, who acted like he was drugged and could hardly walk. He murmured incoherently as they helped him into the Land Rover.

Minneapolis

Darin Harris saw the blue Taurus Cindy Thomas had described to him as he drove into the parking area of the park so he pulled up alongside. "Hi, Cindy. Remember me?"

"Yes," the bewildered woman said.

"Something very unexpected happened yesterday. We must talk. Let's find a place in the park." They took a paved trail leading into the park. The dense foliage of the large oak trees combined with the overcast sky made a semi-twilight as the pair walked. Almost immediately, they saw an octagonal picnic shelter in a hollow with picnic tables clustered under a roof of split cedar shingles. As they walked down the grassy slope, Harris continued, "Keep your voice low and look for others who might be watching us."

As they walked up to the shelter, Harris noticed that a few feet beyond the far side was a small rock garden in which water was pumped from a pool to the top of a six-foot rise and allowed to tumble down large, bluish-gray rocks in a waterfall. He sat down on the table seat closest to the cascade. "The sound of the water will help to drown out our voices if someone tries to overhear."

Thomas was on the point of laughing at the melodrama of it all.

"I know this may seem silly, but let me know what you think when you've heard my story. You may know that George Ratling has been trying to get Ed to go to, of all places, Bulgaria to install the special gantry robots you people built."

She nodded.

"Ed left for vacation yesterday afternoon, didn't he?"

Another nod.

"He and I intended to head out West to do some hiking and camping in the mountains. Well, I'm not there, and neither is Ed. He's been kidnapped, and taken to wherever you sent those robots to supervise the installation. Ed's okay as far as I know, but he's in great danger."

Cindy looked at Darin with a tense frown on her face that wrinkled the skin between her eyes. "Yes, he mentioned that to me about the installation, but he said he wasn't going, and that he wasn't even sure it was Bulgaria."

"It seems Ratling arranged to have him taken to the installation site against his will. But he isn't there yet."

"How do you know this? That's nuts!"

Harris explained that Ed had an Iridium phone in his computer, that it was never intended for this, the encoding scheme, and why that phone was now a key link to him. Then he showed her a copy of the message he had received.

Thomas read it quickly and looked at Darin with anger in her eyes. "That poor guy. Who is George anyway, some sort of evil fiend?"

"I think George's greed got him tangled up with some serious trash. I imagine the money looked good at first. Once hooked, they threatened to either expose him in some way or kill him if he didn't keep on. George is trapped and dangerous. You might want to get out of town for a couple of weeks. Do you know any place you could stay?"

"No! I'm not leaving. There might be some way I can help Ed, and I want to be here."

"Okay. But if George suspects you know about Ed, you'll be in danger."

"I'll be careful. Now, what's this NSA business? Why is he coding the messages?"

"Make some reasonable assumptions. What if these robots are going to Iran or some place like that? Then assume they're intended for the production of weapons of mass destruction. The gantry robots were shipped under false pretenses, which implicates all of you on the project. The CIA doesn't know Ed was kidnapped. Even if we went to them and told the whole story, and, assuming they believed us—a *big* if—they're always looking at the big picture, saving the world while getting themselves promoted. They may say they'll try to save Ed while they're bombing the robots to dust. But realistically, will they care if Ed dies? What's the life of one man compared to the hundreds or thousands who would theoretically be saved by preventing the use of the WMDs?"

This was all so new to Thomas that it was hard to believe. She shrugged her shoulders as she replied, "But how would they know Ed sent an e-mail to you, why the code?"

Harris realized that Cindy was not familiar with the NSA, the Echelon system, and their on-going eavesdropping , so he gave her a short history of it.

"During the Second World War, it became evident that knowledge of an enemy's radio communications was very important to fighting a war. The information could be used either to eavesdrop on them or to jam the signals so they could not communicate. As World War II ended and the cold war started, the NSA was set up. Electronic Intelligence, ELINT, became a serious pursuit for all the major powers. The United States had ships full of listening gear. The public became aware of this when North Korea captured the *USS Pueblo* in 1968. As soon as artificial satellites were possible, some were designed for ELINT. The NSA was the agency charged with gathering intelligence from listening in on electronic signals of all kinds.

"With the end of the cold war, did the NSA shut down? Of course not. Governmental agencies never shut down. In 1995, the NSA had thirty-eight-thousand employees and many more were on the payrolls of companies like Lockheed. They switched their activities to listening to virtually all communications from everybody. Ostensibly, they were looking for terrorists, but they used the information any way they pleased. This is an agency where computing power is measured by acres of computers. With voice recognition in all major languages of the planet, they listen to telephones, faxes, and e-mails, follow money transfers between banks, everything. This massive amount of collected data is screened for what they call flag words and phrases, hundreds of them. The U.S. is connected with Canada, England, Australia, and New Zealand to collect and trade information. The governments involved don't acknowledge this system exists, so oversight is nil. And there is no safety in encrypting your message. The acres of NSA computers were designed to break the best coding systems the Soviets could produce, so anything a commercial operation like a bank did was a piece of cake."

"So if they're so good why does Ed bother to encode his messages?"

"There's a system of encoding called the one-time-pad that's theoretically unbreakable. If you use a set of truly random numbers to encode a message, and use the numbers only one time, the code is unbreakable. At the start of the robot project, Ed had an Iridium phone built into his personal computer with the intent of capturing random noise from atmospheric static. The project had a requirement for a high degree of security, so he used this random noise to encode the documents and drawings for the project. It was sort of an engineering challenge for him, too. When he was taken, he had a set of CDs of random numbers in his computer bag. He sends me a set of his discs now and then so he has an off-site set in case of a fire. If he succeeded with his system, he and I are the only two people who can read these messages."

Thomas was thoughtfully looking at her hands on the table. "I suppose that's why he mentioned he was afraid of them checking on you."

"Yeah, so I'll have to move. I have to simulate Ed and myself being on vacation. Can't even use my phone. The NSA could be monitoring it. If I'm gone, why am I here using it?"

"Maybe they'll bring him home."

"Could be. But, if there's anything illegal going on where those gantry robots will be used, he'll know what it is before he leaves. In that case they won't dare let him go." They sat in silence as a few drops of rain spattered on the rocks and pool. Then Harris continued. "I don't know if there's anything we can do right now except wait for Ed to send another message. Maybe he'll be able to tell us more. I'll call you from time to time from a pay phone. Keep an eye on Ratling."

After Harris left the park, he went to the corner fast-food place to make a phone call. "Hello, Helen? Is Keith in?" Keith Gibbon was the only person Harris knew who had even been to the Mideast.

"Who's calling?"

"This is Darin Harris. Remember me? I landed the airplane in your backyard."

"Of course. How are you?"

"Oh, fine. Is Keith there?"

"No. Actually, he's out of the country, Saudi Arabia again. I do hope this is the last time. Those trips are getting hard on him. Is there anything I can do for you?"

That was something Harris hadn't planned on or even thought of. If that's the area Breckon was headed, then maybe there was something Gibbon could do to help. But until they found where the site was there was no point in pursuing this angle.

"No. I wanted to kick an idea around with him if he were home. I'll call again another time."

After an hour, Breckon decided it was time to act a little. He started to wake up, groan, and thrash around. Mueller stopped so they could take him out of the vehicle. Breckon saw a tire iron lying on the floor as Mueller momentarily turned on a flashlight. Najafi gave Breckon a pill, and in a few minutes he pretended to settle down as Rollins helped him get back in the rear seat.

As they started off again, Breckon knew he could grab the tire iron and club Najafi, who was in the seat in front of him. It would be easy after they all started to doze off. But it was one thing to fantasize about doing it. When faced with killing another man in cold blood, it was different. He had had outrageous treatment, but was it reason enough to kill a man? He contented himself with the thought that it might not be all that advantageous to escape his captors in Libya anyway.

By ten-thirty, they were driving into town. "This Matratin," said Mueller.

"Good. You made good time. You are a good driver. Go to the airport, fast please." He shook Rollins. "Wake up, we're near the airport."

He knew that Rollins would take this as a signal to be watching for parked airplanes. There was more than a half moon that would set soon. As they drove along the perimeter fence, several airplanes were visible. He saw Rollins nod his head.

They drove up to the main gate where there were guards posted. "Hans, they are guarding the airport. I am sure there is a plane here that can help us, but I must get to a phone. Back on the road was a hotel, that's a good place to call from. Take us there please."

Mueller shrugged and turned around. At the hotel, as Najafi was paying Mueller the other five hundred dollars, Rollins shook Breckon. He woke up with a start. Rollins put his hand over his mouth.

Rollins whispered. "Ed, quiet. We're at the airport, act drugged."

Rollins cursed under his breath as he struggled with Breckon's inert body. "You don't have to do such a good job of it." He then took out Breckon's canvas bag, Najafi's bag and his own bag and cart case.

"Thank you much, you did a good job." Najafi said to Mueller. "Now be off so you are back in time and there is no trouble for you."

Mueller was glad to have the money and sped away.

They picked up their belongings and, while watching in all directions, set off toward the airport. They walked for half a mile before they came to the fence. The airport had a small control tower and a flood light, which shown down the line of parked airplanes. At their distance, they were safe from the feeble light.

"Maybe not as good pickings as I thought," whispered Rollins. There were several small single-engine propeller airplanes and one twin. Closer to the tower was a large plane the size of a DC-9.

"Could we take that big one?" asked Najafi.

"That's too much, too valuable."

"There, this side of the big one, in its shadow cast by the flood light," Breckon was pointing. "Isn't that a jet something like the one we had?"

"Where? Oh, yes. You can barely make it out. We'll walk along the fence and get a better look. We all stay together," Najafi said as he was trying to get control again.

Soon they were right behind the smaller plane but still outside the fence.

Rollins whispered, "That looks like a Leer Jet, certainly newer than the one we had. I've more hours in those things than any other type. That'd be a lucky break. How do we get to it?"

Breckon pulled on Najafi's arm. "There's a small gully we crossed a hundred yards back where the fence doesn't quite reach the bottom. I think we could crawl under the fence there. But how do we get into the plane and get it started?"

Najafi whispered back, "I have done it before."

"Somehow that doesn't surprise me."

They found the gully. After some feeling around in the dark with a stick to chase away poisonous critters, they managed to squeeze under.

"We'll stay here until the moon sets in half an hour," Najafi said. "Maybe we can sleep a little. Wish we had something to eat."

Breckon fished around in his bag for a few minutes and pulled out a plastic zip bag. "Here's some smoked, dehydrated, dark turkey meat if you want to try some. It was in my frame pack for the hiking trip."

Rollins took a piece. "That's very good. A little chewy, but it tastes like bacon."

"Alwan? You want some? You're going to need some strength in the next hours. Here, try some."

"No, do not eat pork."

"It's not pork. Rollins said it tasted like pork."

"Yeah, it's turkey. That's like a big chicken, and the meat has been dried. Try some. You'll like it."

Najafi took a piece and tried a small bite. Then he ate several more pieces. He was thinking again how there were so many coincidences. It was hard to believe even Mueller was in on the plot. He seemed to be who he appeared to be. But a Lear Jet, his plane of choice, a place to get under the fence, food on demand, taken together they were making him suspicious again. On the other hand, if Breckon was real and he was going on a trip into the wilderness, he would have food, and dried food was light and did not spoil. He would bring some along from the plane because you never knew when you would get hungry. It all made such perfectly innocent sense.

"I wish I had a small light. It would be a great help on the airplane's door lock."

"Just a minute." Breckon rustled around in his bag again and produced a small, black flashlight. "You twist the end to turn it on."

"Where do you get all this stuff?" Najafi demanded. Though his voice was hushed, his tone was severe.

Breckon did not know what was eating at him as he answered, "My friend and I were planning to be in the wilderness for at least two weeks. Do you know what that means? There's no human civilization, no stores, no doctors, and no other people. We prepare very carefully or we could easily die."

"You have such large, empty places?"

"Of course, and the terrain is very rugged. Look at all the empty land we've seen here. These are deserts, we have mountains, and deserts too of course. The U.S. is very large."

— 12 —

Libya, 0110 hours

The three fugitives sat in the gully, alternately dozing and standing watch. Eventually Najafi was up on his knees looking around.

"It looks like there is no activity. Time to go. We stay together and take everything. Stay along the fence and no fast movements. Fast movements catch people's attention. You two stay down low under the plane while I work the lock. Let's go." Najafi was more relaxed as things seemed to be going his way again.

Once at the plane, Najafi worked the lock. This one was not as easy as the padlock. After a long time, he had it. The door released, half rotated down and half up.

"Okay, in with all the stuff," Najafi prodded. Once inside, they closed the door and pulled the shades on all the windows.

"Now to defeat the dashboard lock," said Rollins. It was already two-thirty, and they had only three hours before dawn.

As Rollins examined the locking mechanism he said, "This is a new plane, and the anti-theft measures are pretty good."

It was getting noticeably light when finally they had it, and the instrument panel lit up. "How's the fuel?" asked Breckon.

"Nearly full, enough to get across the pond at least."

Najafi looked worried. "What do we tell the tower? They must know whose plane this is."

Breckon was sitting on the edge of the seat outside the cockpit. "I was afraid you hadn't given any thought to that. While you guys have been messing around in the wires I've been looking around the cabin. I collected all the paper I could find, went in the back, and turned on a little light. It looks like the guys who use this plane are German or Swiss. Anybody do a good impersonation of a kraut?"

Najafi shook his head. "I speak Arabic, English, and some French. No German."

"Rollins?"

"No German. What about you?"

"Oh, no. You guys are the airplane pirates, not me."

Najafi was tired and out of ideas again. "Get off it, Breckon. Right now we have to get out of Libya, and that includes you. Now, do you know any German?" he shouted.

"I took a couple of German classes in college and worked with some Germans on a project once. Don't get mad if I land you in a dungeon like you deserve. Give me the copilot's seat." Najafi got up and Breckon plunked down. "Where's that radio mic!" Breckon was tired and irritable too.

The number one engine started to spin up and caught on the first try. Number two started just as easily.

Rollins looked at Breckon. "Everything looks okay. Try the tower and see what happens."

"Tower, 7-7-5-2-1 Del-tah request O-K to taxi."

Short pause. "Roger, 77521 Delta. I didn't see you folks come on to the flight line, hold position." The voice was a woman's with a heavy accent.

"They don't have a record of us coming through the guard station," said Rollins matter-of-factly.

Breckon paused a few seconds. "7-7-5-2-1 Del-tah. Vee cum last night to fix luft . . . ah . . . air probe system. It vas kaputt. Fritz good at fix, but much hard to fix, much time. Got fix gut. Go now?"

"Hold 521 Delta."

Najafi was sitting on the edge of the seat where Breckon had been. He got up and stuck his head in the cockpit and said nervously, "She's checking with the guards, we should go. The large plane blocks our view of the tower area. They're probably sneaking up on us right now."

"Take it easy," said Breckon. "Let her be the boss. That's her job. Maybe she's trying to spook us."

"521 Delta, taxi to runway 32 and hold. What is your destination?"

"Vee go Athens. Get pump-e parts."

"Roger 521 Delta."

"See, so far so good. Maybe she has something else to do besides attend to us."

As they taxied from behind the DC-9, they saw no unusual activity in the tower area. Rollins continued to the end of the runway, turned ninety degrees, and stopped. They waited five minutes.

Najafi hated to have others deciding what to do. Finally he couldn't stand it and blurted out, "They're checking the guard report. I know it. There, see," he said pointing out of the side cockpit window, "they're moving a fire truck or something out to the runway. They intend to block us! We should go like we did in Morocco. We made it there."

Rollins was a good pilot in his unflappable demeanor. "There's a military base fifty miles to the west. We wouldn't make it this time. We mustn't let them suspect anything."

Breckon added, "Well, if they want to block our takeoff, it's too late anyway. They could have that truck onto the runway long before we got past them."

And if they were CIA, then what? With so many conflicting possibilities, Najafi once again could not make logical decisions.

Finally, Rollins pointed out the right window. "There, see it?" A faint trail of smoke with a small airplane in front of it wove its way toward the runway, the smoke sometimes changing in intensity and color. A few seconds later, the small jet fighter flew across their front, and they could see smoke streaming out of a service panel on the side. The pilot slid the plane onto the runway, almost going off, then skidded back on. The pilot was fighting it and doing a commendable job. Finally he licked it and turned off at the end of the runway. The emergency vehicle raced toward it.

They were all startled when the cockpit speaker sounded, "77521 Delta, you are cleared to take off runway 32."

"Ro-ger tower, 'ave gut day."

Breckon thought he could hear a faint chuckle from the tower radio. "521 Delta, safe trip."

Rollins rotated the throttles forward, the engines spooled up, and they were rolling. "This is a smooth baby. Everything's in top condition. What a dream." After gaining flight speed, they rotated and were airborne. As they cleared the end of the runway, they saw a small man in a flight suit, the pilot of the disabled plane, hopping around with his hands raised in the air fists clenched doing a victory dance.

Breckon went back into the cabin and strapped himself into a seat opposite Najafi, who said, "That was a nice job, Breckon. Why are you helping? Without that job with the German accent, we might not have made it. And the suggestions, food, flashlight, all of it, why?"

"After the crash landing it looked like you were going to need some help. That's the short answer."

Breckon finally seemed to be opening up. Najafi had to use every opportunity to find out who he was. "What other answer is there?"

"The long answer. You see, for a long time moral philosophers worked on the problem of when a person can do something that had both good and bad effects. They came up with what is called the principle of double effect, sometimes called twofold effect. There are rules that govern such situations. First, the act itself cannot be bad. Another rule is that the bad effect can't be the means of achieving the good effect. The end never justifies the means. It also requires that the good effect outweighs the bad effect. Finally, the bad effect can't be desired, only tolerated."

"So how does your helping me fit into all that moral-legal tangle?"

With a smirk Breckon replied, "I made a decision, admittedly a little subjective, that the good of keeping me alive outweighed the evil of keeping you alive, so I helped."

Najafi's face flushed at the pompous implications of the statement. "And are you so perfect?'

"Hey, you asked the question. Never ask a question if you don't want to hear the answer. And, you've probably not spent too many sleepless nights worrying about the morality of the things you do. Anyway, let's get some sleep—we'll need it."

Najafi lay back in his seat in a funk, thinking Breckon was a real jerk. He did what he was ordered to do. So he enjoyed killing people now and then, so what? As he pondered the situation, it occurred to him that this man did not sound like CIA. Anytime he had come up against the CIA they had been as ruthless as he was. Najafi spoke up, "We'll see what happens to moral philosophy when the going gets really tough—and it will." He leaned back and closed his eyes, implying that he wanted to end the debate with the last word. He wished again that he had had a chance to search that building back in the Libyan Desert.

Breckon hoped he hadn't riled Najafi too much. Rollins had his alarm clock out so he must be asleep. Below them, Breckon could see a few puffy clouds were forming. A pair of jet fighters, little more than specks, passed in front of a cloud going in the opposite direction. Then they were past the cloud and lost from sight. He laid back and closed his eyes, but even though he was tired, he couldn't sleep. He opened his eyes and looked out again.

Bam, there were two F-18 Hornets just feet away. Boy, they moved fast! He hoped they weren't looking for a stolen airplane. Sliding out of his seat, he crawled on hands and knees to the cockpit. The door was tied open as usual. Breckon reached up and pulled on Rollins's arm.

"Rollins, wake up. We have company."

"Huh, what? Leave me alone."

"Look out the right window."

Rollins turned his head and sat up with a start. A chart on his lap flew into the air. He grabbed the yoke, disengaging the autopilot, and the plane pitched up and down. He frantically reached for the buttons on the radio and within a few seconds the cockpit speaker came alive.

" . . . 21 Delta respond."

"They're F-18 Hornets from a U.S. aircraft carrier," Breckon prompted, while keeping out of sight.

"Roger Mister F-18, er, sir, ah, 7721 Delta here. You guys look so big and mean you scared me almost to death."

"Roger 77521 Delta. What's your story."

"Okay, sorry, ah, there was a mining accident in Chad and, since I was available, I was called yesterday afternoon to help. I'm heading for Athens. Got a couple of guys in bad shape. I had it on autopilot and must have dosed off. It's been a long day, I mean night, well day I guess." Rollins ran his hand over his face. "It's been kinda hectic."

"Roger, we watched you on radar coming out of Libya and you are headed for our carrier group."

"Roger, I had to land for fuel, they let me do that. Should I change course?"

"Negative. We'll keep an eye on you. Stay alert. You're headed for Athens."

"Roger, I'm alert all right. Now if I could get my ticker started again, it'd be ever better. By the way, it's kinda nice knowing you guys are on the job."

"Thanks 77521 Delta. Out."

They watched the F-18s peal off and disappear. Rollins sat there for a minute rubbing his face then said, "Well, I guess we're headed for Athens for sure now, half the world knows it. We'll need fuel anyway. Thought they were here to bring us down."

After refueling in Athens, Breckon intended to make careful observations of their route so he could tell where they were going, but he fell asleep. He was slowly awakened by the bouncing of the airplane in the air currents. He looked out and saw they were very low, preparing to touch down in yet another arid land. His watch said he had slept for nearly three hours—more bad luck.

On the ground Najafi said, "Grab your stuff and let's go."

Getting off the plane, the heat hit him again, something Breckon was coming to expect. They saw four men in desert camouflage clothing walking toward them. They greeted Najafi in a foreign language and gathered around Breckon as if to shield him from the view of others. They walked toward another airplane.

As they approached the plane, Najafi said "Get in and don't show your face."

The plane was a contradiction to what Breckon had come to think of as an airplane. It was a biplane with the lower wing shorter than the upper one. Although it was a single-engine tail-dragger, it was very large, having an interior cabin larger than the business jets but far more utilitarian. The cockpit in the front was enclosed with windows that bulged out on each side. The door was located near the tail where the inside deck was waist high. Breckon carefully heaved in his bag and climbed in after it.

To his right was a bulkhead with a small door that led to a compartment in the tail cone. To the left the plane angled up towards the cockpit. There were web seats along either side facing the opposite wall. These could be folded against the wall to make room for cargo. There were two steps from the cabin up to the flight deck. Here there was no need to tie the cockpit door open since it was missing.

There were assault rifles lying on some seats. Breckon thought it wise not to use one of those. These were Najafi's people, but he guessed they weren't in his homeland yet. They seemed worried that someone would see him. Breckon heard the scream of jet engines and saw a white Lear Jet taking off. Rollins was getting out, his job done.

Breckon could see the men outside the plane discussing something. Finally, the voices raised. Najafi was arguing with another man. The man threw up his hands and climbed into the airplane followed by a second man. The first one, obviously the pilot, stomped past Breckon, giving no indication he even saw him. He plunked down in the left seat in the cockpit, and the other man in the right seat. Najafi and two others climbed in, picking seats so as to leave empty seats between them. It was midday and very hot. The pilot and copilot were flipping switches and talking as if going through a checklist. Finally the engine cranked over and came to life. The pilot and copilot were both busy. It seemed to be a complicated plane to operate.

They taxied to the runway and opened up the throttle. From where they started, there was less than half the runway left. But it was soon obvious this was not a mistake. The plane had good short-field capability. From the shadow of the plane on the ground, Breckon could tell they were headed nearly due east. The noise made it impossible to talk, so the others sat and looked bored.

Breckon surmised that they were close to their destination, since they could not possibly cover vast distances in this plane. They were hardly going a hundred miles an hour. After two hours, they landed on a paved runway. Breckon's ears rang from the silence when the engine stopped.

Najafi told Breckon to get out and sit in the shade of the plane. One of the men with an assault rifle stayed by the plane with him. The rest of them went to one of the buildings. They seemed a lot more relaxed now, laughing and talking like this was home.

Breckon sat with his back against one of the tires and looked up at the underside of the lower, sand-colored wing. The wings were fabric covered while the fuselage was metal. There were a few drips of oil coming from the engine, a common thing with radials.

When the sun was an hour above the horizon, they took off again. Now their direction was southerly. Soon they were flying scant feet above the sand and scrub brush. Whenever possible, they flew in ravines where sand dunes rose above the plane. They were obviously trying not to be seen.

Through the afternoon, Breckon had thought of nothing. He found he could not keep his mind on the real life he had left behind less than two days ago. It was becoming like a vaguely remembered dream. Now his stomach started to hurt. He knew he was close to his journey's end. The uncertainty of what lay ahead put him in agony. At times he was so distressed, he thought he'd vomit.

After sundown, he saw a road that ran roughly northeast to southwest, though it was hard to tell in the failing light. The plane banked sharply to the right as they lined up with the road and the pitch of the engine dropped. He glanced over his shoulder and saw the edge of a runway out of the small round window as the wheels touched down. The runway was a widened part of a road. Once the plane had stopped, Najafi motioned for the other men to leave. When they were gone, Najafi got up.

"Here we are. Grab your bag, and let's go." As soon as they were out of the plane, the pilot gunned the engine, swung it around, and took off in the direction they had come.

The sun had hidden itself behind the dunes half an hour before, leaving the sand with a strange color to it, the color of prison. In Libya he had seen the desert as a given, part of the background, something he and his companions would be leaving. Here the sand was different. It was permanent. The sand dune toward which they walked could just as well have been a huge wall with razor wire and guards on top. From the miles of barren land over which they had flown, Breckon knew it was a long way out. Out, but to where? Some small Arab town was all he might find if he walked a hundred miles. Utter hopelessness grabbed his stomach, and the pain was the worst he had experienced. He was forced to set his bag down and fell to one knee. He could feel a chill sweat like he was going to vomit.

Najafi turned. "Are you all right? Come on, we're almost there. Don't die on me now."

That last remark struck Breckon as if he had put his finger on a live 460-Volt circuit. He was nothing but a piece of apparatus for this barbarian's depraved plan. If he malfunctioned, that dirt-bag wouldn't get a gold star on his homework paper. A torrent of hate poured adrenaline into Breckon's blood. It forced him to realize that there was only one person who would get him out of here alive, and that was him. He had heard it said of sick people, of people in terrible situations of all kinds. It's what's in your mind that counts. If you allow your will to be beaten, you're done. You absolutely must want to survive. It filled him with a terrible resolve to beat these people, beat them all.

He stood up and grabbed his bag. He staggered a few steps but stayed up. "A little down on sleep, I guess. I'll come back." And when I do, you had better not be in sight, he did not say.

He breathed deeply and once again was alert. To the southeast, the direction they were headed, was a large sand dune with a fifty-foot opening in it. On the right of the gap, the sand was held back by a thirty feet high retaining wall. To the left of the hollow was a huge concrete door twenty feet high. It stood partially open, leaving a gaping entry to a cavity off to the left. Najafi led the way into the break in the façade. Once inside, there was enough light to see an arched roof. It appeared to be an aircraft hangar that had been covered with sand and could hold four or five fighter planes.

"This is your new home. I'll show you your quarters so you can sleep. The equipment you shipped is in them," he said, pointing to two steel shipping containers.

Najafi walked along the wall on the left, and Breckon followed. Neither of the containers looked like the one Breckon had loaded back at the plant, but at this point, he didn't care. On the far side of the containers was a large pile of broken-up concrete, and near the part of the door that was not open stood two military trucks.

Upon reaching the far end of the hangar, they turned to the left, through a cleverly concealed doorway. The door led to the top of a stairwell, which they descended for what seemed like forever. Finally, they emerged at the bottom into a long, round, concrete tunnel with a flat floor. As they proceeded to the far end, Breckon noticed doors on either side. They went through the last door on the right.

After Najafi flipped on a light switch, Breckon saw they were in a larger horizontal tube. It was filled with stacked up cots and piles of wooden crates with a narrow aisle winding its way among them. There was a small opening in that space with a cot set up.

"This is your place to sleep. You'll remain separated from others in this complex. When you come into here to sleep, close and bolt the door." Najafi showed Breckon a latrine at the far end of the tube. "This room was designed to house up to one hundred troops in time of emergency. Use the water sparingly. You may take a shower every second day if you use only cold water." Returning to the cot Najafi continued. "Here are some cans of food. Now wash, eat, and sleep. Remember to bolt the door after I leave."

It was cool this far underground. In fact, after the heat of the desert, it was cold. He remembered that the temperature of the earth was fifty degrees Fahrenheit a few feet down, away from surface effects. Here he was, in a prison where the vast desert formed the walls and he had to lock himself in for protection. Nothing surprised him anymore. He showered, found that there actually was hot water, and ate some of the food. Near the bed was a large cardboard carton containing wool blankets. He put four of them over himself. That was all he remembered.

Colonel Faisal Basheer sat in his office off the hangar rolling his swagger stick in his fingers. He had been given the job of on-site commander for the renovation of the underground spaces, and getting the secret project started. His job was to manage the work force, arrange transportation, and see to the food. There were the conscripts who did all the hard labor, and there was a contingent of East German technicians. Only the company of hand-picked guards was not under his direction. They belonged to Shahid Arzika, who was in charge of security. Arzika, along with Alwan Najafi, now sat in front of him.

With a sharp snap, Basheer laid the little rod, his constant companion, on his desk. Breaking his steel glare of silence, he spoke. "Najafi, I understand you crashed your plane and lost some vital tooling for this project, in addition to some special ordnance. General Majeed will be most unhappy that he will not get the depleted uranium tank rounds. He wanted some of the American armor-piercing shells to trade to the Russians. But you did deliver your main item, the American engineer. You expressed concerns, tell me of them."

Najafi described the conflicting things that he had noted since Breckon had been abducted. The lost wallet, the way he did not cooperate at first, but later did. His seeming personality change in the desert building, how he had not seemed to recognize the name of CJ that he had given himself, and all the rest.

Najafi said, "He will need a handler who speaks English and who is knowledgeable in engineering. I suggest Arzika take a large role in coaching the engineer you assign to Breckon. With time, a man skilled in intelligence and security will be able to determine if he is a CIA agent or a stupid engineer. I correct myself. Whoever he is, he is not stupid. You will see that soon enough."

Basheer had a hard expression on his face. He did not like this. "Can we kill him and get the job done by ourselves?"

Najafi clenched his teeth. Then glaring at Basheer, he said. "Emphatically no! We need him! This is a very advanced system, beyond what we could master in the time available. TAC Corporation has supplied complete manuals, but we need *him* to get it up and running. Once properly installed and commissioned, it practically runs itself. Those machines will make the difference between success and failure on this project!"

"This is what we will do." They both knew Basheer had made up his mind, and there would be no more discussion. "We have one of our own engineers here for this project. His name is Ashrof Mohed. He attended a university in England. He will stay with this American, be his interpreter, and watch him. Arzika, you meet daily with Mohed. Suggest things to discuss with the American. We will find out who he is."

After they left the office, Najafi turned to Arzika. "I know Basheer would never understand this, but this American is not in good health. He almost died from the heat when I locked him in that building in Libya. Then, yesterday, while we were walking from the airstrip to this hangar, he almost collapsed flat on his face. He is no good to us dead. As hard as it will be for us, we will have to humor him a little and not be too severe with him at first."

Arzika gave Najafi a knowing glance, "And that means we must keep him out of Basheer's sight."

Breckon was roused from sleep by the harsh sound of a buzzer. As he opened his eyes, he had a hard time placing where he was. He looked in the direction of the offending device, and the curved ceiling reminded him. He sat up on the edge of the cot and rubbed his face. At that moment he heard the door open, and Najafi appeared around the boxes.

"Ah, you are awake? You slept a long time."

"I have to go to the john." Breckon got up and walked away. When he returned, Najafi was sitting on a crate.

"What was that buzzer all about?"

"That was call to prayers. You will hear it at 5:45, 11:45, and 9:00 in the evening. Normally, five prayer times are observed, but the Qur'an only calls for three. This is a military compound so three are observed. I'll be back in thirty minutes. Clean up, have something to eat and drink. There are people you must meet. You must get the installation of the machines started." Najafi left.

Breckon pulled out his computer bag and went through it. Everything seemed to be as he had left it. He washed and dressed. Not knowing what he would encounter, he decided to put on his trail clothes again. Then he opened another can of "food." Most of all he needed a cup of coffee.

A half-hour later Najafi was back. They went to the other end of the corridor and entered the room on the same side as Breckon's quarters. Mohed and Arzika were already there. They were sitting on the bench attached to the metal table. Mohed had an olive complexion, dark hair, and brown eyes. He looked like an Arab, which Breckon thought was not surprising. He was about thirty, and looked very uncomfortable.

After the introductions, Najafi announced he would be leaving in a day or so. Thereupon the chain of command as well as rules were firmly stated, especially the rule that Breckon had access to the work bay strictly from 6:30 p.m. to 6:00 a.m., and never was he to go there any other time. There was another crew working on other machinery during the other hours with a half-hour gap on both ends. Since it was still early, he wouldn't be shown the area where he would be required to install his robotic machinery for several hours.

When they had finished, Breckon began the little speech he had prepared. "I see that all three of you speak English pretty well, and I know nothing of Arabic, so we must communicate in English. If you do not understand what I am saying, say so. To start with, I was brought here against my will. That aside, my aim is to get these machines installed and operating as soon as possible and get out of here. I do not know what you will be doing with them, and I do not want to know. I must tell you this, when these machines were shipped, the programming was not complete. There was no final acceptance test as the contract specified."

Najafi was stone faced, but the others were looking at him in a mixture of anger and disbelief.

"Is that true?" Arzika almost spat the words out.

"Yes," Najafi said firmly. "Ratling had received word that the export rules would change on August first, and we might not get the machines out of the U.S. There was no alternative."

Mohed looked at Breckon. "Can you finish the programming in a short time?"

"The answer is yes, if . . . . " He let it hang there for effect. " . . . if I get the support I need."

Breckon had an attentive audience but was not sure they believed him. "What I am going to say now is most important. The software I need to finish the programming is on the computer I brought with me. It is not on the computers shipped to you. Furthermore, my computer is configured to do software development, and the system computers are not. Therefore, if anyone tampers with my computer or damages it, there will be no system, period. I suspect you're all worried that I'll do something sneaky or tricky, and you would like to snoop in my computer. In your position, I would feel the same. Well, don't! You wouldn't understand what you saw anyway."

After a pause, Breckon asked. "Please, is there any way to get a cup of coffee? I can hardly function without coffee."

Mohed spoke up, "We have coffee, but coffee maker is failed."

"Is it an electric coffee maker?" Breckon asked.

"Yes electric, why do you speak?"

"I know something about electrical stuff. Maybe I can fix it. You say I can't do anything for a few hours anyway."

They had the coffee urn brought to him. Najafi and Arzika left. It was an institutional unit that could make a hundred cups at a time. They found a few small tools, and, after a short inspection, Breckon found the thermal over-load had tripped. It was not the type that reset itself and was inside the base. But, he was able to reset it easily.

After Najafi and Arzika left, they chanced to meet Colonel Basheer in the hangar. "I want to meet this American engineer. Where is he now?"

"I believe he is in tube number eight fixing the coffee maker."

"Why is he not preparing for his work? He does not have time for such foolishness."

"Sir," said Najafi, "He cannot start working until 6:30 anyway. Let's see if he is any good at electrical . . . . "

"That is not his job!" shouted Basheer. "He will do what he is told, and nothing else. If there is no one here to keep him in line, I will demand that Arzika assign one of his guards to do it, with full authority to beat him if needed!" Basheer's face had gotten red, and both Najafi and Arzika knew there was no stopping what was going to happen.

Mohed had gotten the kitchen crew to fill the urn a third full of water and, yes, it was getting warm. The young Arab who had brought the water was smiling. Everyone would like to have coffee again.

Basheer walked in. He expected Breckon to come to attention, but Breckon did not know who he was.

Basheer said something in Arabic in a rather high and agitated voice.

Mohed said, "He says you must stand when he comes into the room."

Breckon had one leg on either side of the plank seat attached to the table. He idly lifted one leg over the seat and at the same time casually replied, "And who's this?"

Mohed translated, but there must have been something lost in the translation. Basheer's face got red, and he hit Breckon on the side of the head with his baton. Breckon instinctively raised his arm to ward off additional blows, which quickly came. Najafi yelled, "Stop!"

By this time, Breckon was on his hands and knees crawling away. Finally the blows stopped. Basheer was yelling something in Arabic.

There was a large guard with an automatic weapon near Basheer who had entered with him. Breckon got up and could see that he couldn't overcome them all. If it hadn't been for the guard, he would've tried.

They stood there, Breckon and Basheer, glaring at each other. If hate could have been weighed by the pound, this was the time to do it. Basheer jabbered something in Arabic.

Najafi translated. "He says you are not to spend your time in such foolishness. You are under his command, and you will work or you will die."

Basheer turned on his heel and left, followed by his guard. After he had gone, Breckon glared at the rest of them and walked out of the room down to the tube where he had slept. As he walked, the disbelief at what had happened turned to anger. Adrenaline was pumping into his blood by the gallon. After he closed the door, he heard it open again behind him. In his extreme state of agitation, hearing it open gave Breckon a sense that even inanimate objects were conspiring against him. Glancing over his shoulder, he saw Najafi come in and close the door behind him.

Najafi began, "That was an unfortunate . . . . "

He did not finish the sentence. Breckon spun around and smashed his right fist into Najafi's kidney with all the force his 170 pounds of anger could deliver. Najafi flopped back against the wall, having been taken totally by surprise. Najafi was thirty pounds lighter than Breckon.

A second blow with his left fist caught Najafi in the stomach, who convulsively bent forward. With his left hand Breckon grabbed him by the throat and slammed his head and upper torso against the wall while pounding him in the stomach with his right fist.

As he looked into Najafi's bulging eyes, he said. "You know how on the plane I mentioned the evil of keeping you alive? Well I'm dangerously close to sacrificing my life to kill you and everyone in this stinking place! Do you understand? Blink once for yes and twice for no."

One blink.

"Good!" Breckon's voice rasped on. "Now you go back and tell that bag of camel turds if he wants to get anything out of me to keep his ornery butt out of my way!"

Breckon gave him another punch in the stomach and pounded his neck against the wall again. Then he reached for the latch, opened the door, and threw Najafi out into the hall. With all his might he slammed the door with a bang and bolted it from the inside.

Mohed looked down the tube and saw Najafi lying on the floor. He hurried to him as Najafi was trying to get up. Lifting him up he asked, "What happened?"

"Do not go into that tube with the engineer for at least an hour. He needs time to cool off." Najafi was breathing unevenly and winced with pain with each move. "Help me up the stairs to Basheer's office and find Arzika. We must have a talk with the colonel."

When the four of them were seated in Basheer's office, Najafi was still dabbing blood oozing from wounds on his neck made by Breckon's fingernails. He was leaning to one side trying to ease the pain in his abdomen. "Tell him to get out," Najafi snapped, indicating the guard.

Basheer nodded and the guard left. "What happened to you? You look terrible."

"I will talk, and you will listen. To answer your question, the American engineer almost killed me because of you and that stick!"

Najafi took a deep breath and as he did Basheer broke in. "I thought you were skilled in martial arts. If he could do this to you that proves he is some sort of agent."

Najafi's rage was barely under control. "No! I made a mistake. I did not realize how angry you had made him. He caught me totally by surprise. I have never seen such a concentration of anger in any man. His moves were clumsy and unprofessional. But the power his anger produced was something I could not stop."

"Maybe he is clever enough to make you think that."

"Think what you want! In any case, he would have killed me, I am sure, if he had not wanted me to deliver a message to you."

"Are you his messenger boy?"

"Enough!" Najafi was getting near his limit with Basheer. "The message is this. He said he is willing to sacrifice his life to kill you and everyone at this site. He wants you out of his way. Make that happen! We had him where he might have been able to convince himself that he would actually get out of here alive. Now that's gone. Someone who feels he has nothing to lose is dangerous. In spite of that, we must get two things out of him. First, get the machinery working, and second, find out if the CIA has learned of the project, and if so, how much."

Najafi leaned over, glaring at Basheer. "Now a message from *me* to you. I have spent two years on this project. The president assigned it to me personally. Tens of millions of U.S. dollars have been spent. Now we are within two months of completion, and, if you cause it to fail, you will die! If you have to lick that man's shoes, you will do it. If you want a truck to run, you put diesel fuel in it. If you have to put coffee into this man to make him go, do it!" Najafi was talking through clenched teeth from the pain and from his anger at Basheer. "After he has finished, we can all take turns killing him, but you do not decide when he is done, is that clear?"

Basheer was not accustomed to having someone other than his direct superior talk to him this way. "You speak boldly. Can you back it up?"

"I report to the president regularly. What I say about you concerning this incident will depend on what I see and hear in the days to come." Najafi paused as he fought off waves of pain. Then he snarled at Basheer, "If this project fails, you die!"

Basheer, still defiant, looked at Arzika. A confirming nod of the head was all it took. Basheer's complexion went white.

Breckon was breathing hard and sweat was dripping off his face. His throat was dry. Eventually the ringing in his ears subsided along with his anger. He went to the latrine and threw cold water on his face. He noticed his wrists were bleeding again. "Now I've done it. I've signed my own death warrant," he said aloud. The agony would be not knowing when death would come.

It occurred to him that what he had done to Najafi was exactly what he had thought of doing to George Ratling a dozen times. What had he become? Those fantasies had never been meant to be actualized. How horrible a person was he really? It was like living with himself for twenty-five years and suddenly finding a stranger.

As his thoughts drifted back to how he wouldn't leave here alive, his real life flooded down on him. It was not like when he thought he was going to die during the accident at Altus Air Force Base. That passed in seconds. Now he had time to think of all the people he would never see again and who would never see him. The vacation to the mountains with Darin was put off for all eternity, never, ever to happen. His family would miss him. He tried to pray, though prayers did not come.

— 13 —

31 August, National Security Agency, Ft. Mead, Maryland

The machine made its characteristic buzzing and clicking as it dispensed the cup of coffee, dark with sugar. On Monday morning, it was tough getting psyched up for another week of work.

The weekend had been good. Greg Daley and his wife, Ann, had taken their two boys and daughter out to the mountains southwest of Washington. They had camped two nights. The boys were six and nine. Joan was four. Getting out of the hot, noisy city for a break before school started had been good for everyone.

In addition, since they were pretty sure Ann was working on number four, this was the time to get away. Greg and Ann had wanted to get a larger house but now that would wait. They were of like mind. If you had room in your heart, there was always room in your house.

Daley had come to Washington right out of college to work as an aide for his congressman from Illinois. He had a political science degree from Northwestern University. When his congressman lost the election, he was looking for a job, so he applied at the NSA. He liked science and was well read on technical subjects. In addition he had a knack for solving Mensa-type brain twisters, which where part of the selection tests. His score was well above average, and the combination landed him a job as a signals annalist.

As he logged onto his computer terminal, he had a sense of anticipation about what the day would bring. At various times of the day, analysts were logging on in the same way in Canada, England, Australia, and New Zealand, as well as other minor nations in the system. Echelon listening devices included huge antenna farms, special satellites, simple-looking black boxes inserted in fiber optic lines, and dozens of other devices used to scoop up virtually all communications on the planet. The data were then fed into the largest computer system ever made.

All messages, including business calls, calls to friends to wish happy birthday, pilots calling airport towers, faxes, e-mails, telexes, everything, were sucked into Echelon and sorted. Each of the five countries had a "dictionary" of key words, which included people's names, telephone numbers, names of ships, and other data strings that might yield useful information.

Each of the nations screened all the messages it received through the dictionaries of the five member nations. If a key word from a member nation's dictionary were found in a message, the message was routed to that nation with no further action. It was illegal for any part of the U.S. government to eavesdrop on American citizens without a wire tap authorization, so the NSA had Canada collect all communications from the U.S. and feed them through the U.S. dictionary. The results of the search were sent to the NSA. A reciprocal agreement was in place.

The messages were sorted into categories. For example, 5768 could be the code for diplomatic transmissions to Taiwan from Canada, 2345 might be the code for biological agents that could be used as weapons.

Daley entered 6223 for his specialty, North Africa, military. On Monday, the search yielded the whole weekend's worth of "catches." All of them already had a short, machine translated synopsis so he could get a quick idea of what was going on. He saw that a good number of them concerned the crash of one or more airplanes in Libya. He sorted again, gathered all messages dealing with the plane crash, and began his work. Soon another disturbing fact began to emerge. Rods of heavy radioactive material were on the crashed airplane. Several messages speculated on it being uranium, and whether it was weapons grade. There was one fairly complete report that he selected and sent to the professional translators for immediate translation.

"Morning, Greg. How's the day starting?" It was Doug Evens, Daley's boss and mentor. Daley was still a trainee, spending an eight-month tour in an operational division before going back to the classroom. This process would go on for at least two more years. Evens was an old hand. For nearly eight years he had been working North Africa, and was in charge of the daily signals report for the whole region. He had majored in Middle Eastern studies in college and was reasonably fluent in Arabic. Daley did most of the military signals, and from time to time he helped Evens with diplomatic traffic.

After greeting Evens, Daley briefed him on what he had seen so far. "It's shaping up like there could be a nuclear incident in Libya. I'd like to work that, if you don't mind."

Evens agreed. "But," Evens said sternly, "don't get carried away and spend all day on this one item and forget the other stuff."

By this time, the report came back from the translators, and Daley was engrossed in the incident. It seemed there were no bodies in the plane and no survivors to be found. There was even some question as to when the plane had crashed.

The fact that the plane got well into Libyan air space without being observed on radar led to several traffic items dealing with the lack of alertness of radar operators. This in turn produced several counter accusations about outdated radar equipment. That sort of thing was to be expected in tense situations like this. This is what made the job interesting for Daley. He could watch people grapple with their problems.

By late morning, Daley had prepared a "special alert" report and had given it to Evens for review before sending it up the chain of command. "They really had a time of it," Daley said as Evens read his alert.

SPECIAL ALERT: NORTH-AFRICAN SIGNALS ANALYSIS

Time and Date of Alert: 1720 Zulu, 31 Aug 1998

Prepared By: Gregory Daley

Synopsis

Aircraft of business jet type crash-landed in Libya between 1800 and 2400 hours local time 29 Aug 1998 in oil field south of Matratin. Aircraft burned. No bodies or survivors have been located. Appears Libyan air defenses did not detect aircraft penetrating their air space. Libyan military discovered rods of slightly radioactive metal in wreckage. They assume it's uranium. Tail number of crashed aircraft is X7250B, X represents unknown digit.

A Lear Jet belonging to Canadian Occidental was reported stolen from Matratin Airport 30 Aug 1998. Tail number of stolen aircraft is 77421D. Two F-18s from the carrier *Dwight D. Eisenhower* intercepted this plane at 0646 hours local as it was headed for the *Eisenhower's* task group. Pilot said it was bound for Athens.

Assumptions

The reason no bodies or survivors from crashed aircraft were found is survivors made their way to the coast and stole the Lear Jet at Matratin.

"This looks okay. Keep an eye out to see if the stolen plane turns up anyplace." With that, the report was dispatched. It would be in the hands of the CIA within minutes.

After lunch, they both had their hands full with diplomatic traffic concerning the unpublicized visit of some Arab leaders to Cairo. Because of this, a special message that had been passed on to Daley shortly before lunch was forgotten. Before he left for the day, Daley went to Evens's desk and said, "Doug, I got a message from a guy in the Technology Department charged with bringing that new Iridium satellite system on line for NSA. He mentioned there was a coded message from Libya over the weekend on that system. Since there was no key word in Echelon for it, the message didn't show up on my intercepts."

Evens looked a little annoyed. "But Iridium isn't in operation yet. It could be nothing more than a test."

"Yeah, he said nearly the same thing, except the message couldn't be decoded. It apparently used a one-time-pad code and looked professional," Daley said handing a sheet of paper to Evens.

Evens saw the page starting with "Insert CD as indicated, type in sector(s) shown, press Ctrl Alt Y keys at the same time. Disk and sectors: F4-22." This was followed by half a page of random characters.

Daley continued, "See, it's either a very special test or a coded message. That line of clear text describes how to decode it or how to use it."

"Could be," agreed Evens. "See what else you can find on it, and we'll discuss it in the morning."

Several technical briefs on the Iridium system had been circulated to the analysts in recent weeks. The NSA had dibs on all new satellites. A little known feature of all U.S. communications satellites were the two special circuit boards that the federal government required to be built into them. One circuit board made it possible for the feds to take control of the satellites in time of national emergency. The other permitted the NSA to directly access all of the messages that passed through them.

Most communications satellites were in geosynchronous orbit. At approximately twenty-three-thousand miles above the equator, they orbited the earth at exactly the same rate as the earth rotated, so they stayed stationary above a certain point of the earth. The Iridium system used satellites in low earth orbit. The low orbit of 485 miles above the surface of the earth was necessary for the low power of the user handsets. Messages were transferred from one satellite to another until it neared the destination, at which point it was beamed down to an earth station and fed into the local phone system.

Each Iridium satellite covered a circle twenty-seven-hundred miles in diameter. This area was further subdivided into forty-eight over-lapping smaller circles covered by spot beams. As the satellite passed over the caller on the ground, it transferred the call from one spot beam to another. When the caller was in the spot beam at the edge of the satellite's coverage, the caller was passed to the next satellite. This process made it possible to determine the caller's location within a mile or two.

Though Daley's day was officially over, he stayed to make a call to Rodney Bolton, the man who had sent him the alert. "Is there anything else you can tell me concerning that coded message from Libya last weekend? There was something going in northern Africa there during the last couple of days, and this may be connected with it."

Rodney was glad to know his information was valuable to someone and was happy to be of service. "Even though all the satellites are in orbit, they're still 'beta testing' with only five hundred users. I've been watching all of them to see that we're properly sweeping up all the calls. Let me see what else I have on that message." Daley heard a keyboard clicking in the background. "Okay, here we are. The sender was located at these coordinates, 17:30 E, 29:48 N. The call came from the ground. We know that from the frequencies used." More keystrokes. "That phone is assigned to a Joe Rogers in Minneapolis. He has two beta phones. Even though a call from the desert of North Africa is what this system was designed for, I'd caution you not to put too much store in it. We've monitored other traffic that shows the Iridium people still have some bugs in the software."

"Thanks, you've been very helpful." Daley sat there for a few minutes thinking of what he should do. It would be great if he would find out that one of the phone owners was in Libya, and this was a secret message associated with the plane crash. But, he could end up looking foolish too. He thought awhile longer and finally decided to go for it.

He placed a call to the CIA and explained what he had in mind. It took some time as he was passed from one department to another. Finally, he convinced someone that it was important to find out if the Iridium intercepts were valid. The guy agreed to have someone from the Minneapolis Joint Terrorism Task Force do a check on Joe Rogers. They'd find out what he had been doing with his phones. If all went well, Daley would have an answer sometime the next day.

What was that pounding? Breckon could not place the source. Then he realized someone was pounding on the door. He expected to get dragged out and beaten again when he opened it. Pausing a moment he made sure his facial expression was as neutral as possible. He threw back the bolt and stepped away.

The door opened, and Mohed stood there, looking apprehensive. "Hello. I enter?"

Breckon was relieved to see it was Mohed. "Of course. Come in."

"You are difficult man to understand. I studied some time in England. Know Western people are strange by our ways, but still you difficult." After a pause Mohed continued. "There is small chance for me to use English, so I'm poor on practice. You understand?"

Breckon replied, "I understand you fine." Then his expression hardened. "I'm being difficult! Being beaten for no reason that I could possibly understand is outrageous. What kind of animals are you people? Now I suppose there are a lot of folks around here who would like to see my head on a stick."

"That is a bottom statement."

Breckon was confused for a moment and then smiled, "I think you mean 'an under statement'."

"Yes, that is it."

Breckon sat on his bunk and looked at the floor, shaking his head. "I'm not myself in the morning before I get a cup of coffee. Is the coffeemaker working?"

"Yes. Many men say thanks. I will exactly tell the cooks you have coffee when you get up. You will not last if you start all day like today. Story travels fast. It is small place. All here know what happened. They like that you can fix, but they make bet how long you live. Best money say life short. Alwan is taken out for medical. It strange. He upset with

Colonel Basheer more than you. He acts as whole project was his brain son, you know."

"Ah . . . I think you mean 'brainchild.'"

"Yes, brainchild," Mohed corrected himself without flinching and continued at once, "Sees Colonel Basheer could upset whole thing when near done. Basheer knows not of American ways."

Breckon wanted to say it had nothing to do with cultural ways, but rather with that man being a jerk. He said, "Yeah, I see that. They need me but hate me too. By the way, could you see if there's something to put on my wrists?" Breckon said holding up his arms displaying the bruises and lacerations. "This was done to me when I was abducted a couple of days ago."

Something in the way Mohed looked at him made Breckon think that for the first time it was clear to him that the man he was talking to had been taken by force and was a prisoner. Mohed left.

When Mohed reappeared a few minutes later, he had some antiseptic, gauze, tape, and a cup of coffee.

Breckon helped himself. "That's the best cup of coffee I've ever had, but any coffee would taste that way about now." The lights dimmed for several seconds and then came back on. "I've seen that happen several times. Do you have a power problem? Those computers needed to control the robots won't like a shaky power system like that." They went on to discuss the installation. Breckon explained the concept of operation of the robotic system in general terms since the documentation had not been located yet. He learned that Mohed was a mechanical engineer but was not conversant in the electrical area.

"Captain, message for you on the sat-phone," yelled Sergeant Rodriguez, who was taking his watch in the communications tent, as the rest of the men were relaxing after another field-ration meal. Captain Rebic got up and walked to the tent. He hoped this would be orders to pack up and go home, though he didn't really believe it. Today had been like the last five since they had gotten their forward base set up fifteen miles southeast of Ar'Ar. They had taken three Abrams tanks today and after traveling a hundred miles had seen two Iraqi tanks three miles off. They had seen nothing on the two night patrols they had mounted. There was not enough activity to keep the crews engaged in the mission. This was causing the men to complain and, worst of all, to become lax.

"Thanks, Sergeant." He unfolded the paper and read.

Captain Rebic:

Meet me at your maintenance base near KKMC at 0800 hours on
1 Sept. 1998 to report on activities since deployment.

Yousuf Hamoud, Special Agent, CIA

Today was the thirty-first, so tomorrow he would find out what was
going on. He went to where some of the men were talking and located
the warrant officer in charge of the Blackhawks. He made arrangements
to leave at 0610 hours in the morning.

———————————

At six-thirty, the night shift started deep underground far from the
sunset. Breckon and Mohed left from the tube with the coffeemaker.
Mohed opened a door immediately across the corridor. Breckon noticed
it had a special airtight seal that his tube did not have. They went into a
rectangular cavern with the long axis extending out from the central corridor tube. The ceiling was four feet above his head. They stood on the
landing of a metal stairway that led down six feet. This gave a total
height of the bay close to sixteen feet. It was perhaps forty feet wide and
one hundred feet long. Near the far end, there were several large objects
covered with tarps.

Mohed proudly explained, "To make height for robot machines, floor
of this big room was moved down two meters."

"What's under the tarps at the far end?"

"They covered to keep dirt off. I will also say you always not look
under the covering. Don't ask why not. Not to look."

After that, Mohed led the way up the long stairs to the hangar floor.
They first went to the containers still on the truck trailers that had been
used to transport them. Again, Breckon saw neither of them was the one
he had loaded the gantry robots into.

Mohed pointed to the container on the left. "This one holds robot machines. See, seal still on latch." Next he walked to a part of the floor
made of wooden planks laid in flush with the concrete. It was ten feet to
the rear of the container and was six feet square. Breckon noticed a heavy,
steel lifting ring in the center of it. "This cover," Mohed said tapping his

foot on it, "of, what do you say, up and down tunnel to room below. We lower parts for your robot things down through this."

Breckon was looking around the hangar. "What do you have for a hoist? All I see is that pulley attached to the roof with a rope over it."

Mohed pointed up. "See, rope comes down, under other pulley," Mohed said pointing to a pulley attached to the floor. "After rope moves under pulley four, five men pull hard on rope. Lower parts that way."

"That'll never work," said Breckon shaking his head. "It'd take fifteen men to lower some of the beams. First, let's open the container and see what we have."

They broke the seal, unlatched and swung the doors open. What they saw were the ends of boards that completely filled the doorway. "Oh, I get it," Breckon said sarcastically, "this is a super secret furniture factory and the precision gantry robots will be used to assemble tables."

Mohed's face was blank. "I do not know what happened."

Breckon remembered they were told to leave the last several feet of the container empty. He had imagined some other equipment would be loaded in that space. "These boards fill only the back of the container. They're packed in real tight so inspectors would think the whole container is full of boards. Get the crew and have them remove the boards and see what's behind them."

Back in the underground room, Breckon inspected the concrete footings for the support columns. They had been poured with four bolts protruding as Breckon's drawings showed. They measured the distance post to post, and it was exact.

On the end opposite the door through which they had entered, another metal stairway led up six feet to a platform. From the platform, one could access two doors, one in the direction of the long axis of the room and the other into the right wall. "Where do those doors lead?" asked Breckon.

"One to the right is short tunnel to workshop, the other door to room of things we not need. We can use shop."

Breckon nodded. "We'll have need of the shop. Let's go see it."

Mohed was apprehensive but followed. They found a workshop with the standard tools—lathe, vertical mill, drill press, and the like.

When they returned to the hangar, it was as Breckon had suspected. Behind the boards was a wooden crate containing a motor-generator (MG) set, and his equipment. They removed the MG set by sliding it down some planks. Using pieces of pipe as rollers, they transported it to

the generator room in the corner of the bay, which was diagonally opposite the hidden entrance to the catacombs below. The generator room
contained two diesel-powered generators, one of which was running.
There was a new concrete pad for the new generator. They got the MG
set up on the pad and left it there. The crew took a break. "I think that's
all they have in them for tonight," Breckon said looking at the men. "Tell
them to go back to the container and wait."

The diesel exhaust was piped into the floor—and then? Breckon
looked around. There was a personnel door in the wall that would be at
the end of the large hangar door. "Where does that go?" Breckon asked
as he pointed to the door.

"Leads to, what you call it, cave that big hangar door moves into
when open."

"Oh, yes," Breckon replied. "A giant pocket door."

Breckon could see the door had a horizontal handle on the inside that
could be latched by putting a pin through a stationary bar and into the
handle. A shudder went through him as he realized once again, they
weren't in the least afraid of anyone escaping since the door was locked
from the inside.

He pulled the pin out and tried the handle. It complained, with a me-
tallic squeal but rotated with his persistence. He swung the steel door
into the generator room and saw only darkness. There was a battery-
powered lantern on a metal shelf. He went and got it.

Mohed tugged at Breckon's sleeve and shook his head. "Nobody to
go there."

"Then we will investigate," Breckon responded. Breckon entered a
cavity six or eight feet wide, and somewhat higher than the hangar door.
The exhaust from the diesel engine came out of the floor in the pocket.
Breckon could see the clever idea. The hot exhaust mixing with the air in
the pocket would equalize with the outside air before flowing out over
the desert. No infrared signature would be seen by surveillance aircraft.

To his left, the beam of the lantern showed the shiny rails the door
rode on and, farther on, the closed end of the pocket. There were no
doors or passages in the walls in that direction. To the right, he saw the
rear edge of the huge door, which was two feet thick. It was closed now.
When it opened, it passed in front of the generator room door and pre-
vented exit. He switched off the light, and they stood there for a minute.
As their eyes became accustomed to the dark, they could see the lighter
area of the night sky to the southwest outlined by the end of the pocket.

Only a few stars were visible because of the moonlight. The wind brought the scent of desert dust. This was becoming almost a normal smell for him. They returned to the hangar and found the crew sitting on some of the boards by the container.

Breckon had gotten back to his quarters after his shift when he heard the annoying sound of the buzzer again. He ignored it and got out his computer to start drafting the next message he would send. It occurred to him that he had to write macros for his computer to inconspicuously send and receive messages without drawing attention to himself. A macro was a special program that repeated a series of keystrokes when a special combination of keys were presses to start it. He also had to figure out a way to get outside with his computer.

Even if he had little hope of leaving alive, he still had to get word out, telling where he was and what was going on. He was sure this was a weapons plant of some kind. The air seals on the doors to the room for the robots certainly indicated they were setting up to protect the rest of the site from what went on in that room. And it was certainly secret.

After a half-hour of working with the message and macros, he was fatigued again. He put his computer away and went to sleep.

At 0610 hours, the Blackhawk was spooling up as Captain Rebic climbed aboard. He had only a case of maps and reports with him because he expected to be back by noon. It was 250 miles as the crow flew from the base to KKMC. It was a little further as the Blackhawk flew because they had been ordered to detour certain areas. They were flying directly into the risen sun, and out the side door he could see the long shadows portraying how rugged the seemingly flat terrain really was. There were no high mountains or even hills, but the relief caused by the blowing sand, natural outcroppings of rock and clay, and dry water courses made it all too easy to hide something the size of a tank. Most of the undulations were gradual, so on the ground one frequently got the idea he was looking over a flat plane and could see everything for miles. The shadows cast by the early sun gave lie to that notion.

Yousuf Hamoud arrived at the maintenance base south of KKMC at seven thirty. He had stayed at KKMC overnight. It was important for him to be waiting at the base when Captain Rebic arrived. It gave him a psychological edge.

At seven-fifty, the rotor beat of a Blackhawk could be heard, and in another two minutes, the craft was on the ground. Captain Rebic walked to the building where they had set up a briefing room, as the local crew started to refuel the Blackhawk.

Hamoud could see the captain was disappointed to see he was the second to arrive. They sat down at an old wooden table. One of the Filipino cooks brought a gallon pitcher of tea and two mugs. There was ice in the tea! Where they had gotten the icemaker, Hamoud did not know and decided not to ask.

When they were alone, Captain Rebic gave a rundown on what had happened. He had clear plastic overlays for the map on which he had drawn with grease pencil the routes they had patrolled each day. Points where they had seen Iraqi tanks or other vehicles were also marked, along with the times. Captain Rebic concluded his report by saying, "As you see, there's a lot of desert, and we only can put out two patrols at a time, so the likelihood of running into Iraqis by shear chance isn't good. It doesn't appear they're up to anything sinister along the border."

Hamoud noted that Captain Rebic had spoken with a tone of resignation and exasperation as he made his report. "Yes, I see that. Today I'll give you information to give you more contact. You managed your deployment somewhat faster than we thought you would. As a result you were ahead of our intelligence gathering." This wasn't true, but it had the desired effect of getting the tank crews into a rut.

Hamoud opened his briefcase and took out a sealed brown envelope. Tearing it open, he pulled out a map of the area around Ar'Ar and a list of coordinates. "Our information shows that the Iraqis appear to run the same mock battle with different commanders to see which are the best leaders. Here are the areas they like to use," he said pointing to several red ovals on the map. "It all looks innocent enough until all at once they make a drive deep into Saudi Arabia. Ideally we want you to see them start such an incursion and then swing around and cut them off several miles into Saudi territory." Hamoud made a sweeping motion with a pencil to show what he had in mind. "This would cause them to tip their hand as to their true intentions. Here's a list of locations to approach on each of the next six days." He used a list that had been in the envelope with the map, and wrote the dates on the various red ovals.

"There's no guarantee that they will stick to their old habits, but out of these six locations and times you ought to make contact at least three or four times. There will naturally be no air cover for them because this is in the southern no-fly zone. We have our secure radios, so, if you have difficulties, call me, and we'll get backup for you at once. We'll meet again in a week." With that the CIA agent got up and left.

When Yousuf Hamoud reached his apartment in Jubayl after his meeting with Rebic, he dispatched a message to General Raja Majeed in which he listed the locations, dates, and times he had set up with Captain Rebic. This would get the two forces together and General Majeed could use the encounters any way he wanted to test and probe the Americans for the final, deadly clash.

— 14 —

The evening of the same day that Captain Rebic talked to Hamoud, Breckon was hard at work again. Mohed insisted only manpower could be used to lower the large parts down the shaft to the room below. They tried hoisting one support column with most of the crew pulling on the rope. The process worked, but it would take forever. The men were already tired. Breckon had no desire to see the job completed. Yet, he knew beatings would follow if progress were too slow. Breckon stood looking at a five-ton truck in the hangar, then turned to Mohed, "Does anybody know how to operate that truck?"

Mohed translated, and one of the crew said he did. Breckon lowered the end of a rope down the shaft until it touched the floor below. After that, he walked toward the large hangar door pulling the rope with him until the end came out of the shaft. He could see there was room if they tied the rope to the front bumper of the truck and had the truck back up to lift the support columns. Then, driving the truck forward they could lower them down to the room below.

Breckon looked at Mohed, "We'll use the truck to lower the columns and beams down the shaft."

Mohed shook his head and blurted out, "Not permitted. Diesel smell from truck get into air system. Very bad."

Breckon was undeterred, "Okay, open the hangar door. It was open when I arrived."

"Opened only six to six-thirty morning, night, exchange air. That is all. If satellites come over time is changed."

Breckon put his hands on his hips and said, "We have five hours until six, and in that time we can have all the heavy stuff down. What if the truck disappears? What do we do then? We'll do it. My decision. Colonel Basheer will be mad. Tough luck. He plans to kill me anyway. What do I have to lose?"

With this last comment, Mohed turned his face away from Breckon. Breckon was a little surprised that they thought he could not possibly know what they intended.

Breckon continued, "We'll only run the truck when we're actually moving a beam. While we're preparing one or stacking them in the room below, we'll turn it off. It won't run much." After careful preparation and instructions, they started. Mohed would supervise down below, and Breckon would use hand signals for the driver.

They had four support columns down, and it was working well. Breckon was thinking this was too good to last, when his eye caught some movement by the stairwell. A hastily dressed Colonel Basheer strode toward Breckon, his face set and grim.

Basheer yelled something Breckon did not understand, but he surmised the meaning. He motioned to the man in the truck to stop, and the truck was turned off. Basheer continued to yell. Breckon walked to the side of the shaft opposite Basheer, and yelled down.

"Ashrof, please come up here and translate. Colonel Basheer is here."

Colonel Basheer stood glaring at Breckon. In a couple of minutes, Mohed appeared at the entrance to the stairwell, out of breath. He looked from one to the other. The colonel's face was red, and it seemed he hardly knew where to start. When he started into a tirade, he seemed to be angrier with Mohed than Breckon. Finally he stopped.

Breckon said. "Tell him it was my decision to use the truck, and that you had no choice."

Mohed looked unsure.

"Go on, tell him," Breckon snapped.

Mohed translated.

After the translation, Breckon went on. "I was aware this could cause some discomfort for others, but we got two days work done in an hour. Wouldn't it be possible to open the large door now if we turned the lights off? That will clear the fumes out."

Alwan translated. Basheer glared at Breckon. Then snapped a reply, turned, and stalked to the door.

Ashrof swallowed hard. "Colonel Basheer said you will not use the truck, or you will be beaten. Also, you will be put on half rations for two days, no coffee."

Breckon shrugged. "Okay. Tell the crew from below to come up here. We'll do it the hard way.

At the time Ed Breckon's evening shift started, Cindy Thomas's day started too. She was working at the main plant most of the time now. She was finding it hard to believe Ed had been kidnapped, though it had been gnawing at her more and more. The shipping records for the container were kept at Plant 2. She made an excuse to go there midmorning so she could review the shipping documents. There were only a few contract engineers still working on the project bringing the prototype machine up to the configuration of the shipped ones. Thomas hoped to be able to make a few phone calls without being overheard.

As Thomas walked into the office area, she saw Brad and one other engineer discussing a drawing. "Hi, Brad. How's the progress on the prototype?"

"We're getting it up to snuff. By the way, do you know how long Ed'll be gone?"

"Two to four weeks, I guess. Didn't he say anything to you?"

"We knew he planned a vacation, but that's all. Ratling doesn't say much, but he did an odd thing. He gave two of us access to the coded CDs containing all the drawings and software for the project. It seems strange considering how closely that was guarded until Ed went on vacation."

Cindy tried not to show emotion. "Well, I suppose now that those things are shipped, TAC can get on with making a product to sell in the U.S. Anyway, I've got work to do. See ya later."

The shipping records were kept in a safe in the office Ratling had used during the project. As she went into the office, she pondered the chilling news about the security. It was almost as if Ratling did not expect Breckon to return. He had mentioned that the security was as much to keep contract people from walking off with information as the provisions in the contract.

Even though she had taken care of the shipping papers, she had forgotten the details of the actual movement of the container. She recalled that the greatest difficulty had been with the export papers, commodity codes, and all that. After working the combination on the safe she found the shipping file and sat down at Ratling's desk. The container had gone to a freight forwarder in St. Paul where it was transported by rail to New York. She decided to give them a call.

"Ga' morning, Global Forwarders, Roberta speaking."

"Good morning. This is Cindy at TAC Corp. A month ago, we shipped a forty-foot container of machine parts to you for shipment overseas. I was wondering . . . ."

"Glad ya called. We were talking about that shipment earlier today. Wa-da-ya want to do with that container full of lumber?"

Normally Thomas would've blurted out, "What lumber?" but after the last few days she was more guarded.

"Yes, ah, the lumber. That's a problem. Ah, how much is there?"

"Well, maybe you weren't directly involved in all this, but the odd little guy sure was. There's almost a full container of it. Where should we send it?"

She needed time to think. "You're right, I wasn't fully involved, the partner of George Ratling did kind of take over once the initial shipment left the plant."

Roberta responded with an edge to her voice, "George who?"

"George Ratling. He's the manager of the division that manufactured the machinery shipped to you in the container. Now I have to try to get everything straightened out. We've been so busy, I'm afraid this was forgotten." Then something occurred to Thomas. "You wouldn't happen to have a number where I could reach Ratling's partner?"

Roberta's exasperated voice responded, "That's what we'd like ta have. Seems like he left no information at all, no business card, nothing."

"Do you suppose I could come to your office and work through this with you? I think it would save time."

"Sure, come on over. I'm kind of interested in finding out what was going on anyway. After lunch sound okay?"

"Fine, I'll see you then." After she hung up, Cindy let out a deep breath. How did a container full of lumber fit into this? She called the main plant and said she would be occupied at Plant 2 the rest of the day. A plan was forming in her mind. At lunchtime, she went home. After a quick bite to eat she changed into the most unattractive, baggy clothes she had. She took off all of her makeup and put her hair up in a bun. She wanted to look like an overworked employee always stuck doing unpleasant jobs.

Thomas entered the freight office and approached the only person in sight. It was a woman of fifty-five, overweight but not too bad, frizzy hair, and cracking gum as she talked on the phone. "Yeah. Yeah. Jigs, it's always a hot one with you. The east bound'll head out in five hours, and she'll be pulling it. Yeah, I'm sure. Stop worrying. Yeah, I'll check.

I have to go. I have another customer. I actually do have other customers, ya know. Yeah, bye." She slammed the phone down. "What a pest!"

Thomas approached the desk trying to look timid, which wasn't all an act after what she had heard. "Hi, are you Roberta?"

"You must be Cindy." Thomas nodded. "Roberta Swanson. Glad to meet ya. Come on in here and take a load off."

Thomas was not sure how she should start. "It was nice of you to let me come to see you and discuss this shipment. I'm afraid Ratling, my boss, might have his wires crossed. He's always wheeling and dealing and usually gets the short end of the stick, after which he proceeds to blame me. I do hope we can sort this out."

"So do I, 'cause the money's starting to add up. The bill went out yesterday. There's labor to repack both containers, and storage and rental of the first container. Why didn't you send shippers on the lumber?"

Thomas slowly shook her head. "That's what I was afraid of. He probably intended to tell me to do it but forgot. Now if he's true to form, he'll make up a note telling me to do it, date it a few weeks ago, and stick in it a file some place to be 'accidentally' discovered." Thomas didn't know if Ratling would actually do that to her, but it was in keeping with his character. "What did you do with the two containers?"

Roberta retrieved a file folder and flipped through papers. "Clyde actually oversaw the work, so if you have any questions you can ask him. It seems the container you sent with the machinery and another one with the lumber arrived the same day. This little foreign guy, with a pretty thick accent, showed up and said he worked for the buyer of the stuff. He was quite a talker in his funny way."

Roberta took a sip of coffee from a cup with a globe on the side. "Hey, where're my manners? Ya want a cup of coffee? There'll be some of this acid left if the guys didn't get it all."

Thomas managed a thin smile and said, "No, thank you. I had some with lunch."

"Suit yourself. Seems that some of the lumber had to go to the same place as the machinery. But rather than filling up the empty space in the back of the machinery container with lumber he had them unload everything. Then they loaded the machinery in the front of the lumber container. There was this crate showed up for a company called Alcem International. That was Mr. Accent's company. Well anyway, they put that extra crate in with the rest of the machinery. He had the guys fill the end with short boards. Jammed 'em in. After that, the remaining lumber went into the container that originally contained the machinery."

This was all new to Cindy. She replied, "The engineers thought it was odd they were told to leave the rear of the container empty. It was difficult getting everything in with that limitation, but they managed. Do you know where the machinery went?" Cindy asked worriedly. "Right now that's my main concern. Ratling's lumber I can handle. With all the switching around, did the bill of lading get changed? It was supposed to go to Bulgaria."

Roberta drew in her breath. "Oh, no, that's not right. The little guy changed it. It went to Kuwait if I recall." Roberta flipped though the folder in front of her. "Here it is. Yeah, Kuwait City."

"What is the name of the company receiving it?"

"No company. It was to be forwarded again."

"To Bulgaria?"

"No, no. To get to Bulgaria it would go into the Black Sea."

"Can you trace it?"

"How much is it worth to ya?"

Thomas looked apprehensive without having to fake it. "Well, the contents of that container represent millions of dollars, so any reasonable amount, I guess, as long as you can bill us next month. I want to get this sorted out before Ratling sees the bill or I'll get yelled at."

"He sounds like a beast. Why do you stay at that place?"

"Other than him, it's a great place, and I'll soon be done working for him anyway. Can you try to trace it now?"

"Grab your socks. We're gonna chase that tin box across the planet." Roberta gave her complete attention to the computer terminal on her desk. After five minutes, she looked up. "It made it to Kuwait City, where it disappears—just dis-ap-pears," Roberta said thoughtfully.

"That can't be." Cindy was now genuinely alarmed. "What could have happened? What do you mean, 'disappears'?"

"The bill of lading doesn't show up again anyplace. We track container shipments first by the bill of lading and use the container serial number if necessary. The bill of lading number never appears again. See here," she said pointing to the last of a series of lines on the terminal. "Even if it was sitting on a dock someplace, there would be at least one more entry because some freight-forwarding outfit would've had to take custody of it."

"Can you track the container by its serial number?"

"Yeah, but it's hard. Got to say, though, now I'm curious."

"Go ahead, we're this far. I've got to find it."

Roberta went at it again. This time it took longer. "Yeah, it got to the dock in Kuwait City and, well look at this. A new bill of lading appears, new bill number. It's for lumber again, but shows the shipment originating in Brazil. Then it goes to An Najaf, Iraq. It hasn't left Iraq. Both the serial number search and the search on the new bill of lading number show nothing after An Najaf."

Thomas sat trying not to form the inferences of what this meant. "When did it get there?"

"All I can say is, it entered Iraq a week ago today. We wouldn't see anything until the container comes out of Iraq. Here, I'll write the container number down for you in case you want it." After a pause, "That was some fancy machinery as the guys told it. Are you sure it was legal to ship it into Iraq? There're a ton of restrictions on stuff going into that black hole."

Thomas tried to look casual. "I suspect with all the changing around, the lumber is what went into Iraq. This sounds like one of Ratling's little scams. I want to talk to others at TAC before Ratling hears of this. Maybe this time, he'll get his fingers slapped. If anyone calls concerning this in the next few days, will you please play like you know nothing or I could be in trouble again?"

"Don't worry, us gals gotta stick together, or the beasts'll win. We can't have that."

Cindy thanked Roberta and left. This was getting out of hand. She half expected to see black helicopters swoop down and snatch her. If the gantry robots were in Iraq, that must be where Ed was. Which meant Ed's friend, Darin, wasn't crazy after all. And, how does anyone escape from Iraq? After leaving the freight yard, she drove down an old boulevard with large elm trees on either side, their gracefully arching limbs nearly meeting over the center of the street. The dark green of the late summer leaves gave a dark, brooding mood to the street. Finally she pulled to the side and started to cry. After two years she had finally gotten together with Ed. Things were going so well; they really got along. Now this. It was like one of those silly action movies. Only she was in it.

At two-thirty in his afternoon, Breckon was awake, and he was hungry. That demonic buzzer had awakened him at eleven-forty-five again, and he had not been able to get back to sleep. This was his third "morning" at the site. He had not seen the sun or sky for three days, and it bothered him. While he was working, he could occupy his mind. Times like this, were hard, though. The black mood of despair was fighting its way back. There seemed to be no way out. He knew if he were particularly intractable, it would be suicide, and he wouldn't do that.

He was an engineer. He resolved to do the work he knew how to do, and God would have to deal with the consequences. He certainly wouldn't go out of his way to help. While in high school, he read a lot of books about Russia. In one, he remembered a Jesuit priest who spent fifteen years in the Russian prison system, the Gulag Archipelago. What was his name, Father Walter Ciszek? This priest had a duel of wits for years with his captors while held in Lubyanka prison in Moscow. Finally, one day he said, "God, I can fight no longer. You will have to fight for me." After that, he found peace. It was still hard to make the decisions forced upon him, but his days were easier. So it must be with me, Breckon thought.

It was a bright end-of-summer morning in Washington, D.C., and Jason Hughs wished he could spend the day sitting in the sun on a park bench and let the world go by. But unfortunately, he had business to attend to. As his bullet-proof limo wound its way through the barricades up to the White House, he thought of the meeting ahead. He had managed to get a few minutes scheduled with the president before they both started their busy days.

"Good morning, Mr. President," he said to the sleepy looking chief executive as he entered the Oval Office.

"Good morning to you, Jason." The president supported his head by putting his chin in his palm with his elbow resting on the desk. He motioned to a chair. "Sit and tell me what you have on the operation in Saudi Arabia. Calling it Operation Sand Fire, I'm told. Not a bad name as those things go."

The DCI wished he had better news but knew he had to lay it out like it was. "It took longer than we thought to get the Abrams tanks in shape to travel. The reason they weren't brought back to the states after the Gulf War was because they were worn out. But now we have six tanks running and in the area where the Iraqi armor has been operating."

As he expected, telling this man about difficulties was like not saying anything at all. "How long before they make contact and we can expect some results? I need something pretty soon."

This wasn't much but Jason was playing every card he had. "We have had one thing go our way, though." Jason paused a minute to let the expectation build. "It appears either luck or the lowest bidder has helped us. A critical component of the fire-control system, that's what aims the gun, has gone bad. It's called the cross wind sensor. They're all bad, and they're of an obsolete vintage, so there are no replacements."

"So what does this wind thing do? Does it make it so they can't shoot?"

"No," Jason said slowly, "They can shoot, but they can't hit much. This thing corrects for the amount the wind will blow the bullet off course. The wind's always blowing over there. One of the big advantages of the Abrams tank is its ability to hit a moving enemy tank at one, two, or even three miles away while the Abrams is itself moving. Without this sensor, there's no chance."

"Fine, very good. That's what I wanted to hear. No screw ups."

"Yes sir, we'll do it. The agent in the area in direct control of the operation is very good. We can relay on him absolutely."

Cindy Thomas arrived at work at seven-thirty the next morning and took care of the things that had piled up the day before. She was anxious to get to the other plant to unravel the mystery of the lumber. Maybe it would lead to who was behind this.

At eight-fifteen, Brad called and asked if she could order some parts. That was a perfect excuse to do some more digging. As she walked into Pant 2, she saw Brad look up from his computer terminal. "Morning, Brad. Is George in?"

"Hi, Cindy. No, as I understand he's out until Friday. The requisitions for the parts I want you to order are on your desk. We could use them the day before yesterday, of course," he said smiling.

Cindy had started calling in the orders for the parts when a clean-cut man came into the office. He waited until she hung up the phone, opened his badge, and said, "Hi. My name's Mel Winger. I'm with the CIA. I wonder if you know where Mr. Edmund Breckon is vacationing." He had sandy hair, and though not muscular, was trim. He had a soft, professional manner.

She blinked a few times, wondering if this could be happening. Before she could say anything, the man continued.

"I was at the main office looking for Mr. Breckon and was told he was on vacation. I was also told his boss was out of town. Is there anyone here who could tell me where I might contact him?"

Hoping her expression did not betray the excitement she felt, Thomas replied, "May I ask why you're inquiring about Mr. Breckon?"

"I'm making a routine inquiry."

Cindy glanced away for an instant as she thought how crazy this was getting. "Is there some problem? Do you think something has happened to him?"

"Please don't be alarmed. I honestly don't know why the information's needed, only that I was asked to locate him."

"I must say, this does seem very odd." She thought a moment. "I know he mentioned going out West to do some hiking and camping in the mountains. He said that when they hit the mountains, it's as if they're swallowed up. They see no one for however long they're there, and that's the way they like it. He mentioned that trails were for sissies, so I guess it would be hard to locate them. That doesn't sound like a vacation to me at all."

He smiled. "I guess I'm not that type either. You said 'they.' Do you know who he went with?"

"He mentioned his friend, but not a name. I gather they've done this before."

"There are a lot of mountains out West. Did he give any indication what area he would be in?

"Not that I recall. You see, Mr. Breckon didn't say much about his personal life. He worked hard and expected the same from everyone else, or they were gone." The man seemed to accept what she said.

"Okay," he said, "If he should call in, will you have him contact me? Here's my card. Please don't forget. It's possible he knows something that could be of great help."

After the agent left, Cindy was surprised at how quickly the bizarre, incredible, unbelievable, could become the norm.

Breckon had been awakened again by the buzzer at noon. He had taken a screwdriver and disconnected one of the wires from it. That would solve the problem. It didn't change the fact that when six-thirty rolled around he entered the robot room hungry, tired, and out of sorts. To his surprise, an additional four support columns, and four lengths of rail had been lowered during the day. When Mohed greeted him, he didn't reply other than to ask, "How'd they get them down here?"

"They use truck," Mohed said in a matter-of-fact voice.

Breckon snorted, and said, "Figures." Following that, he pulled his none-too-willing crew together. Using sharp orders, they got the first two columns set up in three hours. From this, they had a system worked out. Breckon had Mohed order the workers to continue while they went to see why the power was so erratic. He was afraid of electrical spikes from the old generator being induced into the computers.

Breckon took his computer bag, which contained his computer, a test meter and assorted small tools. They went to the room where they had placed the new generator after unloading it. Electrical generators had carbon brushes contacting the rotating armature. Breckon turned to Mohed, "The brushes are probably badly worn, and this causes the lights to dim. This will have to be corrected. Please, find an adjustable wrench so I can take the access panel off and inspect the brushes and armature."

As usual, Mohed looked apprehensive. "Colonel Basheer not to permit that. He worried power go out for always. Has orders no one to touch generator."

Breckon was firm "This must be fixed in the next few days before any of the computer equipment is connected. Get the wrench, and we'll see what it looks like."

As Mohed disappeared, Breckon looked out after him. In the far corner of the hangar, he saw movement. It was hard to tell with the poor lighting but it looked like one of the crew, the one who had been the truck driver for lowering the rails. Breckon suspected he was a snitch.

He let the door to the generator room "accidentally" swing shut after which he braced a piece of pipe against the latch. He grabbed the computer from his bag, flipped the light off. By feel he pulled the pin out of the latch of the door leading to the outside, putting it in his pocket. Wrenching the door open, he stepped into the hangar door pocket. Pausing a few seconds, he listened for sounds. Nothing but the stirring of the wind as a few sand particles pelted against his cheek. He walked quickly into the open, unlatching his computer cover as he went.

The three-quarter disc of the moon bathed the stark landscape in pale light. Nothing moved. Immediately falling to a sitting position Breckon saw the computer had not completed booting up. He waited in agony.

Finally, he could invoke the macro that sent his message. It seemed to work. Then he accessed his e-mail inbox. Five messages, two from Darin. One by one he down-loaded them onto his hard drive, and immediately shut down. By this time, he was rushing back to the pocket. Inside, close the door, light on, computer in bag, pin . . . pounding on the door . . . pin in door latch. Almost lunging back to the door he rattled the latching handle and opened it.

Mohed was standing there with a fifteen-inch adjustable wrench in his hand. Breckon ran his fingers through his hair and said, "That door swung shut, and it must have gotten stuck. Sorry, but I sat down, and dosed off. Haven't slept well since I got here, hungry all the time."

Mohed didn't reply other than to say, "This I could find. Will work?"

Breckon nodded. "A little large, but it's okay." Soon Breckon had the access plate off the generator using the ungainly tool. The continual arcing of the aging carbon brushes filled the room with flashes like distant lightning. Then he froze at the snarl of an all-too-familiar voice behind him.

"*Wakaef!*"

"Colonel Basheer said stop! He very angry," translated Mohed.

Breckon slowly turned to face him. The grip tightened on the large tool he was holding in his right hand.

"*Eermiy el-menchar, hallan!*" roared Basheer.

"He says drop the wrench, now," Mohed said in a pleading tone.

After a pause the wrench dropped.

The sound of the guard jacking a round into the chamber of his weapon at the same time raised the tension of the situation even more. Breckon stood motionless as the guard stepped closer. Breckon now spoke slowly and evenly as Mohed translated one sentence at a time.

"He says the generator is not working well enough for a plant with computers in it. The new generator will be affected by electrical noise from this one. The carbon brushes should not be making the flashing. They are badly worn and will fail soon. There must be spare parts here for them. They must be found and installed."

Colonel Basheer's eyes glared from the lack of respect he had been shown. This man had once again disobeyed a direct command. He swung with his baton to whip Breckon on the face. Instinctively a hand came up and caught the end. Breckon pulled on it and then colored lights exploded in his head.

Gradually the aching in his head pushed back the gray fog of oblivion. Breckon felt water running off his head and into his eyes. His face was lying on the concrete floor. He raised his hand to protect his head against further blows. None came. But someone was talking, saying the same thing over and over. Finally, it registered. It was Ashrof asking if he could hear him.

"Is he gone?" Breckon gasped out.

"He is gone. You are like dead for many minutes of time." With Mohed tugging at his upper arm, he managed to sit up. "I pour water on your head so you wake up. Help, I think, yes?"

Breckon nodded. Wincing from the throb in his head, he looked at Mohed. "Let me tell you something. I'm not trying to be ornery. I'm trying to get the system to work. It was never designed to operate under primitive conditions like this. Even the new generator may not provide steady enough power for it. If I had been told about this, I would have specified special power-generating equipment. Do you understand?"

Mohed nodded. Then Breckon added, "Now, I'm going to my quarters and rest. If I don't get some food soon, there will be no system."

Sitting on his bunk, Breckon held his head in his hands. He was shaken beyond the shock of having been knocked unconscious. Now it hit him that he would die here. Though he had said it before, it was almost as a denial mechanism. There was no hiding the fact that he had a few days at most to live. With a surge of fear, he realized he wasn't ready to die. He had spent his whole life putting off any real effort to correct his faults, to make atonement for his sins. He envied those that hadn't had hell and the fear of the Lord pounded into them as they were growing up, the way his parents had done to him. He felt he was in no condition to meet his maker, though he couldn't imagine what he could do under these conditions to make things right, to clear his conscience.

Harris saw Thomas's car in the supermarket parking lot, drove up beside her, and gave a short beep on the horn. Cindy jerked as the horn startled her. She left her car and got in the passenger side of Harris's small pickup. Harris thought she looked dejected.

As Harris started to drive, he said, "You look depressed."

Thomas nodded without a word.

Harris's concern was obvious as he said, "I suppose this business is getting you down, but you never know, maybe things aren't as bad as we've assumed."

She shook her head and slowly said, "They're worse than we assumed. I found out where the container went."

Now Darin could hardly contain himself, "So, where'd it go?"

"Iraq of all places."

Darin was stunned. "Oh, boy, oh, boy. That really does it up nicely. First, Ed gets kidnapped in broad daylight. Then we find he was taken to Iraq." After a pause, he said. "We should get something to eat. Fast food all right with you?"

Nodding she said, "Fine, I haven't eaten much today."

Thomas proceeded to describe her trip to the freight forwarders, and how Roberta had traced the movement of the gantry robots. As she finished she said, "Then there's the next problem."

Harris was agitated as he was maneuvering through the drive-through lane of a burger place "What do you mean? What else did you learn?"

"Not so much what I learned, as what happened. A guy from the CIA came in, wanting to know where Ed was vacationing."

Darin tightened his grip on the steering wheel and hit the brakes so hard the truck shuddered. The driver behind him nearly rear-ended him and gave a salute with his horn. "Wait. This is too much. Here, we gotta order. What'll ya have?"

"I don't know. A fish sandwich, fries, and a Coke." Harris doubled that, ordered, and paid.

As he pulled forward he said, "So, what'd ya tell the CIA?"

"I said he was camping in the mountains out West with a friend, said I didn't know the friend's name. He asked if I knew where, because they're a lot of mountains out there. I said I didn't."

Harris picked up the food. As he pulled onto the street, he was trying not to have an accident with so many things going on in his head. "Let's find a place to stop and eat. How serious did this CIA guy seem?"

"He was very low key like it wasn't important, but before he left he gave me his card and asked me to call him if Ed called in. There was urgency in that request."

Harris pulled onto a side street, and they got the sandwiches out of the bag as he said. "My guess is they're uncertain as to the authenticity of the message because the Iridium system is still being tested. If it checks out that he's on vacation out West, they'll probably let it go until more coded messages appear. I'll have to send another one soon to tell him where he is. After that I have to mess up my apartment and clear out. Hope I messed up his apartment enough."

Then Darin said, "I'll have to go over there."

Thomas had not realized how hungry she was. In between bites she asked, "To Iraq? Why? You can't expect to walk into Iraq and say 'I want you to let my friend go'."

"There's a guy I know who's in Saudi Arabia working on a petro plant. Keith Gibbon. Maybe he'll have some ideas. And I hate to put the profit motive into this, but this'll start to cost me money. There might be a good story in it some place. That would logically be a reason to go. Anyway, as soon as I drop you off, I'm going to send Ed another message with what we've learned. We'll meet again in two days."

Harris sat ten minutes in his car watching his apartment. He drove around the area several times looking for a car with someone waiting in it but saw no one. Then he went in and prepared a message, coded it and sent it to Breckon's e-mail box. He made a point of not turning on lights that could be seen from the street. When he left, he took his laptop computer and the code disks. He drove to Keith Gibbon's house where he saw there were lights on. He pressed the doorbell and waited. The door was opened by a woman in her late fifties with graying hair.

"Hi, Helen. Remember me?"

"Of course, Darin. Come in. It's been awhile since you and Ed were out here. How is he these days?"

"Fine, I guess. He's on vacation at the moment."

Harris walked into the cozy, three-bedroom, ranch-style house. It wasn't fancy, but it was comfortable. Maybe it was because he was always welcome that made it seem so warm. "I was wondering if you could tell me how I could contact Keith. You said he was in Saudi Arabia the last time I called. I have an idea for a good photo story if I could get into that country."

"He's up by six in the morning. If I have to talk to him, that's when I call. If you stay around for a couple of hours, I'll call. It'll be nice to have the company. Have you had something to eat?"

"Unfortunately, yes. If I had planned it better, I would've come at meal time," he said smiling.

— 15 —

The buzzer blared out its message of prayer time in Breckon's bunker at eleven-forty-five as usual. He awoke with a start. "The stinking brain dead rag-heads!" he said aloud. Sitting on his bunk rubbing his eyes, he muttered, "They know perfectly well I'm not a Moslem. Never have there been people so fanatical in their meanness. They hate everybody, and then pray and pray." Then a thought hit him. How did they even know he had disconnected it? They must have some sort of line resistance test to be sure the buzzer would sound. Couldn't care less about the generator, and the possibility of the whole site going dark, but heaven forbid that someone should miss a prayer. He pulled a crate under the offending device so he could examine it. Sure enough, it was direct current on a separate circuit, battery powered. Using his multimeter, he measured the DC resistance of it. Now, all he needed was the right sized resistor.

He lay down again, and the next thing he remembered was pounding. Dragging himself to the door, he opened it and saw Mohed. Looking at his watch, he saw it was quarter to six.

Breckon motioned him in, walked to his bunk and pulled on his pants.

"Here is food," Mohed said, his voice void of inflection.

It was like one of the cans of food Breckon had been given the night he had arrived. Using the can opener from his pocketknife to open it, he was soon gulping it down. Mohed watched from a few steps away. Ed glanced at him from time to time, and finally stopped and looked at him. Something was wrong. He looked at the half empty can in his hand, then back at Ashrof.

"Wait a minute. This is your food, isn't it?"

Ashrof said nothing.

Ed demanded, "It is, isn't it? Come on. Tell me."

Ashrof nodded.

"Why would you do this?"

Ashrof hesitated. Ed motioned for him to talk. "I charge to get machines to work. Have wife, two boys. If machine not work, family punished."

Breckon put the spoon in the can and handed it to Mohed. "You eat the rest. I insist!"

Mohed took it and started to eat. Breckon buried his face in his hands. Aargh! What a position to be in!

Soon the clanking of the spoon on the can bottom as Mohed gleaned the last morsels caused Breckon to look up. "Thank you, Ashrof. That's the first kind thing anyone's done for me since I was kidnapped. Now what do we do?"

"When work time starts, we get crew to stand up more columns. Then, you, with me, look for generator brush parts. Orders for that. Generator need fix."

Breckon let out a loud breath, "And who fixes the lump on my head?"

Mohed said nothing.

An hour later, Breckon and Mohed were both searching shelves in the workshop tube for generator parts. Breckon noticed that at the end of the workshop opposite the central corridor there were doors to the left and right. As Mohed was looking in boxes and bins, Breckon quietly walked to the doors. The door to the left led to a tunnel from the robot bay. The one on the right was the entrance to a new tunnel that ran between the workshop tube and the next tube. At eye level in the door was a small window. Through it he could see a door at the other end where the tunnel entered the next tube. Breckon guessed the next tube must be associated with the gantry robot project too.

As Mohed continued with his search, he was out of sight from Breckon between rows of shelves that extended perpendicular from the walls. "Be sure you look carefully in every box." Breckon said in a loud voice. "If we don't find the parts, we don't want to have to start over."

"Yes, I do that," responded Mohed.

Breckon slowly opened the door into the tunnel on the right. He closed it quietly and quickly walked the thirty feet to the door at the other end. He cautiously brought his eyes up to the small window in it.

The room was well lit. A small man stood with his back to him. The man was wearing a dirty white lab coat and appeared to be talking to himself. Breckon froze as the man turned toward him as though some noise drew his attention. The man held, of all things, a white rabbit. As he stroked the furry animal, he continued to mutter. He started to walk slowly toward the door where Breckon was, but a muffled clacking sound halted his movement. The man turned, walked to a cage, put the rabbit in beside a second one, closed the cage door, and picked up a telephone. There was muffled conversation, and the man replaced the handset and walked away. The light in the room dimmed as some of the lights went out. Breckon heard the faint sound of a door opening and closing at the far end of the tube.

Breckon realized he had been hardly breathing, and after taking a deep breath, tiptoed back to the other end of the joining tunnel. Looking through the window, he saw a man talking to Mohed. Neither was looking his way. It was one of his crew, the truck driver. Now he knew that man was an informer.

Breckon tiptoed back to the other end of the tunnel and slowly brought his eyes up to the window in the door. The lighting was still dimmed, and he could see the rabbits munching pellets out of a cut-off tin can. He slowly turned the door handle and pulled it toward him. A distinct chemical aroma greeted him. He carefully looked into the tube and saw no one. He stepped in, closing the door behind him.

The rabbit cage was in a large fume hood with shelves on three sides. Breckon had seen hoods like this in chemistry labs to carry off the fumes of chemicals by sucking air through the back of the hood creating an air flow away from the worker in the front. The work surface, waist high, was six feet wide by four feet deep. There were two hinged doors in the front that had been left open when the man left.

Curious, Breckon walked over. The shelves were filled with various canned products. He stopped short as he saw a TV camera in the upper left corner of the hood. It pointed at the rabbit cage. He did not know if he had been seen. He slowly backed away. There was also an electrical instrument on the wall above the rabbit cage that might have been a thermostat, though it looked more complicated than that.

The rabbits continued contentedly munching their food. One whole side of the hood contained aerosol cans of all types, and many were recognizable U.S. brands. Most were disinfectants, antiseptics, cleaners, insect sprays, and other products that might be used in or around homes, hospitals, and clinics.

The back of the hood had shelves of canned food from vegetables to salmon and whipped cream, as well as canned beverages. He noticed all the cans had been damaged a little where the tops joined the sides, as if a can opener had been used on them. The third side of the hood had other commodities in plastic bottles, some with pump sprays. Staying close to the left side, he carefully lifted the closest aerosol can off the shelf. It was a disinfectant. The weight felt normal for a full can that size. Replacing the can, he walked past the hood, keeping as far back from the camera as possible.

To the right of the hood with the can collection was a special hood used for working with hazardous materials. There were two holes in it with long rubber gloves attached to them. Between the gloves was a window. Inside there was enough light to see some machines. There were several aerosol cans with tops that had the same marks as the ones in the hood. Some were damaged as if the reattachment of the top had failed. The machines were obviously used for filling and sealing aerosol cans. Further to the right was a pressure bottle similar to a propane canister used on backyard grills. It had oriental characters on it. Under a warning label were the words "Peoples Republic of China." Breckon mused that there were lots of people in on this act.

A click from the connecting tunnel startled Breckon like a pistol shot. Someone was coming. Glancing around, he saw no place to hide. He swung the door from the can hood partially closed. There was room to stand between the two hoods. As soon as he had the door into position so it hid him, the door from the connecting tunnel opened. He stood motionless. His heart was pounding like beating drums. The man who came into the room walked past the can hood several paces until Breckon could see part of his face. It was the snitch. He stopped, paused a moment, then turned and returned to the connecting tunnel. Breckon waited until he heard the door at the far end open and close, then he ran on tiptoes to the opposite end of the tube, slowly opened the door, and entered the main corridor.

Hurriedly he went to the far end and into his quarters. Taking a few seconds to settle down, he picked up his computer bag, reached into a pocket, took out a connector for the rear jack, and nonchalantly reentered the corridor carrying the bag. A few seconds later, the snitch stepped into the corridor from the workshop. "Having trouble with the columns?" Breckon asked. He did not know if he understood English or not. He walked past the man and into the workshop. The snitch followed.

Breckon's hands were slick with sweat, but he dared not wipe them on his pants. Before the others could say anything, Breckon spoke to Mohed. "Why isn't this man working?"

"Where you been? We much look for you." Mohed said.

Looking as stern as he could Breckon replied, "In my quarters finding this connector for my computer," he said pointing to the bag he carried. "Now, what's this man doing here? Can people leave their job and wonder around for no reason? We have a schedule to meet! I have other things to do besides see to it that these men work. I will tell Colonel Basheer his men are without discipline and they are lazy. Tell him what I said, and get him to work!"

Breckon was raising his voice and looking at the snitch with hard eyes. He surmised the man understood a little English, but could not follow the rapid pace at which he spoke. Inside, Breckon was quaking, hoping his ruse would work.

Mohed spoke several sentences to the man, who turned on his heel and left.

When the man had gone, Breckon spoke in a composed voice to Mohed. "Find anything that looks like a part for the generator?"

"No, this mechanical stuff—nuts, bolts, and that like."

Anticipating the reaction he would get, Breckon asked, "Can we look in the tube next to this one?"

Mohed shook his head like he was dealing with a slow child. "No, no. Very bad. You never go in that one, only where I say. Other extra things in tube across where you sleep. We look there." Mohed led the way.

This turned out to be much better. They found the generator parts in the first five minutes, but no resistor that even came close to what he needed to defeat the buzzer in his quarters.

Breckon didn't like what he had to say now, but there was no choice. "Ashrof, it isn't enough to simply replace the brushes in the generator. It must be disassembled, and the rotating part removed. This must be put on a lathe in the workshop, so the place the brushes touch can be machined smooth. Otherwise, the new brushes will wear out in a few days. You must tell people to do that. Is that clear?"

They were seated on crates facing one another. Mohed nodded.

They sat in silence for a minute. Then Breckon asked, "How old are your sons?"

"One two years, one eight years. Older one thinks he be engineer like me. Don't see how."

"If he were to be an engineer, he'd leave and go to a country like the U.S. or England, and you'd never see him again."

"Yes, could be, but like him for better life than me. You married?"

Ed sat there for a minute and said, "I guess it's time to go see if the men are still working."

Keith Gibbon had been up ten minutes when the phone rang. He was glad to ear from Helen, but when she called this time of day, it was usually bad news. "What's up?" he asked.

"Don't worry, dear," she said, "I know you're always worried when I call you. Darin's here. You know, Ed's friend. He wants to talk to you."

"Okay, put him on." After a pause, "Hello, Darin, this is a surprise. Looking for a job in the land of the sand?" he asked with a chuckle.

Darin was grinning as he answered. "Actually, that's pretty close to the truth. I have a line on what could be a good story in that part of the world, and I was wondering if you could give me some pointers on how to get over there."

"To begin with, Saudi Arabia doesn't permit tourists except for Moslems who visit their holy places on the west coast. Other than that, anyone coming must be invited by a Saudi citizen, and there must be a specific purpose for the visit."

"Then what can I do?" Darin said in a dejected tone.

Darin heard another chuckle, "Well my friend, you're in luck. Not many people want to come here, especially this time of year with the heat and all. But, I could use some help making 'as built' measurements in the plant addition we put in. My partner, Fred, had to go back to the states due to a family emergency, so I'm alone. It'd be two weeks of hot work, but we could arrange to have you stay on so you could do some of what you have in mind. And ArmCon would pay for most of the trip. How's that sound?"

"Perfect. What do I do?"

"Call AM-PM Temps. That's the overload personnel company Arm-Con uses. Tell them what you want, and that you were sent by someone from ArmCon. I'll contact my office in Minneapolis, and they'll handle the rest. The visa, forms, shots, and stuff like that will take four to six days. Then plan on a long plane ride."

"Well, I hope I can do what you need. I'm not an engineer, ya know."

"You'll do. I assume you'll have your camera, and that will be helpful in some of the hard-to-describe tangles of pipes and conduits. By the way, be sure your camera is empty when you go through customs. It's easiest that way. Also, be careful about what's on your computer, if you bring one, and any CDs. They check these for pornography, and if they don't like what you have they'll destroy it, or send you packing home. They have all the latest equipment, and they know what they're doing."

"I can handle that. Thanks a lot. This is really great. I owe you one."

"Tell me that after you've cooked your butt for a few days."

"Okay, you're on. I'll see you when I get there. Here's Helen, she wants to talk to you." As soon as Darin handed back the phone, it occurred to him that there would be a huge paper trail as he went to Saudi Arabia. Well, the bad guys who stole his AOL password also stole his passport. He had to help Ed, though he had no idea what he could do.

Back at his apartment, he checked and found the message from Ed. He put in the code disc and the sector numbers indicated and was rewarded once again with a decrypted message.

Darin,

Am at the site, which is deep underground. It's very hard to send messages so I add a little each day and send when I can. Have not had a chance to try to get any from you but if they're in my AOL box, they should come. Hope to get them if I get outside. Very high security, always watched.

Site is in the middle of desert. No mountains, lakes, rivers near that I know of. Flying in saw small town mile or two north of site. Here is how we got here. After last message went to coast of Libya. They stole another jet plane. Refueled in Athens. After Athens, I fell asleep—bad luck. Three hours later landed on paved strip. Still desert. Switched to funny biplane. Large like DC-3 but one big radial engine, flies slow. Cockpit windows bulge out on side. Flew southeast another hour and landed in desert again. An hour before sunset took off and flew mostly south and a little east in same plane 1.5 hours, but we jogged around to keep low so not so far in straight line. Landed on paved highway strip running roughly northeast to southwest.

Site is buried at least fifty feet under a hangar. Hangar is covered with sand and looks like a sand dune. Hangar door is two-foot thick concrete that slides into a pocket in the sand dune perpendicular to the runway. Thirty feet in front of the hangar door is a concrete wall with sand behind it so the whole thing looks like a sand dune with a vertical slit in it from the side. Airplanes must turn ninety degrees as they exit the hangar to avoid the wall. Assume the wall is to prevent the door from being bombed.

Possible to see the door from just the right angle from across the runway. No planes here now, none come and go. Door leading to steps down to site hard to see. Located on same side as door opens and at far end corner. Hangar door is opened part way twice daily to exchange air, 6:00 to 6:30 a.m. and p.m. I recorded eight-hour time shift coming, standard time here I think, so nine time zones.

At bottom of steps from hangar is long corridor tube. The robot room and other larger tubes go off at right angles to this on both sides. Gantry robot room is the only rectangular room. Rest are tubes. All look very strong. Robot room is first door on left. Actual room is sixteen feet high, thirty feet wide, and 100 feet long. I sleep in last door on right. I work 6:30 p.m. to 6:00 a.m. Others work other shift, never seen any of them. They work in robot room on other machines that are always covered for my shift. Don't know what they plan to do here but assume WMDs. Doors have tight seals.

My AOL password is "joker5." Clean out junk mail and leave only what is from you and is coded. If NSA watching, they'll assume bad guys did this. Any sign of them? Am still okay. Ed

Darin let out his breath with a long sigh. "At least he's still alive and thinking," he muttered. He printed two copies and stored the decoded message. He was planning what to do. He could still sleep here tonight if he left early in the morning. Then he could not come back. He sent a quick message to Ed saying he got the message and that he planned to go to Saudi Arabia.

Breckon was dead tired when he got to his bunk. There was a can of food on it. After he had eaten, he felt somewhat better.

The evening before with the lump on his head he had forgotten about the messages from Darin he had downloaded. He turned on his computer and called up the messages. They were coded. That was good. The first one came while he was in Libya.

Ed, got your message and decoded it. I'm thinking, you play it cool, don't antagonize them. Play along like you think you're coming home. That's all I can offer. If you can, send short message so I know if I'm doing it right. Darin

He was glad he was getting the messages to him, and supposed the NSA was getting them too. He decoded the second message.

Ed, good news and bad news: Good news, Cindy found out where the gantry robots went. Bad news, they went to Iraq and as far as she could tell that's where they stayed. That's most likely where you're headed. They were consigned to a furniture factory in a town called An Najaf located on the Euphrates River. (The Tigris River is to the east.) Closest boarder is Saudi Arabia, 150 miles to the southwest, solid desert the whole way. But don't assume that's where you are.

The CIA was at TAC wanting to know where you went on vacation so they could verify your whereabouts. I messed up your apartment and will do the same with mine and get out. I'll keep you informed by this method. Be careful. Darin

He laid down on his bunk thinking it made sense that he was in Iraq. Pulling another blanket over himself, he fell asleep.

Harris was up at five-thirty. As he ate breakfast, he was pondering the situation. He had to locate Ed exactly to have any chance of getting him out. He needed maps, but where? Then it hit him, aircraft navigation charts. He dug around in a pile of junk mail he had in a corner by the bookcase, and found a mailing from Sporty's Pilot Shop. It was a mail order place offering all kinds of stuff pilots used. He located the page with million-to-one charts of the whole world. By calling in an order with a credit card today and having them sent out next day air, they'd arrive tomorrow. This would leave more paper trail, but it couldn't be helped. He'd have the maps sent to his folks' house in Bloomington and stay there a few days, saying his apartment was being painted.

At the NSA, Daley was feeling pretty good about himself as he walked to his boss's cubicle. "Hey Doug, we intercepted more of those coded messages from the Iridium system. This time they came out of Iraq and Minneapolis. What do you think of that?"

Doug Evens said, "I thought you put that to bed when the CIA found that the guy who owned that phone was on vacation. Why waste more time on it?" Evens was thinking Daley would be good at this business if he ever learned to sort the wheat from the chaff.

"Someone said he told them that's where he went. Not exactly verification. So, I put his AOL address and the address of the guy who received the message in the dictionary and caught two more. All were encrypted with code that we haven't been able to break."

Evens smiled at his protégé and said, "Did it occur to you that the reason the code can't be broken is that the random numbers *are* the message? The Iridium guys are in beta testing and rather than send '1,2,3 testing' all the time, they send a batch of random numbers. Maybe the satellites have a program to send these random number messages at odd times to be sure the system can cope with them."

Sorting through the papers in his hand, Daley replied, "I don't think so. We copied the L-band up and down links to and from one of the hand-held phones for each of the messages."

"Well, where's the hand phone located? With the Iridium phones you can locate the sender within a couple of miles, can't you?"

Daley felt the sting of Evens's question. He was sure he was onto something, and Evens had managed to find the one flaw in his theory. "Yes, you can, and that's a problem. The messages are coming from the middle of the desert."

The smugness in Evens's reply came through clearly as if to underscore the value of experience in this business. "There you are. Now start on something worthwhile. And don't call the Iridium Company and ask what these messages mean. They all know we can do what we're doing, but it does no good to remind them."

———————————

It was Friday afternoon when Darin Harris arrived at his folks' house after a day of project orientation at ArmCon.

"Hi, Darin," his mother greeted him as he walked into the kitchen. "It'll be nice having you around for a few days. We can get caught up on what's been happening. By the way, I ran into Mrs. Hendrickson the other day. Her daughter was with her. You know, you met her at Uncle Freddie's eightieth birthday party. She's such a nice girl."

Harris knew this was the price for bunking with his parents. "Mom, stop trying to fix be up with your friends' daughters. And it must have been five years ago when I met her."

Undaunted, as mothers always are, "Yes, and she has changed. She's quite an attractive young woman and unattached as far as I know. We'll be having a get-together for our anniversary in a few weeks. I think I'll invite them, and you *be* here."

He opened the cupboard door where the cookies had always been kept and helped himself to some Fig Newtons. "I'm sure she's nice, but right now I'm working on an important story, and won't have time. By the way, did anything come for me today?"

"You never have the time! Before you know it your life will be over, and what will you have?" His mother sighed. She returned to his question. "Yes, something did come. A special delivery right off the airplane. It must be important."

Darin took the package of maps to the family room in the basement and unfolded them on the floor. After sorting though the maps, he started with ONC G-3, which included Athens, and laid ONC G-4, which covered the eastern Mediterranean, Syria, and northern Iraq, next to it. The maps were forty inches by sixty inches and were awkward to handle until he folded them to show only the areas of interest. East of Athens he marked off twelve hundred miles, which was the nominal three hours times four-hundred miles per hour the business jet flew. This put him in Syria. From there, one hundred twenty miles southeast in the biplane, followed by a hundred or so miles south and a little east. Nothing.

Failing that, he started at the destination and worked back. Northeast-southwest highway strip. The prevailing winds were northwest-southeast from the orientation of all of the airstrips. Still nothing. The next map to the south was ONC H-6. Near the top he spotted a northeast to southwest strip, and it was a highway strip, with a small town to the northeast. Ed had said to the north, but that was close. No other highway strips and no others oriented northeast to southwest. Working backwards would put the second to the last stop at Hi New, and northeast one hundred twenty miles to Dayr Az Zawr. It all fit. That must be where he was, at the Nukhayb airstrip.

— 16 —

Deep underground, Breckon had seen the first bridge that spanned the space between the two rails put up, and the carriage placed on the bridge. After the telescoping mast was fitted to the carriage, they were ready for the cabling. Back in Minneapolis, they had done such a good job of labeling the cables and documenting the order in which parts were to be installed that the final assembly was going much too fast.

Midway through this shift, the first robot was up and ready to test in manual mode. None of the scanning lasers or the other components for the automated operation were in place yet. The new generator had been installed and separate wires run for the gantry robots. The unused worn generator had been repaired with the parts Breckon and Mohed had found, after which it became the primary generator.

Mohed and Breckon were in the control room as they prepared to operate the machine for the first time. Built between the wall of the gantry robot room and the workshop tube, the control room was centered in the long dimension of the robot room with a large window looking down into the bay. It was entered from the workshop tube through a short tunnel. From this connecting tunnel, there were steps up to the control room and several steps down to the utility room under it. The floor of the utility room was on the same level as the floor of the robot room with a door that opened into the bay.

After an hour, they had made corrections to a few wiring errors, and verified the proper operation of the end-of-travel limit switches. Now Mohed used the joystick and began moving it around. "This is nice. You have do good job. It operates quickly. We better the planned installation time, so good."

"It will be weeks before we get the laser transmitters installed and the automatic operating features checked out," Breckon said with a hint of nervousness in his voice. "This proves the motors work, but little else." Even though things had gone well, he hoped Mohed wouldn't be reporting that they were nearly done.

"We have mile rock in two days."

Breckon thought for a moment. "Ah . . . I think you mean 'milestone'?"

"Yes, milestone. I show important people how robot machine work with other machine. After that we very fast get rest of things out from ship container and lowered here. Container much wanted to get out sooner. Colonel Basheer not wanted messy for showing. Container leave in four days. Now we put arm on. That make it better for sure."

Breckon had been expecting something like this. "What arm do you mean?"

"You see. There two," Mohed said holding up two fingers. "One on each up and down robot mast. I show you. After we get arm installed, I practice much, using with other machines. You will go out of here for that time." Mohed led the way down the stairs to the utility room and then into the bay. He pulled a tarp off four large wooden boxes. They cut the metal bands on a crate marked "1 of 4" and pried off the lid using the only suitable tool, an eighteen-inch screw driver.

It was a complete robotic arm from the shoulder down, beautifully made, with care, in Russia. Breckon examined it with interest, noting the precision bearings on the joints and the intricate network of wires going into the shoulder, elbow, and wrist joints of the assembly. Except for a few parts, it was made entirely of shiny stainless steel.

Breckon examined the attachment plate where it would mate to the bottom flange of the vertical mast of the gantry. Without making measurements, it appeared to match the drawings he had submitted.

The crate beside this one was marked "2 of 4." "This one will have controls, cables and, I hope, manuals in English for the first arm," Breckon said.

When the crate was opened they pulled back the packing material and found the rest of the number one system. On the top of the metal control enclosure was taped a large envelope marked "Open First." Breckon's curiosity was up as he pulled a string that sliced open the end. On top of the pile of documents was a letter in English on company letterhead. It was from the Moscow company that built the robot arms. It began: "Greetings Mr. Breckon,"

That was a shock. The Russians knew he would be on site for the installation. It almost made him ill to realize that as he had been going along with his life, others had been planning to use him without any regard to his wishes. He wished it had read "Dear Mr. Installer" or something similar. It was like arriving in a hospital with a broken leg only to learn the room had been reserved for you a year in advance. He read on.

> The manipulator arms are designed to fit on the flange of the vertical mast according to the drawings you submitted. We received the electrical and pneumatic connectors you sent that mate to the connectors on the end of the mast. As a result, there should be no question of these fitting. The cabling likewise was designed to fit the gantry robot drawings we received. Installation should be direct if you follow the procedures outlined below.

The letter went on to describe how the controls should fit into the control scheme. It also mentioned a closed circuit TV camera and a monitor that were included with each arm. It half apologetically said they knew this would be a surprise for him, but the customer had demanded it. They hoped it wouldn't be any great inconvenience to incorporate the camera, cables, and monitors. There was no phone number to call in case of questions, which didn't come as a surprise. There were, however, a few paragraphs at the end of the second page that did not seem to make any sense as he scanned them.

Mohed was standing by watching the expression on Breckon's face. "Does paper say it not work? You look funny."

"They will work," Breckon said after a pause. "They did the best they could to make an English translation, but there is always a bit of uncertainty as to the meaning. I will read it again, and when we study the drawings they've provided and compare them to the actual equipment, I think it will be clear. When did these crates arrive?"

"Day that come before now. We lower down same day."

They carefully piled the cables, junction boxes, and other items out of the crate, and slid the hundred-and-fifty-pound control cabinet into the utility room. For manual operation there was something that looked like a prosthetic device to strap on the arm with sensors at each of the joints to encode the movements of the operator's arm and hand. The robot arm would then mimic the motions of the operator.

This was the most sophisticated end effector Breckon had ever seen. He had planned for all of the motions except for the wrist. He'd simply freeze those motions in automatic mode.

Breckon connected power to the control cabinet from the circuit breaker panel connected to the new generator. He hoped that overhauling the old generator had eliminated most of the electrical spikes. No matter. There was no choice but to proceed, whatever the risk.

The installation of the manipulator arm and cables went surprisingly well. During the last hour of the shift, Breckon sat at a little table in the utility room pretending to study the rest of the documentation. He was really interested in the last paragraph of the cover letter. He read it more slowly this time.

> We are very intrigued by the control system you have designed for this gantry robot. This is a revolutionary concept. As it now stands, I will be part of a small delegation coming to the site in the southwestern part of the country where you are by now working. This is an entirely different mission, but I will plan to see you while I am there. The key date on the other project is 20 September, so I hope to get to that wretched country a day or two early. I think by the time you read this, you will be sharing my opinion of the site location.
>
> Until then I am,
>
> Sergie Musatov
> First Deputy, Automation Technology Directorate

Breckon read this last paragraph several times, and checked that the letter had been addressed to him. As crazy as it seemed, this Russian thought Breckon was one of those world-traveling engineers. It made sense, in a way, because everything concerning the project had been sent to Alcem International, which obviously distributed the documentation and materials as needed.

Breckon wondered if anyone at the site would know of this letter. Not likely from the "wretched country" remark. And he wouldn't mention it. Due to the Iraqis' need for the robot arms, the Russians learned of the project. They would simply steal as much of the robotic design as they could with no regard for the wishes of the Iraqis even though the Iraqis paid for it. Beyond that, the other project with September 20 as an important date was interesting. He decided to mention it in the next message he sent out to Harris.

————————

Mohed was summoned to Colonel Basheer's office at three the following afternoon along with Shahid Arzika.

"What have you learned about the American?" asked Arzika.

Mohed was on the spot. "He tells me things concerning the work, but nothing more. The only thing I have learned is that he worked day and night almost every day for two years to make the automatic system. If I casually ask something else, it is as if he doesn't hear me. The fact that he has been beaten, knocked unconscious, and is living on half rations doesn't help."

Arzika's displeasure was apparent as he faced Basheer. "What else have you done to that man! A hungry man does not perform well. This will be reported to the president!"

Basheer was prepared for this. "Before you do anything rash, remember that the project is on schedule. We are ready for the demonstration. That also has been reported to the president. Perhaps I should report that *you* have failed in *your* assignment. We still know nothing about who this man really is."

Arzika didn't flinch as he turned to Mohed, "Have you noticed anything suspicious. Does he try to hide things? Does he go where he is told not to go?"

Mohed was afraid they would misconstrue the quick trip into the door pocket, so he did not mention it. Besides, he was never explicitly told not to go outside the hangar. "I have never seen him do anything except what is needed to get the job done. For example, he went to the generator room when he did not have permission. But I was with him, and Colonel Basheer was there. His assessment was correct. The generator was close to failing and now we have it fixed." As an afterthought, he added. "That means we can pump all the water we need. Everybody gets a shower."

Colonel Basheer was fidgeting with his swagger stick. "In other words, you have learned nothing."

"That is not true," Mohed answered defensively. "I know he is a very good engineer who knows how to get things done. I also think he is getting sick. He says he needs to get outside and get some fresh air and exercise. Sufficient food would help too."

Arzika looked at Basheer with clenched teeth. "Starting this evening he gets all the food he wants. Is that clear?" After a pause with no response, "Is that clear?"

Basheer nodded. Arzika continued. "I have completed the work that has kept me away and will be here for some time. This will give me an opportunity to work on the American. Tomorrow at dawn I will go outside with him for fresh air and exercise."

The sunlight was dimming as it characteristically did when there was a lot of dust in the air. Yousuf Hamoud looked toward the west and saw the sky becoming darker. This could be a real blow or a twenty-minute dusting. The desert was like that.

As he hurried to get into his apartment building, he saw another man coming out. As they passed, the man brushed against him. After he passed, Hamoud realized there was a small envelope in his hand. It always surprised him how some people were so good at that. It was one of the wiles of the trade he had never mastered.

Once in his apartment he opened the envelope and read the letter. It was from the general in Iraq. He was invited (ordered) to come to a meeting to discuss an upcoming operation. This had to be the one in which the Abrams tank would . . . well, change hands. He was to travel to Al Basrah in southern Iraq, where he would be met in an alley beside a small grocery store. He had no illusions. He would be transported in the back of a completely closed truck so he would have no idea where the meeting was held. Such was the intelligence business.

At five-thirty the next morning, Arzika showed up in the underground bay. "Breckon, do you remember me?"

Breckon looked up and saw a man he would've been happy never to meet again. "You were at the first meeting where Basheer beat me with his stick!"

Breckon could see a motion in the man's cheek muscles as he momentary clenched his teeth. If he had planned to make this a neutral meeting, he had lost the advantage, and Breckon knew that angered him. "I have been told you want to get outside for fresh air and exercise. Come with me."

Breckon shrugged and followed.

At the top of the stairs from the underground tubes, there was a concrete tunnel running parallel to the hangar. At the end was a door with a padlock. Arzika produced a key, removed the lock and the door opened with a complaining squeak. They exited next to the large hangar door. Dawn was breaking with a mild wind. Breckon followed Arzika as he walked onto the sand away from the exit. Arzika motioned for Breckon to come over by him. As soon as Breckon was within arm's length, Arzika grabbed his right hand, pulled it toward him turning the palm up. With his other hand, he slapped the underside of Breckon's elbow. This caused Breckon's right knee to come forward. Arzika reached down, grabbed behind Breckon's right knee, and with the other hand pushed him backwards. Breckon landed on his back. As Breckon got up, he put up his hands to defend himself. Arzika grabbed his left hand, and in two seconds Breckon was on his back again.

Arzika stepped back. "You soft Americans . . . . " Breckon came up with his head lowered and made one step as if to charge Arzika. Breckon figured this was the typical response of someone unschooled in martial arts. Arzika got set to respond. But after the first step, Breckon dodged to the side out of Arzika's reach and was off running. Breckon was a pretty good sprinter, and Arzika was having a hard time catching up. It was hard running in the loose sand, and Breckon noticed his breath coming hard after a few dozen steps. Breckon glanced back after a hundred yards and saw that Arzika was almost on him. When Arzika was two steps behind him, Breckon fell. As Arzika came lunging over him, he caught Arzika's foot and sent him landing on his face. Breckon was up in an instant and, as Arzika was coming off the ground, Breckon kicked sand into his face. Then he backed off.

"You stinking Arab, what were you trying to do? You have cockroach dip for brains." Breckon stopped and gasped for air. "Is that all the better you can do—cheap tricks?"

Arzika was on his knees, trying to get the sand out of his eyes and spitting sand.

"You dip head," yelled Breckon, still trying to catch his breath. "You're in top physical condition and know how to fight. You can break me in half any time you want!" Breckon was shouting the best he could between gasps. "I won't stand for it, do you understand, you slimy maggot? You wanted to get me mad? Well you did. You happy? Slide back into the snake hole you came out of."

Arzika was on his feet still trying to get sand out of his eyes as tears streamed down his face. "You won't talk to me that way."

"You Iraqis are all the same, a bunch of stupid losers. Eat some sand. That's all you've got." Breckon immediately realized he shouldn't have given away that he knew where he was.

Outraged at being spoken to so rudely, and taken off guard by the remark, Arzika replied. "How did you know you were in Iraq?"

Breckon seeing the surprised look on Arzika leapt to the occasion. "I didn't, I only guessed. Now you've confirmed it, you dumb camel jockey."

Arzika shot back, "I did not. I just asked a question."

Breckon was still livid, "Stuff it. I saw the expression on your face. It was a dead give away!"

With that Breckon turned and started back to the hangar. Arzika came from behind, tripped one foot behind the other and sent Breckon on his face into the sand. As he raised his head, a boot caught him in the side of his mouth. "How's that smart boy!" Now Breckon was the one spitting, and trying to get sand out if his eyes.

———

When Breckon got to his quarters, the feeling of being a trapped animal came back to him as he carefully touched the bruise on his cheekbone. He had considered the possible ways to get out. Every idea he came up with was a dead end—with him being dead. The dark mood hung in the air as he showered and ate the yucky food. He shook his head as the thought of all the good things Americans take for granted. Something had changed, though. Now, he had all the food he wanted.

He thought of Cindy. What must she be going through? Not knowing what was happening could be worse than enduring it. The imagination had such an ability to embellish the possibilities. Would they ever be together again? It looked doubtful.

He tore his mind from such thoughts by planning the next day's work. There was one shift left before the demonstration. He thought how he'd like to be a fly on the wall. Then it hit him. The TV cameras! The wheels started turning. If he could clear out a large chunk of computer memory he could record what went on in the view of one camera. No, it wouldn't work. He would have to record ten or twelve hours and that would take up more gigabytes of memory than in all the computers.

How could he have the camera record only what he wanted to see? What if it recorded only when there was movement in the view of the camera? He could program it to compare each frame with the one before to see if there was any change before the frame went into memory. There would be enough memory if he could make that work.

Two hours later, Arzika was in Basheer's office with Mohed. Arzika was still reproaching himself for his compound error. Revealing that they were in Iraq could get him into serious trouble. Then giving into his rage and kicking a man in the face when he was down was nothing less than cowardly. The combination was totally unprofessional.

"How did it go? What did you learn? What happened?" Basheer snapped off the questions betraying his eagerness.

Arzika glanced at Basheer then looked away. In addition to his failures, he had learned nothing.

"Come, tell us," Basheer prodded.

Arzika licked his lips, scarcely conscious of what he was doing. "He kicked sand into my eyes and said I had cockroach poop for brains."

Basheer took a quick, deep, breath through his nostrils. Mohed coughed and clamped his hand over his mouth more tightly than was normal for that small act of etiquette. Basheer's stomach muscles tightened and started to quiver. The uncontrollable tightening of the muscles in his neck caused pressure behind his eyes.

Then, Basheer's eyes met Mohed's for an instant and they both realized it was lost. Exploding in laughter, Basheer roared as he beat his fists on the desk. Mohed held his abdomen and tried not to fall off his chair. He slapped his knee fighting to get his breath. Finally Basheer got up and turned away as tears streamed down his cheeks.

Finally he sat down and said, "Of course that's not funny . . ." and broke out again. Basheer totally lost the struggle to compose himself.

Arzika did a slow burn as his humiliation was complete. He resolved to get his revenge.

The levity stopped as fast as it had started.

Basheer, now dead serious, spoke in rebuke. "So, once again you learned nothing. I suggest you take your job more seriously and get results. Stop pointing fingers at others. Dismissed."

Arzika's face was ashen. His insides churned with rage as he left the room.

The military truck with a canvas top and back finally stopped. Hamoud hoped they were at their destination this time. He had been bumping around in the back of this truck all night. He looked at his watch, nearly seven o'clock. Over the sound of the idling engine, he heard a deep rumbling sound like a mountain moving. The truck lurched forward. These guys could not seem to get the hang of a clutch. They stopped and the rumbling started again. When it was finally quiet, he heard voices, and someone opened the tarp that covered the back of the truck. He stiffly rose and gingerly got down from the truck.

A cavernous building greeted him. An Iraqi army colonel approached looking at him suspiciously. He stiffly said, "The general will meet with you after noon. Meanwhile, go to that corner of the building," he casually pointed with his swagger stick in the direction of the stairway. "You will find a stairwell. Go to the bottom. After entering the corridor take the first door on the right. They will give you something to eat. After that, they will show you a place to rest."

Coming closer, the colonel said sternly, "You are not to go any other place. This is a highly secure facility. You will be treated harshly if you do not follow instructions exactly!"

"Yes, sir." Hamoud turned and walked in the direction indicated, still stinging from the abrasive treatment. He found the stairs and started down. The stairs were of poured concrete with a center wall in the stairwell, and handrails on both sides. At each landing, the stairs proceeded down one hundred eighty degrees from the last flight. Each landing had a light high up on the wall.

Hamoud was beginning to think he had found the wrong stairs since there seemed to be no bottom. Finally, he arrived at a door. He went through and was in a long tube with a flat floor. He stood in confusion. The extreme attitude of the colonel had caused Hamoud to forget what he said. He opened the door to the left. Such a large room so deep under ground didn't seem right, but then the stairs didn't seem right either. He could see a door on the right side of the bay half way to the far end. Descending the steps to the floor he proceeded to the door and opened it. Just a bunch of electrical equipment.

He turned and quickly looked around the bay and marveled at the array of equipment. Dread grasped him. This must be the high security area that made the colonel so unhappy to see him. He ran to the steps and up to the door. He crossed the hall and opened the door as casually as he could. There was a dining room of sorts. He got some coffee and food.

He was shown to another tube with a place to wash up and rest. All the time he was hoping no one had seen him in the wrong room.

General Raja Majeed sat looking at the maps laid out in front of him. He had commandeered the tube beyond the one with the rabbits in it. He smiled to himself. What had started out as little more than a flight of fancy would actually happen. He would settle his score with the American M1 Abrams tanks from the Gulf War. In Desert Storm, it had been the Americans with numerical superiority, and the initiative of when to engage in battle. This time it was entirely reversed. Through his intelligence asset, this double-dealing CIA agent, Hamoud, he would direct the movements of the Americans. When the CIA agent had suggested selling an Abrams to the Russians, it had made the plan that much better. He could get a lot of much needed equipment in exchange for one of those.

General Majeed turned to his aide and said. "Go get our Mr. Yousuf Hamoud."

Hamoud entered the tube where the general sat. Large gray eyes looking out from under oversized eyebrows examined him.

"Yousuf Hamoud, report . . . . "

He was interrupted with a brusque, "Yes, have a seat. You come here as a wonder worker. You did manage to get the Americans to appear at the times and places you said they would. That was quite a feat. Now we must see if you can make them march to their death."

Hamoud blinked. "I could only suggest what they do. I did not order them to do it."

Continuing to scrutinize Hamoud, Majeed replied, "Come, come, this is your plan, and now there are expectations in high places. You have asked for a handsome payment. In exchange, you must deliver."

This was getting ugly sooner than Hamoud had planned. "I will provide information to the Americans that you specify."

With no softening of his demeanor, Majeed replied, "You must deliver the M1 tanks to a point we will agree upon here today between 0700 and 0730 hours on September 20. We arranged that date with the buyer some time ago. There will be no room for mistakes."

Wishing he could get some leeway out of this block of steel confronting him Hamoud said, "They may have other orders."

"Make sure they do not have other orders!" Majeed snapped. "Precision in time and placement is necessary because the forces used for this operation must come from many directions and converge on the area as they are needed. Once an American tank is captured, it must be transported out of the area immediately. The logistics of that operation are as involved as the capture itself. These resources cannot be in place for more than an hour or some fly-over by an aircraft may spot them. And once the Americans know we have captured one of their tanks, they will shoot at anything that moves."

Since the meeting had become confrontational, Hamoud decided to play his best card. "We must have some means for me to communicate with you. The CIA could give me different orders. No one can control something like that."

Majeed fell into the little snare Hamoud had set. "How do you propose to deal with that possibility?"

Being careful not to have a hint of smugness in his voice Hamoud replied. "The CIA has provided some 'scrambled' satellite phones that use the Inmarsat system of satellites. The tank commander has one, the American officer in KKMC has another, and I have one. I was supposed to give the tank commander two of these, but I told him one wasn't working. The fourth phone is for you. It is in the bag I brought with me. You see, I'll hold up my end of the deal."

Hamoud continued, "There is one operational problem with these phones. Iraq is not one of the countries that has been authorized by the satellite company to use these phones. As a result, it will only work near the border with Saudi Arabia. We'll do some tests to see what coverage you have."

Majeed was satisfied. "I'll put this phone in the hands of my commander at the border. He will relay information to me."

After a pause Majeed continued with a hint of softening in his voice, "We will plan for the Americans to have few contacts with our units between now and the twentieth so they will get bored and careless. Now let me show you what we want them to do on that morning."

With that, the plans were laid out. It all seemed so easy, so inane. Hamoud's orders from the CIA were to get some American tank crews killed, and that was exactly what would happen.

— 17 —

Breckon had been told he would be on his own for several hours. He could be only in the utility room and the robot bay. That was all. Everyone was tired after the demonstration. When he was alone, he opened the video file hoping the recording idea had worked. He was rewarded by seeing a faithful recording of activity in the bay. The first ten minutes were of people entering and uncovering the other machinery. Then they prepared for a presentation. There was a pause of twenty minutes after which a man walked up to the utility room door, opened it, looked in, closed it, and looked around the room. He turned to the right and hurried out of the field of view.

There were a few short periods where someone walked through the field of view. At ten o'clock—Breckon had set it up to imprint the time on the frames—he saw Colonel Basheer come in with several others. He recognized his old buddies, Najafi and Arzika. Mohed was in the background along with the snitch. There were four others, two wore military uniforms that matched the design of Basheer's so they were Iraqi officers. After a minute, Mohed left, and shortly, the camera started to zoom in, meaning Mohed was at the controls.

The audience sat on chairs arranged in front of the table, with Najafi as the instructor. He held up an aerosol can. He made a point of showing the label on it. Mohed zoomed in. It was a can of hair spray. Najafi set the can on the table, and flipped back the cover page of a twenty-four-by-thirty-inch tablet on an easel showing a cutaway diagram of the can. There was a dome inside under the top push button. Attached to the button was a sharp needle poised to pierce the dome. The second sheet showed a finger pressing down on the button forcing the needle through the dome and spray coming out of the nozzle.

The show-and-tell was going well. Najafi pressed the button on the can on the table and a mist sprayed out. He waved his arms as if to accentuate the fact that the contents of the can were filling the room. Grabbing his throat, in mock anguish, he unmistakably showed that any person in the area was dying. After a minute the spray stopped. With another chart, he showed how, if this were set off in a large building, its vapors would penetrate many rooms and floors by means of the heating and air-conditioning ducts.

The next sheet was a table of data. The first column on the left contained names in both Arabic letters and English. It didn't come as any surprise to Breckon that there was also a column of oriental characters on the chart. In the next column were letters starting at GA and going to GH. The first line across was GA, Tauban, 240° C, followed by columns of other data. The second was GB, Sarin, 147° C.

Breckon stopped the video in shock. That was a list of nerve agents. Then he understood the hood full of cans. He remembered seeing on TV guys checking the strategic stockpile of nerve gas in long rows of tanks. They carried a cage of rabbits with them because rabbits were very sensitive to nerve gas. That gadget on the wall of the hood was a gas sensor, and the rabbits were a back-up measure. The TV camera was there to monitor both from a remote location. Those cans in that hood were filled with nerve gas!

With the video running again, Najafi appeared to be explaining why the second one had been selected for this use. From motions, it seemed like he was saying sarin would feel most like the product that would normally be in the can. Since nerve agents were liquids with high boiling points, the aerosol cans were ideal for converting it into a fine mist. A drop of the mist on the skin would kill a person. After the mist evaporated, the resulting gas was lethal if inhaled.

Now he held up two clear plastic spheres the size of golf balls. He dropped each in a jar of water, screwed covers on the jars, and appeared to pressurize them. There was a gauge on the top of each jar. As on cue, Mohed zoomed in on them. One gauge showed positive pressure and the other a partial vacuum. In a few minutes, a strip of tape wrapped around the diameter of the spheres started to peel off as if it had been put on with water-soluble glue. Nothing happened. Najafi held up his index finger as if to say "now see what happens." He flipped the small ball valve in the cover of the pressurized jar. The two halves of the egg parted and a large bubble of gas came out and vented out of the valve. Proceeding to the jar with the vacuum, he repeated the demonstration with identical results.

The next sheet Najafi turned over showed a regular can of food with a cutaway section showing a small sphere inside. After a few minutes of explanation, he turned the next sheet showing a hand with a can opener opening the can and the can exploding.

Breckon replayed the sequence again thinking through the demonstration. The aerosol can was obvious. The jars seemed to demonstrate that in cans under vacuum, like canned tomatoes, the sphere would open, triggering an explosion when the vacuum was released with a can opener. Similarly, the cans under pressure, like soft drinks, would cause the sphere to explode when the pressure was released by opening.

Najafi picked up a cardboard box from behind the table and began setting out sample products in front of each demonstration. In front of the aerosol can, he placed a half dozen real products. All were typical of the aerosol cans Breckon had seen in the hood. In front of the vacuum jar, he set canned goods like peas, corn, and spaghetti sauce as representative of products sealed under vacuum. All were top U.S. brands. In front of the pressurized jar, he set cans of soft drinks and beer. No major manufacturer would be spared.

That appeared to be the end of the program. The audience got up and handled the various parts as they asked questions. The operation of the camera could not have been better if Breckon had directed it. Najafi showed them to the machinery. The camera moved in that direction. Mohed was using the mimic arm.

From the first demonstration, it was apparent that great flexibility was needed in the machinery to handle the large variation in size, shape, and type of containers. Breckon realized the machinery that had always been covered was canning machinery. Its purpose was to open existing cans, add the new contents, and put a new top on them without the appearance of tampering.

As the demonstration continued, Breckon saw the manipulator arms on the gantry robots were an integral part of the operation. They would be part of the can tampering operation, as well as changing tools for different can types. Mohed adroitly removed a failure with the manipulator and deposited it in a trash can.

Finally, Mohed demonstrated replacing a sensor module on the canning machine. He deposited the special gripper used for the can-filling operation in a receptacle, and attached a combination wrench tool. As is common in robotics, the "hand" of the robot arm can be replaced with a variety of special purpose end-effectors. The audience paid rapt attention to this as several screws were removed, set carefully on a ledge, and the module removed. Another module was put in its place, and the screws one by one replaced, thus demonstrating the ability of the machines to repair themselves.

Mohed backed off the arm and ran the gantry robot through a series of maneuvers to demonstrate how smoothly and quietly it functioned. This caused the camera to pan around and show the complete bay. Following this he picked up a tray with the manipulator arm that had a coffee cup on it and set it under the spout of a coffee urn. He turned the spigot and filled the cup. He brought the tray with the cup of coffee on it to the most senior man in the audience. They all applauded.

In all, Breckon's system had resulted in two and a half hours of video with one and a half hours of good material. To the end, he added thirty seconds of the camera recording himself in case there was any doubt as to who sent it. Using data compression, he got it on a single CD-ROM, and password protected it.

Now that he had the evidence of what they intended to do here, Breckon was planning how to get it into friendly hands. The only thing he came up with was to send it out on the container. It would logically go to the Persian Gulf where there was a chance someone could intercept it.

He wanted to take one of the test cans from the rabbit hood and send it out with the CD. It would be risky, but necessary. This was the early morning of the tenth, and Mohed had said the container must leave on the eleventh. Since he was not watched much tonight, it was now or never.

After another half-hour in the utility room during which nothing happened, Breckon went up the steps, through the short tunnel, and into the machine shop. No one. Proceeding to the tunnel leading to the rabbit room he looked through the small window in the door and saw nothing out of place. He opened the door and ran to the end of the tunnel leading to the next tube. As he looked though the small window, he saw the doors to the hood were closed, and the lights were dimmed. He turned the handle and pulled. The door opened. The chemical smell was stronger. Carefully closing the door behind him, he tiptoed to the hood.

He did not know if the hood door was in the field of view of the TV camera, but he had to chance it. He unlatched the door and pulled back the wing on the side with the aerosol cans. The hinge squeaked. He was annoyed that everything was in such poor repair. There were a few cans on the lowest shelf in easy reach. He took the can nearest him. His presence woke up the rabbits, who probably thought it was feeding time and hopped around.

Quickly he closed the door, latched it, and returned to the tunnel. He covered the distance to the other end in seconds, and was going to open the door into the workshop when through the small window he saw a shadow move. He pressed himself up against the wall beside the door and saw the light coming though the window darken as someone looked into the tunnel. After what seemed an eternity the face disappeared from the window. As he waited, wondering what to do, he glanced at the other end of the tunnel and saw the main lights come on in the tube he had come from.

He surmised the owner of the face at the window to the tunnel was now in the "rabbit" room. As quietly as possible Breckon opened the door to the workshop. He scooted across the tube and opened the door leading to the far end of the main bay. In the bay, he dropped the can in a garbage barrel, made sure it was covered with cardboard, and went behind the canning machine pretending to measure and mark the wall.

"Ha, there you are! What are you doing? You were supposed to be in that small room."

It was Arzika. He obviously had planned to make a surprise check on Breckon and catch him doing something incriminating. There was irritation in his voice when he found Breckon doing nothing more incriminating than his job.

In as calm a voice as he could muster, Breckon replied, "I was told I could come out here. I needed to check the height for placement of the laser scanners. It's necessary to know this for the next sequence in the programming." Breckon's hands were trembling.

"Did you look under the covers on the machine? You are not permitted to do that," Arzika's voice conveyed more malice than suspicion. "If you leave this area to snoop around, you will regret it." After a pause, "I frequently see you trembling. What are you hiding?"

Breckon waited a few seconds before answering. "The air is bad down here, and I don't get exercise. I'm getting sick." He hesitated, then continued. "You're trained in self-defense. I am not. If we went outside, you could be sure I didn't run off."

Arzika sensed an opportunity. "We can arrange what you request. I have taught self-defense. I will teach you some basics. It is good exercise for the mind as well as the body."

Breckon suspected some sort of trick but needed the fresh air. "Okay, but no stupid stuff like last time. You could've seriously injured me," he said touching the tender black and blue spot on his cheek.

After Arzika's departure, Breckon was struck with the feeling that there was something that man was after. Maybe it was as simple as payback from their first session. No. These people were too serious for that. Yet, there was no reason not to continue on the course he had planned. He had to plant the CD and the sample can on the container. Then he had to get outside to send a message to Harris describing what he had done. It all seemed so inadequate.

Back in his quarters after his shift, Breckon could not shake the despair that gripped him. He had a little saying, "It's always darkest before it goes totally black." For the first time in his life, he saw nothing humorous in that. And then he prayed for something he had never prayed for before. He prayed for deliverance. As he prayed, the load of it all became almost crushing. With what strength he could muster, he heaved himself onto his bunk and pulled up some blankets as he slipped into a deep and dreamless sleep.

0700, 10 September, King Fahd International Airport, Saudi Arabia

"Sorry, gee, I'm real sorry." He had stepped on a man's foot pretty hard. It must really hurt. From the string of angry words, Harris knew he was being cursed, and was glad he didn't understand Arabic. Here they were, squashed in the aisles, and all they did was wait. It took forever for a 747 to empty. He hoped he was at the right airport. When they spoke English, the accents were so thick he couldn't understand them. Anyway, the plane tickets were all gone so this was as far as he went.

Harris was dead tired. He hadn't shaved for two days. Changing planes in Turkey had been especially trying. He hoped Gibbon would be there to pick him up. He was sick of fumbling around finding his own way. He groaned as he remembered he still had to fight his way through customs.

When he came to the door of the plane at last, the bright sun blinded him. The heat took his breath away. He nearly tripped going down the steps. The tarmac was black asphalt, so much the better to soak up the heat. He was sure the temperature never fell below the flash point of molten sulfur. He shambled along with the ragged line of humanity to the terminal. Looking to the right, he shook his head in amazement. There was another jumbo jet in the process of disgorging its five million passengers at the same time. Great planning.

First, he had to recover his suitcase. With his bag in hand, he got in line in a large hallway to go though Immigration and Naturalization. On the wall in bold letters was a sign in seven languages saying that drug dealers lose their heads. After dragging himself along at a glacial pace that seemed to account for the Precambrian Epoch, it was finally his turn. He pulled his passport out of his back pocket and presented it to the clerk. The guy rather carefully compared the photo with Harris.

"Purpose of visit?" He asked.

Harris had been warned not to say anything that would imply he was actually doing something an Arab could do so he replied, "Technical meetings." The passport was stamped with a thud, scribbled on, and returned. The clerk made eye contact with the next one in line, so Harris assumed he was done.

He grabbed his suitcase and computer bag and headed to the customs line. This was different. There were six stations and only a half dozen people in line by each. When it was his turn, he thew his suitcase on the low, metal-topped counter and set his computer bag next to it. The inspector, an Arab in uniform, motioned him to open them. As usual, as soon as he had it half open the inspector was all over it.

Since Gibbon had told him how they searched for pornography, he made sure there was nothing in his possession that showed a woman. But, he had the disk of random numbers that he would need to decode Breckon's messages. There was no point in hiding it so he turned out everything in his computer bag. The CDs were handed to a man sitting at a computer terminal. They had the latest computers and knew how to find what they were looking for. There were several blank CDs which they verified immediately. Next was the disk of random numbers.

The guy at the terminal looked at Harris and said, "This is coded, I must see what is on it."

Harris was aware this could be trouble, but he was too tired to be smooth. "That disk has random numbers on it. There's nothing to decode."

Suspecting some sort of scam, the man responded, "I have never heard of that. Why do you have it?"

Harris couldn't think of what to say. He blurted out, "I've come to document a new petro plant with measurements and photographs. I use random numbers to edit and clean up the digital photographs." He stood there thinking that was the dumbest thing he had ever heard. Who would believe it? He rubbed his hand across his face, and stared blankly at the inspector through slitted eyes.

The first inspector fidgeted, not knowing what to do. The people in line were making sighing noises, unhappy with the slow progress. The inspector held up the disk in front of Harris. Harris didn't change his gaze. The man picked up a booklet and said in a high pitched voice as he tapped his index finger on it. "This is a booklet of our laws. Notice especially this section." He opened it as he spoke and taking a pen made a dark circle around a section labeled "Pornography," wrinkling the page as he did so. "Read this well and do not think that because you are an American you will not be held to our laws. Islamic law prevails in Saudi Arabia, and it applies to foreigners as well as citizens!" Harris took the booklet in a mechanical movement. The inspector made a terse gesture for Harris to slide his belongings to the side on the metal counter and out of his way. Looking at the next person in line, he smiled mechanically as he motioned to have the bags opened.

Harris packed up his stuff as well as he could and started to walk toward the exit when he heard a familiar voice beside him. "Guess you charmed 'em. What was all that about the CDs?"

Harris turned and looked in the direction of the voice. He looked again. "Glade to see you, Keith." Harris extended his hand and felt a firm handshake. "I hardly recognized you, you're so brown. You must visit your local tanning spa every day."

Gibbon smiled, "As a matter of fact, I do. And starting today you'll join me." Gibbon led the way through the people to his car. "How are you doing. Have a good trip?"

Trying to keep up with Gibbon's long stride Harris replied, "I'm tired and miserable. My eyes are so blood shot, I'm afraid if I open 'em I'll bleed to death."

As they stepped outside Harris stopped, put down his bags, and put on his sun glasses. "Man, look at all those foreigners, like a supermarket in Northeast Minneapolis."

Gibbon chuckled. "I see you haven't changed. It'll be nice having you around. Since Fred went back, there have been no Americans to talk to. I like the Japanese and the other nationalities. For the most part they're good people, but a person gets kind of lonely for his own kind." They walked up to Gibbon's rental car, a green Nissan. "Excuse its appearance. They all have paint on them when they get here. They aren't very good drivers. At least we have a set of wheels. With you coming out, I convinced them back home we'd need our own car."

As Harris and Gibbon pushed the bags into the small trunk, Harris asked, "How long does it take to get to Al Jubayl? I've had all the traveling I can take."

"It'll take an hour, less if traffic isn't too bad." They drove five miles east from the airport on a two-lane road and then headed northwest on a four-lane divided highway. The stop signs for cars entering from side roads were universally ignored. At the sight of another vehicle approaching the main road, Gibbon reduced speed and made sure to accommodate entering traffic. They were on a highway with two lanes each way and paved shoulders, much like a stretch of U.S. Interstate highway. The only problem was there were four lanes of traffic. The locals used the shoulders as another traffic lane, and lane markers were ignored.

As they drove, Harris pulled a small pad of paper out of his computer bag and started writing on it. "Oh, by the way, your wife sends her love. She was in good spirits, but she misses you a lot."

"Thanks. I'm glad you said that. Sometimes I'm not sure how she's doing, and she naturally wouldn't want to worry me with anything she could possibly handle."

Harris held up his pad so Gibbon could see it. *Do you know if the car is bugged?*

Harris held his index finger to his lips to indicate a non-audible answer. He indicated an answer by moving his own head positively and then negatively.

Gibbon looked at him quizzically, and shrugged. Harris wrote on the pad again. *Urgent that I talk to you soonest in place where we cannot be overheard in any way.*

Gibbon gave him a "you must be nuts, but I'll play along with you" look. "Where are you staying?" he asked.

"I'm staying at a hotel called . . . let me see." Harris dug through his pockets and finally came up with a crumpled piece of paper. "The Al Shaq Hotel. Know where that is?"

"Yeah. I was planning to drop you off so you could rest up, but check-in time at the hotels around here is noon, so let's go to the plant first, and I'll show you around."

"That's fine. Mind if I put my head back and rest a little?"

"Wake up, Darin, we've arrived."

Harris awoke with a start. "Sorry, I must have dosed off for a few minutes."

"You were dead asleep for the better part of an hour."

There were two others in the construction trailer. Gibbon made introductions, and with hard hats, they were off. "We'll take the elevator to the top and work our way down. It's the equivalent of nine stories to the product receivers on top of the storage silos." At the top of the silos they stopped. Stepping off the elevator Gibbon motioned to the right. "Let's keep walking while you tell me what's going on."

Harris walked beside Gibbon as he began his story. "That CD-ROM you saw me having trouble with in customs is part of it. It contains random numbers used to decode secret messages. Have I got your interest?"

Gibbon thought for a moment. The CIA agent who had visited him came to mind. "Yes," he said slowly, "you do. Let me have it, all you have a mind to tell."

"Do you know where Ed Breckon is at this time?"

Gibbon glanced quickly at him, and Harris continued without giving him a chance to answer. "Well, the whole world thinks Ed and I are in the mountains camping. But neither of us are. I'm here. That you'll believe. Ed is in a deep, underground, secret site in Iraq, having been taken against his will, and being forced to help build a factory to manufacture weapons of mass destruction. I have proof. And I'm here to ask your help in rescuing him."

Gibbon thought a minute, and looked Harris in the eyes. Harris looked worried and stressed. "Either the sun got to you sooner than I expected, or one young man has gotten himself between the proverbial rock and a hard place. You'd better start at the beginning and tell me the whole story."

They walked as Harris talked, with Gibbon interrupting from time to time to tell Harris what the various parts of the plant did. Harris showed the messages he had received as they fit his narration. In an area where they could not be seen, Gibbon read each carefully several times.

Gibbon said, "The part where the CIA checked up on Ed is very troubling. You'll naturally be looking for more messages from Ed. That means you'll have to access your e-mail on a daily basis, which means you, or whoever stole your identity, e-mail password, and all the rest, will be traced here. That assumes that all you've told me about the CIA and the NSA is true. If the CIA can establish that it's really you here and not someone using your AOL account, your alibi will be blown, and with it Ed's. In addition, your association with me won't help protect your cover."

Harris looked at Gibbon a little bewildered. "Why would my association with you mean anything?"

"I've been contacted by a CIA agent to gather information from a certain person. This could get very messy very fast. I'll tell you more tomorrow. For now, let's get you back to your hotel and rested. We'll need clear heads." After a pause Gibbon continued. "When you said you were coming here because you had a line on a story, you weren't kidding, were you? But it'll have to be told as fiction, I'm afraid."

— 18 —

Breckon was at the picnic table having a cup of coffee and thinking he'd like a decent breakfast, when Mohed walked in. "Haven't seen you for a while," Breckon said. "How did your demonstration go?"

"I think all work well."

"Does that mean I get to go home?" Breckon always got an odd reaction to that comment.

"Let us not discuss such things. You to get better food for today. Be happy there."

The breakfast was better, though still out of cans. After they had eaten, Breckon grabbed his computer bag, and they went to work. He had placed the stolen aerosol can and the CD of the demonstration in his bag. It was a risk, both from leaks and discovery, but he was beyond caring much about either. His main concern was getting up to the hangar and planting the evidence on the container before it left.

As soon as they opened the door to the bay paint fumes hit them.

"What have they been doing in here?" asked Breckon. "We can't work in here, we'll get sick."

As they entered, Mohed pointed at the ceiling and walls, saying, "They paint brush on walls and ceiling to cover cracks. This is bad. Come after me, maybe I found idea."

Mohed led the way to the far end of the bay, and up the steel stairs to the original level of the floor. He led through a door into a room beyond the far end of the bay. Breckon had seen the door before but had not had an opportunity to investigate.

"What's that?" Breckon asked, pointing to a steel cage that looked like a small elevator.

"That up-down lifter used to lower food for kitchen, lift out garbage." He pointed up and continued, "Top in room by corner of hangar. Now out from working order." Mohed pointed to a centrifugal fan that clearly had not run for some time. Its outlet duct went up beside the elevator shaft. "Blowing fan used to clean cooking air out before fixing for machines." He pressed a green button. Nothing happened. "Maybe you fix and lift out bad air," he said as he lifted both arms up.

Breckon nodded, "Yeah. We need to get those fumes out or it'll never be habitable in the main room. If we use something to brace the door open that leads from this room to the robot bay it'll work." Breckon set to the task of checking the wiring. He saw at once that, when the kitchen had been decommissioned, the start-stop push buttons had been relocated to this room. Since the fan wasn't essential, nobody cared if it worked.

"Let's find the control panel. I'd guess it's up in the hangar someplace. If the fumes get into the rest of the facility we'll all be sleeping out on the sand dunes."

As they proceeded across the bay to the steps, Breckon was looking at the paint drips on the floor. He looked up and saw drips on the rails and the bridges. "Whoa, Ashrof. Look at that. They slopped paint on the rails. You know how smoothly and silently that gantry robot operates? Well, all that dripped paint must be scraped off or nothing will work right. Next shift that must be done, period. And please, tell them not to use solvents or this place will smell even worse. Tell them to find sharp tools and scrape it off."

"Yes, this is bad job. I see it make good."

As they entered the hangar, Breckon saw to his relief that the container was still there. In the corner of the hangar diagonally opposite where the large door opened was a tank which apparently contained aircraft fuel. It was set back in an alcove that once had a wall in front of it that the renovators had partially knocked down. Breckon knocked on the tank with his knuckle as he passed and discovered to his surprise that it was full. To the side of the tank was a doorway with no door leading to a dark room. Breckon found a light switch and flipped it on. The light revealed the top of the elevator. "There, on the far wall," Breckon pointed, "is an electrical panel, and beside it a circuit breaker panel."

It took half an hour before Breckon had the problem solved. He found a wiring error such that each time the start button for the fan was pressed, the circuit breaker tripped. Someone had taken a control relay out of its socket rather than correcting the problem.

When Breckon had the fan starting and stopping via the buttons on top, he said, "Okay Ashrof. It works from up here. Go down below and start the fan from the button there. I'll stay here and watch the circuits. We should be able to talk to each other through the elevator shaft."

As soon as Mohed was gone, Breckon went out to the container, scanning the hangar for anyone watching. He saw no one but could never be sure the snitch wasn't around. Walking around the container he saw there was no place to hide anything that wouldn't be easily seen. Since the container was on the transport trailer, it was easy to see under it. The structure supporting the floor was made of "C" channels going crosswise and spaced every fifteen inches. The channels were five inches high and the bottom, horizontal leg of the "C" was two inches wide, forming a series of ledges going across the container.

Feeling up in the space, he discovered it was relatively clean. With some duct tape—the Iraqis had discovered "the handiest tool in the world" too—he could secure the CD and aerosol can. If the container were intercepted while it was still on the transport truck, retrieving the items would be easy, or else forget it.

Breckon ran back to the elevator room just as he heard Mohed call from below. He quickly flipped the circuit breaker for the fan to the off position. "Yeah Ashrof, give it a try."

It didn't start. "Still a problem with the switch connection from down there, Ashrof. Stay there and give me a few minutes while I check the wiring in the panel again, okay?"

"Yes, I wait."

This was it. Breckon hadn't seen anyone around, but if he were caught in the next few minutes, he knew it would be death. His heart went into high gear. He grabbed a partial roll of tape, the can, CD, and a rag from his bag. He ran to the front of the container on the right side. For retrieval, it would be on the opposite side from the driver. One, two, three, the third "C" channel from the front. He wiped the area clean of dirt and taped first the CD, and then the can, into place. There, one last strip of tape for good measure. He stooped down and looked up under the container. In the dim light of the hangar, it was almost invisible.

With the rag and tape in hand, he ran back to the elevator room. In his excitement his finger slipped off the circuit breaker. On the second try, he got it. "Okay, Ashrof, try it now."

The fan started as expected. "Come up, and we'll finish unloading the container."

Breckon put the rag and tape among some trash in the corner of the room and went into the hangar. He sat on a pile of empty pallets and wiped the sweat off his face. For the first time he noticed there had been some changes up here. The rubble from the renovation was gone and some sort of structure was being built in the hangar. He walked over to investigate. Some papers on a table caught his eye. That was odd. There was a drawing of a tank he recognized as the M1 Abrams. Yes, seven road wheels, that's the M1. The British Challenger, which looked quite similar, had only six. He had read that someplace. It was an exploded view with numbers with "kg" after them. These were weights. There were U.S. Army manuals lying around too. Some had Arabic words written above the English.

In his concentration, Breckon did not hear Mohed come up behind him. The tug at his sleeve startled him. "No, no, Ed, not look at that!" he said in an emphatic but hushed voice.

"Interested in technical stuff where ever I find it. It's the way I am, I guess. What are they planning to do here?"

"They do vehicle fix-up, I think. Does not be some of our work." As they walked back to the container he added, "Ed, hands shake again."

"Must be the bad air, and then breathing those fumes. I'm starting to get a headache. How about you? Anyway, let's see where we are with the unloading."

As Mohed took each item out of the container, Breckon checked it off against a list in his computer. If parts grew legs and walked away, he wanted to know for sure they had been packed in the first place. Along the way, he was adding a few comments to the message he hoped to send. Keeping his eye on the time, he was not surprised when he heard a buzzer sound at nine o'clock. It was a daily misery to him as it sounded every morning in his room just before noon. He had been unable to find a ten-watt resistor to put in its place.

"Time for night prayer," remarked Mohed. "We go down now."

Breckon shook his head. "No. We're almost done here. I'm not going to walk those stairs again just for this. I'll wait in the generator room. You pray up here." Without waiting for a reply, he turned and walked to the far corner of the hangar.

Entering the room, he glanced out as he closed the door. A couple dozen men were assembling. As before, he braced a pipe behind the door, flipped off the light and went out. It was dark in the pocket, and his eyes had not adjusted to the low light. Immediately he opened his computer cover so it would start to boot up. He ran out into the open and saw only stars. The moon had not risen yet. He managed to send and receive messages and hurried back inside. He replaced the pin in the door, turned on the light, and removed the pipe from the door latch. Opening the door a crack, he watched as the men were getting up. That was some strange religion. Nothing but hating, fighting, killing, and praying.

After unloading the container, Breckon and Mohed checked the air in the robot bay. The fan was helping. Air flowed down the shaft through which they had lowered the equipment from the hangar and up the fan duct to the outside. Breckon decided he'd leave that rear door propped open and run the fan every day. It would help get some good air into the underground spaces.

Maintenance base, south of KKMC

The Blackhawk was barely on the ground when Captain Rebic was out and headed to the corner of the nearest building where Warrant Officer Boyd had set up an office. When Boyd saw the captain, he gave a salute and extended his hand.

"How's it going, Charles?" Although they were on a first-name basis in informal settings, "Charles" was as informal as Warrant Officer Boyd would allow. Other than a few idiosyncrasies, the men found Charles a fair and helpful boss. As long as it was kept within bounds, he always said he'd rather have his men ask forgiveness than permission. This attitude was particularly beneficial out here where they were short of almost everything.

"Have a seat Captain. Ah, well, you may have to move something. It's hard to keep a tidy office around here." This was an understatement. There were manuals, binders of reports, vehicle logbooks, gears, bearings, electrical modules, and junk everywhere.

Rebic paged through an M1 logbook, and his expression was not happy. "Charles, this is a terrible maintenance record. This one hasn't run more than fifteen miles between breakdowns. I hope this is the worst one."

One of the Filipino kitchen staff had been standing outside the door, and Boyd motioned him to come in. He had a pitcher of iced tea and two tumblers. "Thank you," said Boyd. "As I was going to say, Captain, we may not get more than one or two decent tanks out of the junk that's left.

We've exchanged parts repeatedly, and we have little to show for it. Come on, I'll show you what I mean."

Boyd led the way past where the men were working. Rebic saw one tank with a drive sprocket off, another with the engine compartment doors open and hydraulic hoses and electrical cables hanging over the sides. They all had some major defect. When they were nearly to the last tank, they ran into two specialist E4 mechanics working in the engine compartment. "Hi, Charles. Hi, Tom," one said.

The other looked up, smiled, gave a thumbs up, and in a low voice said, "Think we've got another one."

Rebic looked at Boyd, as Boyd gave a slight motion of his head to the side, at which the two men went to nearby tanks and started examining parts. "What's going on, Charles?"

Boyd gave a proud smile as he began, "We know the Filipino kitchen helpers are spying. We've even found notes they've made. They probably even take pictures. Those two guys I motioned away are making sure we're not overheard. The logbooks are coded so anybody reading one would think, as you did, that the tanks are junk. We take them out for trials and nearly always tow them back. Or else, the drivers jerk them around, so it looks like they hardly run. They're getting pretty good at that. Truth is, we have another four in good shape. Give us another week and there could be four more."

Rebic was skeptical as he replied, "But there's not one tank that I saw that would run."

Boyd pointed to one of the tanks, "That drive sprocket could go on and the tread ends joined in an hour. The one with the hydraulic hose hanging out of it is in great shape. Those hoses are hanging there not connected to anything. Pull them out, close the engine compartment, and you have a one-hundred-percent tank.

"But that's not the best part. We only got a few rounds of live ammo at the start of this thing as you know. Everybody, especially the tank crews, were feeling pretty naked, so we asked around. Sergeant Rodriguez knows a guy who knows a guy. Well, it turns out they have a large store of 105 ammo in Qatar left from the Gulf War." Rebic knew they only used the latest model M1s with 120 mm guns now. "Nobody wants the 105 mm ammo. In fact, there was a huge amount of all tank ammo left. One of the guys at the ammo depot said they hauled over two-hundred-thousand rounds of tank ammo for the Gulf War, and expended less than five-thousand. Better to have too much than too little, but that seems a bit extreme.

"Anyway, they're all too willing to get rid of the 105 ammo. It's good stuff too, not a single misfire on the target range. So we have several crates of 'wrong parts' full of 105 ammo, and we can get more. Those tanks that are ready to go have full magazines. We load them at night after the Filipinos go back to KKMC. We'll load that Blackhawk you flew in on tonight so you guys on the line can fill up too."

Rebic was pleased, "Well done, Charles. I assure you, that topic has come up more than once as we sat around in the evening. Everyone suspects that eventually shooting will start, and we have only a few rounds per tank. You'll be 'hero number one' when they see that load of ammo."

0730 hours, 11 September

The meeting was set for 0800 hours at the maintenance base south of KKMC, and Yousuf Hamoud was a half hour early. Captain Rebic was waiting for him. "Good morning, Mr. Hamoud," said Rebic, stiffly extending his hand.

"Yes," replied Yousuf just as curtly as he took the captain's hand. "I take it you had better hunting since we last met."

With a hint of sarcasm in his voice, Rebic said, "Yes, we did. The Iraqis certainly do stick to a pattern. You accurately predicted their movements each day but one. That's phenomenal."

Hamoud was prepared for such a comment. "Ah ha, you sound skeptical that I predicted the movements of the Iraqi armored units. The truth is, I didn't. We have a source inside Iraq. It took him some time to learn how to get the information on their exercises."

This came as no surprise to Rebic. "Does this source tell you what their maneuvers are intended to accomplish other than make tracks in the sand?"

Hamoud replied, "That's the main reason for today's meeting. We don't know of a grand strategy, but we've learned they intend to strike across the border and take out one of the pumping stations on the Saudi Arabian pipeline. This will be September 20th. We don't know the time and place, though we expect to have that before the twentieth. Your job is simply to position yourself between them and their objective and cause them to abort the mission."

As Yousuf stopped talking, Rebic interjected, "Wait a minute. How big will their force be? Have you thought that they might have ten times more tanks than I have and decide to roll over us? Excuse me, but that doesn't sound like much of a plan."

Yousuf said in a patronizing tone. "Calm down, Captain. At the present time, they're planning to use no more than eight T-72s. It will surely be less than that because of chronic maintenance problems. In fact, there will be two tank retrievers following the force, so they won't leave any malfunctioning equipment on the Saudi side of the border. We get regular reports from inside. I'll pass along any changes to the plan with our secure sat-phones. There is nothing to worry about."

That last statement really made Rebic's spine tingle. There was never "nothing to worry about." Putting the thought aside, Rebic asked, "What will be happening between now and then?"

"It appears they will be exercising in areas away from the border. You are to keep up sweeps as you've been doing. If I learn anything, I'll pass it along." With that Hamoud left.

When the car was gone, Captain Rebic got Boyd and Lieutenant Duke Blatz, the platoon leader of the third platoon, to a secure location and briefed them on what he had been told. Then he said, "Pack up and be ready to go. If Charles is the wonder worker he says he is, we'll have three full platoons by the twentieth. We'll work on tactics as if anything could happen. And, Charles, see if you can get a lot more ammo. We took a sweep to the southwest of the forward base, and it's nothing but empty desert. We're going to work on gunnery, and then work on it some more. I want these crews to get more live-fire training in the next nine days than they'd get during their entire enlistment back in the States."

After a pause Rebic said, "Come to think of it, Hamoud didn't show any interest in the equipment. I wonder if the Filipinos are sending the information to him." He shrugged, and giving a sharp whistle to get the "hawk drivers" attention, he motioned to them to mount up. The Blackhawk, fully loaded with 105-mm ammo and fuel, labored to lift off in the hundred-degree heat. If the Filipinos noticed, they gave no indication.

— 19 —

"Hey, Breckon. Let's get some fresh air."

It was Arzika taking him up on his request for fresh air and exercise. Breckon could not remember a time when he felt less like exercising, but he knew he had to comply.

As he emerged from the hangar behind Arzika, it was dawning. Breckon started jogging out along the side of the runway toward the southwest. After a hundred yards, Arzika was beside him. "Now that we're warmed up let's try a few basics."

To start with, Arzika covered in detail the first thing necessary, and that was how to land without getting hurt when you were thrown. Breckon didn't like this man in any way but had to admit he was a good instructor.

The sun was starting to streak the tops of the sand dunes to the west when they stopped for the day. Breckon was sure he'd have a few bruises, but he felt better than he had in a long time. This did not change the nagging feeling he had. Arzika was after something, and it worried him that he couldn't figure out what it was.

Breckon was deep in his own thoughts as he entered the hangar and descended to the underground spaces. Immediately upon arriving at his quarters, Breckon showered and ate some of the "food." He opened his computer and decoded the message he had gotten from Harris and saw the following:

Minneapolis, 9/5/1998

Ed, I have located your site to at least a 98% certainty as Nukhayb, which is located 60 miles NW of the nearest border with Saudi Arabia. This is based on the info you sent in your last message. You are really out in nowhere, so don't try to walk out or something like that.

On 9/10, I'll arrive in Saudi Arabia on the gulf coast. Keith Gibbon is there for a new petro plant installation, and I hope to get help from him to get you out of there. I'll be working for Keith to document the new installation. Otherwise, I couldn't have gotten into Saudi Arabia.

So far, we have not contacted any governmental agency. Let me know if you want me to do that. It's your call unless you stop communicating. Then we'll use our own judgment.

Keep the faith, Darin

Breckon was thinking that having both Harris and Gibbon in Saudi Arabia here greatly increased the odds that they could retrieve the stuff from the container. "Here's hoping you're the most inventive guy in the world," Breckon said aloud.

Harris was up and shaved by 5:30 a.m. He booted up his computer, and connected to the hotel's Internet jack, to see if he had a message from Breckon. It took longer than normal to connect to his mailbox, but he was rewarded with a new message.

After the decoding process, Harris had the message on his screen. He read through it rapidly and sat back in his chair. His mind was racing. If he could recover the evidence, he should be able to get someone to help, maybe even the UN. He was mystified as to the meaning of the tanks. His first impulse was to call Cindy and get a track on the container. Then he thought he should discuss it with Gibbon first. Harris did not have a printer, so he put the message on a floppy disk.

When they arrived at the construction trailer, Harris handed Gibbon the disc and quietly said, "I received a message from Ed. Can you print the file on this disc without anyone seeing it?"

Gibbon nodded and slipped the disk into his computer. Seconds later a printer fifteen feet away spat out a page. Gibbon was waiting to catch it. After casually returning to his desk, he read it. His expression was one of intense interest. As he came to the end he fidgeted and rubbed his hand across his mouth in agitation. "Come, grab your tape measure and these drawings. I'll show you where to start."

Harris didn't know what was wrong, but Gibbon's alarm was genuine. He gathered his stuff as fast as he could. Harris held a messy wad of drawings under his arm as he ran after Gibbon to the elevator. The elevator stopped at the fourth floor. Gibbon raised the gates and strode off the lift. He turned onto a catwalk running to a cluster of large tanks. In among the tanks was a place where the noise from the construction was lessened. When Harris caught up, Gibbon was reading the message again.

9/10/98 11:45 p.m., from the rat hole

Darin,

Things are progressing well on the installation. Don't know if that's good or bad. They got a very sophisticated robot arm for each robot, made in Russia. Each of these arms has a closed circuit TV camera on it, and that has been a real benefit.

They had a demo a few days ago to show some VIPs how the project was coming along. I knew about this and rigged up a system so the camera on one of the robot arms recorded the demonstration. The Iraqi engineer who is my immediate supervisor, the nicest guy here, loves to play with the robots. His name is Ashrof Mohed. He was in the control room watching the demo on the closed circuit TV. He even went through a manufacturing sequence in manual mode for the guests.

Watching the video you'll see what they intend to do. They will put these products, all of which will contain nerve gas, on store shelves across the country, in military post exchanges, everywhere. As the video shows, once you press the button on an aerosol can, the entire can empties. They have hundreds of products. The government will have to recall first this product, than that, and pretty soon the store shelves will be empty.

I have sent a CD-ROM of the demonstration, and an engineering prototype of one of their aerosol cans, out on the container that the gantry robots came in on. I found the can in a fume hood in the tube third on the left as one enters the corridor tube. The second tube is a workshop. They seem to have made these as prototypes.

If you manage to recover this stuff, BE VARY CAREFUL WITH THE CAN, IT CONTAINS NERVE GAS. The container is

HANJIN, number HANJ 014639 7. I was told it would leave 9/11/98, but that's Friday, their equivalent of our Sunday. It may go a day later. The CD and can are attached to the underside of the container. "C" channels running across the container form the floor support. The items are in the third "C" channel from the front on the right side looking from the rear doors forward. They're attached with tan-colored duct tape. While the container is still on the transport truck, they will be easy to get. Once the container is stacked on others, it will be impossible. The CD-ROM isn't coded. I password protected it. The password is "iraqsucks."

If Cindy found the container when it came here, maybe she can find out when it will leave and where it will go. This container won't contain any of the production cans filled with nerve gas, they aren't that far yet, but getting close.

This last item is sort of "to whom it may concern." In the instructions that came with the Russian robot arms, the head engineer sent a letter addressed to me. Obviously, he thinks I came here willingly. He mentioned he intended to meet me here. Following is a verbatim duplicate of that part of his letter.

As it now stands, I will be part of a small delegation coming to the site in the southwestern part of the country where you are by now working. This is an entirely different mission, but I will plan to see you while I'm there. The key date on the other project is 20 September so I hope to get to that wretched country a day or two early. I think by the time you read this, you will be sharing my opinion of the site location.
Until then I am,
Sergie Musatov
First Deputy, Automation Technology Directorate

Stay cool, buddy. ED

PS Last minute addition.
Just saw M1 Abrams tank manuals and a drawing in hangar. Was exploded view with weights of turret, gun, engine, etc.

written in. Putting up crane of sorts for heavy lifting. Seem to be preparing to disassemble an M1. Why?

As Harris watched Gibbon read the letter, he saw the muscles in his face twitch. Gibbon unconsciously rubbed his chin. When he looked up, there was a wild look in his eyes. Not certain what to make of it, Harris could only watch.

Suddenly Gibbon blurted out, "My friend, this part of the world could blow up, and only I have the information to stop it!"

Stunned, Harris replied, "I don't follow. How?"

"You see, the UN inspectors have been in Iraq for years and have found nothing. They know there are WMD programs going on at some level, but their hands are tied at every turn. Finally, someone high up has gotten pissed."

"Slow down, Keith. I still don't see it."

Gibbon slowed down but was still pacing the enclosed area. Turning to Harris he said, "Here's how I put it together. The officer I met is using old, dilapidated tanks for some special operation west of here along the Saudi/Iraqi border. They have some of the newest M1A1s with 120 mm, smooth bore guns over here. When you go to war, you use the best equipment you have, not obsolete junk. I think they're deliberately being put in harm's way. Coincidentally the Iraqis are planning to disassemble an M1 tank."

"So, how does this make this whole part of the world blow up?"

"The U.S. has decided to finish what the Gulf War started. My guess is the tank operations have nothing to do with Ed's site. The reason the M1s are here isn't exactly clear. But, it's not normal training. That tank commander said as much. If shooting starts on the Iraqi border at the time these aerosol cans show up in the U.S., everyone will assume they're linked. Two dirty tricks started for different reasons, one by the U.S. and the other by Iraq, will collide. Each in itself would be hard to manage. Together there's no possible way for anyone to control the outcome. Rockets with chemical warheads could start falling on Israel, followed by nuclear bombs on Iraq."

Harris was still skeptical as he replied, "Okay, I'll grant you this could get real messy, but what can you do to stop it?"

Kieth seated himself on a six-inch horizontal pipe running two feet above the decking, and six inches away from the silos. He leaned his back against one of the tanks. Holding his hard hat in one hand, he ran his fingers through his thin graying hair. Gibbon continued, "A few years ago I saved the life of a young man on a job site in Kuwait and was almost killed in the process. His father is the second richest man in the world. He owes me big time. I have never asked for anything because I was afraid of the power associated with all that money. But, I could call in the debt.

"I certainly don't want to see the Iraqis hit the U.S. with those little gas bombs, nor do I want to see Ed die. I also want to save the tank crews. On the other hand, people in high places in the U.S. probably think charging into Iraq with some old tanks and getting some crews killed, is a good Idea. Similarly, someone in Iraq thinks gassing the U.S. population will gain them something. In any case, neither side will welcome interference."

Gibbon stared at his hard hat for some time. "I'm sitting right in the middle. I know I have to do something, and, in the end, win or lose, there's a good chance I'll be dead. Do you understand, Darin? That includes you! These are the big guys who kill a couple of little guys like us before breakfast every morning." Gibbon looked up at the patch of sky visible between the catwalks above and said with a touch of languor in his voice, "I hated coming back here again, and now all I want is to go home and see Helen—and rest. What a crap game."

"He's really the second richest man in the world?" Harris asked quizzically, too stunned to form an intelligent comment. "And most of all, does he like you?"

Gibbon managed a thin smile. "I don't know if he likes me or where he ranks in wealth. I assume everyone knows who the richest man is, so I think of him as the second richest. He's worth billions, if that helps put it into prospective.

"Darin, the guy who's commanding the Abrams tanks in Saudi Arabia could be near where you described the location of Ed's site. From what Ed said, the Iraqis plan to capture one or more M1s, probably by drawing them into a trap. If they could disassemble some American tanks and ship them to Russia, Iraq could get a lot from Russia in return."

Harris was trying to keep up with Gibbon's reasoning. "Keith, you're only guessing at all this."

Gibbon shook his head, "The rich guy's son mentioned Iraqi tanks marauding the Saudi pipe line near the border. Then I found out about these M1 operations. Now this message saying the Iraqis plan to take apart some M1s. Ever since I met that Captain Rebic, I've been wondering what could be going on." Gibbon sat a few moments, resting his fore-arms on his thighs. "I know I don't have it all figured out, but if you have an innocent explanation for this, I'm listening."

Harris was now pacing back and forth in the small space. "How can you get hold of this powerful man? No matter what happens, we're going to need some serious help to get Ed out."

Gibbon nodded in agreement. "I can reach him through his son. That's not a problem. But we must go to him with a plan. Asking him to start a war with his neighboring country to save one American is pushing gratitude a bit too far, even if he likes me a lot."

"And the war is out in any case," Harris interjected. "Ed and I both accept the fact that if we contacted the CIA, or the U.S. Department of Defense, in all probability they'd screw it up. Either they'll bomb the place to rubble, or they'll fiddle around until Iraq figures out there's a leak, assume it's Ed, and he's dead."

Gibbon looked up at the tall polycondensation towers that stood beside the storage silos. They seemed to soar up like skyscrapers. There were catwalks like gossamer webs between the structures. Hundreds of tons of steel would be rubble again if this thing got out of hand. "I agree we shouldn't get the U.S. government involved." He was remembering his own meeting with the sleazy CIA guy. "Okay, here's what we do. You call this woman, Cindy, and try to find out where we can intercept the container. That's vital. The sheik, through his son, has invited me for dinner before I leave, so that'll work. But, we must have the evidence before we see him. I must also contact the tank commander. Counting today, there are nine days before the twentieth. That isn't much time."

After a pause, Gibbon continued. "Keep that code disk where it won't be stolen. We'll have to send and receive more messages. That code disk could become a hot commodity."

Gibbon saw a cloud come over Harris's face as the situation hit home. "I see what you mean," Harris said. "Since the NSA is alerted to our messages, they'll want to read them. They'll need the disc. Now with one end of the messages in Iraq and the other suddenly in Saudi Arabia their paranoia will become intense. They'll be looking for the one sending and receiving the messages. And another problem. I got Ed's message by plugging my computer into the jack on the phone in my hotel room. They'll know where the guy getting today's message is staying. If they have a mind to, they'll be able to identify me and prove that I'm not on vacation."

Gibbon got up slowly as he spoke, "You'll have to stay there tonight and then move to another hotel. In the future, you'll have to check your e-mail from a pubic place. In addition, you must get a lot of work done so your cover isn't questioned. Let's get to it." Kieth took the pack of drawings from Harris and laid them out on the deck. "As you see, the dimensions I've highlighted in yellow on the drawings are the ones I want you to verify by actual measurement. The blue marks show where additional dimensions must be measured and entered."

0600 Minneapolis

"Hi, Cindy. Did I wake you? This is guess who from out East. Be careful not to use identifying words."

"My alarm went off a few minutes ago. I've been going crazy. What's happening?"

Harris could imagine what it must be like for her. "Some progress. I got another message. I met my friend, and, from the information I got, we have a lot figured out with some ideas of what might work. It's more complicated than we imagined, and I can't go into it. Do you understand?"

"Yes, I think so," Thomas replied. "But, slow down so I can put this together."

"Yeah, sure. Our friend still seems to be okay. I need you to do something. Do you still have the number of the box the goodies went in?"

"Of course."

"Good. Use your source and find out where it goes next, and when. I think it's scheduled out in the next few days, which means there should be plans made for it. Others may be looking for it, so tell the source to throw them off if they ask. Can you do that?"

"If it's possible, I'll have it today."

"That's good." Harris paused a moment, then continued. "Do you remember I mentioned Helen?"

"Yes."

"Go to her place at nine-thirty this evening and have her call her husband. Tell him what you've learned. Tell Helen what you must."

"Yeah. But I don't really know much. I'll let you go. Stay safe. Bye."

"Bye, don't worry, we'll make it."

NSA Headquarters, Ft. Mead, Maryland

"Mr. Daley, may I have a moment of your time, if it isn't too much trouble?" Evens was deliberately being caustic with his trainee who had returned from across the hall.

"Yeah. What's up?"

"You're very busy buzzing around other departments and not very busy with the work I've assigned you. We have requests, and they're starting to back-up."

Daley was hurt by the reprimand because learning how to interface with coworkers covering other parts of the world was part of his training. "We have more of those Iridium messages, and I think we're onto something. More activity is coming out of Iraq, and now the other end of the messages is in eastern Saudi Arabia. Without my input, neither the Iraqi nor the Saudi sections would've picked up on it."

Evens was getting a bit impatient, "I must insist you give this little game your lowest priority. We have to get our work out."

Daley nodded but added, "The guy sending from Iraq is way out in the desert, *but* he's located at a small air base, and there's been a lot of Iraqi armor activity in that area lately. Also, there's an American armor unit operating opposite that site on the Saudi side of the border."

Evens turned to face Daley squarely. "We have to assume the guys covering that part of the world will handle it if they think it's important. You found it, and then passed it off to them. That was the correct thing to do."

Daley persisted, "They say there won't be time to look into it for a day or two, and things can get away from us in that time."

"Okay," Evens replied in exasperation, "alert CIA and suggest they try to locate the Saudi Arabian end of the messages. I'm only doing this to prove to you that there will be some perfectly simple explanation."

Feeling he had scored a great victory, Daley went to his cubicle and made the request to CIA.

1345 hours, 12 September, Nukhayb, Iraq

The small man in the dirty lab coat walked to the field telephone and turned the little handle on the side a few times. In the kitchen, a clacking could be heard at the switchboard. It was located there because this was one area of the compound that had someone present twenty-four hours a day.

"Switchboard."

"Colonel Basheer."

"Basheer," the voice on the other end said after the connection was made.

"Colonel, this is Prakash in the test lab. Will you come down here as soon as you are free? We have a serious problem."

"A leak, is that it?" The test lab was where they made the prototype cans filled with nerve gas. He was deathly afraid a leak would prove the design of the cans was defective.

"No, but something almost as bad. Come down and I'll explain."

Basheer hung up and left for underground immediately. Now what? This had been nearly an impossible assignment from the start. Then the decision to bring that captured tank here. Of all the stupidity.

As Basheer entered the lab tube, he saw Zafar Prakash look up, and with his little finger push his glasses up on his slanted nose.

"If we don't have a leaker, what's so important?

"One of the test cans of nerve gas is missing." He raised his hand with the palm facing the colonel. "I know what you will ask. No, it is not lost or misplaced. It is missing. Someone has taken it."

Basheer with his typical tact almost shouted, "How can you tell with all of these cans?"

Zafar, accustomed to the man's demeanor, calmly explained, "Each can has a serial number. I did a complete inventory, and that one is missing. It is special because I had detected the faintest trace of a leak with the new German sensor we received recently and had placed it right here," he said putting his hand on the place. "It was a yellow, black, and white antiseptic can. The only one of that kind. If our thief had taken any of the other cans, we might not have missed it. The last time we know for sure it was here was the day before the demonstration."

Zafar went on to describe how they had searched through the garbage cans in the large bay and the other shops. They even searched the food garbage. "We searched all the tubes, even that of the American engineer. It isn't here. It's a mystery."

"Maybe not such a mystery." The colonel went to the telephone and rang the switchboard. "Find Arzika and have him come to the laboratory tube immediately."

When Arzika arrived a few minutes later, Basheer explained what they knew.

After listening intently to Basheer, Arzika said, "I see two possibilities. There has been quite a bit of traffic associated with General Majeed's project."

"And the other?" Basheer asked.

"The American."

Basheer slowly shook his head. "I knew you would say that, but I don't see how. He'd need an accomplice, in fact, several."

Colonel Basheer sat down on a stool by a workbench, and Arzika sat on a crate next to the curved wall. Zafar took the hint and sat down on the crate beside Arzika. Looking up, Zafar said thoughtfully, "If the can has been stolen—and it doesn't matter by whom—there are three obvious facts that we must deal with. First, there is someone in this site, or who has been in the site, who knows where the cans are, and who had access to them.

"Second, there is someone on the outside who knows something is going on here who is to receive the can. The third fact is we must recover the missing can before it falls into the wrong hands."

They sat for a minute thinking. Then Basheer rose and in his typical manner said, "Arzika, check every vehicle that has left here from 8 September until now. I will talk with General Majeed about all his people who have been here. Zafar, keep the doors to this tube locked at all times, and make a daily count of the cans." With that, each left to begin his assignment.

As he stooped to put the key into the lock to his apartment, Hamoud hoped his brief absence had not gotten him into trouble from one or the other of the governments he served. He spent Friday visiting relatives and stayed the night, deciding to return Saturday. It was nearly 6:00 p.m.

Once inside with the door closed, he walked into his small kitchen with his bag of groceries. He noticed the light flashing on his answering machine. With one hand, he put an earphone in his right ear as he started emptying the contents of the grocery bag with the other. A female voice said in Arabic, "Call your mother sometime, son. It's been a long time."

"Piles of camel dung to you," he said under his breath. This message from "mother" meant he had to go to his contact and pick up an assignment from the CIA. He quickly ate and in ten minutes was leaving.

His contact ran a little jewelry shop in the *souq*, the traditional market place, which was still thriving in the older parts of towns. This was only three blocks from his apartment, so he walked. Back at his apartment, he put on water to heat for tea.

The assignment was typical of what he called "junk work." "Identify, determine business of, associates of, and other relevant information about, occupant of room 205, Al Shaq Hotel, Jubayl. Two days." From the date and time, he could see one full day was already gone. He thought of the other things he had to do, and decided the morning would have to be soon enough. He needed some sleep. He wished the CIA could get more help out here to handle their low-priority stuff.

1830 hours 12 September

Breckon walked into the robot bay. He was tired and in a low mood. The cup of strong coffee he had finished minutes before had done nothing to revive him. The stress was wearing him down. This combined with the bad air, and the continual physical beating, was taking its toll.

What was Arzika after with this hand-to-hand training? To his surprise, Breckon could see he was learning a few things. But, there was one move he could not master. He did exactly as Arzika told him and always landed on his back. It was beginning to seem like Arzika was using this "training" as some sort of sadistic game. It occurred to him that he was spending a lot of time trying to figure out how to beat Arzika at that move.

As Breckon walked to the center of the bay to organize the day's work, he noticed something on the make-shift workbench. Of all things, a machete. From the chips of paint on it, he realized this was what they used to scrape the drips of paint off the rails. Being in a lethargic mood, he examined it in detail. Stamped on the blade near the handle was "USN, MK2, Legitimus, Collins & Ott, 1945". He chuckled, imagining that if it could talk, it would have some strange story to tell.

"You plan to chop down doors to go out?" asked Mohed as he came up behind Breckon.

"Look," Breckon said pointing to the inscription. "Compliments of the U.S. Navy. New too. Made in 1945."

"Used to chop dead branches off date palms. Common tool. We grow much dates."

"What, Iraq is a big producer of dates? I didn't know that. So much for our geography lesson."

Mohed gave Breckon a wry smile.

1900 hours, 12 September

As soon as Arzika had closed the door to Colonel Basheer's office, the colonel began. "Timing is very important. Every second we lose, the trail grows colder. I got little from General Majeed. He is totally absorbed in his plans. Arzika, is it possible any of the vehicles leaving here took it along?

Arzika settled on a hard metal chair. "There seem to be two possibilities, the truck that transported Yousuf Hamoud in and out, and the container truck that left on 11 September. General Majeed vouches completely for Hamoud and the drivers. This leaves the container. It went directly to Al Kufah, where it was immediately loaded with dried dates and will leave the country by way of Kuwait. It is scheduled to sail from Jubayl, Saudi Arabia on 16 September. We kept it here overly long, so it will move fast to meet its sailing time. Iraq has a good agent in Saudi Arabia. I will have him start at Jubayl and work his way north to intercept the container, and search it for the missing can."

Basheer nodded, "I agree with your plan. We have the option of locking down the whole country and in the process alerting hundreds of people to our project, or taking a few swift moves ourselves to get the can back. Besides, we still are not sure it left this site. Have Prakash keep looking."

— 20 —

0530 hours, 13 September, Sunday, Jubayl, Saudi Arab

It was approaching daylight, but the sun wouldn't be visible for some time. An unobtrusive Toyota, looking like any other Saudi car with its dents and scratches, sat among the cars parked along the street across from the Al Shaq Hotel. Only the lack of dew on the windshield set it apart. The man in the driver's seat watched as the light in room 205 came on. After a few minutes, he left his car and walked across the street, through the revolving door, up a half flight of stairs, and into the lobby.

Since it was early, there wasn't much life stirring as Hamoud walked up to the long counter with a folded newspaper under his arm. "Would you recognize the occupant of room 205 if you saw him walking through the lobby?" he asked the clerk, an Arab of not more than twenty with fine facial features.

"Let me see, 205," he replied in Arabic as he tapped a few keys on the computer terminal. "Oh, yes, I'm good at connecting the face with the name."

Hamoud slipped his hand over the counter and put a folded fifty-riyal note on the keyboard. "I must have a business meeting with him later in the day, and I want to fix in my mind what he looks like. I would appreciate you giving me a sign when he comes down. Move this plant to your right when he comes," Hamoud said, nodding to a potted plant sitting on the counter. "Can you do that?"

The clerk pocketed the note and nodded.

In front of the desk was a lounge area with several wicker chairs with stuffed cushions. Some were arranged around tables. Down the hall from the check-in desk was a small bakery that sold cakes and coffee. Two chairs faced away from the wall with an end table between them.

Hamoud took a seat in one of the chairs where a potted plant partially shielded him from the front desk. He unfolded his newspaper, pretending to read. He hardly noticed the man who sat down in the chair on the other side of a small table and unfolded the front page of his newspaper as he said, "I hear the rains may come early this year."

Intent on observing the front desk over the corner of his paper, Hamoud almost didn't hear the other man. After a moment of mental confusion, he recognized the statement as the sign of his contact from Iraq. "If it pleases Allah, the desert will bloom early," was the counter sign.

"You have been hard to find," the second man said in a hushed but stern tone.

Hamoud was taken aback by the comment and tried discretely to observe the other man who had lifted his paper as if reading something near the bottom. This movement of the paper obscured Hamoud's view of the front desk. Out of sight, and momentarily out of mind, Hamoud turned his attention to the man beside him and responded "I have many assignments. But, if you have one for me, it will be acted on promptly."

"It is top priority," the man said with his newspaper still held in front of him. With that, the man folded his paper and casually laid it on the table between them keeping his face turned away. He got up, turned, and left by the back door.

Hamoud waited thirty seconds as he watched the front desk impatiently. He folded his paper and laid it on the same table. He bent to check his shoelace and glanced at the front desk as he did. He stopped half upright. There was a man standing there wearing faded jeans with his back turned. He instantly tried to remember if the plant had been moved. Just as quickly his mind snapped back to the newspaper the other man had left. He casually picked it up.

Slowly unfolding the paper he saw a small envelope with a black strip across one end taped to it. He gritted his teeth since it was top priority. He was required to go to his apartment or other secure place to open it. It meant he would miss Mr. 205 for today. When he glanced back at the front desk the man was gone. Serving two masters was tough.

––––––––––

Darin Harris glanced at his watch and bent to pick up his only suitcase. He had let Gibbon take his computer and camera equipment to his apartment the evening before. He made his way through the revolving door with his bag and stepped into an eighty-five degree morning. Scanning the cars on both sides of the street, he saw Gibbon parked up the street half a block and walked to the car. Dumping his suitcase in the back seat, he got in the front. As Keith drove away, Darin said, "I'm checked out of the Al Shaq. Where do I crash tonight?"

Gibbon hit the brakes hard to avoid a car entering the street in front of him and said, "I've had the guy who acts like a gopher at work looking into that. He thinks there's a small apartment in the building where I'm staying that'll open soon. Until then it'll be another hotel." Keith laughed. "For a gopher, I guess he does all right. He has three wives. Talk about masochism. One wife is quite enough for me."

As Gibbon got out of the worst of the traffic, he said, "Helen called me earlier. Seems the girls had a heart-to-heart talk. She's worried but glad she knows. She can keep her mouth shut. Cindy told her the container is scheduled to sail out of Jubayl on the *Orient Mist* Wednesday. That means it must be at the port on Tuesday at the latest. As of a few hours ago, it hadn't crossed into Kuwait. I suggest we put in a long day today and start early tomorrow morning, checking containers on the road as we drive to the border with Kuwait. If we haven't met it on the road, we'll wait for it."

Back in his apartment, Hamoud opened the message. "Intercept a shipping container and search for an aerosol can of antiseptic hidden on the outside. Assume can is dangerous. DO NOT press the button on top." There followed the number and description of the container. From the information, he could see that early the following morning was soon enough to drive north.

14 September, Jubayl, Saudi Arabia

Harris was out on the street a block northwest of the Holiday Inn where he had spent the night. It was showing first light in the east. He saw the lights of a car approaching, and it was Gibbon.

As they started their drive north, Gibbon was working on the situation, half talking to himself and half to Darin. "It shouldn't be too hard to spot. If we meet a HANJIN container, we have to turn around and follow it to check the number. There shouldn't be that many."

When they got to the outskirts of Ra'sal Khafji they stopped, not having met a single HANJIN container on the way. Gibbon found a place to park on the west side of the southbound lane. It was a short distance past the last traffic light on the road heading south out of the town. "This is less than ten miles from the Kuwaiti border, and I don't want to chance going into the town and getting stopped at a check station. If our container comes by, we'll easily be able to read the serial number on it."

It was eight-forty and already above ninety-five degrees. Darin asked, "What do we do if we see it? We can't flag it down and tell the driver we want to search his vehicle."

Gibbon waited before he answered then said, "Follow it, I guess, until he stops. Maybe one of us will have to start a disturbance while the other one grabs the stuff. We know where it's stashed so it should be quick."

They were parked among a few other cars that appeared to have been left there as a park-and-ride. Time dragged as they sat, sweated, and drank water. Suddenly there was a squeal of tires. They both watched a dark-red car entering the intersection against the red light. He swerved to the right and then left between two cars with horns blowing and tires skidding. Once through the intersection he accelerated to the north.

Gibbon shook his head. "They drive like fools around here, but that guy is really something."

Harris laughed, "No wonder his car is so dented. What would've happened if there had been a fender-bender."

"I'm told all parties go to the police station and make their statements and generally the guy with the best insurance pays regardless of fault."

They settled down to boredom again. They watched intently as each truck hauling a container passed by. "I'd say that isn't it, agreed?" The reply was, "Agreed." This kept them alert so they wouldn't get dopey and miss it when it finally came.

To pass the time, Darin fished something out from between the front seats. "Where in the world did you get this thing?" It was a stick not much thicker than a toothpick, ten inches long, and was bent over on the end where a fuzzy bumblebee hung on a rubber band. As it bounced up and down, the wings made a fluttering sound.

"When I filled up with gas last night, the guy gave it to me as a premium. The Arabs like to fix up the interior of their cars as you'll see if you ever take a taxi."

After a half-hour, Harris pointed, "Hey look, there's that beat-up red car, the Toyota that almost caused the accident. It's pulling off the road on the north side of the traffic light." They watched as the driver got out of the car to stretch his legs.

Gibbon put his hand on Harris's wrist and said in a whisper. "Don't move except to slowly slide down in the seat so you're not visible. I think I recognize that man." Gibbon was scrunched down so his head could barely be seen.

Darin could sense the tension in Keith's voice. "So, who already?"

Gibbon watched out of the bottom of the driver's side window. "If that's who I think it is, he's the CIA agent who wants me to spy on 'the second richest man in the world' the next time I see him."

Harris slowly adjusted his position so he could see the man clearly. "You think he's following us?"

"No, dummy, he's after the same thing we are. The CIA obviously knows enough to be looking for this container. We figured this was a good place to wait for it so why wouldn't someone else? He scooted up to the border, found nothing, and decided to wait here."

Harris slid down out of view from the road. "Maybe he's an Iraqi operative. They found the can missing, and told this guy to look for it. How can you be sure he's a CIA guy? These Arabs are hard to tell apart. Anyway, if he's after the can, what do we do? We can't just whack him on the head."

They quietly discussed their options as Darin kept an eye on the man. After a few minutes, the man got back into his car. Darin was watching the road as Keith stayed out of sight. "Here comes a container. It'll have to stop for the light. 'Toyota man' is giving it the once over, and is consulting a sheet of paper. Light turned green. Truck's moving, Toyota's moving. He's blowing his horn and waving something out of the driver's side window at the driver."

Gibbon hissed between his teeth as the truck came past in front of them. "That's our container. He'll find the can and the disc!"

The truck pulled off the road a couple hundred yards past where Gibbon and Harris were parked, with the Toyota in front of it.

Harris had a broad brimmed felt hat. It was his "hiking in the woods hat." "Keith, quick, the bee on the stick. Start the car." As he was talking, he put the stick in his hatband so the bee bobbed up and down above the crown of the hat.

"He'll show the driver some credentials and demand to search the container. Pull up behind and to the right of the truck. I'll go around the left side and distract them while you get out and go along the right side of the truck and get the stuff. Then come back and get down on the floor in the back. Let's go."

Harris grabbed a map and was out of the car as soon as it stopped. As he walked around from the back of the truck, he could see the truck driver was not being cooperative. Harris waved at the two men and said, "Yo, there, good buddies, speak any English lingo?" He walked toward them unfolding the map. They looked at him with expressions that ranged from incredulous to annoyed. He stopped with them between him and the truck so they were forced to look away from the truck. "Looky here, Ah been driv'in an driv'in an kan't find this here place, Ra Aha Zar. Kan't ya help me? Ah'm lost as a puppy," he said pointing to one of the first towns he saw on the map.

"This is official business, and you are interfering," said Hamoud. "Go on your way."

Harris's face lit up when he heard English. The man's expression portrayed the realization that he had been a mistake as his eyes were drawn to the dumb thing on the hat.

"Hay, ya talk my lingo. Put it here, good buddy." Harris reached out, grabbed his hand, and started pumping it. Hamoud wrenched his hand free, looking in disgust at the image in front of him and that irritating flapping thing.

The truck driver was smiling ever so slightly, amused at the scene.

"Okay, where? Show me. You mean Ra's as Awar. You are too far north. Go south fifty kilometers and watch for the signs. Now leave."

"But where, good buddy, am ah now?"

"Here, here. Give me the map." The "you imbecile" was not spoken but was apparent in the tone of his voice. "Ra's al Khafji!" Hamoud said stabbing his index finger at the map.

"Wall, Ah thankyee, good buddy. Mucho gracias." Harris reached out as if to grab his hand again, but Hamoud snapped his hand away and stepped backwards.

"Go now. Go," he said motioning with his hand. Harris smiled broadly, turned, and walked away with his bee flapping merrily above his hat, hoping that Gibbon had had enough time to get the stuff.

As he got into the driver's seat of the car he whispered, "The keys, Keith, the keys. You must've put 'em in your pocket." There was bumping around in the back seat and soon a hand reached up with keys in it. Harris started the car and could see Hamoud looking under the

container as he drove by. He waved his hand out of the driver's window
and above the roof of the car and yelled, "Good buddy!"

Seconds later Darin asked, "Did you get it?"

"Yeah, I got it. Stop in a couple of miles, so I can get out of here. It's
really cramped. Lucky the driver left the truck running. Thought sure
they'd hear me pulling the tape free." Gibbon got up and peeked out the
back window. The container truck was rapidly disappearing in the distance. "That was some act back there. What was the idea behind the
bee?" Gibbon sat up sort of sideways in the back seat.

Darin glanced over his shoulder and grinned as he said, "I read in a
western novel once that a gang of outlaws held up a bank, and each one
had a sillier hat than the next. After the successful robbery, the sheriff
questioned the witnesses, asking them to describe the malfeasants. All
they could remember were the hats. I had the sun to my back and with
the distraction, I doubt either man really saw my face."

"Well, it seemed to work. Now to get back and see what's on the disc.
I don't know what we'll do with this can. I hate to be near it."

Hamoud watched this horrible man in the faded jeans walk away glad
to be free of him. He had been brought up in America and had not found
the people *so* repulsive. And, for a moment, he had a sense of déjà vu.

As Hamoud stood there searching his mind for the connection, the
truck driver's voice sternly jerked him back to his senses. "You have
your job to do. So do I! Do your inspecting or whatever you have to do,
and let me be on my way."

A thorough search revealed nothing except a place under the right
side near the front where there was no dirt. It looked like it had been recently cleaned. He asked the driver where he had been earlier in the day
and found he had stopped to eat before leaving the environs of Kuwait
City. It was possible something had been there that was taken while the
driver was eating.

At last, Hamoud let the driver go on his way. He checked the serial
number on the container once more. It was an intense disappointment to
come up empty handed, but he had searched every place the aerosol can
could have been hidden.

Gibbon and Harris got back to the job site at 1:00 p.m. and went to work. At seven, they went to Gibbon's apartment to eat and watch the CD on Harris's computer.

"Here goes, the feature presentation," Darin said as he inserted the CD. The screen flickered a few times and the show started. From Ed's message, they knew it shut off when there was no movement, so scenes jerked from one action sequence to another. They ate sandwiches and drank soda.

At first, they saw two workmen uncovering the can closing machinery. Following that a table was set up. The next scene showed a man walking into the field of view of the camera, looking around the room, and then right at the camera.

"Stop it there!" Gibbon heaved himself out of the only easy chair in the room and stooped by the computer screen.

"No mistaking it," said Darin as he ate the last bite of his sandwich. "That's the guy in the beat up Toyota. No question. I was standing two feet from him. Now is that the CIA guy you met?"

Keith studied the still frame on the computer. "It looks a lot like him, but it's been a few weeks. I'd say yes, but I'm not positive. Start again and let's see what else there is."

Harris was making another sandwich. "You could set up a meeting with him before we visit the sheik and refresh your memory."

"Yeah, I suppose I could, but I'd rather not."

When they came to the end, Keith said, "That's an impressive system they have. I guess I'm convinced they can do everything they plan to do. With that thing on automatic mode, they could really turn out the cans of nerve gas."

Gibbon sipped some bottled water. "If he's not the CIA guy, he's obviously an Iraqi associated with the project looking for the missing can. If he is the CIA agent, then it's complicated."

Darin suggested, "Maybe the guy who approached you wasn't CIA and was faking it. What then?"

"He's CIA all right. I went to the consulate in Dhahran to check on him. That's where I met Captain Rebic. He has to be a double agent. Either the CIA doesn't know he's working for Iraq, or the Iraqis don't know he works for the CIA. Neither option looks good for Ed."

Gibbon was tired. He put his feet up on one to the two dinette chairs as he spoke, "As a more practical matter, we have to assess our situation. You can't wear that hat again. In fact, get rid of it. And never say 'good buddy' to anyone. The bus to the plant comes down the main drag. Flag it down. We shouldn't be seen riding together. That guy'll put it together that your accomplice took the evidence right from under his nose. He'll want the can—and revenge."

They discussed their dinner engagement with the sheik in Kuwait in two days. Keith said, "I've told the people at the plant we'll be gone. The sheik will send a car to pick us up at 1:00 p.m. You take the noon bus back and change clothes. I'll have him swing around and pick you up.

As Harris left Gibbon's building, he thought about the rescue. It seemed the twentieth was the day in light of the business Breckon mentioned with the tanks. There should be a lot of distractions that day. Darin was tempted to send Ed a message that they got the evidence but decided he wouldn't risk it until he knew how and when the rescue would happen.

15 September, Jubayl, Saudi Arabia

Shortly after one o'clock, a gray car pulled to the curb past the intersection that had been arranged. The right front window lowered. Gibbon walked over and asked, "Are you headed south or west?"

The driver in his late fifties, and graying replied, "No, to the north."

Gibbon nodded and said, "Very well," and got into the back seat. Once under way, Gibbon asked, "Are you aware we are to pick up another man?"

"Yes, I was told that. Please tell me where I should go." Then in a more casual tone he said, "I think I recognize you. Are you not the one we know as Mr. OG?"

Gibbon smiled and replied, "Yes, and I remember you too. Your name is Mulla, I believe. But I've forgotten your first name. You drove me around after the accident."

"You are right. Ansari Mulla is my name. We still speak of you from time to time."

They chatted as Kieth gave directions. "The man we'll pick up will be waiting by the store on the right past the hotel up ahead. This may sound strange, but I must get my head down so there won't appear to be anyone in the car with you. Observers must not know he and I are together."

"Is there trouble then, OG?"

"This is something more than a social visit. With luck, it may not be all that important, though." Gibbon didn't believe that last statement, and he doubted Mulla did either.

As the car stopped, Mulla lowered the passenger-side window. As Harris neared, Gibbon said, "That's the guy. Hop in, Darin."

Harris settled in the back seat with Gibbon and the introductions were made. Gibbon turned and looked out the back window. "Ansari, keep an eye on the rear view mirror in case anyone is following us."

Mulla replied, "It sounds like you guys have been real naughty or you think the world is going to end."

"Let's say the latter is closer than the former." They left that topic and spoke of other things. Darin was getting some local color from a perspective not normally available. He endlessly fired questions at Mulla, who was good at describing the culture.

The time passed quickly. At three forty-five as they pulled up to an unremarkable looking gate, Gibbon said, "Don't let the appearance from out here fool you, Darin. This is one seriously beautiful estate."

"And much has been added and improved since you were here, OG. You'll be surprised," added Mulla, with pride in his voice.

As they passed through the gate, there were trees of many varieties from arid climates. The drive turned several times and at last the villa came into view. It was only two stories high, but had spires at several places, a sight common to Arab architecture. The front entrance was meant to give the feeling of power, yet was elegant. Mulla stopped, and an Arab butler in typical Arab dress opened the door.

"Thanks for the ride, and information," said Harris. "I hope we'll see you later."

Gibbon handed the tote bag he had brought with him to Mulla. "Will you please keep this temporarily? It's very important. I don't want to walk into such a beautiful place carrying this."

Mulla agreed and took the bag.

They were escorted through stout wooden doors. The foyer had marble floors of intricate design with slender marble columns along either side. They emerged into a courtyard where the brightness caused both Harris and Gibbon to instinctively glance up to see that they were outdoors. There was a pool surrounded with blooming plants. Near the walls were palm trees that shaded the area. They admired the view for a few minutes. Harris pointed at several things and mentioned how the colors and shading, plants and stone, all blended harmoniously into a whole.

His training and experience as an artist and photographer made the genius of the construction more meaningful to him.

Off to the left, a movement caught Gibbon's eye. Glancing over he saw Ali and his father coming toward them. Keith touched Darin's arm, who immediately turned as their hosts approached.

Sheik Al-Taryam wore the typical garments of Arab males, the white floor length *dishdashah*, and the white shoulder length head covering, a *shora,* with a dark *egal,* or band, around the crown of his head. He looked as Gibbon remembered him except that the lines in his brow had deepened. Gibbon remembered the piercing eyes that could be warm and friendly or harsh and intimidating as a reflection of the mood of the soul behind them. For now, they were warm.

Ali wore a *dishdashah*, but had a bare head, perhaps in deference to his western guests. They stopped a few paces from Gibbon and Harris. Then the sheik extended his hand, and Gibbon clasped it warmly. The sheik said with a soft Arabic accent, "Welcome to my home and my hospitality."

Gibbon replied, "We're grateful for your invitation. You look well, and Ali, as always, a pleasure to see you."

The sheik waved his right hand in a gracious gesture and said, "Come, let us sit by the pool and have something cool to drink."

As they were seated, each was presented with a tall glass of iced drink. It was not alcoholic, but had a delightful blend of fruit juices. They passed half an hour with pleasantries while Harris intrigued himself with the garden. They were given a short tour of it while the sheik explained the meaning and reasons for the features, how they were meant to be beautiful as well as functional. It was so very restful.

Finally the sheik looked at Gibbon with an expression that had changed from his earlier one of amiability designed to put his guests at ease to one showing concern. "I hear from Ansari that you had some concern that you were being followed. Is there some difficulty where I could be of help?"

Gibbon spoke almost too quickly, "Your Excellency, I have a heavy heart that I should come on such a pleasant occasion to your home and bring troubles with me. But troubles have found Harris and me. On one hand, you'll want to know the information for your own purposes, and on the other, I am sorry to say, we desperately need your help. I surely would've preferred to make this meeting some other time, but actions must be taken at once."

The expressions of both the sheik and Ali changed. The sheik's was almost quizzical while Ali was solidly alarmed. "Perhaps after we have discussed the situation, it will not seem so dire," commented the sheik.

"I would hope it would be so simple, but it's not. Is there a secure place where we can go to discuss these matters?"

The sheik nodded and got up. The rest followed. He led the way to a room, well furnished with bookcases on the walls, obviously a study or home office. "This room is swept daily for listening devices, and is completely enclosed in a brass mesh electrically charged so no electromagnetic signals can come in or go out. The windows are randomly vibrated so voices cannot be overheard by sensing the vibrations of the windows. In addition, there is white noise in the background."

Gibbon nodded. "You may think this is unnecessary for the puny problems a couple of guys like us could have. Let me know your opinion in an hour. We're trusting the two of you implicitly, knowing if we're wrong in doing so it could mean death for us."

The sheik flinched in surprise. "You are assured of our trust."

"By the way, I left a bag with Ansari. Could I ask you to have that brought here?"

The sheik made a short phone call in Arabic and then faced Gibbon. "You have certainly aroused my curiosity. Please proceed."

Gibbon and Harris gave the whole story covering the design of the gantry robots, Breckon's capture, the layout of the site, the Iridium phone and the coding of the messages, the suspected NSA surveillance, the suspected CIA involvement, even the meeting with the UN inspector. Harris produced the messages he had received from Ed. The bag arrived and Gibbon took out the disc and the aerosol can.

"Can I have this can tested for traces of nerve gas and x-rayed?" asked Ali.

Gibbon was surprised. "Yes, of course, but how?"

The sheik smiled. "My business dealings are mainly in the oil industry, but that can be, shall we say, very involved at my level. Samples must be tested, the competition must be watched. It frequently requires us to do physical testing of various kinds so I have a modestly equipped lab on the premises."

"I see," said Gibbon. The "modest" part was probably a gross understatement. "But," Gibbon continued, "give instructions for the technicians to be very careful. We don't want to be the cause of anyone dying. Besides, I plan to use it later."

After the can was on its way to the lab, they watched the CD from Breckon on a large monitor in the study. Gibbon told what he knew about the strange M1 tank operation.

"You see," continued Gibbon, "there seem to be two operations, one by the U.S. and the other by Iraq, and I suspect neither side knows the intentions of the other. When these collide, as they will in a few days, things could get out of hand in ways beyond what anyone expects, and Kuwait will be right in the middle."

The sheik's expression had changed. Now it was cautious, like a hard-bitten vendor in the *souq*. "For a couple of big city boys you sure managed to step in a pile of camel dung, didn't you?" said the sheik. "Your caution was well founded. I must admit I was skeptical. I should have known, though. You are not a frivolous man, OG."

The sheik sat for a few minutes deep in thought. He was himself a member of the Inner Council of Islam and knew of the project in Iraq, though not its location. He saw how stupid it had been to bring the American engineer to the site. Now the question was how to handle the situation. The cost of exposing and destroying the secret plant was small compared to another war. He thought he might as well learn what these two had in mind.

There was a light knock on the door. The man who had taken the can had returned. He handed the can and an envelope to Ali as they spoke in low tones.

When the man had gone, Ali said, "You were right. The can contains nerve agent, and it has a slow leak at one of the seams. The lab technicians managed to get a large enough sample to make a thorough analysis with the mass spectrometer." Now he referred to the sheet of paper he had removed from the envelope. "The Iraqis are known to have a nerve gas similar to what is called GH. GH is made with isopentyl alcohol, which is hard to get. Their version is unique in that it is made with iso-butyl alcohol. If they were to use that, it would be traced to Iraq immediately. The can doesn't contain their version of GH, but sarin, GB. That's what the United States and the U.S.S.R. made in great quantities during the cold war. Iraq either learned how to make it or they're getting it from some other source.

"The leak isn't dangerous if the can is kept in a well ventilated place. The x-ray analysis was difficult because the internal mechanism isn't made of metal. Using image enhancement of the x-ray plates like is used on aerial reconnaissance photos, we learned the following. When the button on top is pressed, a needle pierces a bladder inside and it appears the liquid will keep spraying out until the can is empty even if the button is released. In the right place, this aerosol can could kill thousands. This matches what you surmised from the video and Breckon's message."

Sheik Al-Taryam was sitting back in his chair with his chin resting on his clasped hands. His son did not know of the Inner Council's existence so he had to handle the situation with care. He could simply make these two Americans disappear. But, he took seriously the debt he owed OG.

Finally Al-Taryam spoke. "The existence of the factory to make the aerosol cans with nerve gas in them was completely unknown to us. I have never known Iraq to do a better job of keeping a secret. We can only hope there are no more secrets they have kept as well as this one. For now, we must deal with what we know. The factory must be exposed and destroyed, and the tank battle must be stopped to prevent a war, if that is the Americans' intent. I am not forgetting your friend, Breckon. The best way to save him is to do the first two things."

"With due respect, Excellency, I disagree." Harris was sitting upright with his eyes flashing. "The reason we did not go to the U.S. government was because we expected that kind of logic. The man on the ground, Ed, says your plan will assure his death in a heartbeat. I'm aware you have many weighty considerations on your mind, but we didn't come here and give you this information to be used as you saw fit without regard to our main goal, which is rescuing Ed. I don't want to use the past deeds of others for my own purposes, but at this point I don't care. When Keith saved your son's life he did not look at the big picture, or at what was good for himself. I can't speak for Keith, but I came here looking for a modest amount of help in rescuing Ed the only way it's possible."

The sheik was moved by the young man's pluck. He had not been spoken to that way in more years than he could remember. It rankled him, but the mention of Ali sent a pang through his heart. "And what assistance can I offer you, young man?"

Harris, realizing he had been very forward, proceeded in a more composed manner. "I've given this much thought. He's gotta be rescued like he was kidnapped. That is, by being snatched. I can only get one more message into him, and he might not get it. If he doesn't, that's too bad. I'll give him an exact date and time when I'll come and get him. It'll be tough, but there's no other way. I understand more of what's going on from his messages than you or Gibbon do because I know Ed.

"In his e-mail he describes the plane that flew him to the site. I looked it up and it must be an Antonov AN-2. Fifteen to twenty thousand of these were made in Russia and Poland. They must be common in this part of the world. I want you to find a way for me to borrow an AN-2 and arrange a flight plan, fuel, a GPS instrument, and whatever else it takes for me to fly in there, land, pick up Breckon, and get out. Flying low should make it possible to get close before I'm detected. Then it'd be good if I could get the engine to run rough and belch some smoke as I land, faking an emergency. I'd land as the large door to the hangar is opened to exchange air. If Breckon's there, we can be gone before they know what's happening. I feel the plan has one chance in four for both of us getting back alive. I've considered everything from dirt bikes to hang gliders. This is the only possibility. By the way, I am a pilot, been flying since I was sixteen."

The sheik raised his eyebrows. "That last piece of information makes more sense of what you said. I'm glad you recognize the slim chances of success such a plan has, even in light of your being a pilot." It also made the sheik relax. The plan made logical sense, but, as Harris himself admitted, was almost surely doomed to failure. This would leave only OG to deal with. The sheik could see it working out for him and fell into a magnanimous mood. "The plane you suggest is perfect from the point of view of being unobtrusive. However, the AN-2 is hard to fly, I am told. It really takes a crew of two. Ali has some experience flying one," he said, turning to his son. "You have been quiet, Ali. Tell them about the AN-2."

Ali was slouching back in his comfortable chair. He did not look comfortable, though. Now he leaned forward, placing his clasped hands on the table. In an even, barely audible voice he spoke. "That's right. It's a difficult plane to handle, especially during take-off when Harris will have more on his mind than getting it off the ground. He will need a second pilot." He paused long enough for the words to register fully with his father. But, before the sheik could say anything he continued. "I will go with him."

The older man's face took on a sickly appearance, even for one whose skin was darkened by years of desert sun. "There is no reason why you have to do this. We can get someone else to go along, a trained and seasoned pilot with thousands of hours in the cockpit of an AN-2. You don't have to go." The sound of desperation in his voice was palpable.

"I must go!" Ali shot back. "You have not lived with the burden of feeling that your life belongs to someone else. The knowledge that there's no way to repay. Now there is a chance. I'll have regrets the rest of my life if I do nothing. I must get my life back again. I must rescue myself from being rescued."

The father, with an act of will that has distinguished fathers through the ages in all states of life, resigned himself to a pain that would never entirely go away regardless of the outcome. "So you must, my son. So you must," he said almost as a last breath. But, his pain went deeper than that of his son's life. Now he had to do all he could to make sure the rescue plan succeeded, thus insuring the site was discovered.

Gibbon more than the others detected the anguish in the sheik's voice. "There's the possibility of some further assistance," he interjected. "If the rescue is attempted on the same day as the Iraqis intend to steal an M1 tank, and I can warn the M1 commander of this, he may be persuaded out of gratitude, anger, or what ever, to dash into Iraq. He could arrive at the site at the same time as Harris to provide cover fire for him. M1 tanks have enough range for that."

Now the sheik got up and paced slowly around the room, deep in thought. For the first time in decades he was feeling threatened personally. If he warned the Inner Council of the rescue plan, they would stop the rescue and kill his son. If the council ever found out he had known of an attack on the site and had said nothing, he could be thrown off the council and reduced to poverty, or more probably killed.

The others waited until at last he spoke. "OG, what is the chance we could get this UN inspector you know to go along with the M1 tank force to the site, assuming they go? This would give a UN presence to it. And it would keep the U.S. in a supporting role, thereby depriving them of the opening they need to renew the Gulf War."

Gibbon responded, "I had thought of the inspector too. If he can be made available at the right time, I think there's a chance he'd go along. We'd have to get him back here under false pretenses because this must be kept extremely secret. Once he's presented with the proposition, he'd have to be kept isolated until after the operation if he agrees to go or not."

"Agreed, I can handle the inspector. When and where do you want him?"

Gibbon felt uneasy at the casual assurance with which the sheik meant to control another man's life. But, this was not the time to object, so he said, "It all happens on Sunday the twentieth. I'd want to present the evidence and the plan to the tank commander by noon Friday so they would have Saturday to plan and position their forces. That means we have to leave from the Jubayl area Friday morning."

Al Taryam nodded. "The inspector will be at Jubayl by, say, eight o'clock Friday morning. We'll work out where you are to meet."

Taking a deep breath, the sheik turned to Harris, "We happen to have an AN-2 in the airplane garage. I suggest you and Ali go have a look at it. There is time before we dine."

After the two left the room, the sheik and Gibbon sat in silence for some minutes. Finally the sheik looked at Gibbon and said, "I have been wondering what had caused the change in Ali since the accident. I never thought he would feel that way. But, now I see it's a natural thing to take hold of a man. After this, I will have either a whole son or no son. The half man will be gone."

Gibbon almost felt ill at what had happened. After a pause he replied, "I have sons too. Something like this never happened to me, but the thought of it happening has haunted me many nights. I guess it's the way of life. I imagine it must be harder for you, though. Most people in similar circumstances will resign themselves to something they could not control. You have command of so much with your wealth and power, and still, in this situation, you are left in the position of an average man. Kids can drive their parents crazy."

Sad eyes peered at Gibbon. "Once again, you know what I am thinking, my friend," the sheik said thoughtfully as he lowered his gaze to the table in front of him. "You feel what other people feel and in some way lessen the pain for them. I thank you for that."

"Now that they're gone, though," Gibbon said, changing the subject, "is there anything else we could do to even the odds a little? Getting some M1 tanks involved is a long shot."

Al-Taryam still torn between his duty and his son slowly nodded thoughtfully. "Oh, yes. There are things that can be done. I suppose we may as well get started."

— 21 —

"Captain, message from Colonel Liston on the secure sat-phone saying you're to contact Captain Adrian Jackson at Fort Hood. Says it's urgent."

Rebic looked puzzled as he walked through the curtained doorway separating the two halves of the command tent. "I know a Captain Jackson, but not terribly well. I thought he had been transferred to Fort Knox six months ago. Since it's urgent, I certainly want to respond, but it's not clicking as to why he'd want to contact me out here."

Suddenly Rebic's neurons got their act together. Not Fort Hood, Saudi Arabia, when he got the mission from the CIA. "That's it! I gave that name and number to the guy who told me how to fix the wind sensors. The name was a code he would use to contact me if he had something important."

Stepping out of the tent, Rebic gave a shrill whistle to get the attention of his officers. As soon as they arrived he passed around the message and said, "That guy sure knew how to fix the wind sensors. And, he seemed to know what was going on."

"You never mentioned anything like that," said Lieutenant Duke Blatz. "I thought he was a rough-neck or something on that petro plant construction."

Rebic was trying to remember the details of his meeting with the man. "No. He was an engineer supervising the construction. He seemed to know people. He mentioned the Iraqi tanks along the border like it was common knowledge. Yet, when we were scrounging parts, icemakers, 105 ammo, you name it, there was no gossip about us or the Iraqi tanks. We all know how rumors travel. The news would've gotten around. He knows stuff, and if he says it's urgent, I suppose I should contact him. Jake, when was the next scheduled run back to the base at KKMC?"

"Tomorrow sometime, depending on operations out here."

"I'll have to go back. Let's plan on leaving at first light. Duke, take out all the tanks tomorrow and continue working on gunnery."

During dinner, Ali and Darin mentioned they had taken the AN-2 "around the patch," but in general they spoke of other things. Shortly before they departed, they spent a few minutes in Al-Taryam's secure study. Darin prepared and coded a message to Ed, giving the timing of the rescue operation. Ali agreed to go to the Kuwait airport early the next morning and send it to Breckon's e-mail box. This would further throw off the NSA if they were watching Breckon's e-mail. Harris and Gibbon were also presented with a container normally used to transport medical pathogens that resembled a thermos bottle. This was for safe storage of the aerosol can. Then they were off, the plans, such as they were, set in place.

0830 Hours, Thursday, 17 September

The phone rang on Gibbon's desk. He felt as if he had been working ten hours already. As the years passed, it was getting harder and harder to make up for lost sleep, and the rapid development of things was adding a lot of stress. He also knew it would get worse before it got better. He picked up the phone after four rings. "Keith here."

The clerk in the general contractor's trailer said, "There's a call for you. Will you come, or do I take a message?"

Gibbon was expecting a call from Rebic or possibly Kuwait. "I'll come," he replied.

A minute later, Gibbon picked up the extension phone on the desk across the trailer from the clerk. "Yeah, Keith."

"I'm looking for Adrian Jackson."

Gibbon lowered his voice and turned toward the wall. "Good. Where are you?"

"At the maintenance base. Do you remember where that is?"

"Yes. The line's very noisy. Can you go into the nearest town and call me back in exactly an hour? I'll be at a different phone then." Gibbon gave him the number of a phone in a store five miles down the road where he could talk without being overheard.

"Sure, in an hour."

An hour later, Gibbon was at the store and in the phone booth. He had arranged with the proprietor to take the call and paid in advance. Trying not to be obvious, he kept glancing out the window to see if he were being watched. Fumbling through some papers, he tried to make it look as if he were preparing to make a call. The phone rang right on time. "Yeah."

"Adrian?"

"Yes. I must see you. This is deadly serious, matter of life and death, your life and death." Gibbon heard a breath being let out as if the man on the other end thought he was dealing with a nut case.

"What do you mean? Nothing's happened, and we won't be here much longer."

Gibbon was getting impatient. "Let me ask you this. Do you have, shall we say, an appointment on the twentieth?"

Silence on the other end.

"Well? Tell me about the twentieth!"

"How could you know . . . listen, who are you anyway. Who do you work for?" Rebic shot back.

There was no question that Gibbon had gotten Rebic's attention. "I work for ArmCon, an equipment supplier for petro-plants. Fate, and I do mean fate, has really been kicking me around lately. There's no government I can go to in an official capacity, so if you ignore me, you and your crews will be dead come the evening of the twentieth. Time is short. You're being set up. I have proof. Listen to what I have to say and see what I have to show. Then you decide. What've ya got to lose?"

The reply came with no hesitation. "Where do you propose to meet, assuming I agree?"

"Out at your base. I feel one or two of your select people should also see what I have. It won't be only your life on the line."

"When?"

"Tomorrow. Today is Thursday and Sunday is *the* day. I'll need a secure place with house power for a computer. Is it possible for you to supply transport? Maybe send a truck to Jubayl to get me?"

"Don't worry, I'll send a Blackhawk helicopter for you. The Jubayl airport, south end. The pilot will have to refuel, and then pick you up at, say 0900. That okay?"

"That'll do. I'll probably have another man along with me. He's reliable, has impeccable credentials. Don't ask any more. Will there be room for him?"

"There's room for a fully equipped combat squad in a Blackhawk. There'll be room."

"See you tomorrow."

———————

When Captain Rebic got back to the maintenance base after making the call to Gibbon from KKMC, he walked to the shop area. Lieutenant Denton could see there was something wrong. "You look like you just lost your best friend."

"Worse. Get Charles very inconspicuously and meet me out at the end of junk row." Junk row was what they called the line of tanks they knew could never be resurrected and were being cannibalized for parts.

When they were all there Boyd asked, "What's up?"

"That guy who helped us with the wind sensors will be here noon tomorrow. I'm sending Jake to Jubayl to get him and another guy. He wouldn't say much, but he knows about our mission on Sunday. He said he also knows we're being set up to be killed. Says he has proof."

Captain Rebic sat down on a crate. They each took a few minutes to take in what Tom had said. Boyd spoke up, "What do you think?"

"I don't know. Let's hear him out. He alluded to something like this when we first met. Either he's so paranoid he puts the rest of us to shame, or we're headed into a real dust-up come Sunday."

"Let's assume for a minute he's got the proof," said Denton. "What can we do to prepare?"

Boyd jumped on that. "If we take this seriously, there are two things we should do. First, we'll send our hired help packing for good. We'll eat MREs for a week if we have to. I don't think the men will complain. Second, we turn out everybody and get every last tank and support vehicle in the best shape we can."

Lieutenant Denton was nodding while Boyd was talking, then said, "I'd also suggest we don't let the CIA dude know any of this."

Rebic added, "It makes sense. If this is a trap, he must be involved some way, though for the life of me I can't figure out a sane situation where that would be true."

Boyd chuckled. "The driving logic behind most wars doesn't look all that sane in hind sight. I don't think giving some consideration to insane motives is completely out of the question here. Besides, that CIA guy gives me the creeps. In case you haven't noticed, he *is* Arab.

Just because he had a CIA badge doesn't automatically make him a true-blue American."

2200 hours, Jubayl, Saudi Arabia

Hamoud sat at the kitchen table in his apartment. He was in a stew. He prided himself in not getting riled up. In his profession that could be fatal. Today he had received a second message from the CIA to find the man in room 205. Earlier, he had been berated from the Iraqis for not finding the aerosol can on the shipping container. Hamoud re-read the message again hoping things weren't as bad as they had seemed at first glance.

1500 hours GMT, Wash., DC
Second Information Request—Urgent

Need information on the man in room 205, Al Shaq Hotel per first request. We need results! Man's name is Darin Harris, though could be using aliases. Known associate is Ed Breckon. Neither man is thought to be in Gulf area. Identities probably stolen. Man using name of Darin Harris arrived King Fahd Int'l 9 Sept. Suspect sent e-mail using Harris's AOL account from Kuwait airport 0720 hours Gulf time, 17 Sept. No plane-fare to/from Kuwait City in the name of Harris. No passport records of either man into or out of Kuwait. Locate, establish identity, and photograph soonest.

"Well, screw you. Only half the world to look in, and I'm supposed to find him. Get real," Hamoud mumbled to himself. He knew the Iraqi request was the most important for the short run. But, he had to do something to keep the CIA off his back. He pictured in his mind what he remembered from the day he was waiting for him in the hotel lobby . . . the guy in the faded blue jeans. Then he thought of the ridiculous man asking for directions at the container. He also wore faded blue jeans. It was strange, that guy asking for directions at the very minute he was going to search for the aerosol can. Maybe it wasn't a coincidence.

Hamoud was putting together both situations in his mind. The CIA was looking for this guy from room 205. He could be receiving messages from Iraq. If he was the guy at the container, an accomplice could have grabbed the can off the container while that clown was distracting the truck driver and himself. He had to admit it was a clever trick. The hotel clerk had given Hamoud the company he represented. Flipping through a notebook he found it, ArmCon Corp. He knew he could locate that company and, with it, Harris.

0750 hours, Friday, 18 September

Gibbon waited at the prearranged place in downtown Jubayl, on the sidewalk outside the Marriott hotel. There was the standard mix of people around him. Most were Arabic, but the Orientals outnumbered the other foreigners by a wide margin. He carried his tote bag and kept a watchful eye on anyone loitering, knowing there was a good chance that he was being followed. Only being watched didn't bother him. That would stop dead at the airport. Then he saw the gray sedan pull up. Ansari Mulla caught his eye and nodded. The rear door unlocked, and Gibbon got in. Instantly they were moving, melding in with the dense traffic.

As he got in, he saw UN inspector Craig Kardell looking very puzzled and apprehensive. "Hello, Mr. Kardell," Gibbon said. "How is everything with you?"

"What are you here for, uh . . . Gibbon, isn't it? I'm on an emergency trip home. My wife has taken very ill. Why are you here?"

Gibbon glanced at Mulla in the rear view mirror. "I gather, Ansari, he has been told nothing?"

"That is correct, OG. There was no other way."

Kardell glanced at Gibbon and then Mulla with quick, unsure movements of his head. "You two know each other? What's going on! I've been abused enough," he said, his voice rising in anger as he realized something was not as it appeared. "I'm not some toy you can throw around as you please! I demand to know the meaning of this!"

Gibbon looked at Kardell knowing what he must be thinking. "First, Mr. Kardell—Craig isn't it?"

"Yes," came the terse reply.

"First, Craig, we're all being used as toys, but this is more serious than that. Second, your wife is fine. A dreadful set of circumstances has developed, and we desperately need your help, both technically and politically. We especially need your UN position for veracity."

Kardell blustered, "Oh, this is ridiculous. I'm nothing but a minor functionary on a large team of UN inspectors in Iraq! And, if it has escaped your notice, we keep getting further from Iraq all the time. And, one more thing. Who are you?"

"The same nobody I was the first time we met. Events have forced a few ordinary people like you and me into a deadly international game. We're on our way to recruit some more ordinary people. Stay with me. Thousands of people could die if you don't."

Kardell sat quietly as they drove into the airport grounds. He nervously pulled on his ear and rubbed his nose. Gibbon was worried he'd jump out at the first chance. Each time they stopped at a guarded gate, Mulla showed identification of some kind, and they were waved through. There was no question, Mulla's boss had good connections.

Gibbon turned and looked squarely at Kardell and in an even tone said, "Mr. Kardell, you came to me and asked for help in learning how chemical plants worked. I did what I could to give you a hand. I don't know if it helped you, but I tried. Never in a hundred years did I think the tables would be turned and I'd be asking you for help, but now I am. I'm asking you to take a big leap of faith and go the next step with me."

Kardell looked warily at Gibbon. "And, what is this next step? Ever since I got picked for this awful UN job, it has been one dreadful thing after another."

They reached the south end of the airport and stopped. There were some cargo facilities and a moderate amount of truck activity on the road, but no aircraft movement and no Blackhawk. Gibbon hoped he could get Kardell more positively disposed before the helicopter showed up. A movement caught his eye over Kardell's shoulder, and he saw the helicopter across the field lifting off. That had been the fuel stop.

Kardell turned to look where Gibbon was looking. "What are we waiting for?"

"This is were we meet another member of our party."

Kardell was fidgeting again. There was the look of a trapped animal in his eyes. "This UN assignment is a messy business all in itself. Why does a citizen of the U.S. have to take an oath to some other organization, and without his consent? I'm really fed up with this whole sordid affair," he said, sighing. Then he looked up, "That was pretty low down to get me here by saying my wife was dying," his anger was building again. "Don't you people have any human decency?"

Knowing that he had to get through to Kardell, Gibbon grasped the man's forearm and in a firm voice said, "Craig, when you say 'you people' you tell me you haven't heard what I said. We're not an organization.

We're average people who by some crazy accident have been put into a position where we'll affect world history if we do nothing or do something. None of us signed up for this. If we do nothing, there'll be another war in Iraq. You've been there. Do those people deserve another war? Do you want to spend the rest of your life knowing you caused thousands of children to grow up in misery without parents?"

The beat of helicopter blades could be heard approaching. The man was confused. He was angry, and he felt sorry for himself. He was a decent man who wanted to do what was right but was sick of being used.

"Take a chance and come with us to see the evidence," Gibbon pressed. "If you want out, nobody will object. With what's ahead, only volunteers will be welcome." Gibbon could see the Blackhawk landing. Kardell had his back to the direction from which it approached. The car was well sealed, so the sound was not distracting.

Kardell looked into Gibbon's eyes. The wild look had softened. "Okay, when and where do we meet the others and see the evidence?"

Gibbon raised his eyebrows, scratched the hair on the side of his head, and managed a wry smile. "Well, if you look behind you, you'll see a big, ugly helicopter. It'll take us two-hundred-fifty miles into the desert where we'll meet them."

Kardell snapped his head around and saw the Blackhawk. Gibbon had to admit it did look big and ugly, almost sinister. "Oh, for Pete's sake!" was all Kardell could manage.

Gibbon hastened to say, "When you get aboard, you'll notice it's flown by men wearing U.S. Army uniforms." Almost whimsically he added, "Think of the stories you'll be able to tell your grandchildren."

Kardell paused and stared into space. Gibbon could tell he was suffering from a serious case of cognitive dissonance, the mind grappling with two contradictory concepts at the same time. Finally, Gibbon said in a low firm voice, "Time to go."

With that Kardell opened the door and started for the helicopter.

Gibbon grabbed his bag and followed. Kardell was in the Blackhawk being assisted with the seat belt by the copilot when Gibbon got there. The seats faced forward, and Kardell was in a seat second from the door. The copilot was a little more than six feet tall and bulged with muscles. His helmet covered most of his head and had a knob on its top that rode in a slot to lower the tinted sun visor when needed. The large knife in a scabbard on his left side was offset by the pistol slung tightly above his right hip. He gave the impression of a man one didn't trifle with.

With a snap of his hand, the crewman directed Gibbon to a web seat next to Kardell. Each was fitted with a helmet containing earphones with a mike to the side of the mouth. The copilot plugged the headsets into a jack by each seat and returned to the cockpit. In a couple of minutes, they were off the ground. The pilot rotated ninety degrees while level, and as the ship tipped forward to acquire forward speed Gibbon glanced at Kardell. His knuckles stood out like little white mountain tops as he grasped some straps on his seat. His eyes were closed tightly as his hair whipped in the wind from the open door next to him.

Gibbon reached over and shook Kardell's shoulder as he spoke. "Craig, can you hear me?" Kardell turned his head toward Gibbon and opened his eyes. The intercom was working. "Don't close your eyes, you'll get vertigo and barf. Look out the side of the chopper," Gibbon nodded toward the open door. "Look at the horizon so you have something that isn't moving as a reference for your stomach." In a couple of minutes, some color returned to Kardell's face.

Soon, they were cruising over open desert. A road passed beneath them and then a small town. There was a click on the headsets. "This is Chief Warrant Officer Jake Fergerson. I'm the pilot. As you boarded, you were met by our charming flight attendant, also my copilot, Warrant Officer Marlo Skradski who sometimes answers to Grog, but 'sir' is best." There was a short, heavy chuckle in the headset as Gibbon saw a fist shoot out and whap the pilot in the upper arm. "In case of an emergency," the voice continued, "don't wait for the oxygen masks to appear from above you. There aren't any. As soon as we hit the ground, which isn't so far away, get out fast, being mindful of the rotor blades—if we still have any. Now sit back and relax, it's going to be a long boring ride . . . we hope."

Gibbon saw Kardell was looking better. Kardell turned toward Gibbon and grinned. Keith could imagine what was going through his mind. Kardell's whole life had become a comedy, and the message from the pilot was part of it. Why not relax and make the best of it?

The noise and rhythmic vibrations of the aircraft were relaxing Gibbon as well. He leaned his head back, and it mercifully rested on a pad of some sort rather than metal structure. He closed his eyes to rest them and went to asleep.

0930 hours, Jubayl, Saudi Arabia

In his apartment, Hamoud figured he had enough information to send a message to Iraq. He had not found the aerosol can but had a strong hunch as to who had it. It took half an hour to write the message and encode it letter for letter using a one-time-pad. The system of couriers that he used was good, but not great. The message would be in the hands of the addressee in Iraq in a day or so.

After leaving the message at one of the drops previously arranged, Hamoud returned to his apartment. It was time to check in with the boys in the desert. Turning on his scrambled sat-phone he pressed the speed dial number for the tank platoon.

After twenty seconds, he got a response. "This is Uncle Fred."

"And this is Uncle Jack. The planned maneuvers for 20 September are still on. Will have final details 0700 tomorrow. Do you copy?"

"Roger, copy, final details 0700 tomorrow."

Hamoud hung up. He was getting a sadistic rush out of bugging those guys, many of whom would be dead in a couple of days.

— 22 —

1100 hours, 18 September, near KKMC

Gibbon awoke after two hours of fitful sleep. He moved around as best he could in the restraints to ease the stiffness in his muscles. Twenty minutes later, the Blackhawk settled down in a cloud of blowing sand. Captain Rebic walked out to the aircraft as the rotors came to a stop. Gibbon told Kardell to stay in his seat as he motioned Rebic to come up into the craft.

"Captain Rebic, we meet again."

"It seems we do. Keith Gibbon, isn't it?"

"Yes. This is Craig Kardell a UN chemical weapons inspector from Iraq. I'd like to speak to you, Captain, and Craig for a minute." After the pilots had gotten their personal gear together and left, Gibbon began, "First, I must ask if there are any personnel here that aren't strictly under your command."

"There aren't any. The men were getting an itchy feeling that something was wrong, so when they heard of your call we let the cooks go. We're clear on that score."

"Good, because his is scary business. Craig works for the Department of the Army as a civilian and is on loan to the UN as a chemical weapons inspector in Iraq. We may need his expertise as well as his position.

"Craig," Gibbon said turning to the man beside him, "Captain Rebic is a company commander in the Armor Corps. He's out here on a mission of some sort using M1 tanks that should be in a museum. Isn't that right, Captain?"

Rebic agreed.

Gibbon got up, "Okay, let's go. I have a story to tell you and some things to show that might start to make sense of this situation."

Gibbon grabbed his bag, and the three men headed for the buildings. They were offered iced tea as two officers joined them. There was a table and some folding chairs. Two fans kept the oppressively warm air moving. Gibbon began with a summary of how Breckon had gotten into the gantry robot project. He covered Breckon's trip to the site and what he found at the site, reading Breckon's first two messages at the appropriate times. He described the Iridium phone in Breckon's computer, the coding system, and that they knew the NSA had intercepted the communications. The location of the site caused the officers who had joined them to glance at one another and shake their heads in bewildered resignation. They couldn't believe someone could invent a story like this.

"That's the context into which I'll now put the hard evidence and my interpretation of what it means. We got a third transmission from the site." Gibbon read the first part of the third message and stopped.

Boyd was too involved to keep quiet. "Did you find the evidence?"

"I thought you'd never ask. We got it a few seconds before someone else would've grabbed it." The description of the pick up of the CD and the other evidence had them really wondering.

"This sounds like you've been reading too many spy books," interjected Rebic. "It's too fantastic."

Gibbon hoped Rebic was expressing healthy skepticism rather than falling back on rote procedures. "I'll admit that it's a lot to believe, so now let's look at the video."

Gibbon told them how the recording was made, that it recorded only if there was motion in the field of view. The first part showing the men setting up for the demonstration was nothing special. Then the lone man came into the bay, looked into the utility room, and looked right at the camera.

"Stop right there," Rebic snapped. He was getting a little pale. "I'm not supposed to divulge this, but most of us here know it anyway. That's the CIA officer who's been directing this operation."

Boyd and Denton agreed they had seen that man here at the base.

With a touch of alarm in his voice Gibbon slowly replied, "That's a turn I never expected. Let's watch the rest of the video."

When it was finished, Gibbon said, "That site is a couple of hundred miles northwest of here. I don't know what you've been told will happen on the twentieth, but let me read the last part of the third message." When he had read it, he continued. "It appears they plan to get their hands on one or more M1 tanks so that they can disassemble them. Whose tanks do you think they have in mind?"

Lieutenant Denton was on his feet and out the door. He returned in minutes with maps under his arm. He laid them on the table. "Where's that site?"

"Nukhayb," answered Gibbon.

"There it is," said Boyd.

Denton pointed at the border between Saudi Arabia and Iraq. "Look, this is the general area where we're supposed to have our little mission on the twentieth. Ninety klicks into Iraq perpendicular to the border is Nukhayb."

"Wait a minute!" Captain Rebic quieted everyone. "Why would they pull the captured M1 tanks to this place where they have this super secret site? Why risk the nerve gas project with the tank capture operation?"

"I've had more time to ponder this than you guys have," Gibbon replied. "See if this makes sense. They select a site for the nerve gas project that's away from the UN inspectors. But, they have to supply it. A lot of unexplained truck traffic into the desert would be noticed by intelligence gathering organizations. They need food, equipment, and building materials delivered to the site. So, they have armor maneuvers in the area, which means a lot of traffic. Next, they see U.S. tanks in the area. Only then did they get the idea of grabbing an M1."

Boyd broke in. "Think of it, they need trained technicians and tools to disassemble the M1s and that site is where they are. It's perfect."

"Plus," Kardell added, "if the UN did get wind of the site, the Iraqis would delay the inspectors getting there like they always do. They'd have time to seal off the underground operation. It's not likely we'd find anything."

"That's a possibility," admitted Rebic, who was deep in thought. "It leaves us with a lot of assumptions, though." He looked at Gibbon, "Can you get hold of this guy at the site?"

"No direct contact," said Kieth. "Apparently he has some freedom of movement in the bay with the gantry robots, but he's in real danger any place else he goes. Remember, he must be outside to send and receive messages. You want more assurance before you make decisions. I can understand that. Maybe the other evidence will help." Gibbon pulled the thermos bottle out of his bag and held it up. "In this canister is the prototype aerosol can that the engineer sent out with the CD. It has a slow leak. Don't ask how I know this, but I did not go to a governmental agency. In case it started to leak more, we won't open the canister in here. We need a large open area with the wind blowing away from any habitation and a nerve gas sensor. Do you have one?"

"We've a couple of CAMs, that's Chemical Agent Monitor, and an M22. What are you proposing?"

"What's an M22?" asked Gibbon.

"Sorry. That's an Automatic Chemical Agent Alarm. It's set upwind of places like a bivouac area to give an audible alarm if it senses chemical agents."

"Sounds good. We'll set up this M22 down wind and then open the canister. If there's a leak, there should be enough gas to detect with a CAM. If our assumptions are right, when we press the button there should be a lot of nerve gas."

They got together a complete NBC (Nuclear, Biological, Chemical) protective suit, both CAMs, and the M22. The five of them drove a mile to the south of the base in a HMMWV. The wind was from the northwest so this was safe. As Boyd donned the NBC suit, the others set up a crate to be used as a workbench. When everything was ready Boyd took the canister and the sensor to the crate and the others moved up-wind.

Opening the canister, Boyd 'sniffed' inside it with the sensor and gave a positive nod that he had sensed nerve gas. Boyd set the can down on the bench, removed the protective cap, and carefully pressed the button. There was a short burst of visible mist and then clear gas. They could all hear the hiss of the can emptying as Boyd used the sensor to test the air near the can and then farther away. The M22 had been set up a hundred meters down wind. After several seconds, its loud claxon could be heard with the chemical agent warning.

After forty-five seconds, the hissing gradually decreased to nothing. Boyd sensed near the can with the CAM and then walked down wind fifty feet continually sensing the air. Satisfied it was all clear he returned to the others and took off his gas mask, hood, and gloves. At this time, the M22 stopped its cry of danger as well. "That was the real thing, no doubt at all," Boyd said in disbelief. "That little can of gas could kill everyone in a movie theater, or worse. And, that's no battlefield weapon, that's clear."

Denton had a catch in his voice as he said, "I've got a can just like that in my bathroom at home."

As they drove back to the base, Captain Rebic was torn. The evidence was good, but was it good enough to risk what he was considering?

When the five somber men were seated in the meeting room, Rebic stood in front of them and began. "What do we have? Somebody can obviously make products, which, if randomly placed in stores in sufficient numbers, will kill many people, and in the process shut down the U.S. economy. We know to a fairly high certainty where the site is located. We know we have been ordered to intercept a deliberate Iraqi incursion into Saudi Arabia in the same area. We have some certainty they plan to be disassembling some of our tanks on the same day as this incursion.

"It seems almost certain that the CIA, or at least one rogue officer, is involved. I can't tell the CIA guy we have a movie of him in a secret facility in Iraq. How far up the line do these rogue officers go? What happens if we alert senior army brass? They will probably say this is a covert CIA operation, and it's our job to follow orders. In any case, what proof will we have for them? What proof do we have for ourselves in the final analysis? We can only look this guy in the eye," he nodded toward Gibbon, "and make our own assessment if he's telling the truth. I tend to believe him."

Everyone in the room felt the uncertainty. It was one of those terrible situations where there were no easy answers to a vitally important question.

History often pivots on some small act or comment made by an individual. Maybe it was the timing or the tone of the voice. When Lieutenant Art Denton opened his mouth to speak, he didn't intend to drive historical events, just voice his opinion. "I, for one, don't want to have one of those things go off in my house. I vote we do something rather than let some pencil-pushing screw-up sit on regulations and in the process kill our families. Ninety klicks is a piece of cake. We can do it." At that point, the mood changed.

Kardell spoke for the first time since the demonstration. "I agree we must act, but how do we justify invading a foreign country with no orders, no declaration of war?"

Captain Rebic had made something of a study of such questions ever since he had been introduced to the U.S. Army booklet *Field Manual 100-5, Operations,* commonly referred to as *One-hundred-dash-five.* This was the U.S. Army's guide to fighting wars. It emphasized speed as well as independent thinking by of the commanders on the ground. It was designed around the M1 tank, or the M1 tank was designed for it. In any case, the M1 tank better than any fighting machine in the world made its implementation possible.

One-hundred-dash-five stressed that once the battle was joined, all national boundaries disappeared and a battle in depth followed. Armored units were to strike deep into the rear of the enemy, disrupting the enemy's ability to marshal second and third attack waves. It emphasized striking hard and dispersing before the enemy had a chance to counterattack, and then striking again where least expected, keeping the enemy's responses uncoordinated and ineffective. It centered on large-scale armor warfare, but it also applied to small-scale operations. Especially in the latter case, there was emphasis on *audacity*.

Captain Rebic looked relieved, as if a huge weight had been removed from his shoulders at the change of attitude he sensed. He smiled and replied, "We've *FM 100-5* to cover us there. We have been ordered to intercept the Iraqis on the twentieth. That we'll do, and from the point where they fire the first shot all bets are off." He explained briefly the meaning of *One-hundred-dash-five*. He didn't mention that he might be taking slight liberties with it by striking deep into a sovereign state because of a small border skirmish. But, he did emphasize correctly and in some detail, the meaning of the section in Chapter 7 on "Audacity in the Attack"—attack where and when least expected.

Lieutenant Denton slapped his hand on his knee and said, "I'll be darned, we've been training for this operation ever since you took over the company!"

It was now 1600 hours, and Gibbon wanted to get back. He asked Rebic if he could give him a lift into KKMC where he might get some transportation back to Jubayl. Kardell decided to stay and be a part of the operation. After the weeks of frustrating failures to find evidence against the Iraqis, this looked like his only chance to do something important. There was also the appeal of being counted among a closely-knit band of warriors. He saw it as an honor he could not refuse.

Rebic turned to call one of his men when Gibbon asked if he could drive him. Getting the message, Rebic said, "I'll drive. Maybe I can get you a ride on a truck, and you won't have to wait so long."

When they were on the way, Gibbon tuned to Rebic and said, "What I am now going to tell you is between you and me. Can I trust you to keep it that way, not only for the next few days, but forever?"

Rebic considered the offer for a few seconds. He decided that whatever else Gibbon knew, he had to know. "Yes."

"The five of us in that room have seen the video, and the gas demonstration. You've heard what I had to say. If you proceed to attack the site as part of the border skirmish, an inferno will be let loose. Even if you manage to save your skin from the bullets, you might end up being killed by assassins for political reasons. That includes me too. Everybody from the CIA to the KGB to the UN to the Iraqi military will want to know how you knew about the site. The question is, how do we stay alive?"

Gibbon proceeded to describe how Harris intended to rescue Breckon. "We need you guys to get there before the plane lands. In the time they're on the ground to pick up Breckon, they will almost surely need covering fire."

Rebic drove in silence for a few minutes then said, "What we need is air cover. If we start blasting away deep inside Iraq, they'll violate the no-fly zone in a heart-beat."

Gibbon smiled. "If things work out, you'll have that. Don't ask how I managed this, but before I leave I'll give you an envelope with some instructions, frequencies, and call signs in it. If you need air support, don't be bashful. Call it in."

They drove in silence again. Then Gibbon continued, "If they do plan to capture an M1, and you do thwart the attempt, they'll know their security's been compromised. They can find the leak by starting at their end, the sending end, or with you, the receiving end. This could ultimately put every man in your unit in danger as they try to squeeze out of you where you got the information.

"But, if you also attack the site, it might look like the battle in the morning was a false start, and the U.S. force was part of a UN operation going after the site all along. After it's finished, however far it goes, you must convince Kardell to put out the word that it was all based on information given to him by the UN. If they deny it, he could say they were protecting their sources. This moves the hidden world of the spooks in different ways."

After a few minutes of silence, Rebic said, "Keith, I'd sure appreciate it if you could confirm that the Iraqis intend to capture an M1 tank. If we don't plan for it and they attempt it, we're in real trouble. If we do plan for it and it's all a hoax, I could be in worse trouble. They could think *we* are trying to start a war by invading Iraq."

Gibbon looked straight ahead as the huge KKMC complex came into view. "I see what you mean. How should I inform you one way or the other?"

"Call that number I gave you and say you're Adrian Jackson again. Leave a message for me to call Adrian at home if it's a hoax, and to call him at the base if it's confirmed to be real. If I don't hear I'll assume you heard nothing either way."

Kieth nodded. "Consider it done."

Rebic pulled into what looked like a freight yard with trucks backed up to warehouses. They stopped at a building with lights on inside. Gibbon reached in his bag and gave Rebic the envelope containing the list of frequencies and call signs. As they sat in the stopped vehicle, Gibbon said, "There's one more thing we must discuss. The American pilot of the rescue plane and I went to a rich man in Kuwait for help. It's quite involved, but he owed me a favor. He's providing the rescue plane. He's helped a lot but doesn't want his involvement known. If you decide to raid the site and are successful, he'll help you get the word out if that's what you want." Gibbon continued with what information he thought Rebic needed.

Rebic shrugged. "There are so many uncertainties, it's hard to give that much thought now. But, I'll keep it in mind."

"Good, the coordinates where you'd land your helicopter if you want to make use of his offer are in the envelope I gave you."

Rebic had become friends with a Saudi officer in the time he had been in the area. This officer found a Saudi Army supply truck that left minutes after they arrived. It would be four hours by bus or truck so Gibbon was glad to get started as soon as possible.

As Gibbon bounced along in the truck on the road from KKMC to Jubayl, there was no conversation because the driver did not speak English. The gathering dusk made him introspective as he meditated on what he had done. His part in it was over. He would be safe as others were facing death. He prayed that as few as possible would die on both sides. The melancholy became more acute as he thought of how he would probably never know how the deadly drama unfolded.

Captain Rebic mechanically guided the Humvee around the worst of the holes hardly aware of what he was doing. His mind was racing, trying to put all the information he had received in the last several hours into perspective. It occurred to him that Gibbon could be the one setting him up, but if his information on the battle of the morning was accurate, it would go a long way in dispelling that worry. One thing he had decided, he would deploy every last man to the west along with stores of food, water, ammunition, and fuel. Logistics would be a concern, but the short duration of the operation made that part of the mission feasible.

They had two five-ton water trucks, a five-ton fueler, and a HEMTT fueler (Heavy Extended Mobility Tactical Truck) pronounced, *hem'it*. The normal HEMTT was an eight-by-eight wheeled recovery vehicle that could tow anything in the army inventory except the M1 tank. The fueler version had the entire back of the vehicle replaced with a twenty-five thousand-gallon fuel tank. Rebic's HEMTT was presently deployed at the forward base.

Doing some mental arithmetic, he figured he had the equivalent of twenty-five vehicles, with the Blackhawks and support vehicles. They all used JP8, a fuel closely related to diesel fuel. Here was where the army's one-fuel policy really helped. An M1 consumed fifty gallons of fuel per hour and there were fifteen. That's 750 gallons per hour. So, he figured a thousand gallons per hour at top ops tempo. After topping off the vehicles at the forward base, the HEMTT would be sent to Ar'Ar to be filled. This would handle the fuel requirements. All the tanks and Bradleys were kept loaded with ammo, and they had five hundred extra rounds of 105 at the forward base.

He had a dozen different things spinning around in his head as he lurched the Humvee to a stop at the maintenance shed. The company first sergeant, Jonathan Hitchcock, approached, and Rebic said with his first breath, "We'll pack up what we can and deploy everyone to the forward base."

The sergeant gave a knowing smile and replied, "Give us another half hour, and we'll be on the way. We got together and came to the same conclusion."

"I like the way you think, John. I don't know what I'd do without you. Carry on." Rebic watched the solidly built six-foot-four sergeant stride away with a bearing any four-star general would envy. If he said half an hour, he meant it. Any company commander relied heavily on his first sergeant. The officers were concerned with operations and tactics. The sergeants and especially the first sergeant handled the housekeeping, as it were, everything from food to tents to daily reports, or as they would say "the beans, bullets, and Band-Aids."

The convoy departed soon after sundown. There were nine M1s, a Bradley, an M88A1 tank recovery vehicle, a water truck, a parts truck, and two Humvees. Already at the forward site were the other six M1s, a Bradley, an M88A1, a water truck, a parts truck, the HEMTT fueler, a

Humvee, and the two Blackhawks. Because there was no moon, going was slow. Seven of the M1s took off ahead since they burned the same amount of fuel regardless of their speed. They could travel thirty miles per hour since the drivers had a night vision system in their view port. Two M1s were left with the convoy under the command of Lieutenant Boyd to ride shotgun. This group of vehicles averaged closer to fifteen miles per hour in the dark. Part of the time, they used gravel roads going in their direction. They stopped at midnight and slept until dawn. Tired men sleep anyplace. Most slept in their combat positions. The M1s pushed on and arrived at the forward base before sunrise the morning of September 19th.

1830 hours, deep underground in Iraq

Breckon sat at his computer terminal in the utility room. He had part of the control program on the screen but his mind was far away. He knew his time was growing short. Mohed could see the system was working better every day. Any time they could decide it was good enough and his services were no longer needed. To stay at the site seemed like certain death, so escape was essential. A faint chance was better than none. The only alternative was to walk out some night and head southwest based on Harris's information on where this facility was.

He decided to make his escape on the twentieth, hoping the project with the tanks would cause a diversion. What he needed was a chance to get outside and send a message to Harris telling his plan. He had decided, if nothing else were possible, to take his computer and send a message shortly after he left saying what he was doing.

He absentmindedly rubbed his left arm in an attempt to ease the ache from a bruise he had gotten the morning before from Shahid during their now routine "frolic" in the sand. The systematic teaching of the first several mornings had gradually turned into a grudge match. By now Shahid had to know that Breckon was a novice. What could he prove? In addition there was that particular move he tried every day when he would throw Breckon so he landed on his back. Then Shahid would berate him for not countering the move as he had been shown. But Breckon was sure that he did it as he had been taught. He was beginning to think he had been deliberately shown wrong, yet he had no idea what else he could do.

The door opened and Breckon was snapped out of his mental digressions to see Mohed. He nodded and said, "Good Morning."

Mohed nodded in acknowledgement, as a second man followed him into the room. "This Sergie Musatov. He would want discuss robotic manipulators. I say to him work good, but he still push on seeing for his self. Wants talk with you."

As he rose from his chair, Breckon saw a bear of a man smiling slightly as he extended his hand. Breckon took his hand and was immediately given a hug. This was the Russian of course. He had a strong frame of six feet, or a little more. His face was Slavic with pronounced features. He was a study in black hair. His black bushy eyebrows, mustache, and beard assisted the black bush on his head, with a symmetrical stump in the center of it all that passed for a nose. His teeth were even and white.

"Well, Mister Ed Breckon," he said with a thick but understandable accent, "I have looked forward to meeting you. Mr. Mohed, we shall be all right. If you have other things to do, we can get along by ourselves."

Mohed looked uncomfortable since he was well aware the Russian wanted him to leave. "Okay, the workshop is place for me for small time."

Breckon was not pleased with the situation either. The last thing he wanted to do was spill his guts about the special programming he had worked so hard to perfect, especially to a Russian.

When Mohed left, Breckon steered the discussion to a problem he had experienced with the manipulator arms. Breckon took the Russian up to the control room and showed how it worked in manual mode, pointing out the jerky motion of the manipulators. He took him out into the bay and showed him where he thought the problem originated. He stressed the need to get this corrected. Breckon did not mention that his programs could compensate for this problem.

The Russian quickly traced the problem to the elbow joint. There were carbon filament "tendons" connecting hydraulic actuators in the upper arm, one for the "biceps" and the other for the "triceps," to the lower arm. The tension on the tendons was set too high. Built-in fittings permitted these points to be adjusted, so the problem was quickly fixed.

Breckon could tell Musatov was getting frustrated at being steered away from discussing the control strategy, but luckily Mohed returned. Breckon looked at him. "Ashrof, it's nine-thirty, suppose we could get a cup of coffee?"

Mohed nodded and led the way. When they were seated, Breckon addressed Musatov. "You came a long way to see your manipulators. I'm happy to say that other than that one small adjustment we made on the elbow joint, they're performing very well."

Musatov nodded and excused himself to go to the latrine. As soon as he was out of ear shot, Mohed said in a hushed voice, "You know this Russian?"

Breckon answered, his voice barely above a whisper. "No, the manipulators came from Moscow, and his name appeared on the documentation that came with them. Why is he here?"

Mohed replied, "He here for plan up in hangar with big tools, lift heavy things. He wants learn down here too. Not good. Must put him up in hangar," he said pointing up. "How do that? You help? His boss, General Majeed, bigger rank to Colonel Basheer, so order cannot do."

This looked like an opening to Breckon, though he could not see how exactly. "You brought him down here. What can I can do? But if he's down here much longer, he'll take the tarps off those other machines. There'll be no secrets then. He may even grab the computers from the gantry robots and walk out with them. Then you'll have nothing."

Breckon had said this to appeal to Mohed's worst fears, and it was working. "Not me bring him! He say he come, not possible to stop. What we do?" Mohed had hardly sipped his coffee as he fidgeted with his mug. "If work goes wrong, I blamed."

"Find a reason why we both have to be up in the hangar. If something were to go wrong with the wiring you would need me to fix it. Then someone could insist that the Russian should not be down here alone."

Mohed glanced up. "He come now. Stay busy by him. How I make something wrong?"

"Pull the wires off something, break something, anything."

As the Russian approached Mohed said, "Mr. Musatov, I leave for some time. Be with Mr. Breckon." With that, Mohed was gone.

When Mohed appeared at Colonel Basheer's quarters, he was out of breath. He told Basheer his concerns, and asked why Shahid was not watching over security. Basheer responded that the general had commandeered Shahid for the tank project. They could both see that the subterranean project stood a good chance of being ruined by this general.

"I agree with your plan. First go into the hangar and break something. Then bring them both up here to see me. While I'm talking to them go back and lock all the rooms associated with the can project. After that help Breckon. Make sure he takes all night fixing things in the hangar. Maybe the Russian will get tired and go someplace to sleep."

When Mohed entered the hangar, it was deserted except for two men in the southwest corner. He made his way unseen to the opposite side of the bay. From his experience working with Breckon, he could see that the temporary wiring for the hoist and special lights was a sloppy mess. It was not hard to peel back the electrical tape from some of the hastily twisted together wires and short them to other wires. The electrical arc sent a shower of sparks flying. It also caused a funny sound in a nearby electrical box, as well as making some lights go out. This was immediately followed by an angry shout and footsteps in Mohed's direction. Mohed faded back into deep shadows and stood motionless.

The men discovered the problem and headed to the offices on the west side of the hangar. For the next five minutes, there were intense discussions between General Majeed and the men. Colonel Basheer soon showed up and upon learning of the problem generously volunteered his electrical engineer and Mohed to remedy the situation so the general's men could get a good night's sleep. After some hesitation, the general accepted the offer.

Mohed found Breckon and Musatov in the control room looking over some flow diagrams. Breckon looked up with an expression that said, "What took you so long?"

"Breckon," Mohed said out of breath, "very bad trouble with wires in hangar. Colonel Basheer order you help fix it up. Get tools. Come now. Mr. Musatov, you request come too."

When the three arrived in the hangar, Mohed looked at Basheer, who gave a small nod in return. Mohed disappeared immediately. There was a moment of confusion as to why Musatov had been summoned. This left Musatov with nothing to do. After a time, the Russian left.

Breckon was surprised by the changes in the hangar. Two huge tracked vehicles stood near the offices. Located in the center to make use of the highest part of the arched roof was the hoist attached to a monorail that had been under construction the last time he was here. The structure was now complete with stairs, platforms and hand railings, lights, and power tools. It straddled an intact Russian tank. They could lift parts off a tank and move the hoist over the bed of a waiting truck set at right angles to the movement of the monorail. On the far side of the bay were two large trucks made for hauling heavy construction machines. These had been fitted with frames over which canvas could be pulled to shield the load on the truck from blowing sand and prying eyes.

Part way across the bay Breckon stopped in surprise, not at what he saw but what he didn't see. The hole in the floor through which they had lowered the gantry robots was gone. The new concrete blended in with the old leaving no trace of the hole.

Mohed showed Breckon where the wires had "accidentally" touched each other. The wiring was truly a mess. "Colonel Basheer say you spend all night to fix. After shift done, go to quarters. Stay in there."

The two men walked across the hangar and said something Breckon did not understand. They were either Germans or Russians. It appeared they had been told the plan of repair and seemed to be watching to see if Breckon knew what he was doing. Their eyes had bags under them the size of canned hams. After a few minutes, it seemed they weren't terribly unhappy this had happened. They walked away talking to each other.

"I think they sleep now," Mohed said with relief in his voice.

The short circuit Mohed had caused had blown two of the three fuses in the temporary three-phase distribution panel. It didn't seem like too hard a job to fix it if there were spare fuses. Breckon made a point of tracing the wires to the various branch circuits so he could see what these guys were doing. At one place, he saw a table with drawings showing exploded views of various parts of a tank. All the notations were in what appeared to be Russian. There were circles with characters in them that probably indicated the sequence of disassembly. Other documentation left no doubt this was an M1 Abrams tank.

After an hour of checking these other circuits, Breckon sent Mohed to look for replacement fuses in the storage tube below. When Breckon had packed up his tools, he had taken everything out of his computer bag except the computer and put in other tools. He made a point of having wrenches, multimeter leads, and other such equipment sticking out of the bag. Now there was no other way. He had to go to the generator room, and from there outside to send his message. His heart was pounding again. He wanted to add something about the tanks but couldn't risk the time. His message was coded and ready to send.

Using the same procedure as before, He opened the door and quickly stepped into the pocket. The air was warm, but it was the harsh wind that surprised him. As he walked out of the pocket, sand stung his face, but mostly he seemed to get lungs full of dust with every breath. There was no moon, and he could see only the brightest stars.

Sitting down he crossed his legs Indian style and opened his computer. The display was terribly bright in the total darkness. He reduced the brightness as fast as he could, hoping it had not been seen. He sent his message. After a quick look around, he started to down load. It took several minutes that seemed like hours. He got the latest message from Harris and was closing his computer when he heard a voice raised in a stern command. He could not see the source of the voice. Closing the computer he got up and moved quickly toward the pocket. A louder shout followed, and Breckon ran as fast as he could. In the pocket, it was totally dark. Out of the direct wind, he could hear footsteps approaching. He felt for the door, wrenched the latch, opened it, and stepped in. As he closed it, he felt a resistance on the latch. The man on the outside was trying to open it. It was a tug of war. Breckon could hold it with both hands. But, if he tried to use one hand to get the pin from his pocket, his pursuer would gain the upper hand.

Finally, as he felt the opposing torque lessen, he took one hand and grabbed for the pin. The moment he had it out of his pocket his opponent gave a sharp twist. The pin flew as Breckon used both hands to slowly force the latch back to the closed position. "Darn the luck!" Breckon whispered. "Now what do I do?" Using his knee to help hold the latch, he grabbed a screwdriver from his shirt pocket and slipped it into the hole. The guy on the outside rattled the latch a few times. Realizing what had happened, he went away. Safe for now! The light was not good, but he could not risk turning the light on. After a frantic search in the shadows hoping he wouldn't put his hand into something poisonous, he found the pin, and replaced his screwdriver.

Breckon grabbed his bag and hurried back to the area where he had been working. As he got to the area lit by the few overhead lights he saw he was covered with sand. His clothes, skin, and hair, were covered with it. He had to think fast. It looked like while sweeping up workers had swept sand and other debris under the scaffolding that surrounded the T-72 tank. There were some wires in the same space. Breckon dove under the cross braces and after grabbing around for the wires pulled them up out of the junk as if looking for a bad splice.

"What you doing?" came the familiar voice of Mohed. Breckon let out a slow breath. It had been too close.

"In a minute." He finished wrapping some electrical tape on a wire junction that needed no additional tape. He slid out on his belly, turned on his side, and managed to get sand pretty well all over himself. When he was beyond the bracing, he got up, all the while slapping the dust, dirt, and sand off while making sure plenty of it fell on his computer bag. "There was another short in the wiring that I couldn't find, and, wouldn't you know, it'd be in such a dirty place. The jolt when you crossed the wires sent a surge through the circuit. It shorted there too." That wasn't what happened, but Mohed accepted it. Then Breckon asked, "Did you find any fuses?"

Mohed produced a dozen fuses that were the same size as the blown fuses and said, "Not look like ones that broke inside."

"Yes, I see. The numbers are the Amps, but we don't know if they are slow-blow, or fast-blow. We'll have to try them." The replacement fuses seemed to work well enough, so they spent the rest of the shift tidying up the messy wiring. At five-thirty, they called it a night. Breckon grabbed his computer bag, and they went to the bunker below. Mohed made sure Breckon went directly to his quarters.

— 23 —

Back at his bunk, Ed Breckon had a gnawing feeling ever since he had gotten in from sending the message. It finally occurred to him what it was. It would be hard to escape with Arab soldiers around. He had been spotted sitting on a sand dune in the middle of the night with no moon and sand blowing. And, from now on they'd be extra alert.

He opened the back pocket of his bag and took out his computer. After cleaning off as much sand as he could, he turned it on and decoded Darin's message.

September 16, Wednesday

Hi, Ed. Hope you're still hanging in there. We have a plan to get you out, but sorry to say it's a mite risky. But stay with me. We'll make it work. We found the evidence you sent out on the container, and it's dynamite. We used this to get help from a rich sheik in Kuwait. A long story. In fact, I'm writing this at his estate. The sheik has instruments that verified the can you smuggled contains sarin nerve gas as you suspected. Through the sheik, I've gotten the use of an Antonov AN-2. That's a big biplane like the one you described flying to the site on. They're common in this part of the world.

There'll be a twenty-seven-year-old Arab man with me. How he gets involved is part of that long story. The AN-2 is complicated to fly. He'll help me or visa versa. We'll arrive at exactly six-twenty-five on Sunday evening, September 20. We'll make it look like we're having engine problems and land as close to the hangar door you described as we can.

Breckon threw back his head and moaned. "And I sent him a message saying I intend to walk out shortly after midnight that same day, eighteen hours before he plans to be here." This business was getting harder all the time. Now what to do? Change plans and wait for Darin? What if Darin changed plans and decided to look for him along the road? He closed his eyes and sat for a few minutes, then read on.

> We think we can be on the ground five minutes without getting into trouble. Ali, that's the Arab guy, will get out of the plane and check the engine. If anyone comes out to the plane Ali will stage a fit saying the dumb airplane isn't working. We know this is the no-fly zone of southern Iraq so I don't suppose you get many planes landing there. This may put them off balance.
>
> For the second part of the plan we're going on the footnote you added to your last message about the tanks. Keith Gibbon knows there are some M1 tanks south of your area in Saudi Arabia. We figure it may be one of those M1s the Iraqis plan to capture and disassemble. Tomorrow Keith will talk to the commander of the tanks. The two met by accident some time ago, another pretty long story. Gibbon will show him the evidence and try to convince the tank commander to make a dash across the border to Nukhayb to provide covering fire for us when we land. You mentioned the locals will probably kill you instantly in the event of an attack, and we agree. That's why we'll come in first in the plane. The plan will be to have the tanks go in after the plane gets off the ground.
>
> If for some reason we don't arrive, or you can't get to the plane, there may be a second chance. That is, there will be a second chance if Gibbon convinces the tank commander to declare war on a foreign state. Might be a big if.
>
> Well, Ed, this isn't the best plan, but it's the best we could do. We'll be there. Good luck. Darin

After reading the message several times, Breckon sat back. They had no idea how risky the plan really was. And worst of all, now he would probably be the cause of Darin and the Arab guy getting killed or captured. His conscience ground down on him like a millstone. He lapsed into self-pity, thinking it would've been best if he had never sent any messages. Now he had no choice but to wait for them. If he did not meet the plane, they'd stay on the ground too long for sure.

Though Breckon was tired, he could not fall asleep. It was as if his body were rebelling against sleep, having been jarred awake at eleven-forty-five every morning. That buzzer was on just long enough so there was no chance he could ignore it and get back to sleep. Twice he had disconnected it only to have it repaired when he returned. He imagined that whoever was in charge of keeping the system functional was well aware that he was not a Moslem and that it caused him pain. Through the simple performance of his duty, he could bring misery on an infidel. It occurred to him how common this was. Everybody did it at some time or other. Each day he tried to offer up the irritation for the times he had done nasty things to others. But, just as often as not, he ended up getting mad at the wretch pieces of camel dung, and his mortification lost its merit.

After being visited by this and a hundred other demons that tugged and pulled at his weary mind, shear fatigue finally pulled him into fitful sleep.

0705 hours, southwest of Ar'Ar

"Captain, message on the sat-phone," yelled the operator from the other end of the tent.

Rebic walked to where the radio operator sat and took the handset, "This is Uncle Fred."

"This is Papa Jack," said Hamoud "I have details for 20 September, are you ready to copy?"

Rebic grabbed a pad of paper as he knelt on one knee by the table. Pulling a ballpoint pen out of his breast pocket he said, "Ready to copy."

"On 20 September at 0600 hours, depart from coordinates 41° 45' east, 30° 54' north and proceed north by northeast keeping to low ground for thirty kilometers. The terrain will guide you. You will meet your party en route. Upon meeting, act as we discussed." After a pause, "Did you get that?"

"I copy."

"Papa Jack. Out."

"Well that was short and sweet," Rebic said to himself. Walking to the other end of the tent, he told Duke to get Art and Gene, the first and second platoon leaders. He got out the map board and found the coordinates he had been given. When the others arrived, he said, "Looks like this is the route they want us to travel to meet the supposed Iraqi raid into Saudi Arabia."

As they studied the map, it became obvious there was no place for an ambush until they were at the Iraqi border. Denton pointed to the map and said, "If we're coming north along this dry river bed as the orders say, we won't be in any trouble until we get a couple of kilometers from the border. Then the ravine is deep enough so we can't see much."

Duke interjected, "Look here. If they had a force behind the crest of this rise, hill 1165, on the east, and hill 1152 right in front of us, they'd have us in a cross fire." The hill tops were numbered by the height of their top above mean sea level.

"See," Rebic pointed to the area to the west of the route near the border, "here's a low area with rocky out-croppings. If we drove in there, our progress would be slow. We'd be sitting ducks. If they had some tanks or TOWs to the west of that, they could see us, but we couldn't close the distance to them. They'd remain at a range of two klicks. Perfect if they thought our wind sensors didn't work. We couldn't hit them, but they could hit us."

Denton pointed to a spot on the map and said, "This draw between hills 1152 and 1165 looks like it's passable. It's impossible to tell from the map, but it might appear to someone coming on the route we have been directed to use that there's cover between the two hills. I'd say that's the way we'd logically go."

Rebic shook his head, "If we only had time to recon the area, it'd probably be clear. That's probably why we didn't get the details of the operation until this late."

"Here," Denton said, putting his finger on the map between the two hills. "Here's where they've laid in antitank mines. If we went through here, the mines would take tracks off at least a couple of tanks. Then with the two forces from the hills converging on us, they'd have us in a killing zone."

Rebic took the lead in the discussion as if it were a routine exercise, rather than one that could easily be the end of them all. He asked the question, "Knowing what we do, and assuming they think we only have five or six tanks, what do we do?"

The three lieutenants put forth their ideas. Gene's was the most audacious. "If we assume they want to get us to go through here," he said pointing at the suspected location of the minefield, "they'll have sufficient forces to ensure that we do that. See this escarpment to the east running roughly southeast to northwest? If one platoon went way around to the east and came up the escarpment early, that platoon could see what was behind the crest of the two hills, and we'd know what to expect. As soon as the first shot was fired, they could shoot a volley at whatever was on hills 1165 and 1152. It's four to five klicks, but from a stand-still, somebody would hit. This would throw off their entire plan being outflanked this way. As soon as the platoon on the escarpment fired, they'd charge off to the west toward the force on hill 1152. Third platoon comes up from the southeast and attacks hill 1165. First platoon does whatever makes the most sense under the circumstances. When we strike, we don't want to be predictable."

The others considered Gene's plan. It had advantages and disadvantages. Rebic expressed probably the worst disadvantage. "This puts one third of our force a long way away, on its own, in Iraq. If you haven't noticed, the best place to come up the escarpment is likely to be here," he said pointing to the map with his pen, "a kilometer across the border."

"Who knows where the border is out here?" asked Duke. "I don't see that's a problem. If first platoon turned up hill 1165, it could join with third platoon coming from the southeast, and we could have *them* in a killing zone."

"Okay," Rebic said. "It's nearly 0800. Clean up and get some rest. At 1800 we'll get together and finalize the plan."

0730 hours, Petro plant north of Jubayl

Harris and Taryam had arranged that Mulla would pick up Darin at a store a few miles from the plant at eight-fifteen. At a little after eight, Harris left the construction trailer with a few drawings and his hard hat. A minute later, Gibbon followed. As Gibbon and Harris drove away, a Toyota pulled into the building site. At twelve minutes after eight, Gibbon stopped at the store and said, "Good luck with your mission. The party's on me after this is over and we get back home."

Harris gave Gibbon a worried smile and nodded. "You're on." With that, Harris opened the door and got out. As Gibbon turned the car to go back to the plant, he wondered if he'd ever see him again.

Immediately Harris was back into his mind-set for what lay ahead. He had sent home everything except a change of clothes and his computer.

He could not hang around this part of the world after the mission. He and Ed had to get back to the United States and get back into their lives to make it appear they were coming home from vacation like nothing happened. How difficult that would be had not been given much thought.

Hamoud parked at the end of a row of vehicles furthest from the trailers. He entered the first trailer and showed a police badge and was directed to the trailer in the corner of the three-by-four pattern of construction trailers.

Inside the corner trailer, Hamoud approached one of the Japanese technicians, flipped a local police badge and asked for Darin Harris.

The Japanese man took a draw on a cigarette and said, "Both he and the other American left with some drawings as if they were going to the plant, but they didn't go there. I saw them walking out to where the cars are parked. You should have seen them as you drove in."

The man's remark confirmed Hamoud had located Harris. He remembered the car driving out as he drove in and hurriedly ran out to his car. If he could spot that car, he'd have Harris. After a mile, he met a car going in the opposite direction. It had only a driver. That was the car. If it were coming back so soon, one of the occupants had been dropped off, and he could not be far away.

As Hamoud was a quarter mile from the first crossroads, he saw a gray sedan pulling away. Stopping by the store, Hamoud looked at the buildings on the four corners of the intersection. Harris could be in any one of them. Then he remembered the gray car. He swung his car onto the road and followed the car to the north. Grabbing his cell phone, he pressed the auto-dial button for the CIA. It was answered immediately. "This is 'delivery 5.' Have found Harris and am following him north on road from Jubayl. Car is gray, didn't get the number . . . . " A hiss on the line told him he had gotten out of the Jubayl cell range.

In the gray sedan, Darrin was unaware of his pursuer. "Ansari, nice to see you again," said Darin as he settled into the back seat.

"Nice to see you too. I've been doing quite a bit of chauffeuring for you guys the last few days. I hope everything works out for you."

"How much do you know about what's happening?" Harris asked cautiously.

"Enough. But don't worry. I wouldn't have my job if I couldn't keep my mouth shut."

They had been silent for some time when Mulla asked, "Would it surprise you if we were being followed?"

Harris carefully looked around. The rear window was tinted so he doubted if anyone could see him looking. "I can't be sure, but if that's a dented Toyota, it's the CIA agent who's been in our way for some time. We think he may be working for Iraq too. Can you lose him?"

"It would be difficult here. Once in Kuwait, especially if we go into Kuwait City, it will be easy."

"That's a good plan. I need to get to a large hotel where I could plug my computer into the Internet and check on messages from my friend. I could do it after we get to the estate, but the NSA would trace it to your employer."

"That would be fine. We can drive into the basement garage of a hotel. I have done this before in similar circumstances."

The car behind them stayed with them as they arrived in downtown Kuwait City. Mulla knew the streets and, after what seemed to Harris like aimless wandering, Mulla suddenly darted into the underground parking ramp for a large hotel. He opened his window and ran a credit card through a slot and the gate opened. Harris kept craning his neck to see if the Toyota followed. It hadn't. Mulla parked, and they took the elevator up to the lobby. Harris went to the front desk and asked if there was Internet access. After some discussion, he paid the clerk a hundred-riyal note. They seemed to have no problem accepting Saudi Arabian currency in Kuwait. "In the room across the way, there are several small cubicles. I have enabled number three for you," the clerk said.

As Harris headed for the room, Mulla said he would stay in the lobby and watch for trouble.

Realizing he had lost his quarry, Hamoud called the CIA office in Saudi Arabia again. He had his cell phone registered in Kuwait City since he came here regularly. They said they would make some quick calls, so stay on the line. Hamoud cruised up and down the main drag without spotting them. After five minutes, there was a voice on the line. "Harris is accessing the Internet from the Phoenicia Hotel located at the intersection of Ai-Hilali and Fahad Al-Salem streets. How far are you from there?"

"A block," Hamoud said, his voice portraying his excitement as he closed in on his elusive quarry. "Do you have a room number?"

"No, didn't have time."

"Okay, I'm there. Call you later."

Hamoud parked, jumped out, and ran into the lobby. Good, no customers at the front desk. Walking up, he asked, "Could you tell me if you have a Darin Harris registered here?"

After tapping on the keyboard a few seconds, the reply was, "No we don't."

Using a different name, is a sure bet, Hamoud thought. "Have you seen a young man maybe twenty-six, rather good looking, Caucasian, probably speaks with an American accent, come in here in the last several minutes? He may have asked to use the Internet."

"Yes, I did. He paid to use one of our Internet connections."

"Good. Where is he now?" Being this close, Hamoud could feel his palms sweating.

The clerk casually pointed across the lobby. "We have a room across the way where guests and their associates can use the Internet," the clerk said pointing to the room where Harris was. "He is still in there, I suspect."

Hamoud dashed for the room.

As soon as Mulla heard Harris's name mentioned at the desk, he slipped into the Internet room. There were six small cubicles along each wall with an aisle down the center. Each cubicle had a work surface and a chair along with the all-important jack where an Internet cable connected the properly accoutered people with the world.

Mulla touched Harris on the shoulder and in a hushed voice said, "We must leave NOW!" In one sweep, Harris pulled the Internet jack and the power plug out. With cables dangling, he was up and following Mulla out the far end of the room.

Hamoud opened the door in time to see the door closing on the far end. As he tried to hasten through the room, a dark-skinned man pushed his castered chair back and turned to talk with his colleague across the way. Hamoud fell head long over the man, and they both tumbled on the floor. There were shouts of pain and outrage. Hamoud helped the man up and brushed him off. Seeing the man was not injured, he turned and renewed his chase. Out the door and . . . nothing. Running down the hallway to the main corridor, he saw a down elevator door closing. It would go to the garage. He ran for the stairs, then stopped. Better to get his car and wait at the garage exit.

Turning, he raced out of the main entrance and ran the half block to his car. How could this be! He had taken a chance and parked in a NO PARKING zone. An officer was methodically filling out a ticket. Hamoud had a few things in his car that he did *not* want discovered. After two minutes that seemed like two hours, the police officer carefully tore off the slip of paper and placed it under the windshield wiper.

Hamoud walked to his car, took the ticket, and nodded to the officer while accepting a glare in return. He got in and drove to the next intersection. The light was red, and he was in the right lane with a car in front of him. As he waited, he saw the gray car roll through the intersection from right to left. The driver had seen him, he was sure, which meant he would take evasive action. When the light turned, he could not get into the left lane in time to gain pursuit. Lost him again!

"I saw our man at that last intersection stuck in traffic. He cannot catch us," Mulla said casually as if this was something he did every day.

Harris rubbed his forehead. "That was close. What would've happened if he had caught up with us?"

"Hard to say. Depends on what he wants," Mulla said with no emotion in his voice. "He might want to identify you, or capture you, or kill you. Just depends," was the answer. "He knew you were using the Internet, by the way."

"That means the Puzzle Palace is watching us in real time now. I hope the message I got from Breckon doesn't need an answer because we have to stop communicating by way of the Internet. Which means we can't communicate at all." Harris turned on his computer, put the random number code disk into the tray, and proceeded to decode the message.

September 18, 7:05 p.m.

Hi Darin,

Things are coming to a head here. I'm nearly done with my work. I've learned nothing more about the M1 tank thing. But, in the last few days it's like they've forgotten my project. I'm going on the assumption the tank operation is distracting them and will use this to cover my escape.

My plan is to walk out in the early hours of Sept. 20, like 1:00 a.m. It's quietest around here from then until six. I'll stay on or near the road heading south or southwest from here. If I can't get out on the twentieth, I'll try each succeeding day until I get out. Not much of a plan, but what else is there?

I doubt I'll get a chance to send this message until I am actually on the road. When I am some distance from the hangar, I'll send it. If you could manage some way to pick me up on or near the road, I'd appreciate it. If I should happen to send and receive before I leave, I'll take into consideration anything you might send.

See you sometime, Ed

Harris was speechless. Was the rescue plan to be for nothing? Maybe they should change the plan to be looking for Breckon along the road. He read it again. Harris assumed that since Breckon has sent a message his had been received too.

Later, when Darin met Ali, they discussed the message and agreed Ed would probably wait. A carefully planned rendezvous was better than a random hit-and-miss one, even if it was right under the enemy's nose. If Breckon did not meet the plane, they would scan the desert to the south with the thermal imaging headsets Ali's father had provided.

By 1:00 p.m., they were in the cockpit and learning to work as a team. The whole afternoon and into the evening was spent practicing flying, navigating, and landing. They landed and took off at all angles to the wind to learn what was possible with the plane.

1540 hours near Ar'Ar, Saudi Arabia

Tom Rebic awakened. Looking at his watch, he realized he had slept six hours. He had laid out a sleeping pad in the rear of the tent where they held their briefings. He was sitting on the pad with his forearms across his knees. Gene's plan was nagging him. He liked it the best, but if there were no ambush planned by the Iraqis, he could get into real trouble if a tank failed on the wrong side of the border. How much was he willing to risk? If he ordered them to use the plan, they'd do it. Even if he asked them to volunteer, they'd go. He knew he could order a different plan less risky for him, but more hazardous for them, and they'd follow orders.

Getting up, he slapped the sand off his clothing and sat on a chair by the table to study the map again. As he pondered the situation, a smile crept across his face. As tough as this deployment had been, he didn't even want to think of the problems he would've faced if he had women to deal with. Then, his stomach sank. This is what he lived for, the summons to battle, pitting his wits against the enemy, getting into his opponent's head. And, it would soon be gone because of that insane policy—doing social engineering experiments in the most deadly business in the world. It made no sense.

At eighteen hundred, they got together. "Charles, what's the status of the equipment?" was Rebic's first question.

"Fifteen tanks, two Bradleys, two Blackhawks, two M-88s are up. Support vehicles are up, with minor gripes, like always, but they'll go. Anything can fail at any time. They're ready as of now."

"Good. On the down side, I haven't gotten confirmation from inside the site at Nukhayb that the M1 capture operation is real." He sat silently for a long time. Finally, he decided not to ask for volunteers. It came down to a tough, fateful, command decision, his decision. "We'll use Gene's plan and assume there'll be an ambush. Gene, are you up to the long swing to the east, and the climb up the escarpment? It was your idea."

Gene responded in his laid-back manner, "We'll be there, don't worry."

They then went over the "Command and Control." This was the frequencies, call signs, way points, forming up points, and all the other critical information needed to keep everyone in the right place and on time. After that, the lieutenants went off to their individual platoons to brief their crews.

Craig Kardell had been in the background during the briefing, and now Rebic was alone with him. It was quiet except for the incessant flapping of the tent by the wind. They had the option incorporated into the plan for a later attack on the site. If they could get away from the morning's action in good shape, they would assemble at a point sixty-five kilometers to the west and five kilometers south of the border where they would refuel and rearm. They would depart at a time figured to get them to Nukhayb at 1825 hours. The two Bradleys and the HEMTT tanker would leave the base before dawn to arrive at the assembly point when the M1s did.

Rebic smiled at him. "Looks like this is where the rubber meets the road, or the tracks meet the sand, as the case may be. Are you up for the trip north if that's the way it turns out?"

Kardell looked nervous. "I see these eager young guys, and it bothers me. I've never been in combat but I've lived long enough to see how easily the simplest plans can go wrong. In a sense, it's refreshing to see their naive youth. I have a deep sense of foreboding. But, I haven't come this far to turn back—count me in."

1900 hours, Nukhayb, Iraq

Breckon was working on a computer program. Today was different in that his work was not on finishing the programming that operated the gantry robots, but setting up a super virus in the computers. Ashrof came in for a brief time, and they chatted awhile. Breckon told him it would take nearly the whole shift to complete the changes he was making before they could do more testing. Ashrof accepted this without comment and left.

The Russian had not been back to bug him. Tomorrow was the day they had planned to capture the tank. Maybe Musatov had his hands full. Breckon was relieved to be alone most of the time this night because his emotional state was not good. The anxiety he felt about Harris and the other man coming because of him was overpowering at times. His stomach hurt, his heart ached, and at times his hands shook so much he could hardly type. He repeatedly got up and paced around in the little utility room, rubbing his forehead, wondering why it had to come to this. He thought through the sequence of events from the start of the project. There had been many times when he could have done something differently, but he hadn't.

Shortly after being kidnapped, he felt anxiety, but there was always at least a little hope for the future. Now the plans were set, and he was helpless to do anything. He didn't want to die. He didn't want anybody to die. Unfortunately, as the earth turned one more time, it would drag him and everyone else towards a conclusion which could only end in the death of some and perhaps all of them. Breckon was young, and he, like most young people, normally didn't fear or even think of death. This night the thought of death was Ed's only companion. But he had things to do, and he hoped this would take his mind off the coming day.

The virus he was preparing was set to attack the system in twenty-four hours if he did not turn it off. If his escape attempt failed completely, he would be here in plenty of time to do that. The virus, when invoked, would proceed to write varying bit patterns on the hard drives again and again as long as the program ran. Because he had been planning this for days, he did not have much thinking to do other than getting the virus installed correctly.

In addition, through the night, he would make one CD containing the programs in their final state. After that, he would fill up the rest of the disk with more video that he had surreptitiously recorded since the demonstration. This disk he would encode with random numbers.

— 24 —

0200 hours, 20 September, near Ar'Ar, Saudi Arabia

The sand stung Lieutenant Gene Chatwin's face as he walked to his M1 Abrams tank. From its serial number he knew it came from the first year's production. He longed for a newer M1A1 with a 120 mm gun, and other enhancements. But one thing all M1s had was the thermo imaging sight (TIS). Through them the tank commander, the TC, and the gunner saw things by their relative temperatures. As a consequence, it didn't matter whether they were operating during the day or night. The imager using infrared, also did a better job in dusty or smoky conditions.

He gave the signal and turbines came to life in Red Horse platoon, his platoon's call-sign for the mission. The steadily climbing pitch as they spooled up always gave him a thrill. As they moved out, Captain Rebic watched from near his command tank. Chatwin gave a salute. In the starlight, it was just possible to see it returned. Chatwin would command four of the most formidable fighting machines ever built for the next ten hours. By the end of that time, they'd be refueled or be dead pieces of metal. The M1s burned fuel at nearly the same rate sitting at idle as they did at full speed. In a combat situation, engines were never turned off. That made the time inviolable. Chatwin knew where the fuel would be, and it was a long way from here.

This was a combat situation so they'd travel with a round chambered. The most potent round was the sabot, so he ordered, "Load a sabot."

Sean O'Brian, the loader, went into action. He moved his right knee to the right pressing on a hinged metal plate. This was the switch that opened the door to the magazine located in the bustle of the turret, on his right, that extended from waist to shoulder height. The heavy steel door opened on the left side of the turret and slid to the right. It revealed the butt end of twenty-five shells in the ready rack. The tank carried a total of fifty-five 105 mm shells, each weighing thirty-five pounds. On the base of each was written with grease pencil an "H" for HEAT, High Explosive Antitank, or "S" for sabot. The TC asked for a sabot so he pushed the base of a shell marked with and "S" in an inch with the gloved fist of his left hand. When he released his fist, the shell was forced to protrude from the rack four inches by a spring. Grabbing the base of the shell with his left hand he drew it out of the rack, and hit the switch with his knee again which instantly closed the sliding door. This kept the ammunition in a compartment outside the turret from where the crew sat. Turning the shell end for end, he guided it into the breach of the gun, then forced it home with his right gloved fist, knuckles up. He instantly drew his fist back to avoid the breach block as it automatically rose into place and locked.

When the loading was done, he moved his arms and legs out of the recoil path of the breach. He hit the safety button readying the gun to fire, and yelled "UP" into the intercom, telling the gunner it was ready to shoot.

O'Brian had arrived at KKMC with the first detachment. He thought of that first night on guard duty. It seemed to him he had matured a great deal in these weeks. Now he was off to battle, or so he imagined.

North of the Tap Line Road they separated into two squads of two tanks each, the normal platoon formation. In this formation, each squad member covered his mate and each pair covered the other pair.

Chatwin carried the AN/PSN-11 Precision Light Weight Global Positioning Receiver (PLGR) assigned to his platoon. For the next three hours, he ticked off one way-point after another, until a little before sunrise, they were driving along the escarpment. Even though sunrise was at 0555 hours this day, there was no sun to be seen. There was a twenty-mile-per-hour wind with higher gusts. A layer of dust in the sky filtered the light, giving the landscape a sickly yellow pallor.

Chatwin did not like what he was seeing. "Sean, this could be trouble. I don't see a way to climb that escarpment." The thirty-foot escarpment was made of sandstone carved out by flowing water in eons past. "It's that crest that'll give us the real problem."

The top few feet were nearly vertical. It was obviously made from a somewhat harder rock than the material underneath. At some places, the blowing sand had filled in at the natural angle of repose of sand nearly to the top. An M1 tank could climb a sixty-degree slope. Piles of sand, as one might see in a gravel pit, averaged fifty-degrees.

Having gone a half-mile past the place where they wanted to go up the escarpment, they turned around. Chatwin had his driver pull over near Red Horse 3 and motioned for him to stop. "Have Randy pick the spot he likes best in the next half mile of bank and get up it," Chatwin yelled.

"Roger," the commander yelled back. Chatwin could see the tank commander talking on the intercom to the driver as they started off with Red Horse 3 nearest the escarpment.

What the driver of Red Horse 3 heard was, "Randy, I guess you're it. Find the spot you like best and give it a try." Randy was reckoned the best M1 driver in Rebic's company. He could feel the tank's movement in his butt, he'd say, and knew from that how far he could push it.

Within a quarter mile, Randy slowed. He had his driver's hatch open, and wore goggles. "I'll do it here," he said over the intercom.

The turret was turned to the rear so the barrel wouldn't inadvertently scoop up dirt. He drove past the spot, and circled so as to come straight at the bank. From out on the level he twisted the motor cycle style throttle on his steering bar. He was going twenty miles an hour when he started up the slope. Nudging the throttle a little as he reached the hard pack, the tracks strained to gain purchase and pull the tank up. The angle became precarious. As it seemed the tank would fall over backwards, he killed the throttle and let it roll backwards. Shifting into reverse, he backed up and took another try. This time he got extra speed, and the tank got up to where the first road wheel went over the top. Randy worked the controls putting power to one tread, then to the other. He used this to scratch away at the hard pack. And then he was up.

"That was a great job, Randy," said Chatwin into the intercom even though Randy couldn't hear it. Looking at his watch, Chatwin shouted, "We should've given our report by now."

Third platoon, call sign Black Horse, commanded by Lieutenant Blatz, left an hour after Chatwin's Red Horse platoon. Whereas Chatwin was making a wide end around to the east, third platoon was to make a less wide sweep to come up from the southeast, protecting Rebic's right flank. The M88s, whose call sign was Chariot 1 and 2, stayed some distance behind Black Horse. The fifteenth tank, White Pebble, stayed with the M88s as a spare. It was crewed by mechanics.

At 0410 hours, Rebic in first platoon, White Horse, moved out with his six tanks. They had the shortest distance to go. Rebic had planned to

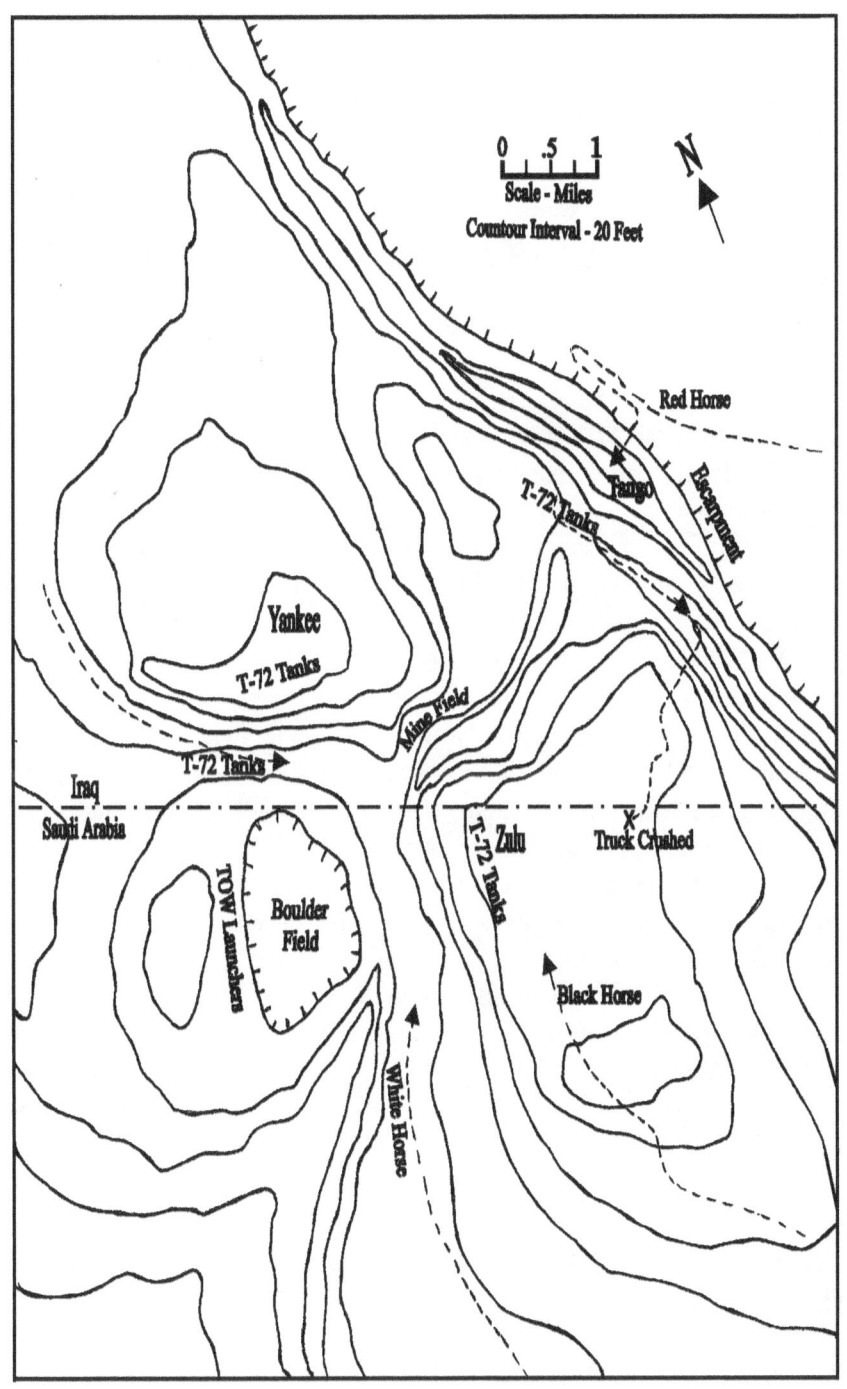

0 .5 1
Scale - Miles
Countour Interval - 20 Feet

N

Red Horse

Tango

T-72 Tanks

Escarpment

Yankee

T-72 Tanks

Mine Field

T-72 Tanks

Iraq

Saudi Arabia

X
Truck Crushed

Zulu

T-72 Tanks

TOW Launchers

Boulder
Field

Black Horse

White Horse

Order of Battle

cross Tap Line Road at the most likely place, planning to be seen in case there was anyone checking on him. As they approached the highway, they slowed down as was their practice. Scanning both ways, his gunner came on the intercom. "Heat image to the left. Possibly a stalled or stopped car, three hundred fifty meters."

"That'll be someone waiting to report that we showed up," said Rebic.

0525 hours on the Tap Line Road

Yousuf Hamoud had done his figuring and come up with the likely place and time the M1s would cross the Tap Line Road as they traveled to their starting coordinates. Every few minutes he used his single-eye, night-vision scope to look first to the west and then to the east. On a sweep to the east, he saw a dark object on the road that wasn't there before. Looking to the north of the road, he saw others. The closest one had the silhouette of a tank with no doubt.

"Well, that's great. Our good little soldiers are following orders like the robots they are," he muttered to himself. He got his sat-phone out, and set it on the front fender. He made sure the switch was turned to scramble, and hit the power button. He pressed the button to speed dial the phone he had left with General Majeed. It took three minutes, but finally there was an answer in Arabic.

"This is Vengeance One. Over." Standard radio procedure was a hard habit to break, though unnecessary here since the sat-phones had two-way voice communication.

"Vengeance Upwind here. Six tanks have crossed Tap Line Road at the point expected 0530 hours headed north."

"Copy, Vengeance Upwind. Out."

Well that was that. Hamoud decided he'd go to Ar'Ar and get some food. Then he'd wait for the call that he was sure would come.

White Horse arrived at the designated start coordinates fifteen minutes early. Everyone was glancing at the sky, wondering what this weather would bring. At 0600 hours, Rebic started out. It would take an hour to get to the suspected point of contact.

After forty-five minutes, Rebic realized they were making good time. Chatwin in Red Horse platoon should have given his report by now. Rebic needed to know if there were enemy forces on Yankee, the code name for the hill that would be in front of them, and Zulu, the hill on their right. Rebic slowed his platoon. He desperately wanted to contact Chatwin, but in keeping with the mission as given to them, he had to maintain radio silence. It's the way they had always operated. And, if he only had six tanks, why would he be making a call to others. Using hand signals, he motioned to the two tanks on his right to fall behind and go up the bank and have a look to the east.

He gave the signal for the other four tanks to speed up when they were half a kilometer away from the area where the bank on the left fell away to reveal the boulder field. The squad on the left had their turrets turned to the left waiting for the open area.

Then, Rebic's gunner called out, "Something coming our way off to the left front between the base of Yankee and the boulder field, four klicks." Rebic could not see what the gunner was seeing because the gunner was using his ten-power TIS. These were supposed to be the bad boys going to do mischief with the Saudi Arabian pipeline. Right on schedule. It also meant Rebic's tanks would be at the point where he could turn off to the right into the expected mine field when these tanks were one and a half klicks away. Good range for the Iraqis, and bad for Rebic if his wind sensors had not been working.

Rebic made the signal to button up. The driver normally operated with his hatch closed, using thermo imaging or normal light through his prisms as the situation warranted. Rebic was still standing in his hatch as he keyed his microphone.

"White Horse to all Horsemen, the fire is lit, the fire is lit." This meant they had sighted the enemy.

Sean O'Brian was in his loader's seat with his hatch closed. While Chatwin was concerning himself with getting his tanks up the escarpment, Sean was occupied with his own thoughts. He was feeling both elated and frightened. Hours before he had loaded a 105 shell that he felt certain would soon be fired in anger. In his mind, it was still in the abstract. Men had been in the armor corps for six, eight, and more years and never come to this point. Yet, here he was, a little past his twentieth birthday, a year and a half in the army, and it was happening to him. His fear was not abstract. It was real. These were live rounds to be shot at live people who would surely shoot back.

It had been drilled into him that the M1 was the best tank in the world. Through his training he had seen many pictures and even some film footage of M1s being hit by projectiles from Russian T-72s. The Chobham armor held. The crews had been safe. Nether he nor any of his buddies ever asked the obvious question. Are these all the pictures? Are there any you aren't showing us, like the ones that punched right through and killed the crew? It had seemed to be unpatriotic to ask that question. There was always a gnawing feeling in his stomach that it was all too reasonable. These tanks were not invincible. What *really* happened in combat? Had M1 tanks ever been in a punch-for-punch battle?

If his mind was refusing to accept the reality of the situation, the rest of his body was another story. They had stopped for a break at dawn. That was less than an hour ago and still his bladder felt like it would explode. He had heard stories of how men lost control of bodily functions in combat. That too had been abstract. Now it was less abstract. His stomach hurt, and his colon was jumping around. But, what could happen, his mind asked. After all, third platoon was off in a reconnaissance role and as a reserve.

Once above the lip of the escarpment, the land still angled up for a quarter-mile to the west. Chatwin wanted to get his entire platoon up before he showed himself above the crest of the hill. He had gone up after Red Horse 3. His driver made it on only the second try. Chatwin was normally laid back, but at the moment he was going crazy. It was taking too long. He held out his arm with his clenched fist and forearm vertical, and was pumping it up and down. This meant to speed it up.

The call he had been dreading crackled in Chatwin's headset, the call from White Horse. He looked back just as his third tank came up. He had no choice. Motioning to his left, he pointed the other two tanks forward in line with him spread out with fifty yards between the tanks. They inched up to the crest of the hill.

Sand was blowing over the top of the rise, but most of it was staying close to the ground. Using his eight-power binoculars, Lieutenant Chatwin swept both hills in a few seconds as the gunner swept the turret looking through his TIS. There were vehicles on both hills.

Rebic had no idea what had happened to Chatwin. Just then his gunner called out in an even voice, "Muzzle flash from the base of Yankee."

This was beyond the Iraqis' effective range. They were firing to get the American's attention.

Seconds later they were clear of the left bank. "Flash to the left beyond the boulders." came a call from the squad on the left.

Rebic keyed his microphone again and said, "This is White Horse to all Horseman, the pan is hot. I say again, the pan is hot." This was the code that meant the war had started and anything not American was a fair target.

Radio silence was no longer an issue, so Rebic, keyed his radio again. "This is White Horse. Red and Black Horse report! Over."

Chatwin had been expecting it, yet he jerked at the startling call from White Horse. The pan was hot, the war had started. In response to the call he transmitted. "This is Red Horse. Delayed by escarpment. Call it two sand burrs on both Yankee and Zulu. Out." Sand burrs were enemy combat vehicles in units of four vehicle platoons.

Blatz responded. "This is Black Horse. Lost our PLGR. Headed your way dead reckoning. ETA five minutes. Out."

By standard arrangement, the tanks on the left would take targets from the left, those on the right, targets starting on the right. Chatwin ducked into the turret and grabbed the TC's turret yoke as he swung the turret so the tanks on Yankee were in the sight. Into his helmet-mounted mike he said, "Gunner, sabot, eight tanks, right tank first." Bart, the gunner immediately switched the TIS from three to ten power, lased the target with the ranger finder and performed the G-pattern lay of the gun, and held on target waiting for the TC to turn over the gun to him for firing. O'Brian, the loader sat on the left side of the turret facing more or less across it. As soon as he heard the TC say "sabot," he knew he had nothing to do. He said "Up" into the intercom indicating the gun was loaded with the round requested.

"The pan is hot," he heard Chatwin tell the rest of the platoon on the platoon radio net.

"Fire!" said Chatwin too loudly.

"On the way," Bart replied, and he squeezed the trigger. *Wham*! The first round was on its way at more than a mile a second.

The breach opened, and the turret instantly filled with acrid fumes as the empty casing made its appearance. "Gunner, sabot, second tank from left!"

O'Brian flew into action loading a sabot. "Up." He'd know soon enough what would happen.

An instant later Chatwin said, "Fire."

"On the way." *Wham*! O'Brian assumed the other tanks were firing also, but with the noise in the turret and on the intercom he could not tell. His was the only position where he had no knowledge of what was going on outside. His main enemy at times was vertigo. With no outside reference, it was all too easy to feel is if the tank were tipping over.

"Gunner, sabot."

Like a well-oiled robot, O'Brian flew into action again, and had another round in the breach in less than four seconds. "Up!" he yelled.

The crews worked in well-practiced harmony. Through the hours and weeks of intensive training, a fraternal bond had developed among the men in each crew and between each crew and its machine. Men have a way of forming a psychological link with inanimate objects. It was this ligature of the crew and the tank that was a necessary element in achieving the final increment of performance necessary for survival on the ferocious modern battlefield. This was another abstract concept soon to be put to a hard practical test.

Rebic pulled his squad ahead of the left squad so the four tanks were in echelon left. This formation gave all four tanks a clear shot to the left without fear of hitting one another. Rebic yelled, "Gunner, sabot, APC, far left, fire!" This was the wrong round for a soft target like an APC, but that was the round in the breach. The gunner lased the target at two-point-one klicks, and said "On the way," as he squeezed the trigger. Almost simultaneously all four tanks fired. The orange muzzle flame from each 105 gun, larger than the tank, momentarily flared out the thermo imagers of the gunners. An authoritative *Wham* struck the inside of the tank, and the crew felt it rock to the right. At the limit of the recoil of the big gun, the breach was inches from the back of the turret. As it slid forward, the breach block automatically opened, and a twenty-five-inch-long brass casing slammed out of the breach hot and smoking. It filled the turret with the smell of cordite. Less than a second after the muzzle flair, the TIS was stabilized again and both Rebic and the gunner saw smoke and flame belch from the APC.

Rebic yelled again, "Gunner, HEAT, next target from left." A flurry of movement and "Up" came the reply from the loader. Rebic replied, "Fire!"

"On the way," from the gunner as he squeezed off another one. *Wham*, the sharp report of the gun a second time. The APCs mounted four TOW (Tube launched, Optically tracked, Wire guided) rockets each, so it was important to dispatch them as soon as possible. The most vulnerable part of any tank, the tracks, were open to their direct fire. The M1s were moving thirty miles per hour at full deflection to the TOW gunners. These rockets were guided all the way to the target by means of fine wires that spooled out of the back as they flew along.

There were six TOW launchers to the left of White Horse platoon, four were APCs and two were trucks. After the first volley, the M1s had taken out two of the six. After the second volley one remained. At two klicks to the side, with the M1s moving fast, it was a difficult shot for the M1 crews, but they managed well.

The T-72s on Yankee and Zulu held their fire to see if the attack on White Horse from the left and front would cause the M1s to head for the narrow pass that had been mined. The T-72s coming around the base of Zulu continued to fire, still out of their effective range.

Rebic's sat-phone was mounted on top of the turret to the left of the fifty-caliber machine gun. He flipped open the lid and hit the power switch. He grabbed the handset, and pressed the speed dial button to call Yousuf Hamoud. "Papa Jack, this is Uncle Fred. Over."

After five seconds came the reply, "This is Papa Jack."

"This is Uncle Fred. We're under heavy attack by a much superior force. Must have air support immediately. Over."

"This is Papa Jack, exactly how large a force?"

"This is Uncle Fred, there are at least twenty enemy tanks, I have already lost two of mine. Send support immediately! We're being cut to pieces. Must have support, or we'll all be down in minutes. Over."

"This is Papa Jack. Okay, I'll get some help on the way."

The hiss of the scrambled transmission was interrupted by a tick as Hamoud hung up, and the line went quiet. Rebic hoped that he had not stated the truth. He'd have to be good *and* lucky today not to lose both men and tanks.

Rebic's third squad engaged the T-72s on Zulu. It was two to seven, one having been taken out by Red House's first volley. Rather than charging in, they slowed almost to a stop. The sand sweeping over Zulu obscured the targets at times so they maneuvered for advantage. When the call came that the shooting had started, there was no choice but to attack. They came fast, taking on the lead tanks first. Suddenly they were the center of attraction with five tanks shooting at them. One of them scored. White Horse six lost his track.

"White Horse 1, this is 5. Where's Black Horse. I've one down."

"Black, this is White. White 5 and 6 are on Zulu among two sand burrs. What's your ETA."

"White, this is Black, have Zulu in sight. Must close to be sure of targets." The silhouettes of M1s and T-72s were quite different and seconds later T-72s started to explode.

At two point five klicks, Rebic's crews started to fire at the tanks coming from Yankee. "White Horse, charge right at them and pass through, speed to forty, watch for rocks." There were two platoons of Iraqi tanks coming at them from the front.

Then, quite unexpectedly, Rebic heard a call for help from Red Horse. Keying his mike on the company frequency he said, "Black Horse, if you can, give Red Horse a hand. Chariots and White Pebble, move in the direction of Red Horse. Stay out of contact. Out."

As it became apparent to the Iraqi commander on Yankee that the M1s weren't going to fall for the trap, he started firing at Rebic's platoon. Rebic had no choice but to take it in the teeth. The T-72s on Yankee were in "hull down" position which meant they had only the turrets of their tanks visible above the crest of the hill. "First and second squad, mow down the guys at the base of Yankee," Rebic yelled into his mike. The fire from the top of Yankee was not accurate, being at the limit of the T-72s effective range. The two platoons on the base of the hill were being reduced to rubble. Traveling at fifteen miles per hour and now nearly straight on, the T-72s were at a good range for the ten power sights of the M1 crews. All four of Rebic's tanks were intact as they passed through the burning hulks at the base of Yankee.

Two of his M1s had been hit, but the frontal armor was so formidable they were still in fighting condition. The sandwiched layering of the M1s special Chobham armor, though classified, was thought to be something like steel, then ceramic, then a gap, followed by uranium mesh, more steel and ceramic, and finally a steel shell forming the inside of the tank. It gave the equivalent of thirty inches of solid steel against the HEAT and sabot types of antitank projectiles.

"Continue around the base of Yankee, follow the tracks," Rebic ordered. He was concerned with the slope on the front of Yankee being mined. Rebic was wondering what had happened up on Zulu, and not a little worried about Red Horse. His crews were trained and well motivated. For the moment, he had no choice but to hope that was enough.

Coming around the west side of Yankee, Rebic turned up the north side. He was first met with two tank retrievers and several support trucks. Vehicles that could not inflict damage were ignored. A half-mile ahead were APCs. "Gunner, HEAT, four APCs left one first, fire," Rebic said. "Up" came the reply. *Wham*! Muzzles flared and vehicles burst into flames. Next came "sabot" as tanks came into view. One platoon of Iraqi tanks disappeared beyond the crest of the hill to the east, leaving the other platoon to defend the position. Shots were fired both ways. White Horse 3 took a hit in the doghouse, the rectangular opening on the top of the right side of the turret housing the sighting optics and the laser range finder. Another lost a road wheel to a T-72 shell. Eventually three of the T-72s were destroyed and a fourth disappeared into the blowing sand.

As the commander of two platoons of T-72s on Zulu was poised to fire on the rear of the M1s below and in front of him, he saw the turret explode on the tank to the left and forward of him. Turning to the right he saw muzzle flashes from a second Red Horse volley in the area of the escarpment. "What's this!" he yelled.

The Iraqi platoon leader's radio blared, "Commander, tanks on our left rear." The M1s to their front were forgotten as two more T-72s were hit.

"Vengeance four," his unit's call sign, "attack to left rear." In a second, he had gone from the hunter to the hunted. He was already down to five maneuvering tanks. Black smoke billowed from the diesels as the Iraqi drivers gunned their engines and wheeled around. The two White Horse M1s closed on the formation at high speed. One of the attackers spun around as its track was blown off. T-72s converged on it like a wounded animal. They didn't finalize their kill as Black Horse closed to where they could sort out the players. Shots were traded, but it was no contest. In seconds the T-72s were out of action. Partial seconds made the difference between living and dying. The speeds of the machines over rough terrain was so great and the munitions so lethal, only young, quick hands, and well-knit crews survived.

"Move out. Four abreast," Chatwin ordered on the platoon net. Red Horse 4 had moments before joined them.

Suddenly the driver yelled into the intercom, "Below the hill, a whole gob of T-72s up real close!" From their firing position the curvature of the hill hid what was in front and below them. A long sloping pocket ran parallel to the ridge. In the pocket, the Iraqis waited. The pocket was low enough so any M1s coming through the mined draw could not see them. Never suspecting anyone could get up the escarpment to their rear, the Iraqis had left no sentries.

"Gunner, sabot, Tank!" Having one in the breach Sean yelled, "Up." The TC talking on the radio was heard by the tank crew on the intercom so Chatwin keyed the radio and yelled, "Tanks up real close in front pick targets relative to your position. Speed up!"

Click. Chatwin switched off the radio so he was only on the intercom. "Bart, pick your targets and fire at will." Click, back to the radio. "Pass through the tanks in front and pick . . . . "

Wham! "Sabot."

" . . . pick up good speed. Second squad, peel off to the left, and go after what's to the south. First squad peel to the right. As we pass through and turn . . . . "

"Up," Sean yelled.

" . . . and turn, squads cover each other's back."

O'Brian knew this call. This was a tactic Captain Rebic had drilled them on at the company level. But in that case there had been three platoons, not two squads. As his squad went through the formation and turned to face the enemy on the right, the relatively soft rear of their tank would be vulnerable to the opposite flank with no one to cover for them.

When they saw the Iraqis, they were less than half a kilometer away. Having been alerted by the first shots from Red Horse, some were gunning their engines. Even using the three-power low-magnification sight, the Red Horse gunners were having a hard time sighting on a target. The close range and fast closing speed made a rapidly changing angle from the gunner to the target. This caused many misses. But even here, the M1 showed its superiority. The T-72 had a crew of three: commander, gunner, and driver. It had an auto loader. That saved one crewmember, but the system could fire only one shell every ten seconds. The M1 with a strong-armed young man could load as fast as three seconds. This was one time when they were loading fast. The M1s were giving two and three shots for each shot they took.

By the time Red Horse platoon passed through the Iraqi platoon directly in front of them, all four T-72s were out of action. Red Horse 3 had taken a hit to the front of the hull, but to no serious effect other than a huge dent in the Chobham armor. T-72s mount an enormous 125 mm gun and even though the technology of their sabot rounds wasn't up to that of the M1 rounds, they made up for it to some extent in size. They had hit the waiting company in the center. There was one platoon of tanks and two light trucks, mounting TOW launchers to the left, and two platoons plus command tanks with support vehicles further to the right.

Wham! "HEAT." O'Brian only had a few H's, one of which he loaded, "Up."

O'Brian heard click as Chatwin changed frequencies to the company net. "All Horsemen, this is Red Horse, we fell into three or four sand burrs, augmented, just west of Tango." This was the code word for the top of the escarpment. "Send help!"

Wham! "Sabot." O'Brian could feel the sweat running down his back. He was the only one actually doing physical work. He used the back of his gloved hand to wipe the sweat off his forehead and out of his eyes. Everybody was sweating, though. The smell of sweat, gunpowder, body odor, urine, bowel, mixed in the close quarters of the turret.

The 105 shells weighed thirty-five pounds, and O'Brian moved as fast as humanly possible, at times faster. He had never had to load so fast. He already felt fatigue setting into his forearms.

All gunners on both sides, most of whom were little more than kids, were over-eager and kept pumping projectiles into the sand and sky. The brass casings were clanging around in the turret and Sean yelled at Gene, "I have to open up and dump casings."

Chatwin nodded. "If we get artillery fire button up."

Wham! "Sabot." O'Brian didn't acknowledge Gene's comment as he went to work loading again.

The TCs hatch can be swung closed and then raised straight up eight inches giving the TC three hundred sixty degree viewing while keeping shrapnel from air-burst artillery off his head. He was in this position now. At this moment, first squad was turning to the right. Chatwin yelled, "Bart, there are two to the south that'll get you from behind. Get around and return . . . . ."

"Red 1, this is 2. We took a hit, but we're okay. Get those guys to the north."

"Red 2, this is 1. Can't, '72s to the south are after our engines."

Click. "Red 3, 4, this is Red 1. Cover our back. Red 2, can you get a shot at the guys behind us?"

"Red 1, this is 2. We're trying. We dropped a shell in here and it got buried under the empties." Red Horse 2 inadvertently left his mike keyed as his crew struggled with the shell. "What the . . . ouch! That empty's still hot . . . use the other hand . . . there, we're loaded. Oh! Sorry, Red horse."

Wham! "Sabot. You're going great, Sean. Keep 'em coming," said Bart in the intercom. "Don't drop any."

Chatwin saw a muzzle flare from Red Horse 2 who had the barrel pointing to the rear. A T-72 jerked up as its hull took a hit and split open. An instant later parts flew from the engine of Red Horse 2 as they took a hit in the rear.

"Red 1, this is 2. We're hit. Lost our engine. They'll get us for sure. Cover us."

"Roger, 2. Bart, get that guy!"

The turret was rotating so fast, O'Brian momentarily lost his balance and put out his foot behind the breach to balance himself. He grabbed a handhold and jerked his leg back a second before the gun lurched back.

"I'm on him." *Wham*! "Sabot." Exact procedure was being lost but the connections among the crew members as well as the crew to the machine were still intact. The seamless functions continued to flow.

"You got his track, but he can still shoot, get him again."

"Up!" *Wham*!

"Got him!" Click. "Red 2, you guys stay inside unless you must get out. Don't see fire, suppressant must be working. You're okay for a few minute . . . . "

Bang! The sudden concussion was overpowering, like standing in the middle of a lightning strike. O'Brian felt the turret lurch so violently he slipped off his seat and stumbled into the empties. Shouting and cursing, he half lunged and half fell back into his position with burns on his left wrist and arm. Chatwin had momentarily lowered his head as the shell hit. A piece of flying metal sent his CVC helmet tumbling down into the turret. Bart snatched it and handed it back. A few seconds later Chatwin yelled into the intercom. "Report!"

"Engine's up," followed by, "turret's up."

O'Brian whacked the switch for the ready rack panel with his knee. It operated normally. Ammo's up." O'Brian leaned back and hit something that hadn't been there before. He snapped his head around and saw the wall of the turret dented in. The armor had held, barely.

Chatwin didn't have time to be relieved. "Red Horse 3 and 4, this is 1. You're in too close," Chatwin yelled into the mike. "Get your frontal armor toward them and put it in reverse. Get out of there."

After the second squad had come past the T-72s the first time, they had turned too soon, giving point blank shots from both sides. After passing through them the second time, they were heading up the incline toward the ridge from which they had taken their initial shots. Since he was on the outside of the turn, Randy banked against the hill for his turn so he could go faster without the chance of throwing a track. One of the T-72s had him in his sights and fired. He would've hit Randy's tank right in the center of the turret except he did not account for the higher than expected speed of the M1. As a result, it hit further back on the bustle. With the M1 on the hill, the projectile hit the sloped armor. It penetrated. In a thunderous clap the whole magazine exploded. The blow-off panels sent the explosive force upward. But, the slender rod of the sabot continued through to hit the magazine blast door. It all happened in a fraction of a second.

The explosion cleared off the top of the turret and eliminated the bustle. It also caused the sliding panel to the ready rack to bow inwards and leave a crack at the bottom. Gases from burning gunpowder sent a shock wave through a crack under the panel into the turret.

"This is Red 4, Red 3 has esppppot . . . . "

"This is Red 1, say again, you're garbled."

"Exploded. I said exploded, Red Horse 3."

Chatwin was too far away by this time to see what was going on.

"Red 4, it he still moving? How bad is it?"

"They're still rolling but the turret's not moving . . . looks like the back of the turret's gone! Red 1, I have two '72's left. Send help."

"Roger, Red 4." Click. Chatwin switched to the company frequency. "This is Red Horse 1, Black Horse, where are you? I've two down!"

"This is Black Horse 1. We're three klicks away with the pedal to the metal. Over."

"Roger, Black Horse. As you approach, be careful of your targets. We're all over the place."

Click. "All Red Horse. Black Horse is coming from the southwest. Watch for them."

The ammo explosion left the three crew members in the turret of Red Horse 3 unconscious. In the lower part of the turret extending inside the hull, called the basket, there was a cutout. This gap was to provide a means for the driver to get out of the hull by way of the turret if the main gun pointed exactly to the front, thereby aligning the cutout with the driver's seat. When the magazine exploded, the turret was turned to the side, shutting off this passageway. Randy was stunned, but in a few seconds was marginally functioning. When he got no response from the turret on the intercom and the turret did not rotate, he assumed the turret had been penetrated or one of their shells had gone off in the turret, killing the crew behind him. The smell of cordite was overpowering.

Unlatching his hatch, he raised it and swung it to the right. In his semi-consciousness, his rote training came though. He made sure the hatch was latched in open position. Raising his seat, he was blasted with wind and sand. Groping around, he put his hand on his goggles. Spitting sand, and blinking the dust out of his eyes, he got the goggles on a little askew. That would have to do.

He had almost come to a stop as he rolled in a tight right turn. He saw Red Horse 4 duking it out with the two remaining T-72s, one of which had lost a track. As he watched, he saw the other T-72 catch fire. Instinctively he hit the power. The tank lurched forward to his surprise. He glanced down. No engine warning lights.

"Four's got it under control. I'm getting out of here before I'm hit and can't move." There was a rise a few hundred yards to the south, and Randy gave his tank all it had. By the time he was over the rise, he was doing fifty miles per hour. There, a half-mile down the slope was one of the TOW missile trucks that had wisely gotten out of the cat fight. "We'd have him but nobody to shoot, not even the coax." The coax was the 7.62-mm machine gun that fired where the main gun was pointed. He knew he had to keep the frontal armor pointed right at him, but had no time to button up. He headed for the truck. He saw the rocket launch. At the same time the truck driver must have thought that unless his missile stopped that huge charging tank dead in its tracks, it would squash him. Randy saw sand fly out from under all four tires, and the truck lurched forward. Guiding the TOW missile to the target was hard enough for the shooter with the truck stopped. With it moving, it was impossible. The missile dug into the sand and exploded halfway to the tank.

Maybe Randy was still dazed by the hit his tank had taken, or maybe he was feeling abused. In either case, he took after that truck like he was back at Fort Hood chasing jackrabbits. The truck had a quarter mile lead on him and appeared to be opening the distance. Then the truck driver did something stupid. If he had continued on down the dry water course, he may have gotten away. But, he started up the bank to the right. He had to shift down to get up the slope, cutting his speed in half. Randy could see the gunner and loader jump out of the truck thinking the M1 driver had gone berserk. Before Randy got to the point the truck had turned up the bank, he veered to the left to use the opposite side of the draw to bank his turn. "You fool, M1s eat hills for breakfast," he sneered under his breath. The M1 with its 1,500 horsepower turbine shifted from fourth gear to third and lost only five miles per hour.

As the tank went up the bank of the draw, Mitch, the gunner in Randy's tank, felt like there was a great weight removed from his back as Sergeant Reemer, the TC, rolled off him. Mitch slowly regained consciousness. His face hurt from having hit the sighting devices as Reemer had fallen unconscious on him. Mitch lifted his head and struggled to get free. Empty shell casings rattled around beside him. He tried to piece together in his mind what was happening to the tank. It was jerking like a bronco. Finally, mostly conscious again, he managed to squirm out from under the sergeant. Grabbing a canteen, he unscrewed the cap and splashed water on first the commander and then the loader. All the time, he was losing his balance and falling down. "What's gone wrong with this demented tank!" he yelled in exasperation. He could hear himself talking in his head, but it was as though he had his hands over his ears.

"Come on, you guys, wake up," he said rubbing his crew mates' heads. Mitch had a throbbing ache in his head and his ears were buzzing. His eyes fell on the magazine door. It was bowed inward. That explained why the three of them were unconscious, but why hadn't the tank stopped moving?

The ammo was supposed to cook-off with no injury to the crew inside the turret. But, anyone who has designed machines knows they can be made foolproof, but never *completely* foolproof. This is because in reality, sometimes the craziest things happen, and sometimes the dumbest fools used them. Here was a case of the former.

Reemer lifted his head. "What's wrong with this tank?"

"What? Can't hear you."

"I said, what's wrong with this tank the way it's bouncing around?" yelled Reemer. Instantly he grabbed his head. Oh, it throbbed.

After a pause, Mitch put his mouth next to Reemer's ear. "We took a hit in the magazine."

"No, the bouncing around. I feel like a cork in a washing machine. Ouch, my back's killing me."

"Let's see," said Mitch leaning over him.

"Oh, boy, be careful how you move. You're back looks like poorly cooked meat. Some is burnt crisp, the rest is bleeding. Don't lean back." They talked by bringing each other's mouth up next to the ear of the one they wanted to hear. Mitch checked out Chris, the loader. He found burns on his right side and arm. The hot gasses came through the crack under the panel and in an instant cooked any flesh it encountered.

When Randy came out of the draw, he was only a hundred yards behind the truck. Now it was cunning against cunning. Randy would close on the truck, only to have to back off on the power as the truck turned sharply to one side or the other. If he didn't slow down, he'd throw a track. Even though the M1 had superb acceleration for a tank, it did not equal that of the truck. On the other hand, when the truck came to patches of loose sand, it slowed noticeably. This had no effect on the tank. He closed, feinted to the left, and immediately turned to the right. The truck driver saw the movement to the left through his rear-view mirror, and immediately turned to the right. Momentarily distracted by a rough spot, he lost sight of the tank.

Accelerating again, the truck driver looked over his left shoulder. No tank! Snapping his head to the right, he saw it ten yards away. The M1 made surprisingly little noise. When traveling more than twenty miles per hour, there was no clanking from the treads, and what little engine noise there was, came out the rear. Randy had the throttle at full and was closing. The truck was still in a gradual turn to the right and Randy was cutting across the turn. The truck driver jerked the wheel to the left just as the left tank tread ground into metal.

In the turret, Mitch grabbed for an intercom headset to yell at Randy, when the tank suddenly lurched up on the left accompanied by a tooth-shattering screech.

In a split second, it was done. Backing off on the throttle, Randy turned to see what was left. He saw a lone tire rolling across the sand. It gradually lost speed and flopped over. The truck was flattened, twisted metal. "Boy, what a stupid thing to do," said Randy aloud.

"What happened? Where are we? What did you do?" a voice in his headset yelled.

Randy froze but was at once grateful to hear the voice. "I thought you guys were dead."

"If you're talking, stop. We can't hear. We took a hit in the magazine and all of the ammo cooked off. It sent burning powder into the turret. Stop whatever you're doing. Reemer and Chris are badly burned, and you're dumping us around back here. Find friendly forces and join up with them out of harm's way."

Mitch worked his way around Reemer and Chris and managed to open the commander's hatch. The air felt good. He pulled himself to a standing position. Looking out, he spotted what looked like the M88s. "Randy, the M88s are to our rear. Go over by them."

Letting out a deep breath, Mitch could hardly believe how the tank had changed. The fifty caliber was gone, the radio antennas were gone, and the bustle was gone along with the crew's personal gear that had been in racks around the back of the turret. There were streaks of smoke from the vicinity of the top of Zulu. He could see more smoke back at the escarpment were the Red Horse battle had been.

When Randy had headed to the rise to the south in Red Horse 3, the T-72 with the track off was drawing a bead on Red Horse 4. A few seconds after Red 4 dispatched the last maneuvering T-72 in his sector, the disabled Iraqi tank sent a shell in the direction of Red Horse 4 hitting his 105-mm tube a glancing blow. The projectile took an angled bite out of the top of the barrel, leaving two thirds of the tube bent down.

"Red Horse 1, this is 4, my tube's been hit, and there's a '72 without a track here that'll get me. I'm backing away and popping smoke."

"Roger, Red 4, this is 1. Black Horse will be here in a minute."

Because of the wind, the covering smoke from the smoke grenade launchers on the front corners of the turret wasn't doing much good for Red Horse 4. They took a hit to the front of the hull. The tank shuddered as it absorbed the shock and kept moving. "That's one feisty bugger," said the TC into his intercom. As he watched, the T-72 took two hits from Black Horse platoon in less than a second. That '72 was finished.

"Red Horse 1, this is White Horse 1. We're coming your way from Yankee. Over."

"Roger White Horse 1. Make a swing to the north to see if they're forming a counter attack. Black Horse is here, and we have the local situation under control. As you approach, let us know. I have some pretty trigger-happy crews."

"Roger, Red Horse 1. Out."

Click. Chatwin switched to the intercom. "How're we doing, guys?"

O'Brian answered first. "I've just about emptied the ready rack. All I've got left are HEATs. We've got to cross load ammo, now." This meant that it was necessary to move ammo from the rack behind the TC to the ready rack, which was almost impossible to do with all crew members at their posts.

"What? In these few minutes, you guys almost emptied the ready rack? That must be a record. We'll cross load in a minute, hang on."

"Red 1, this is Black 1. Looks like you boys kicked some serious butt!"

Inside Red Horse 1, Bart handed empties to Sean, who launched them out the loader's hatch.

Chatwin closed his hatch and hinged it open to get his first good look at the damage from the hit on the left side of the turret. He saw a foot-deep jagged slice in the side of the turret. Looking further, he saw more than a dozen destroyed T-72s and eight or ten other vehicles smoldering. The sound of the M1s maneuvering around the perimeter was interrupted at times by the staccato beat of machine gun fire. A couple 105s fired, as someone suspected a damaged enemy tank might still be operational enough to shoot.

In five minutes, the Chariots arrived, and in another five minutes Red Horse 2 was being towed to the south with one Chariot attached to the front and one to the back. For safety, a second M88 attached to the rear to prevent the towed tank from over running the puller when going down hill. If the second M88 wasn't available, it could get hairy. As soon as they had Red Horse 2 safely across the border, they'd come back for White Horse 6.

As Rebic's White Horse platoon joined the rest, Chatwin pulled up beside Rebic. They stopped, inches between their treads. Chatwin yelled, "Tom, call a Blackhawk, I have injured men in Red Horse 3."

Rebic nodded and got on his radio. "Raven 1, meet us at check point November at 0730. Bring carrion." Carrion was the code for 105 ammo.

"White Horse 1, this is Raven 1. Wilco. Out."

At 0733 hours, they met the Blackhawk at November, five miles south of the Iraqi border. They rearmed the remaining seven combat worthy M1s. Chatwin's entire four-tank platoon was out of action, and Rebic had four of his six unfit for battle. Fuel supplies were adequate until they met the Bradleys and the HEMTT fueler. They would make a final decision to go north to the site later. The attitude of the crews as well as the weather would play into that decision.

While they were rearming, Rebic made it a point first to see the wounded men. He shook each man's hand and said, "Well done, brother warrior. You're now a member of an elite club." That was the Purple Heart club for having been wounded in battle. He made the rounds to the rest of Chatwin's platoon and shook each man's hand, and gave some well-deserved pats on the back. If ever there were some men standing tall, he was looking at 'em. They knew they had done themselves proud. But it was nice to know the brass understood.

By 0750 hours, the Blackhawk was off the ground. It would head straight for KKMC with the wounded. Rebic told Chatwin and Boyd to keep the tanks out of sight. "Use camouflage netting, nestle up to rocks, anything so they're not easily spotted. If we go north to the site, we don't want interference."

Then they parted. The damaged tanks and the M88s headed south to the area of the forward base. The force of seven turned west.

— 25 —

0535 hours, September 20, Sunday, Nukhayb, Iraq

Breckon muddled his way through the night and had gotten the tasks done he had set for himself. He was ready to leave the utility room when Arzika came in.

"Time for some exercise, Breckon. Let's go."

Breckon wasn't interested, but felt if he refused, Arzika would be suspicious. It was half an hour before sunrise when they got outside, but still fairly dark. Breckon jogged toward the southeast to where they usually held their work out. He was surprised to see no vehicles as there had been for the last week. After warming up, the tension from the night was somewhat relieved. He expected the usual contest to ensue. Perhaps it would be the last one between them. They went after each other with verve neither had shown before. Eventually Arzika said, "Ha, Breckon, let's see if you have learned anything."

Breckon knew this was it. Arzika grabbed Breckon's left wrist with his right hand, and Breckon was to break the hold. Arzika had shown him how to do it, but it never worked. Screw it! Today he'd do it his way. Rather than leading off with his right foot as he had been repeatedly told, he led with a short step by the left foot immediately lunging forward, jabbing his right elbow into Arzika's abdomen as he lowered his head. Arzika momentarily recoiled from the unexpected move. Breckon thrust his right hand at Arzika's cocked elbow, forcing it out. With his right hand, he grabbed Arzika's wrist as he went under his right arm. He planned to plant his right foot behind Arzika's right leg and roll him over his hip. But Arzika countered, and they landed in a tangle of arms and legs. Breckon lost his hold and scrambled away. They both came up. Rather than attacking, Arzika dropped his arms and broke into a satisfied smile.

"Got you, you stinking snake!"

Breckon took a couple of steps backwards, bewildered at the remark.

"I knew you'd slip and revert to type if I stayed at it." Arzika wheeled and tromped back toward the hangar entrance, saying something in Arabic at the sky.

Breckon paused thinking Arzika had flipped his cookie. Arzika yelled back, "Hurry up, or I'll lock the door so you can cook outside." Breckon had no choice but to run after him.

A five-ton truck rolled through the door into the hangar at 0630 hours. Moments later, the huge door grumbled as it closed. A sergeant in the Republican Guard got down from the passenger's seat as soon as the truck stopped moving. His walk was unsteady from the long jolting ride. He headed toward the only office with a light that showed through a dirty window into the hangar. He stepped into the room, expecting to see a soldier of lower rank than himself. The sight of a major general seated behind the desk startled him. He came to attention and, producing the sharpest salute he could muster, said, "Sergeant Igbal reporting with a classified message, sir."

"Fine, Sergeant," replied General Majeed, "I'll take it."

"It is for Colonel Basheer, sir. I must deliver it to him personally."

Reaching for the message the general said, "I am the ranking officer here. I assure you I can see to getting it to Basheer."

Sergeant Igbal was apprehensive but had no choice but to turn over the message. "Please, sir, sign the receipt form attached to the envelope. It is a "very secret" document. I must have a signature."

"Yes, yes." The general knew that even he was subject to certain restrictions. He scribbled his signature on the three-part form, looked at his wristwatch and entered the date and time. He tore off the top two copies of the form and handed them to the sergeant.

"You are dismissed, Sergeant."

General Majeed picked up a stub of a cigar from the ashtray and lit it. He blew a smoke ring as he fingered the message that had come for Colonel Basheer. That colonel had not been at all helpful with his mission of capturing an M1 tank. What the big deal was with all the fancy equipment in the rooms below, the general did not understand.

Looking at the sealed envelope, he decided his rank permitted him to open it. Since the message had been hand delivered by courier, it was not encoded. He read with mild interest.

18 September 1998

Jubayl, Saudi Arabia

This is in response to request to intercept shipping container and recover an aerosol can. When container was intercepted in Saudi Arabia south of Kuwait border, can had already been removed. Found likely place where it had been attached to structure under floor with brown tape. Small piece of tape remained, and dirt was pulled off where other tape had been removed.

Through other investigations have learned the man who likely took the can is going by name of Darin Harris, an American. CIA is looking for Harris. Known associate of Harris is Ed Breckon but neither man is thought to be in the Gulf area. Other men are using stolen identities of Harris and Breckon.

General Majeed sat back and thought a moment. Seemed like Basheer and his men were looking for a can of some kind. He'd want to see this.

At that moment, a voice from behind startled the general. "General, word from 'Vengeance' battalion came in," said the head that looked around the door casing from the next room. The general laid down the message as he got up and went into the signal room next door. The first message had said all of Vengeance battalion was in position. This one gave news that six Abrams tanks were seen crossing the Tap Line Road at 0530 hours. "That is good," the general said. At the normal M1 speed over good terrain, that would put them at the intercept point at 0700 hours, right on schedule. General Majeed went to get his breakfast, the message forgotten on the desk.

Hamoud, still in Ar'Ar, was back in his car with the motor running, hoping to hear from Uncle Fred. At 0708 hours, the call came. Answering as Papa Jack, he gave Uncle Fred a little abuse and then promised to send help. "Well, no help. Too bad. Some days are like that," he chuckled to himself. The deed was done. The Iraqi general would get his revenge, the Russians would get at least one M1 tank, Hamoud would get a nice fat fee, and the Americans would get what they asked for. Everybody wins—except the tank crews.

Immediately after the call from Rebic, Hamoud called CIA headquarters in Langley, Virginia. The phone rang two times and was picked up.

It was 11:15 p.m. September 19 in Washington. "This is Golf Tee," was the answer, Harold Stanus's call sign.

"Nine Iron here," said Hamoud. "The plan on this end had been completed. It was quick and professional."

"Roger, Nine Iron. Do you have any independent confirmation?"

"Negative. There's a sandstorm going on. I don't know how to get other confirmation. It's your ball game now."

"Roger, Nine Iron. We'll be in touch. Stay close."

"Roger. Out."

Stanus was still in his office, having planned to be there all night if necessary to get this call. He was a career CIA man, and days like this came with the territory. He called Director Jason Hughs as he had been ordered. The phone was answered with a sleepy, "Yeah."

"This is Stanus. Sand Fire was completed successfully less than half an hour ago."

"What verification do you have?"

"Nothing other than our officer who's directing the field operation. There's a sandstorm in that area now."

"Okay, I'll inform Number One and have the Pentagon get us some verification. Good job so far."

"Thank you, sir. Good night."

Hughs hated to make the call he was forced to make. It made no sense to try to start a war in that part of the world. The night secretary answered at the other end of the secure phone. "Yes, sir, he said you might call. He'll be here in a minute." While Hughs waited, he could hear talking and laughing in the background. Didn't that guy ever sleep? Some of his Hollywood gang must have blown into town.

"Yep."

"Mr. President, I have received word that Operation Sand Fire has been completed successfully."

"Confirmation?"

"Not yet, sir. Our field officer called in immediately after it happened. I'll get aerial recon out to get verification right away."

"We'll meet at eight o'clock."

"Yes, sir, good night."

0700 hours, Nukhayb, Iraq

"Colonel Basheer, thank goodness you're here." Arzika entered the colonel's office breathing heavily. "I believe the American, Breckon, is someone other than who he says he is. Today during our exercise and martial arts training, I tricked him into revealing that he is quite highly trained in hand-to-hand combat. Maybe a little rusty, but he attempted a very advanced move against me that only a seasoned professional would try. I thwarted the move part way through, but he knew what to do."

"Your observations are noted. He is asleep now. Let him be. Today is the big day for our precious General Majeed. They should be cleared out of here in twenty-four hours. Then we will deal with our Mr. Breckon."

As the force of seven set out to the west, the storm increased in intensity. If it hadn't been for the AN/PSN-11 PLGRs they would've had to stop. By 1015 hours, the GPS instruments said they were at the point where they were to rendezvous with the Bradleys and especially the HEMTT. They were at the right spot but no HEMTT. Rebic motioned to Denton to make a circuit around their position. Visibility was a hundred yards. In seconds, Denton's tank and his buddy disappeared. In five minutes, Denton was back and motioned them to the south. Five hundred yards later they made the link-up in a hollow. They needed fuel, water, and food in that order.

By 1040 hours, the tanks were taken care of, dispersed, and the engines of all vehicles turned off. Now the men could take care of their personal needs. It was Rebic's hope that the wind and sand would cool the vehicles and obscure overhead observation, leaving them undetected. After they had eaten, Rebic got Denton, Blatz, and Kardell together in one of the Bradleys out of the wind where they could talk. One of the M1s had developed a problem with the engine control, and Rebic decided to leave it behind with the HEMTT.

"With six tanks, we have Duke's full platoon, and another consisting of Art's two M1s and two Bradleys." Even though Denton had more experience than Duke Blatz, Rebic didn't want to lose the unit integrity after the intensive training. This meant he left Duke's platoon intact. "I'll be in the Bradley that goes in for the evidence. While I'm inside, you're in command, Duke. You guys will provide a perimeter defense. Traveling to the site, we'll stay together. Coming out it'll be dark, and we'll probably be pursued. We'll travel in two platoons, one a mile to the side of the other. We'll keep the Bradleys and your tanks, Art, to the west. Remember, it doesn't matter where or when you get across the border. Just get there."

Kardell was once again shocked by Rebic's dictatorial tone. This was not the type of life he was accustomed to. He understood that there was no other way. Someone had to be in charge, and time was short. It was one man's plan, and that was the way it had to work.

Rebic continued. "Brief your crews and get a sense on how they feel about this excursion. If we go, we'll leave at 1510 hours. We'll meet again at 1430. Art, tell the five guys who'll make up the commando team with Craig and myself to come in."

When the "commandos," really mechanics, arrived, Rebic and Kardell described everything they knew of the site. The Bradley commander and driver were part of all of the briefings. Rebic had a clipboard and sketched the hangar bay. "As we understand, the entrance to the underground bunker is in this corner and hidden. We have no idea what that means, so keep your eyes open and use your imagination.

"Craig, you and Riley," Rebic nodded to the man on his right, "will be in charge of getting the samples. Look for documentation. Two will remain in the corridor as security. The remaining three of us will secure the main bay and look for whatever makes sense to take. Watch the time. Call it off frequently. With time going down and up we'll have less than fifteen minutes at the bottom.

"Most of all, don't shoot each other. Remember, shooting in a closed, concrete space is dangerous from ricochets." After a few questions, the five men were dismissed.

When they were alone, Rebic said to Kardell, "Craig, if we go, we have to figure out what we're going to do afterwards. We have to justify how we got our orders, how we got the information, how we got the tanks, and how we got together. It all has to make sense without making the people who have helped us fall guys."

Kardell sat motionless as he listened. "I know what you're saying, and have given it a lot of thought. It turns out nobody will know the whole story. The CIA will know for sure that something went wrong. If we go public as soon as it's over, they'll have to leave us alone to some degree. So, here's what I propose."

0930 hours near Kuwait City

Harris was in the right seat of the Antonov AN-2, and Ali in the left. They droned through the checklist in the confines of the cockpit. "That's it, Ali. Time to shove off," Harris said. They donned their headsets because once the engine started, it would be impossible to communicate over the noise. The plane sat in the open door of the hangar. Ali gave a hand signal, and a tractor slowly pulled the aircraft out tail first. Members of the sheik's household, one on each wing tip, and one at the tail held it steady. The plane met wind gusts of forty knots as it exited the hangar. Wind rocked the wings of the huge biplane, as the swirling sand pelted the Plexiglas like gusts of silicon dioxide sleet.

Once clear of the hangar, the plane was towed a short distance to get it out of the turbulence of the structure and pointed into the wind. With the pull of a lever, the tractor driver disconnected the tow-bar from the tail wheel and drove the tractor back to the hangar, shielding his face from the stinging sand with his hand.

"Let's see if she'll start," said Harris. Ali hit the contact switch, and the huge four-bladed variable pitch propeller started to turn as the starter engaged the ring gear on the flywheel. The first cylinder caught with a cough, then another, and another. Finally, all nine cylinders of the thousand-horse-power Shvetsov ASz-621R, radial engine (reverse engineered from a Curtis-Wright R1820) came to life, each sending a pulse of power to the propeller shaft in its appointed turn. The air drawn into the engine went through a cyclonic air filtration system to remove the sand and dust.

After several minutes, Ali said into the intercom, "Looks good to me. Okay with you?"

Harris turned and gave a thumb's up. "Advancing throttle, pitch to twenty-five degrees." The plane's vibration increased in proportion to the climbing tone of the engine's sound. "Brakes off, rolling, throttle to full." The plane shuttered at the application of power. Ali immediately gave it some right aileron and right rudder to counter the engine's torque. He continuously worked the rudder pedals and ailerons to stay exactly into the buffeting wind. After a two-hundred-foot roll, the tail was up, and with three hundred feet more, the main gear lifted off. The big biplane, loaded with maximum fuel plus an auxiliary fuel tank in the belly, labored against the wind as it reached 110 knots indicated air speed. They were on their way.

Darin keyed the intercom. "Radar crews in the area will think there's some kind of nut case out flying in this weather." Ali smiled and nodded affirmatively. It would take six hours to get to Ar'Ar.

1430 hours, five miles south of the Iraqi border

Captain Rebic and his lieutenants were standing in the lee of a Bradley. The wind had dropped, and visibility was improving. They all feared recon planes would spot them, but for some inexplicable reason, none came. Rebic looked tired as he spoke. "What's the feeling among the men?"

"They're scared, but all agree to go."

"That's what I figured. Okay, we go. We've got ninety klicks of ground to cover. The route we discussed still looks good to me. Any objections?"

There were none. "We leave at 1510 hours. In keeping with a continuation of the call signs of this morning, we're now Green Horse. Duke, you are Green Horse 1, and the rest of your platoon is 2 through 4. Art, you are Green Horse 5, and 6. My Bradley is Green Horse Light and the other is Green Horse Dark. Any questions?" Again, there were none. They were eager to get back to their platoons and make last minute preparations. "There's one more thing," he said pulling out a slip of paper for each. "If you get into real trouble, use the frequency and call signs on these pages. Give your location from your GPS." He handed a small cardboard box to each. "You'll need these, too. Be sure the color in the call sign matches the color of the flares."

0800 hours, Washington, D.C., the White House

"The president will see you now, Mr. Hughs."

Entering the Oval Office, Hughs felt tired. After he had fallen asleep for the second time, there was another call. The NSA had information on radio intercepts they had made during the tank battle. The guys with the wrinkly brains in that place were paid to analyze messages, but this seemed absurd on the surface, yet something in the back of Hughs's mind made it hard to dismiss.

Seeing the president, he was shocked. His dress was downright slovenly, even granting the time and day. He wore a sweatshirt and sweat pants, had not shaved, and had huge bags under his eyes.

"Okay, what's the news from Saudi Arabia?" The president leaned back in his chair and put his feet up on a desk drawer he had pulled out. He closed his eyes. He had a pleasant expression on his face, expecting good news.

Jason Hughes, seeing the anticipation was all the more uneasy. "We have confirmation of a tank battle at the precise location it was planned."

"Tank battle?" the president asked with hardness in his voice. "Wasn't this supposed to be an ambush with a few American tanks destroyed?"

Hughs winced at the off-handed way he referred to American soldiers being killed. "The weather was atrocious at the time. There's still a major sandstorm, so we don't have all the information we'd like. But, during a lull in the storm, our planes identified no fewer than twenty-one T-72 tanks destroyed, and many support vehicles. No M1 tanks were among them. We . . . ah . . . we can't find the M1s."

The president's face flushed and his mood soured more. "Can't find the tanks! That's stupid. That's incompetent. Doesn't their commander have to call in to his superior? What kind of insubordinate fools do we have driving those expensive machines?"

"Sir," Hughs said timidly, "only one man, a CIA agent, had contact with them. That was for security purposes. His contact was by secure satellite telephone. If the commander's sat-phone failed, we temporarily have no contact with the tanks."

"I'm not interested in excuses. I'm interested in results, understand? Find those tanks!"

Hesitating to proceed, Hughs was silent for a few moments. "Sir, there's some additional information I received as a result of the NSA monitoring the radio communications during the tank battle. It sounded like there were more American tanks involved than the CIA was told about. At the end, the Iraqis were in a panicked retreat, wailing that one or two U.S. battalions were pummeling them. In fact, they could break the news to the world as a full scale attack by the U.S. on them."

Now the president was confused. The lack of sleep and the total reversal of events had shaken him. "Muster all U.S. forces in Saudi Arabia and find out what happened!"

"Yes, sir, we can surely do that. Getting more information on the battlefield won't be possible for another twelve hours, though."

The president held his head in his open hand, obviously nursing a headache. He took a deep breath. "Oh, please, tell me why we can't get information on the battlefield for the next twelve hours."

Hughs could see his boss's exasperation was reaching critical mass. "Sir, because the Saudis have started a surprise training operation with their air force. It includes everything from F-15s to Tornado ground attack aircraft, with AWACS planes, midair refueling, the whole works. And the area of the tank battle happens to be in the off-limits area they gave us. They told us we could not put up one of our AWACS planes to grade their exercise like we commonly do. It's their country. They can do this if they want."

"Yes, yes, but why now? What don't they want us to find? Look into it. Is there anything else?"

Director Hughs nervously rubbed one hand with the other. "There is, ah, well still one piece of information that is, well, for lack of a better word, shall we say, odd."

The president winced and said, "Out with it, man. What else could be wrong?"

"It's the call signs the Americans used during the battle, sir. They were, so to speak, incomplete. The NSA analyst mentioned this immediately."

"What! The call signs, what could be wrong there?"

"I'll say it, and that'll be the end of it. There were, as could be discerned by the radio intercepts, three platoons of M1 tanks with call signs of White Horse, Red Horse, and Black Horse." Seeing the blank expression of the president's face, Hughs continued. "Don't you see. The fourth horse is missing, as if yet to come, indicating that whatever is happening over there in the desert isn't finished."

"Can there be anything else! What are you talking about!"

"Sir, the white, red, and black horses are the first three of the four horses of the Apocalypse. The fourth horse, the green horse, is yet to appear."

"Oh, balderdash. You're getting carried away. That's nuts."

"The folks in the spook business don't think so. When people go out of their way to mastermind a complex operation against a super power, they like to play games. It's too common to ignore. What I'm saying is, we, the United States, your administration, or somebody, is being set up to be foiled by a very complex, well-funded organization. It appears our operation to get some M1 tanks destroyed has been infiltrated, and we're no longer in control."

"Pull out the stops. I want information. Dismissed." The president's displeasure showed in every wrinkle on his face. "No wait," the president put up his hand. "Whoever heard of a green horse anyway. Are you sure that's right?"

"Oh, yes, sir. But, it isn't green like grass is green. It's a light ugly gray-green of an animal after it's been dead for awhile and has started to bloat. According to the book of Revelation the rider of the green horse is Death, and it is followed by Hell. I'd say it doesn't portend well for someone."

The president, rubbing his forehead, gave a flick of his hand for Hughs to leave.

The engines of six Abrams tanks and two Bradley Fighting Vehicles came to life. Turrets turned, check procedures were made of all equipment and sensors. At 1510 hours, Rebic gave the signal to move out. Green Horse 1 platoon went first followed by the Bradleys, followed by Green Horse 5, and 6. There was no joking among the crews. These were serious men. They were going into the jaws of the enemy to hit him where he lived. The wind, still gusting above twenty knots, gave a visibility of half a kilometer. They stayed in single file mainly for safety from obstacles. If the first tank traversed the ground without getting into trouble, the rest could do the same.

Time dragged. Progress was good for the first hour. Then they encountered a watercourse with deep cuts in it and had to turn back. Getting all eight vehicles stopped and turned around without radio communications took valuable time. They had to backtrack two kilometers and take another route. Rebic had planned to be in position a mile west of the site by 1825 hours, a few minutes before the AN-2 was scheduled to pick up Breckon. They were falling behind schedule and had no choice but to pick up the speed.

At the same time, five thousand feet above the desert, a lone Antonov AN-2 relentlessly fought the wind. Ali and Harris traded off handling the plane every twenty minutes. They were above the blowing sand and the majority of the dust, so visibility was good except that there was nothing to see. Below them was an amorphous dark tan cloud. Above was dust-filtered blue sky punctuated by a reddish disk of the sun.

The GPS instrument told Harris they were fifty-eight nautical miles southeast of Ar'Ar and on schedule.

"Looks like it's clearing a little," remarked Ali, just to say something.

"I'll be happy to make Ar'Ar. My butt's numb," Harris answered. Ali smiled and nodded.

The display on the GPS inched them toward the airfield. At last, it came into view. The drop in the pitch of the engine was a relief after six hours of droning at the same level. Harris was at the controls for the landing, and, in the buffeting wind, it was one he was not proud of. It came under the category of "any landing you could walk away from was a good landing." They taxied up to the fueling station as two men came out and lashed down the landing gear. Apparently word of their arrival had discretely been sent ahead. After fueling and other maintenance checks, they taxied to a tie-down. Having secured the plane, they ate food they had brought along. After that, they stretched out as best they could on the inclined floor of the cabin and rested.

At 1740 hours, the engine sounded good. The plane felt good. Ali and Harris, on the other hand, did not. Now was the time for action. Skill, cool thinking, and agile hands were the only weapons they had. The AN-2 took to the air like it was eager, too eager it seemed. They headed northwest for five miles, and then, dropping to two hundred feet, swung to the north and into what appeared all to certain to be the short remainder of their lives.

Harris, being in the right seat, was the copilot, which brought with it the duties of navigator. At 1815 hours he was concentrating on the GPS system, he said, "Three kilometers to the right turn, this will be a tough landing in a gusty cross wind. Once we're stopped on the ground, I'll try to hold it with the door facing the hangar door. That may not be possible with the wind, though."

They had agreed Ali would get out and pretend to make some adjustment to the engine. That wasn't terribly realistic because the hub of the propeller was eight feet off the ground with the tail down, and the engine was buried inside the cowling. It might fool someone who knew nothing about airplanes.

"Turn now." Ali dipped the right wing and swung it around. "With the tail wind the down wind leg will go fast." Harris had programmed the way-points into the GPS. There were two points to go on the in-bound part of the mission. Glancing out the window, Harris saw tanks below. "Ali, there's a bunch of tanks down there. Waggle the wings and make the engine miss. I'll pump some oil into the exhaust manifold to make smoke."

Ali immediately grabbed the throttle and made the engine surge while Darin worked a little lever. "Give me some side slip." Craning his neck to see behind them, Darin replied, "Looks pretty realistic. Guess they bought it. Oh, oh. There's some dark exhaust coming from the back of some tanks. Hope that's not bad news."

"We always knew we could have a reception committee. Comes with the job."

"Yeah. One kilometer to go to next right turn."

"Ready, turn. Five kilometers to the programmed touch down point." They were heading almost exactly south, and the runway ran northeast to southwest. "Look to the left. Can you see the highway?"

Fighting the buffeting of the plane, Ali quickly glanced out the left window. He said, "No," as he nudged the left rudder, applied left aileron, and pushed the throttle forward a tad. The AN-2 was a beast to fly in good conditions, and these were far from good.

"Pull her to the right. The wind is blowing us off coarse. I see a larger than average sand dune to the right of the nose, one klick to go. Look for the road."

Another quick glance as another gust hit the plane. After a few seconds, "Yeah, I think I see it."

"Okay, half klick to go. Slow her down. Take her to the right some more . . . more yet. Okay, hold her on that heading. Land to the right of the sand dune. Put her down now, we don't want to over-shoot."

Whomp. They hit hard and bounced. "That wind is really bad. You won't be able to hold her unless she's into the wind."

Harris pointed with his finger, "That dark area must be the cut in the dune for the hangar door. I'll give her a couple of shots of oil as you taxi forward. As soon as she's stopped, I'll take it. There it is. Stop! The big door is open. I see lights in the hangar. Ali, I have six twenty-four, we stay exactly five minutes, no more, no matter what."

Ali stopped the craft, but the huge wings that gave it its short field capability wanted to lift on the right, so he stood on the right brake and let off the left one so it'd swing around. "She wants to go into the wind. Ready? Okay, take it." With that, Ali released the controls to Harris, yanked off his headset, and unbuckled. Slipping off the seat, he went down the incline to the door near the tail on the left.

"Five minutes, no more," Darin yelled after him.

As Ali jumped out, he was shielded from the hangar. Walking toward the tail of the aircraft, he looked toward the hangar opening.

Harris had the propeller set at nearly zero pitch so he could surge the engine without much thrust. Now and then, he'd pump more oil onto the exhaust manifold to make smoke.

He flipped to the frequency the M1 tanks would be using if they had come. No sound except for a little crackling. With the nose into the wind, the plane was easy to hold. Causally he looked out of the left side window. Some dark objects caught his eye. The strut between the wings was in the way, so he gunned the engine and let up on the right wheel brake. The plane swung to the left. Two objects moved toward him. Straining his eyes, he concluded they were tanks. His heart sank. They might have made it, but not now. If he moved around to avoid their fire, Taryam and Breckon would never get aboard. Any moment he expected to see flame from the gun barrels. His existence was fixed on these tanks. "So this is how we die. At least we tried."

The AN/PSN-11 read-out showed one and a half kilometers to go. Rebic gave the hand signal to slow their pace. He did not want to take the chance of suddenly coming over a rise at full speed only to realize they were in view of the site. Rebic stood in the open hatch of his Bradley with binoculars. The rest of the force held back as Rebic's Bradley moved forward. It was 1819 hours. They had made it with minutes to spare.

"Okay, stop," he said to the driver. "I can see the runway and what looks like the place the door to the hangar should be. Back up and go three hundred meters to the right." The driver backed up slowly so as not to give an exhaust heat plume. Two minutes later, they crept up to the crest of the rise again. "Okay, this is the place. Looks like the man described." Rebic keyed his microphone twice and the M1s moved to position. Green Horse 1 came up around Rebic with Green Horse 3 and 4 off to the left. As planned Green Horse 5, and 6 went half a kilometer to the right. The two tanks in Blatz's team jockeyed into position to get a shot at the base of the door to stop it from closing. Now they waited.

Sweeping the sky to the north with his binoculars Rebic spotted the plane. Low to the ground, it wallowed in the gusty wind. Rebic clenched his teeth as it hit hard in a down draft and bounced. In a remarkably short distance it stopped in front of the door, blocking the shot of the only two tanks in a position to stop the door from closing. The wind swung it around. Rebic looked at Blatz, who was watching too. Keying the mike, Rebic got Blatz's attention. Blatz shook his head. Then Blatz pointed to the right front. Rebic looked. Two tanks were coming up along the side of the runway toward the airplane, and near the top of the dune was a second pair.

Keying his mike, Rebic said, "Green Horse 3, 4, this Green Horse Light. Take 'em out."

— 26 —

General Majeed was in the foulest mood he could remember. Even after the rout by the Americans in the Gulf War, he did not feel such despair mixed with anger. At that time, he had received one order after another to retreat and give ground. Today it was different. It was his plan. He alone was in command. Twenty-two T-72 tanks and as many support vehicles destroyed, and others damaged, and not one M1 tank to show for it. The accounting would be hard, even deadly. The colonel standing at attention in front of him received the full fury of his wrath.

"Colonel, the Americans were tipped off about our plan, and the leak came from here. I demand an accounting of what you are doing here, every man stationed here, the reporting system, security system, everything!" His face was red turning to purple as he bellowed at Basheer.

This meeting was being held in the underground tube where Majeed had briefed Hamoud. Besides Colonel Basheer, there was Basheer's personal guard, Arzika, and Majeed's aide. Colonel Basheer described the Jihad Sting project in as much detail as he thought necessary, stressing its extreme secrecy. At times, he referred to the American engineer.

The East German and Russian engineers and technicians were discussed but there had never been a problem with these nationalities in the past. They had families back home that would suffer for their misdeeds, to say nothing of themselves, if they leaked information.

Finally, General Majeed said, "Who is this American? Isn't it odd to have an American here?"

Colonel Basheer wished Alwan were there to speak to that question. "Only the Americans had the technology to do this project. This engineer was brought here to tend to the installation and start-up. He is nearly finished, and our own engineer has been trained to handle the equipment after the American's work is complete. He is constantly supervised. As the commander of the site, I saw to that," Basheer added.

"And who is his supervisor?"

"The Iraqi engineer, Ashrof Mohed."

"Get him. Tell me the American's name again."

"Ed Breckon. He was brought here under the careful eye of Alwan Najafi the whole way."

The general bent over and whispered something to his aide. He promptly got up and left as Mohed entered.

After strained introductions, General Majeed said to Mohed, "Has Breckon ever been out of the hangar where he could signal anyone?"

In a typical maneuver of a man under pressure, Mohed tried to direct the attention to another. "He goes out nearly every morning with Arzika to exercise."

The general leveled his gaze at Arzika, who responded tersely, "That is true. But, I have been in physical contact with him as we practice martial arts. I assure you I would have detected any signaling device on him." Arzika proceeded to explain why he had started this and took a chance by revealing what had happened that morning.

Majeed looked at Mohed again. "Think hard, has there been any other time when he has been outside, on a mission to fix something, or similar reason?"

Mohed related the time he walked out into the door pocket, and the time he went into the generator room during the prayer time. Following that, Arzika mentioned the incident of the other night when one of his off duty guards had chased a man into the pocket. They were all starting to get an uneasy feeling. "Where is this man now?" asked Majeed. "Get his computer, and let us examine it carefully, and keep a guard with him at all times."

Breckon hadn't slept much. His anxiety was mounting with each passing minute as zero hour approached. His heart was heavy as if God had totally abandoned him. Nothing was right. Those days before, he had abandoned himself to his maker, but nothing had changed. Events still pushed and shoved him with a life of their own. His solemn prayer for deliverance had resulted in this? His having to run out to meet an airplane that probably wouldn't get this far and be destroyed on the ground if it did? He was too deep in enemy territory, the site too well defended, for any of this to work.

Grappling with these thoughts, he headed for the robot bay. Today was the day of the tank project. He had expected to hear the rumble of the large door opening at least a few times as they hauled in an M1 tank or parts of several of them. But, he had not heard it once.

He knew it was early, but he started work this early before and had not been told to do otherwise. He headed to the utility room so it would appear as though he were starting a normal day. He would leave at six-fifteen for his rendezvous with the airplane at six-twenty-five. It would take three minutes to get to the top of the stairs without running and getting out of breath. He would take some tools and act like he was there to fix something. He would work his way to the big hangar door, and at six-twenty-five he'd dash out. If the plane wasn't there, he'd have to decide on his feet what to do. He'd have no food or water but had decided this was the day. All-in-all, a terrible plan.

Once in the utility room he took his computer from his bag. He found his hands were shaking so much he could hardly manage them. He kept telling to himself to calm down with little effect. There was a steel shaft four feet long and an inch and a quarter in diameter sitting against the wall. He had used it to prop open the door to the bay when he and Mohed were doing testing so they could talk to one another. It weighed about fifteen pounds and had successively smaller diameters machined into the ends until on one end there was a one-inch-long by quarter-inch diameter stub.

He grabbed this shaft with both hands, and using it as a barbell, exercised his arms. He had to do something to relieve the tension with only minutes left before he'd leave. He heard someone coming from the workshop. Leaning the shaft against the wall behind his chair he sat down in front of the computer console and appeared to be working. Basheer's guard appeared on the stairs coming down from the workshop tube. He was carrying his AK-47 as usual. The door from the bay opened and Mohed stepped in followed by the snitch. Breckon glanced at his wristwatch. Six-fifteen. He should be leaving now!

Mohed spoke. "Colonel Basheer like much to see your computer, Ed. This man take it to him," he said nodding to the snitch.

People all over the place, and time to go. "Whatever. Remind him the development software is on it. If he trashes it, what you have now is the best you'll get." He handed the computer to the snitch who left by the rear stairs leading to the workshop.

"This man staying by you," Mohed said pointing to Basheer's guard.

Suddenly the realization struck Breckon. He wouldn't get out of there without dropping the guard, and possibly Mohed. He had hoped against hope it wouldn't come to this, but there was no other choice. The option to stay and sacrifice himself no longer existed. It would lead to his friends getting killed along with himself.

It was time to invoke the virus he had prepared, but he needed a distraction. Sitting down in front of the console of the control system computer, he loaded a test program used to test the ability of the two robotic systems to work together. One manipulator would pick up two-inch wood cubes from a random pile, travel some distance to where it met the companion gantry robot and pass the block to the other manipulator. The second robot traveled fifteen feet and piled the blocks in a pyramid.

He made sure the screen was turned so the guard could see it. As the program started he said, "Ashrof, could you stick your head out into the bay and tell me if the manipulators are moving together?" Mohed went to the door to the bay.

"No Ed, they are moving apart. What is wrong?"

Breckon hit a few more keys to feed the video from one of the manipulator cameras to his monitor. "That can't be," said Breckon in an irritated voice, knowing they would be moving apart exactly as Mohed had reported. "Someone has been messing around down here." The guard, understanding little English, was unsure what was going on. He was afraid of a trick and was becoming agitated. "Here, let me see," Breckon said as he got up. At that moment the monitor started showing real time video as one manipulator very gracefully handed a block to the other. The guard momentarily watched the scene with riveted attention. Being distracted, the guard did not notice as Breckon turned his body to shield his movements. He grabbed the shaft standing against the wall. "Come on, Ashrof. You must be mistaken," Breckon said as he wheeled around and rammed the small end of the shaft into the side of the guard just below his ribs. He thought it would be like punching the man in the stomach with his fist. He put his full weight into the thrust, and to his horror, he saw the shaft bury itself deep into the man's side.

As Colonel Basher's guard, the snitch, and Mohed went to find Breckon and his computer, the others headed to the workshop tube. This was at Arzika's suggestion because the necessary tools were there. It was then that the general's aide arrived with the message that had come early that morning. Majeed took it and casually handed it to Basheer as he instructed his aide to wait there in the planning room and to inform him immediately if any messages were called down from the signal room. General Majeed said to Basheer, "That message arrived this morning. It didn't appear important at the time."

Basheer read it and stopped. "You fool," he said showing no respect for rank. "This is proof that the American is a spy. He isn't Ed Breckon, but someone who has stolen his identity. Our site, my project, and your project have been compromised for days. When did this come. Let's see. You signed for it at 0635 hours. If you had delivered this to me immediately, I would have known what this meant. There would have been time to warn your armored forces that the operation had been compromised. The defeat of your armored unit is entirely your own fault!" Basheer's temper was up, and he didn't care. They were all doomed now.

Rather than getting lashed at by Majeed as he expected, the general was quietly composed. "Colonel, what we need now is damage control. We do have a very important spy in the palm of our hands. Let's think this through. We must find out how he communicated, and with whom."

As they arrived in the workshop, the snitch emerged with the computer. He opened the computer, and it booted up. Arzika took over. "If this contains a communication device, it would need an antenna. The logical place for that would be the cover, perhaps behind the flat screen." In a few seconds he had the two screws out and very gently separated the screen from the cover housing. "There, that is a high-gain directional antenna. This is definitely a piece of spy gear."

In the utility room, the guard lurched from the thrust of the shaft. Out of habit, he flipped off the safety as he tried to bring the gun to bear on Breckon. A three-round burst exploded with a deafening roar in the small room. The bullets impacted the glass of the monitor, causing the cathode ray tube to implode in a shower of glass. Breckon felt something hot go through the hair on the side of his head as a ricocheting slug whipped past him. Breckon released his grip on the shaft and grabbed the barrel of the AK-47. The guard was down. The thrust had sent the shaft completely through him. Mohed stood at the door staring in disbelief as Breckon swept the automatic weapon out of the guard's hands and rushed toward him.

"Go home to your family," Breckon said in almost a conversational tone as he brought the barrel down on Mohed's head. Breckon dropped the weapon and grabbed Mohed's limp body so he wouldn't fall and hurt himself. He laid him on the floor. "Hope I didn't kill him," Breckon said aloud. "What am I doing?" He felt sick as he saw the guard, now in a pool of his own blood, feebly tugging at the shaft. The destruction of the monitor had no effect on the operation of the robotic systems since the computer and servo drives were in a rack under the table and were undamaged. The robots continued with their task.

The sound of the shots made everybody in the workshop freeze for a moment. Majeed was the first to speak. "Those were shots from an automatic weapon!"

They all agreed. Basheer sent the snitch into the utility room to check, and for good measure Arzika to the end of the bay with the old elevator in it. "Take a quick look, if that man accidentally let a burst out of his '47, I'll have his hide," Basheer said more out of irritation than concern. "That fool is always fiddling with the safety on that weapon."

"Got to move," Breckon almost yelled at himself to gather his wits. He stepped out the door leading into the bay and was met with a burst of automatic weapons fire. The slugs grazed along the wall and one spattered against the steel door jam sending fragments of metal into Breckon's arm. Another creased his cheek. "He's got a guard on the service platform and I gotta go—now!" Breckon said to himself. Grabbing the guard's AK-47, he made sure the safety was off. He had seen guards absentmindedly flipping their safeties on and off a hundred times. He stepped out, saw the guard, fired a burst, and stepped back in. Only one round fired. "What's this? I thought these things never jammed." Looking out again he saw the bullet had found its mark. The guard had dropped his weapon and was teetering at the edge of the catwalk.

In its normal cycle, the second robot was close to where the guard stood. As he fell, he landed on the festooned cable pack along the side of the bridge beam feeding power and signals to the trolley. His foot caught in the cables, leaving him hanging. Blood dripping from him left a pattern on the floor marking the machine's path.

As Breckon stepped into the bay again and started for the door leading to the stairwell up to the hangar, a voice behind him bellowed. "I've got you now." Breckon recognized Arzika's voice immediately. Breckon fumbled with the automatic weapon as Arzika came toward him drawing his own gun as he did. The magazine fell out of Breckon's AK-47. It had come unlatched when he dropped the gun to grab Mohed. Breckon aimed at Arzika and pulled the trigger. Nothing happened. Seeing Breckon was without a weapon, Arzika holstered his gun and menacingly advanced. "Crushing out your life with my bare hands will be a pleasure, Breckon, or whoever you are."

Breckon threw the gun at Arzika. As he turned, he saw Arzika sweep it aside like a piece of straw. Breckon took a few steps and was beside a worktable. There were tools, electrical components, and the random pile of blocks the robots were using for the test program on it. Breckon grabbed a twelve-inch adjustable wrench and threw it at Arzika. This time Arzika was not so quick, and it grazed his head. Momentarily stunned, he slowed down. Breckon wheeled to make a run for it when he spotted the machete on the table. With his back almost turned to Arzika he grabbed the handle with both hands and glanced over his shoulder. Seeing Arzika pressing his attack, he made two steps backward and spun fully around swinging the blade at arm's length.

Arzika saw what was happening too late. He raised his hand to ward off the blow. The sharp edge cut deeply into his fingers followed by the main force of the slashing blade landing on Arzika's neck, nearly cutting though. The momentum thrust Arzika's body toward the worktable sending it sprawling on top of it, his head dangling by a few uncut muscles. As the main artery to Arzika's head was severed, Breckon was drenched in blood. Arzika twitched a few times and lay still.

Breckon could feel himself becoming sick. His head was light, and he thought he might pass out. Never had he imagined he could do something like this. It wasn't him. Who was it? A horrid noise seemed to come from inside him. What was happening? Suddenly he realized he was screaming like a banshee. The revulsion at what was happening was gushing out the only way it could.

Breckon turned to see the snitch standing in the door of the utility room. Upon entering the small room, the man had stopped to see if there was anything he could do for the guard or Mohed. He opened the door and stepped into the bay in time to see Breckon slice the head off Arzika with the machete. Now he saw Breckon's flaming eyes fix on him as the wrenching shrieks petrified him. He backed away toward the opposite side of the bay from the utility room. His foot caught on some steel banding on the floor. He fell backward. At the same time Breckon lifted the machete above his head with both hands and threw it at the snitch. It made one complete revolution in the air, looking as if it would strike low. But due to the snitch's backward fall the man landed on his rump with his back against a wooden crate just as the whirling blade found its mark. It sliced easily through the man above his hipbone and imbedded itself in the crate.

In the workshop, General Majeed and Colonel Basheer heard the additional shots and Breckon's howling. "What is going on around here?" Majeed said looking at Basheer. "It sounds like someone is being killed! And why haven't your men come back?"

Basheer was suddenly concerned too. He wanted to find out what was happening, but he didn't want to get into some disagreement where there was shooting. If he went through the utility room, he would be at close quarters with whatever was going on. "I'll find out immediately," he said as he started for the far end of the workshop so he could enter the bay at the far end.

"And if you don't come back, then what?" Majeed retorted as he followed Basheer.

Breckon was still yelling. The devilish assault on his psyche wouldn't end. Out of the corner of his right eye, he caught sight of a movement. It was Basheer with Majeed behind him coming from the far end of the bay. When Basheer saw Arzika on the crate, he stopped and took a quick breath. From the intense wailing, he thought Breckon had gone mad. As Basheer reached for his pistol, Breckon grabbed the first thing that he saw, a ten-foot coil of roller chain that would be used to drive a conveyor. This was a big brother to common bicycle chain.

Basheer's hand fumbled with the leather flap over his pistol. This gave Breckon the time he needed. Grasping the chain by one end, he swung the now extended steel strand around over his head, dashing madly for Basheer as he did so. Basheer had his pistol out of the holster, and with his left hand was pulling the receiver back to chamber a cartridge. The chain whistled through the air. As the bolt snapped forward, Breckon lowered the swinging chain and hit Basheer in the neck seeing it wrap around once, twice, three times. Breckon pulled sharply on the chain setting it deep into Basheer's throat. Basheer lurched forward clawing at the chain as it crushed his windpipe. For an instant, the scene struck Breckon as totally incongruous. That was number fifty ANSI roller chain, yield strength six thousand pounds, and Basheer was trying to break it with his fingernails.

As Basheer fell, the pistol clattered to the floor. Instantly, Majeed made a scramble for it. Breckon seeing another man dead caused his piercing cries to be louder than before. Breckon released the end of the chain and backed up. The glint of metal caught his eye. It was the eighteen-inch screwdriver used to open crates. He grabbed it by the blade. Majeed had his hand on the pistol, which lay partway under the table. This action caused Majeed's head to be turned sideways to Breckon for a moment. Breckon threw the tool with as much force as he could, hoping to throw Majeed off balance while he found something heavy to hit him with. The screwdriver made half a revolution in the air and penetrated Majeed's temple. The shock of the sudden damage to the man's brain caused the general's legs to stiffen, lifting him up, and then letting him fall on his side. As he hit the floor, the screwdriver was shoved completely through his head. He didn't even twitch as instant death enveloped him.

Breckon grabbed the pistol and swung around looking for others. None came. He looked at his watch—he had lost precious time, but he could still make it. He sprinted to the door forty feet away. As he approached the stairs, he saw the door handle turn. He dove for the side of the stairs, tucking his head under as he tumbled over. Messing around out in the sand with Arzika had taught him more than he realized. Two men armed with automatic weapons rushed into the room and down the stairs. Breckon stepped back from beside the stairs and methodically pumped one bullet into each one. The first tried to get a burst off. But, the falling body of the second left them both in a pile at the foot of the steps. Coming around with the pistol held with both hands straight in front of him, Breckon put another round into each man's head. He was no longer howling. It was as if he was watching a robot perform a routine task. Satisfied they were dead, he dropped the pistol and grabbed an AK-47. Pausing an instant to consider, he reached down, released the magazine from the other, and stuffed it in his belt. Stepping over the bloody mess, he bounded up the steps and opened the door.

Strange, nobody around. The heavily sealed door to the bay as well as the closed door to the dining tube across from it had muffled the sound of the shots. Weary men eating their insubstantial evening meal weren't inclined to check on strange noises for fear they would miss some food.

With difficulty, Breckon kept himself from running the steps too fast lest he be winded at the top. On the second to the last flight of steps, he heard the door above open. As he rounded the concrete center wall to the last flight, he saw a man start down. He also had an AK-47. The man backed up before Breckon could shoot and stepped into the hall leading to the locked door he and Arzika had used to go out for exercise.

Then he heard it, the tinkle of a small piece on metal on the concrete—a hand grenade. Four and a half seconds to detonation raced through his mind. He had read it in a book on Vietnam. One-one-thousand, he started to count off the time. Come on, throw it you slimy lizard. Breckon stepped around the wall dropping the gun from his right hand. Two-one-thousand. *Bonk*, here it came bouncing off the wall. He lunged up two steps and caught it in both hands. Three-one-thousand. With his forward momentum, he continued up two more steps transferring the instrument of death to his left hand as he grabbed the handrail on the right. The weight of the grenade swung his hand back. Using the grip of his right hand as a pivot, he swung his left out to the side in an arc and lobbed the bomb up the steps behind the center wall at the top. As soon as it left his hand, he fell back, still holding the handrail and thrust out his lower jaw. This would open the Eustachian tubes in his throat equalizing the pressure on both sides of his eardrums. He had lost his count, but it didn't matter because at that instant—*WHAM!*

The pressure wave collapsed his lungs, forcing the breath out of him and gave a prickling sensation on his chest. Dazed, he almost fell backward. Falling to his knees, he scrambled backward and around the center wall to the second flight of stairs. Taking deep breaths, he recovered quickly. Palming the AK-47 he had let fall, he waited another ten seconds. The ringing in his ears made it impossible to hear any movement from above. Swinging the weapon around the wall, he saw nothing. He went up the last flight of steps slowly two at a time squinting through the smoke. The grenade had bounced off the top of the door when it went off, destroying the light for the landing and knocking the door off its upper hinge. As he reached the top, he held the weapon vertically as he stood by the dividing wall. He swung the gun horizontally as he stepped partially around the wall and let go with a burst down the hall, immediately stepping back. He could hear some groaning, and cautiously looked into the hallway. In the dim light coming from the far end, he could see men on the floor, how badly wounded he did not know. In the shadows, he saw a black pool forming by the nearest man. He hardly noticed the weapon in his hand, though it weighed slightly more than eleven pounds with a full thirty-round magazine. He kicked the door open and sprang out, immediately dodging to the right. The grenade blast and shots had gotten everyone's attention. He knew what to expect.

He immediately fired a burst in the direction of human forms. Men hit the floor and scrambled for cover. Across the bay, he saw a muzzle flash. Concrete chipped off the wall near his ear. He fired two short bursts. A man fell. His bullets made a funny thumping sound. He had hit the large tank of aviation fuel. No time to worry. Glancing toward the large hangar door, he saw it half-open and slowly closing. He pointed the weapon at three guards coming in through the large door and fired. One man fell, and the others raced for cover behind a truck. By now, he was at a dead run. Once he fired a burst to his left without looking to keep heads down.

A man with a thick accent called out, "Ed Breckon." He recognized it as the Russian's, just as he saw a blurred movement. The Russian had a pistol pointed at Breckon. Breckon brought his gun to bear and squeezed just as the Russian fired. A bullet went between the stock of the AK-47 under Breckon's right upper arm and his ribs, creasing the wood of the rifle stock, and cutting his skin in a long gash. The Russian folded over as bullets spent their momentum in his chest.

Twenty feet to go. It seemed like he had been running and shooting for an hour. He turned and ran backwards now, sending a short burst back the way he had come. On his first step out of the door, he sent a flight of bullets into the deeply shadowed pocket. He whipped his head around a hundred and eighty degrees. Would it be there . . . unbelievable! A biplane was sitting right in line with the pocket with its engine idling and a small man in front of the lower wing.

From the cockpit of the AN-2, Harris watched the tanks bearing down on him, transfixed. Maybe they would only use their machine guns to rip the plane to shreds without wasting rounds from their main guns. He heard a click on the radio and then, "Green Horse 3, 4, this is Green Horse Light. Take 'em out." The corner of his right eye caught something orange off the cowling of the engine like a lightning flash. He jerked his head to see what had caused it. More flashes appeared to the left. Swinging his head, he saw one of the tanks erupt in flames. Dust or smoke puffed out of the side of the second tank near the ground. Seconds later its turret lifted up as a round ignited the ammunition. More muzzle plumes from the right, followed by explosions on the top of the dune. More tanks being destroyed that Harris hadn't seen. The M1s had come! A surge of emotion flooded Harris as tears welled up in his eyes. At once, he was happy he was not going to die, but mostly he was so proud of those guys risking their necks to come and help. Those were some real warriors, real Americans!

Breckon was out of breath. As he ran backwards, he saw men come to the edge of the hangar door. Breckon fired a burst. The weapon stopped firing as the magazine emptied. Dislodging it from under his arm, he yelped in pain. Some of the wooden splinters from the stock of the gun had imbedded themselves in his skin from the passage of the Russian's bullet. Looking around, he saw he was headed toward the tail of the plane.

Throwing in the AK-47, he jumped in after it. "Darin, go, go, go! I'm here," he yelled, panting. The engine revved and the plane swiveled to the left as Harris held the left brake while releasing the right.

"Get the little guy," Harris yelled. Breckon glanced out to see the small Arab running alongside the plane near the door as the plane started to move. Breckon grabbed the shirt over Ali's shoulders and heaved him off the ground and into the plane on top of himself. Breckon rudely dumped him off with a yell as he grabbed for the automatic weapon.

"Darin, we're both in. Move it! Get out of here!"

Taryam scrambled up the inclined aisle of the plane, momentarily frightened, as Breckon was a blur of motion grabbing up the AK-47 and swinging the muzzle around. He slapped his hand at his waist. To his surprise, the spare magazine was still there. Unlatching the empty, he let it fall. He grabbed for the spare from his waistband. It snagged on his shirt, and he lost his grip on the magazine. It clattered to the deck and out the door. Lunging after it, he snatched it as it was on its way into the slipstream. Regaining his balance he shoved it into the bottom of the weapon and jacked a round into the chamber.

Harris fought the crosswind. He got the tail up and the weight of the plane was only on the left wheel. The plane wanted to tip to the left. A little more speed, and he'd have the wheels clear of the ground, and he could let the plane drift with the wind. Stars appeared in the Plexiglas near the top of the windshield. Harris felt small pieces of the plastic falling on his face. He shouted to Breckon and pointed at the bullet holes.

Looking back, Breckon could no longer see the hangar door, though men were running out to shoot at the fleeing plane. Breckon could not shoot back for fear of hitting the tail surfaces of the aircraft. He saw muzzle flashes off toward the left front of the plane. That's what Harris had meant about the bullet holes in the windshield. Two men were shooting at them. He heard tap, tap, tap, as bullets hit the plane. "Not now you scum suckers. Not when we're this close," Breckon howled. He unleashed a burst at the men. One fell, the other kept shooting.

Finally, Harris got the last wheel off the ground. The plane instantly slid to the left with the wind and the wings started to come level. As they did, an unexpectedly strong gust of wind nearly dropped the wing tip into the ground.

Breckon finally made contact with the second shooter as he saw several slugs hit the soldier in the upper chest and neck. In his wrench of death, his weapon dropped as he stood straight up. The left wing was coming up as Harris fought for control. The lower wing interrupted the man's death stride, striking him in the lower chest. He momentarily folded over the leading edge of the lower left wing and was picked off the ground. The sudden impact sent blood gushing down the top cord of the wing. As the wing rose, the man fell free. Breckon's eyes unconsciously followed the man as he tumbled in the sand mere feet from him. The body quickly passed from sight behind the buffeted plane. Watching in detached curiosity, Breckon saw the dark stain on the top of the wing smear along by the flow of air. As it reached the trailing edge, black drops flicked off into the slipstream of the airfoil. He felt his mind had been beaten until it gave up its sanity.

They were still taking small-arms fire from the Iraqis at the hangar, but, the soldiers, not taking into account the side drift of the plane and increasing distance, were hitting only the lower right wing. Harris watched with alarm as the side drift carried them toward the sand dune on the southeast side of the runway. He had been keeping the plane near the ground to gain speed and hence distance from the hangar. Suddenly he needed altitude, and needed it now. Banking the plane to the right, it looked like the sidewise drift would smash them into the sand. To his relief, the stream of air being forced up by the sand dune carried the plane on its oversized wings up with it, and they cleared the top with feet to spare. They were up and free of the site.

Rather than diving behind the dune, Harris climbed into the wind. Keying his mike, he said, "Green Horse this is Gold Trumpet. Over."

Nothing. "Green Horse this is Gold Trumpet. Over."

Harris thought it was likely they weren't expecting a call from him so he checked the call sign. He wondered who had come up with these call signs anyway. It sounded like something Gibbon would do.

Then, "Gold Trumpet, this is Green Horse Light. Go ahead."

"This is Gold Trumpet. Thanks for the help. But, we saw two dozen Locusts five miles to the north, northwest of Bottomless Pit. We have Jasper Stone. Do you copy?" Locust was the code name for Iraqi armor.

"Gold Trumpet, this is Green Horse Light. We copy. Thanks for the warning. Out."

NSA headquarters Fort Mead, Maryland

White horse, red horse, black horse, and especially green house had been put into the top priority list of flag-words to all of Echelon's listening stations. If they showed up, these transmissions would be sent to the sponsor in real time. Greg Daley was feeling pretty good that his dogging of the messages surrounding an ill-fated flight in the Libyan Desert had reached a top-priority task. He was doing some routine analyses when a message appeared in a rectangle on his monitor. It read, "A priority intercept has occurred. Do you want to see it now?"

He clicked on the "YES" button with a swift movement of his mouse.

At the top of the screen that appeared next was, "Flag word: Green Horse." Under this was the text of messages as they were being intercepted. Near the bottom of the screen was more information such as the receiving station as England, and the origin of the message as Iraq.

He scanned the messages transcribed into text from the voice intercepts. Associated messages in Arabic were also translated into English, and then transcribed, all in real time by the powerful NSA computers. Daley reached for his phone and punched in a phone number.

"Sir, they're at it again, and yes, as we thought, Green Horse has appeared. It's hard to tell the exact location since we're in real time, but it appears they're some distance inside Iraq now. Yes, sir, thank you. I'll stay on it."

— 27 —

Green Horse 1 and 2 watched the hangar door close but couldn't shoot for fear of hitting the plane. The shallow angle made it look like the door was nearly closed when the plane finally swiveled counter clockwise and started to move. Instantly the gunners of the two waiting tanks pressed the fire button. Two bright orange plums of flame pierced the gathering dusk. Dust erupted from the base of the door as first a sabot and then a HEAT round struck. Seconds later two more projectiles hit their mark. The 25-mm canon on Rebic's Bradley sent armor-piercing rounds along the edge of the base. The door stopped moving. Rebic keyed his mike and said, "Green Horse 1, this is Green Horse Light. Forward."

The four M1s and two Bradleys charged across the kilometer to the hangar. Streams of 25 mm exploding shells from the Bradleys destroyed the few vehicles in the area. Green Horse 5 and 6 made a swing several kilometers to the south to check out the path of egress. Green Horse 3 and 4 probed north toward the expected advance of the Locusts. Green Horse 1 and 2 patrolled closer in. Green Horse Light entered the hangar. As the turret of the Bradley panned back and forth, men began stepping out with hands raised. Green Horse Dark came as far as the door, and after searching the dark pocket with a long burst from the coaxial machine gun, swiveled around and faced partly into the hangar and partly toward the runway.

Green Horse Light proceeded toward the back of the hangar, crushing work tables, crates, and anything else in the way. The gunner spoke in the intercom first. "Tom, what's happened here? These men are tending wounded. Look, to the right on the floor. Bodies are laid out." Rebic moved his Bradley to the far end of the hangar and the driver, pivoted the machine in place to face the hangar door from the northwest corner. The Iraqis stood transfixed as Rebic opened his hatch on the Bradley.

"Okay, Chuck," Rebic said to the gunner, "Keep 'em in line. Lower the ramp and we're off."

The ramp lowered and the first two to exit took up kneeling positions one on the right and one on the left with their M16s at the ready. "Guess the concealed door won't be a problem," said Riley pointing to a partially open metal door hanging on one hinge. Two men dashed for the door. In seconds one appeared and motioned for the others to come. Rebic was next, followed by the other four in pairs. Rebic saw the badly mutilated body of the man who was closest to the hand grenade when it exploded. From the tracks in the blood, it looked like others had been carried out leaving the dead man for later.

Descending the steps, seven men were accompanied by a sense of foreboding. The inadequately lit stairwell smelled of smoke and blood. They had a wracking horror of someone waiting at every flight of steps, the fear of being shot at in the confined space. The strange echoes might be someone below them or the lonely sound of their own foot falls. As they descended ever deeper into the earth, the sense of dread grew worse.

At each landing, the lead men cautiously peered around the center wall, and then proceeded. Finally, the lead men were at the bottom. There was no way to go but through the door. Rebic at the top of the last flight of steps motioned them on. One man pulled the door open and stepped back as the second swept his M16 from vertical to horizontal through the door. The corridor tube was empty.

As silently as possible Rebic joined them followed by the others. Rebic motioned to Riley and Kardell to go to the third tube. Rebic noted with a moment's amusement that Kardell was really getting into the "Delta Force" thing as he held his M16 vertically and moved silently behind Riley, looking all around. Riley tried the door. It was locked. Riley examined it with a small flashlight. He motioned to Kardell, who pulled a bolt cutter out of Riley's pack. Kardell put the handle of the cutter through the door handle loop. Slinging his M16 over his shoulder, he leaned on the cutter with all his weight. A snap and crunch sounded as the handle turned. The door opened. They rushed in. There was a shout and then silence.

One of the two corridor sentries looked in. He nodded okay. Rebic motioned to the bay door. It was not locked and one by one the three entered. Two on the metal landing inside the door and one on the steps searched the bay as they held their M16s poised to fire. Rebic and his men expected automatic weapons to appear and blast at them. Two-thirds of the way to the far end of the room, they saw men lying on the floor and one lying on the worktable.

Hardly looking where they were going, they slowly descended toward the floor of the bay. They constantly swept their ready M16s from side to side thinking each breath could be their last. As the first man reached the bottom of the stairs, he stepped on one of the dead guards. Looking down he gasped. "Tom, look at this. Each with a bullet hole in his head."

"Quiet," Rebic whispered as he motioned him on. All three stepped over the corpses as best they could. As they cautiously moved forward, they looked for a possible ambush. The only sound was the hushed whine of the servo motors, the only movement the ballet of the machines as they passed blocks from one to the other. The dead man hanging by his foot in the cables rhythmically swayed to and fro as the robots went about their task. They approached the three dead men. They stood frozen, looking at the scene of horror before them.

Finally, the man on Rebic's right said, "Couldn't he have shot them? My God, look, this one has a screwdriver rammed right through his head. How could anyone do that?"

"And the guy with the roller chain wrapped around his neck," said Rebic's other companion. "And, yuck, the one with his head chopped off," wincing as he pointed.

"I'd say this," said Rebic. "Somebody was *really* pissed off. If you ever run into him, be nice."

Harvey, one of the men with Rebic, said as he watched the robots, "These machines are positively spooky. Look, they've been trained to pick up blocks and pass them from one to the other. Now the blocks are getting hard for this one to find, so it's digging under that headless man's body and pulling them out dripping with blood. It doesn't seem to faze them. Well, why should it? They're only machines." After a pause he finished, "I guess."

As he said that, the first robot could not find any more blocks. Both robots stopped momentarily. Without a head, the man's torso did not match an anatomically correct human form, so the corpse was identified as a piece of debris. The first robot grabbed an arm and tried to lift him off the remaining blocks, but the corpse was too heavy for the grippers. After a second unsuccessful try, it stopped a few seconds. Then an amazing thing happened. The second robot came to help. Together they managed to roll the beheaded remains of Arzika off the blocks and onto the floor. It was the cooperation of the two machines to perform an unprogrammed task that was the unforeseen and totally unintended result of Breckon's algorithm.

At that instant to their left and somewhat behind them, a terrible groan crashed against their mental fixation on the robots. Instantly the three men snapped out of their stupor, spun and dropped to the floor, weapons at the ready. The closest man inched closer and gradually got up with his mouth open. Motioning the others to advance, he said, "Here's one that's still alive, but probably not for long." The three stared at the pathetic man nailed to the crate with a machete.

Rebic held the men back. "Doesn't look like we can do much for him. We can tell the men in the hangar to come down after we leave. What could have happened here? This doesn't seem real."

One of Rebic's men wiped cold sweat off his forehead. Suddenly he stooped and heaved his lunch. "Okay," said Rebic, "take it easy, Virgil, but get done fast. We've lots to do. Harv, take a look at what's in the far end of the bay. See what's through that door that's standing open. Looks dark. Take my flashlight, and be careful."

The door to the utility room stood ajar. Rebic reprimanded himself for being distracted from his mission. "Virg, back me up," Tom snapped.

Virgil still had a green pallor on his face and was spitting the remnants of bile from his mouth but got up and held his weapon at the ready. Rebic pulled on the door as Virgil swept his M16 into the opening. Nothing moved. Cautiously they entered, almost stepping on Mohed as they fixed their attention on the guard with the steel shaft sticking out of his abdomen.

"Oops, didn't see this one," Virgil said stepping aside. Mohed moved and Virgil pointed the muzzle of the gun at him.

"Don't think he's got much fight in him. Here," Rebic said grabbing a half-full bottle of water. "Let's see if he'll come around." Splashing water on Mohed's head got a response. He opened his eyes and looked up at the two men.

"Do you speak English?" asked Rebic.

Blinking a few times he said slowly, "Yes, pretty good."

Rebic knelt down by him and said, "Let me help you up. What's your name?"

Sitting up with his back against the wall, Mohed answered. "Ashrof Mohed." He winced as he touched the lump on his head.

Rebic recognized the name from one of the messages the engineer had sent from the site. "I am Captain Thomas Rebic, U.S. Army. We have only a short time. Can you tell us what happened here?"

Mohed's eyes fell on the guard. "Oh, look, poor guard. Look like he bit the large one."

Rebic turned to Virgil and said, "Do you feel up to checking out what's up those stairs?" Glancing at his watch he said, "We've seven minutes left. Be careful, but find what you can."

With that, Virgil was off. Rebic returned his attention to Mohed. "That man is only one of those killed. There are more in the big room. Who did this?"

"Was Ed. Guard wanted to shoot Ed. Ed pushed shaft quick at guard. Now he dead," he said looking at the man on the floor. "Ed grabbed guard's gun, could killed me too, but say 'go see your family,' then hit my head." Looking away from the man and focusing his eyes on nothing in particular he continued, "Ed was strange."

Rebic could see the man wasn't completely recovered but being desperately short on time coaxed him along. "We don't have much time. Can you stand?"

Mohed struggled as Rebic helped him up. "Ashrof, I'd like you to tell me what's going on out here in this large bay." As they walked out Mohed saw the men on the floor and froze.

"Who are they?" prodded Rebic.

"Oh, this is bad, there be much trouble. Th-there with the tool though head," he said pointing, "Major General Majeed. He here for special job about tanks. And this one, oh . . . ," Mohed shuddered, "Ed easy to work with things, good with hands . . . chain is tight around neck . . . that chain to drive rollers on this conveyor trail, or what it is called . . . ?"

"Yes, who is he?"

"He Colonel Basheer, he command this base. He and Majeed not get along. And see no head, how could Ed do that? That Shahid Arzika, security top man. He found out Ed. He say Ed not Ed, other person. Ed nice man if he treated good, but fire in him when they treat bad. Poor Ed. They force him to come here. Ed dead too?"

Rebic's patience was almost at an end but this man appeared to be the best way to learn what the factory was for. "I think he got away. What's all this machinery?"

Mohed pointed to the can closing machines. "Those for closing aerosol cans. Moving machines—they now do test job. Smart robot. Their job to help can machines. Help many ways, even fix can machine when fail. Can fix one other too. Won't tell more."

A low moan and disjointed talking startled them. "I almost forgot," Rebic said, "there's one more we found back here by this crate."

Mohed covered his mouth with his hand when he saw the man. "This is bad. They force Ed to come, ruined project. Alwan Najafi say no other way. He need Ed. Now all ruined." Mohed knelt by the man. "Ed say big knife, he call machete, has marking of U.S. Navy. I think we pull knife out man die quick, if no he die slow." Mohed was running on like a man in a trance. "Ed call him snitch. He watch Ed, then talk to Arzika. Ed know he snitch first day. Ed smart man."

"What is he mumbling? Can you understand him?" Rebic prompted.

Mohed began to talk to the man in Arabic and in spite of the obvious pain and loss of blood the snitch perked up and started to talk more forcefully. Mohed replied several times, clarifying what was being said. "He talk like Bedouin, live in west Iraq. I understand pretty good. He pain from terror too, and knife. Say Ed not man, but spirit. Much magic. Only touch thing, then weapon, want blood. Spirit of wild thing," Mohed was shaking his hands in expression as he spoke. "That mean Ed, made sound of demons. I think that hearing come me too. Anguish was on Ed."

The man spoke again. "He say sound like spirit of big cat." Mohed talked in Arabic again. "Yes, tiger, huge rage. He say . . . how I say . . . yes, English say Ed is tiger's fury."

The man's eyes suddenly became very large, and he held out his arms in front of him with his hands facing out. He said something very loud. His arms dropped, and his head rolled to the side as he died.

"What'd he say at the last?"

"He say, no to catch Tiger's Fury—eat your soul.'"

Virgil had returned from his missions and stood behind Rebic and Mohed to hear the last of it. He was carrying a small satchel of stuff he had found.

Harvey ran up, a little out of breath. "Tom we gotta leave, now! This place will blow any minute. In the far end of the bay is a small elevator shaft that goes up to the hangar. There's gasoline running down it. Add to that, the guy hanging in the cables back there's causing the strain relief on the cables to fatigue. If those cables pull out, there'll be sparks as the live wires fall. That'll ignite the fuel. Let's move!"

Glancing at his watch, Rebic replied, "Time to go anyway. Ashrof, you can come with us if you want. We're headed south and can drop you off whenever you say. You've helped us. We'll help you. You won't be our prisoner. If this place burns you'll die."

"I come. Ed say to see my family again. Others no see me leave."

"Agreed."

As they started for the door, it opened. One of the sentries waved and pointed at his watch. As they got to the door, the sentry said, "Riley and Kardell are starting up with their bags."

"Good," said Rebic. "This man is coming along. Others must not see him leaving with us. Let's go."

Arriving at the top of the stairs out of breath, they paused at the door. Chuck, the gunner, had the rear ramp down and was waving them to come. The crew ran the few steps from the door to the Bradley surrounding Mohed as they made the dash. They were temporarily packed in as the ramp came up. This would have to do until they got away from the site. As soon as Green Horse Light started to move, Green Horse Dark disappeared from the doorway.

In the robot bay below, the cable harness yielded to the stress of the dead man's weight and broke off at the carriage. As the frayed cable ends hit the floor, live wires touched grounded wires and made a shower of sparks. The gasoline vapors were waiting, and a conflagration filled the bay. The burning vapors caused an overpressure of one pound per square inch in the bay. This was more than enough to lift the six inches of concrete out of the hole in the hangar floor through which the equipment had been lowered. A vicious tongue of flame gushed out of the opening. Air flowed down the elevator shaft to the bay along with the fuel, and flowed out of the bay through the hole, creating a wind tunnel of fire.

A din of pain and horror arose as men ran for their lives before the searing flames spreading into the hangar. Green Horse Light made the right turn out of the hangar bay as the inferno reached the door.

Rebic keyed the radio transmitter and said, "Green Horse Light is clear of Bottomless Pit, Green Horse 1 report."

Green Horse 3 and 4 were two kilometers to the north when they spotted the lead element of T-72s approaching. It was now fifteen minutes since Green Horse Light had entered the hangar.

"This is Green Horse 3, four Locusts coming from the north."

Blatz patrolling a klick south replied. "Green Horse 3 and 4, this is Green Horse 1. Take them under fire. Then back off to my position."

The M1s sent off two well-aimed rounds each. Three of the T-72s were hit and the fourth turned around. "Green Horse 1, this is 3. Three are down, but we glimpsed many more coming. We're backing off."

"Green Horse Dark, this is 1. We have a swarm of Locusts coming. Speed it up."

"Green Horse 1, this is Dark. Until they show from underground there's nothing we can do."

Green Horse 3 and 4 formed up a quarter kilometer north of 1 and 2 and waited. Then, Blatz was on the radio again. "All Green Horse, this is Green Horse 1. When the main body arrives, they won't turn back. Green Horse 3 and 4, watch for a right flank attack. We have to hold them off until Light appears."

At eighteen minutes, Green Horse 1 platoon spotted armored vehicles on the road as well as on both sides of it. The on-rushing tanks stayed behind dunes as much as possible.

Green Horse 3 and 4, being positioned more to the north, fired first. Immediately they started taking fire from their flank.

"Green Horse 3 and 4, this is 1. Fall back. Green Horse 2 stay with me and keep those on the flank under fire."

This was a practiced maneuver for withdrawal under fire. Green Horse 1 and 2 stayed on high ground so they could see the enemy as they kept firing. They kept moving, changing direction and speed frequently to make a more difficult target for the enemy. At times, they traveled in reverse. When Green Horse 3 and 4 had retreated half a kilometer, they took up the fire so 1 and 2 could get into defilade and withdraw. It was with considerable relief that Blatz heard the call that Green Horse Light was clear of Bottomless Pit.

"Green Horse Light this is 1. We're under fire from many Locusts that are closing fast."

"Roger Green Horse 1. Green Horse 5, Report."

"This is Green Horse 5, looks good for plan Alfa."

"This is Green Horse Light to all Green Horse. Plan Alfa is in effect."
Plan Alfa required Green Horse 5 and 6 with the two Bradleys to run

west and retrace the route they used coming in. Green Horse 1 platoon would head southwest along the road, running at high speed and then stopping to wait for the T-72s to catch up, get into range, fire a few times and charge off again. The intent was to make the Iraqi force follow them rather than pursue the others. The purpose of the mission was to get the Bradleys with their evidence out of Iraq. Plan Bravo was in case everything fell apart. It would be made up on the spot.

As soon as the two Bradleys started southwest along the runway, they saw two pairs of M1s race down the west side of the sand dune southwest of the hangar at nearly fifty miles per hour, on a heading that angled across the runway. With their turrets turned nearly to the rear they fired every few seconds as they went. The Bradleys' top speed of forty-five miles per hour allowed them to keep up with the M1s under most circumstances. This was one case where they would fall behind until the M1s hit rough country and were forced to slow down.

Through their thermo imaging sights, the Bradley gunners saw some enemy vehicles burning. Then the view went red. The image in the Bradley sights was on a red background, unlike the familiar green background used in the M1 tanks. The fire in the hangar had reached the tank containing aviation fuel causing it to explode. Flame gushed out of the hangar door as well as through air ducts that had gone unseen.

Two kilometers to the west, the formation of two tanks slowed as the two Bradleys stopped so half of the men and evidence from Green Horse Light could transfer to Green Horse Dark. The ramps were lowered while still moving. The men were out and in the other vehicle in six seconds. Dust and diesel fumes flooded the interior of the vehicles as they were on the move again with the ramps coming up.

Having left the hangar behind, the Antonov headed southwest. Harris and Taryam both noticed the engine was not running smoothly. "Ali, when those bullets came through the windshield I think the engine took a few too. I hope this sucker hangs together. I think we lost a cylinder."

Back in the cabin, Breckon sat back on his heels for a few moments looking out the open door. Looking down at the AK-47 in his hand, he released his frozen grip, letting it rattle to the aluminum deck beside him. His mind went back to the final man he had shot. Of the two men out on the sand shooting at them, he had hit the first one at a hundred yards. He could not hit the second man until he was point blank. Whatever it was that had happened to him had disappeared. The thoughts of his escape came back in rapid replay. Every move he had made meant life or death. Every one was perfectly executed. His balance, coordination, aim, his entire mind and body flowed in perfect unity. At the end, with that last man on the sand, it seemed as if he knew it was over and the unity was lost. His thoughts went back to the feeling he had had after the Altus accident, that he'd have control next time. Was this it?

As he reflected, he relaxed. The pain in his body lashed out, drawing his mind to more immediate matters. Slowly he got up and balanced himself in the swaying plane. He walked forward. The cockpit door was still tied open. He went up the two steps and stuck his head into the cockpit tapping Harris on the shoulder. Harris slipped the head phone off his left ear and leaned toward Ed.

"Hey, Darin, when you can spare a minute, can you give me a hand?" Breckon yelled above the roar of the engine.

Harris said into the intercom, "What do you say, Ali? Ed needs a little help. Looks like you can handle it alone as long as we aren't being shot at."

"Yes, help Ed. I'd hate to lose him now after all of this." Harris slipped out of his seat and went down the two steps from the flight deck to the cabin, closing the cockpit door behind him to reduce the noise. He also steadied himself with both hands as he went to the rear of the plane and swung the entry door closed. Harris switched on a small light that shown from the rear of the cabin forward. "Man, you're covered with blood. That can't be all yours."

"No, most of it's from when I chopped a man's head off with a machete. But screw that. There's a first aid kit by that bulkhead. Help me get patched up. The wound under my arm really hurts, and it's bleeding a lot, and I'm in a pretty ornery mood. Now that the adrenaline is wearing off, I everything hurts. I'm thirsty, hungry, and tired. By the way, thanks very much for coming to get me."

"Well, you're welcome very much. Let's see what you got. Lift up your arm. Oh, man, what did you do to yourself? There's a long gash cut in your side with what looks like splinters of wood sticking in you. You look like a pin cushion. I can't pull them out bouncing around in this airplane. Here's an aerosol can of antiseptic. I'll spray some of that on first. Hope it's not filled with nerve gas."

"Oh, stuff it!" Breckon erupted in agony.

"Okay, okay, just kidding. You *are* in a sour mood, aren't you."

"Yeah, I am! I've had half the Iraqi Army trying to kill me. They didn't miss by much. Those splinters came from the stock of an AK-47 I was holding."

As Harris knelt beside Breckon, he sprayed the wound with the antiseptic while trying to keep his balance in the bouncing plane. Breckon winced but didn't complain. "I'll put a pad on it and wrap gauze around your chest. Here goes. Bite on a bullet or something."

Breckon gave a short yelp as Harris pressed the cotton pad on the wound. The sweat ran down Breckon's face as he gritted his teeth. "Oh, that hurts. Is there anything in that kit for pain?"

"What happened to the Russian?" Harris asked as he used a flashlight to look closely at the various items in the kit.

"I killed him, what'd you think? Boy, I killed a lot of 'em back there. I know when I calm down and reflect, I'll never be the same. That rat Alwan was right. Moral philosophy doesn't hold up when the going really gets tough."

"What are you rambling on about?" asked Harris.

"Oh, forget it."

"Here's a brown box that has stuff written on it in four languages, and believe it or not, one's English. It contains five syringes of morphine. It says each contains one adult dose. Wanna try?"

"Yeah, the pain is getting worse all the time, and I suppose we're not out of this yet. How long before we get to where we're going?"

"Here, let me put this in your right leg. Your pants are torn so it's easy to get at." Harris used a swab out of a sealed package to wipe the skin, then injected the morphine. "We took a few bullets in the engine, so we're only doing a hundred knots indicated. If the engine keeps going, and if we keep the twenty-knot tail wind, four hours should do it. This will take us to the outskirts of Kuwait City. How you feeling now?"

"Still hurts all over. What's this blood running down the side of my head?"

"Looks like a bullet grazed your noggin and another your left cheek. You were really in a scrap." Harris sprayed the wounds with antiseptic and wrapped gauze around his head. "Where else you hit?"

"There's some metal fragments in my left arm where a bullet hit a steel door jamb an inch away. That's starting to hurt too. Probably can't do much about that, though."

"You'll start feeling pretty good. You'll be on a drug high. But, don't forget you have some serous wounds. Maybe you can sleep. Here's a bottle of water. You've lost blood, and your body'll be craving water."

Breckon drank deeply and sat on the web seat swaying with the airplane when there was a loud *thud* and the plane lurched wildly as the engine surged. Harris fell and leaped up. "Ed, put on a seat belt. Hope the engine didn't blow." Harris went a couple of steps forward, opened the cockpit door, and yelled, "What?"

Taryam spat out, "That Iraqi Mig hit his afterburner two meters above our head. We have big trouble."

Then another flash and thud to the right as another one lit his afterburner ten yards from the right wing tip. The plane rocked violently to the left. Harris lost his balance again, bumped his head on the door jamb and righted himself. He vaulted into his seat, snapped on his seat belt, and put on his headset.

"They'll break this thing apart if they keep that up. Why don't they shoot us down?" asked Harris.

Looking scared, Taryam said, "They want us to turn back. They want us alive!"

Harris frantically looked through sheets of paper he had pulled out of a pocket on the right of his seat. He flipped unwanted items on the floor. "Where's it, that list from Gibbon? I thought I put mine in this pocket."

Taryam glanced down and pointed, "On the floor?"

Harris swooped up the manual and slipped the paper out. "That's it. Okay, let's see if this works. Harris adjusted the radio frequency and keyed the mike. "Sharp Sickle, this is Gold Trumpet. Over." Nothing. "Sharp Sickle, this is Gold Trumpet. Over."

Some crackling sounds came in the radio headset, "Gold Trumpet, this is Sharp Sickle, we have your position. Over."

"Sharp Sickle, this is Gold Trumpet. Request immediate assistance. Red Dragons are buzzing us and igniting afterburners within meters of our aircraft. They'll break us apart if they keep doing that."

"Roger, Gold Trumpet, Try to maintain course. ETA twenty seconds. There are many Red Dragons near you. Out."

Taryam turned to Harris, "Who are they and how do they know where we are? I thought this was a secret mission."

Harris was as surprised as Taryam. "These are the frequencies and call signs OG gave us. Both the U.S. and the Saudis have AWACS planes in the area. They could have been watching us the whole time." It was now 1835 hours, twenty minutes after sunset. Twilight would last for an hour this day.

Harris saw the white knuckles on Taryam's hands as he gripped the steering yoke. He spoke his thoughts. "We have fifteen minutes before we get to the border. If they're going to do something, it'll be soon."

"Hey, guys," Breckon yelled as he poked his head into the cockpit and pointed to the left. "Don't look now, but we have company." They watched as a Mig came past them from the rear a hundred feet away with its landing gear and flaps down. He was flying a barely above stall speed at one hundred thirty knots. That was as close as he could get to matching the AN-2's tortoise pace. As he went by, he motioned for them to turn back.

Harris looked at Breckon, "Thought you were almost dead," he yelled above the engine noise. Once again he slipped the head phone off his left ear to hear Breckon.

"That morphine kicked in, and you're right. I feel pretty good. That is, until they pop us out of the air. He wants us to turn back. What're we gonna do?"

The Mig passed on ahead and swung in front of the AN-2 causing the biplane to bounce around as they hit the jet's wake. The Mig continued its turn and passed out of sight to the rear. Seconds later it came alongside again as the pilot made the same motions along with pointing down indicating they should land.

Harris started to speak, "It's not what *we're* going to do, but what *they're* going to . . . . " The Mig had pulled a couple hundred yards in front of the AN-2 with the landing gear coming up when suddenly the afterburner came on sending a shudder through the biplane. As the Mig made a climbing turn to the right half a mile in front of the biplane, a streak of flame passed over the AN-2. They saw the air-to-air missile change course as it followed the fleeing Mig, and exploded in the tail section of the jet. The rear of the plane sank as most of the empennage broke off in fluttering pieces. All control lost, the stricken Mig-25 tumbled end over end until it left a smear of flame across the desert.

Another shock wave buffeted the biplane as Taryam fought to keep it from colliding with a sand dune. They were about to curse the Iraqis again when the unmistakable shape of an F-15 Eagle and its wingman sped past a hundred meters above them.

The entire cockpit roof of the AN-2 was Plexiglas so the view was good as they watched high-performance jets battle it out. Tracks of missiles cut through the evening sky.

Breckon craned his head, watching in stupefied amazement. "Hey, you guys go first class. Where'd you come up with the F-15s? I didn't think anybody would take my situation so seriously."

Harris could see some hurt feelings coming. He shouted at Ed, "Ed, get back there and get strapped in, or you'll get killed. Remember, you are still seriously wounded. Go on now, no arguments!"

Breckon looked surprised but did as he was told.

After Breckon was gone Harris spoke into the intercom, "Ali, as you can see, Ed can't behave himself. I'm going to be sure he straps himself in." Taryam nodded as Harris started back, closing the cockpit door behind him.

Breckon fumbled with a seat belt as Harris got to his knees and helped. "Ed, that hypo will last three hours at most and you won't get another one until we land. You had better get some sleep. Lay across some of these seats, and I'll put two or three seat belts around you."

"Kind of harsh up front, weren't ya, buddy?"

"Ed, there's no way you could have known, but those F-15s aren't here to protect you but to protect Ali."

Breckon frowned not understanding.

"It's like this. A few years ago Keith Gibbon saved Ali's life and almost got killed himself in the process. Ali's father is the richest man in Kuwait, and one of the richest men in the world. Both he and Ali were very grateful. The only chance we had of rescuing you was to go to Ali's father. That's where we got this plane.

"Anyway, Ali insisted on coming on this mission as a way of atoning for having been saved. His father was deeply grieved but couldn't stop him. Well, with wealth comes influence. Those are probably Saudi F-15s shooting at Iraqi Migs. That's something Saudi Arabia would never do, except for one reason, that being, to save Ali as a personal favor to his father. Ya done good, Ed, but in this world, virtue seldom measures up to the raw power of money. Get some sleep now. I mean it."

After Harris left, Breckon lay thinking. He had almost ruined his health trying to do what was right, doing his job the best he could and all that. Then, who saves the day? A poor little rich kid feeling bad because he's alive. But, he had to admit, the little guy had grit.

Plan Alfa was working well for Green Horse 1. Their only fear as they came to within ten kilometers of the border was how far into Saudi Arabia the Iraqis would chase them. The Iraqis were understandably very irritated. As the M1s stopped each time to shoot at the pursuing T-72s they weren't hitting them very often. Maybe the wind sensors weren't working again, but more likely the men were tired. They had not slept well the night before with the anticipation of going into battle. And, it had been a long day.

Six kilometers from the border the call they all feared came in. "Green Horse 1, this is Green Horse 2. I lost my transmission. The engine is still on line, but the transmission's in neutral. All four speeds forward, and both for reverse are gone. I can't move."

It was a no brainer for Lieutenant Duke Blatz. "Green Horse 3 hook up a tow for 2. Four, team up with me. We'll cover you." Each M1 had a large cable fixed to each side of the turret. This was specifically for emergency towing. The crew of Green Horse 2 was already out getting the cables ready. It was dark now and the danger of working with these huge machines in close proximity in the dark was immense. There were two tie points on the front and two in the rear of each M1. They attached the clevis of the cables to the front of 2. Green Horse 3 came up on the left two feet away and then pulled in front, to back up. They made the connections and were off, top speed fifteen miles per hour.

With the engine of Green Horse 2 still running, they still had power to the brakes. Towing would be risky but there was no choice but to take chances. Going uphill would be safe. Going downhill Green Horse 2 would have to ride the brakes to keep the cable tight, and this would slow things down even more.

"Green Horse Light, this is Green Horse 1," Blatz called. "We have Green 2 down and must tow him. Locusts are closing the distance. We'll need help."

"Green Horse 1, this is Light. Use the package you received. Don't wait. Use it now! Out."

Blatz had the frequency set into his radio and pressed the button to select it. Grabbing his sheet of paper, Blatz scanned it in the red light of the turret. He keyed his mike, "Two-Edged Sword, this is Iron Rod Blue. Over." Was he making a call to space aliens on Mars? Who could this possibly be?

Almost instantly, the radio responded in a heavy accent. "Iron Rod Blue, this is Two-Edged Sword. What is your position? Over."

Blatz looked at his PLGR and keyed his mike. "Two-Edged Sword, this is Iron Rod Blue, position is 31° 21' east, 14° 24' north. Many Locusts closing in on me from the north. I have one Iron Rod in tow."

"Roger Iron Rod Blue. Pop two flares in twenty seconds. ETA thirty seconds. Group around the tow. Out."

"Minnelli, watch the time. Twenty seconds. Let me know," Blatz said to his gunner.

"Right," responded the gunner. "*Who* is Two-Edged Sword, anyway?"

Blatz immediately prepared his flare gun with one blue flare loaded and one ready. "I have no idea. We were given that frequency and call sign to use in case of dire emergency." Blatz and his companion M1 headed for Green Horse 2 and 3.

"*What* is Two-Edged Sword?" asked Minnelli with a hint of irritation."

"Don't know that either. Scan to the south, southeast, and southwest, I guess. See what shows up."

"Coming up on time, eighteen, nineteen, twenty." With a thud, one flair went up followed a few seconds later by a second.

Minnelli scanned the horizon by rotating the turret. "There's 2 and 3 a quarter klick to the left making slow progress."

They had closed to a hundred meters of the two tanks when Minnelli said, "There, to the southwest. Aircraft so low they're sucking sand off the tops of the dunes. Must be four, no, six of them . . . can't make out what kind . . . moving fast."

Blatz looked up to be sure the two flares were still dangling from their parachutes. The T-72s were in range and were firing. Green Horse 2 and 3 were taking a devious path to keep to low ground. Blatz in Green Horse 1 kept maneuvering, always staying close to the locked together pair. They fired back at the advancing Iraqis as the opportunities presented themselves.

Minnelli tracked the aircraft with his thermo imaging sight. "I don't recognize the type, certainly not A-10s. There go missiles."

Blatz could see the missiles followed by the fire from 30-mm cannons as they got within range. The planes wheeled and were gone.

Blatz, switching back to his platoon frequency, keyed his mike. "Green Horse 4, this is 1, stay with me. Three, make a direct line to way-point Hotel." The M88s and HEMTT fueler would be monitoring the frequencies and would meet them at Hotel.

Blatz started a swing to their rear to see if they were still pursued. After fifteen minutes of probing the area, he was satisfied the fight had been taken out of the T-72s, so he headed southwest to join up with Green Horse 2 and 3.

By 2150 hours Rebic had crossed into Saudi Arabia and was calling a Blackhawk to pick him up. "Olive Tree 2, this is Green Horse Light. Over."

"Green Horse Light, this is Olive Tree 2. Go ahead."

"Olive Tree, meet me at Oscar. Over."

"Roger Green Horse Light, meet at Oscar. Out."

By 2210 hours, Rebic and the rest of his force were at way point Oscar. A few minutes later, they heard the beat of helicopter blades, as the Blackhawk appeared as a silhouette against the starlit sky. The wind had nearly calmed, and the temperature was in the low eighties. It wouldn't be many days before the winds changed to the damp, chill, southeast winds called the *sharqi*.

From here the armored vehicles would head to way-point Hotel, refuel, and the entire force would head back to the forward base southwest of Ar'Ar. Rebic and Kardell had taken eight of the aerosol cans and most of the documentation with them on the Blackhawk. Mohed asked to come with them to Kuwait. Rebic agreed.

It would take three hours flying time. The Blackhawk had its ferry tanks nearly full of JP8. Normally, the ferry tanks fed directly into the fuel system of the Blackhawk. But, these had been modified so the ferry tanks could be used to fuel M1 tanks and other vehicles. They would have to land on the desert and refuel themselves.

Rebic and Kardell decided to go to Kuwait City. Here they hoped to get some help from the sheik to make their findings public. They saw clearly that they had to go directly to the major world media to get the story out. There would be many people who wanted to keep the story of what really happened untold. At 2230, the Blackhawk lifted off.

— 28 —

1845 hours, 20 September, Jubayl, Saudi Arabia

Yousuf Hamoud thought he had never been so weary as he turned off the engine to his car. He arrived at his apartment after twelve hours of solid driving. The road from Ar'Ar was long and monotonous. He slowly climbed the steps to his second-floor apartment. The light was flashing on the answering machine. He decided to let it be. After having something to eat, he went to the shower. As he was drying himself, the phone rang. He thought a minute. If he didn't answer it and someone had seen him arrive home, it could be big trouble. With a scowl, he picked it up.

"Yeah."

"At last. You must come immediately. Your brother is much worse." Hamoud knew any mention of his brother meant Washington wanted to talk to him by means of a secure line at the consulate in Dammam. He had no choice but to go to the consulate in spite of the hour. He decided he'd take a taxi so he could sleep on the way.

It was nearly nine-thirty at night when he arrived at the consulate. He showed his badge and went up to the CIA offices. The watch officer greeted him. "There's been several calls for you, Yousuf. Here's the name and number to call. You can use the phone in the squad room. It's set for secure communications."

Hamoud looked at the slip of paper. He was surprised to see the calls were from Harold Stanus. Why hadn't he used the sat-phone? He punched in the code for the system to auto dial the number followed by the extension. It was mid-afternoon in D.C. Those desk jockeys never cared about what time it was where they called, as long is it was convenient for them. The phone rang three times.

"Stanus here."

"Hamoud. What's going on? Why'd you make me come here rather than using the sat-phone?"

"Where've you been? This place has been a zoo all day. Must be nice to be out in the boonies where there aren't ten rabid dogs breathing down your neck. Something's wrong with the sat-phones. Somebody in Iraq is using one with our encryption algorithm. That why you didn't call? Most of all, though, what went wrong with *sand fire*?"

Instantly alert, Hamoud replied tersely, "What? Wait a minute. Nothing's wrong. In case you haven't looked at a map, it's six hundred hot, boring miles from Jubayl to Ar'Ar. I drove twelve hours up there yesterday and twelve hours back today. I'm shot. It went as planned."

"No it didn't! There was a big battle out there. More than twenty Iraqi tanks, and a bunch of support vehicles were destroyed. It's a smoking junkyard." The agitation in Stanus's voice was almost palpable.

It still wasn't making sense to Hamoud. "Did they think the M1s wouldn't shoot back? Huh? You wanted a filthy war, you got one. What's the big problem? Someone must have rocks in their head, though. How could six M1s do all that damage? There were only six. I was there and saw them go across the Tap Line Road."

Stanus's breath was strained, "NSA intercepted the radio communications. There was at least a whole company of M1s, that's fourteen, not six. And the M1 guys knew what was coming down. They had been tipped off. They attacked a full battalion of Iraqi armor from three sides, all at once, and cut 'em to ribbons." Stanus continued, his voice was just above a whisper. "Ya really gotta hand it to those tank jocks, though, don't you? They're real professionals. They knocked the snot out of that Iraqi battalion. I never did like this business, and this kinda does my heart good." Coming back to reality, the tone of voice changed again. "But, my friend, our back-sides are grass, and there are some mighty revved up lawn mowers around here. Try to find out where the extra tanks came from, and how those guys found out what was . . . . "

"Wait a minute," Hamoud interrupted. "The brass got what they wanted, some M1s destroyed and some dead soldiers, right? So why's everybody in a lather?"

"That's another problem. There were no destroyed M1s. In fact, there were no M1s found at all. They all disappeared. How could that be?"

Hamoud had to chuckle at how out of touch his counterpart in Washington was. "You knot heads sitting behind desks, that's simple. There was one knock 'em dead sandstorm out there most of the day. I could hardly find the road half the time coming back. Those tanks are probably lost out there some . . . . ”

“Wait. I got a report tossed on my desk. Hang on there a minute . . . . You’re wrong. They weren’t lost. About eleven-thirty this morning, D.C. time, an air base at Nukhayb was attacked and destroyed by some M1s. What’s that, 6:30 p.m. your time? You know where this Nukhayb is?”

Hamoud’s stomach fell. Not only had Rebic learned he would be ambushed, but he knew about the plan to capture the M1. Then they dashed off deep into Iraq and got revenge for someone having the nerve to even attempt such a thing. Who’d have guessed they’d be so mean? This all amounted to double cross layered on double cross. His blood ran cold as a thought hit him. The Iraqis would think he sold them out, that he was a double agent working against them rather than for them.

“Hey, Hamoud, you there?”

“Yeah, yeah, I’m here.”

“Thought I lost you for a minute. You know where that place is?”

“Yeah, it’s eighty or ninety kilometers north of the Saudi border.” Not only could Hamoud see he’d lose his big fat finder’s fee for the M1 tanks, but he’s be lucky to escape with his head. “Tell you what, I’ll poke around and find out where the leak came from, okay?”

“Good man. We have to find out what happened.”

“Don’t worry, I’ll get to the bottom of it. Bye.”

Hamoud sat for a minute thinking. This whole operation had gotten totally out of control. It was time for his backup plan. The plan where he disappeared. His life as a spy was over.

1645 hours, Washington, D.C.

Jason Hughs paced nervously in the entry outside the president’s personal quarters. “The president will see you now, Mr. Hughs,” said the secret service agent at the desk. Hughs opened the door, and the president motioned him to a stuffed chair.

“You sounded concerned on the phone, Jason. What’s happening?” Hughs’s face was expressionless as he began the report that he knew wouldn’t be welcome. “As we guessed, sir, Green Horse appeared along with the rest of the Apocalypse.”

“Jason, my head hurts. Why don’t you tell it to me without riddles, okay?”

"Sorry sir. As I mentioned earlier, the Saudi Air Force had a major exercise going on. Then, Iraqi fighters violated the southern no-fly zone and got in a fight with the Saudis. It seemed to start when a biplane called Gold Trumpet asked for help. That biplane, along with some M1 tanks, code name Green Horse, attacked an airfield sixty-five miles inside Iraq. The Iraqis wanted to get the biplane back undamaged, and when that appeared impossible the pilots were ordered to destroy it."

The president was seated on a sofa with his foot on a coffee table. "What's going on? Did this all grow out of our plan? What happened to the M1 tanks? Did any of *those* get destroyed?"

Hughs was shaking his head, a pained expression on his face. "It appears not. The American tanks destroyed a hangar at the airfield, along with some more Iraqi tanks, and then took off for the border. About five miles short of the border, one of the tanks broke down. They were being pursued by a company of Iraqi armor and would've been captured, but . . . . "

"But what?" the president shouted, "They got away! Is that it?" His face was lined and squished up in a gruesome expression.

Beads of sweat appeared on Hughs's forehead. "They got away, but they had lots of help. With one tank towing the broken down one, there was no way they were going to pull this out of the bag. The best we can tell, there were six or eight ground attack aircraft that pounced on the Iraqi armor. The strange part was it seemed to have been set up in advance. One call from the M1s and, bang," Hughs hit his right fist in his left palm, "the air support was there."

"What," the president was on his feet pacing, "could be so important about that airfield, and what's with that small plane? We need answers! Call Packard and Winton. We meet at 7:00 p.m. here. I want information. All of you do whatever it takes, and get me some answers!"

2345 hours, 20 September, near Kuwait City

Pain and thirst awakened Breckon. His head ached, and his right arm hurt from having lain on it for so long. The plane gently bounced around as before. The drone of the engine seemed more erratic than he remembered. Gritting his teeth, he got out of the seat belts and sat up. Even his shins hurt where he had skinned them getting into the plane. He found the light switch and flipped it. There was a box of water bottles and candy bars tied down to the left of the cockpit door. Easing his way over to it, he fell into a web seat. Grabbing a bottle, he opened it and drank.

To get his mind off the pain, he turned off the light and looked out a window, trying to see anything that would give him hope that his ordeal would soon end. For the next hour he looked in vain. Finally, he saw lights on the ground. There were roads with vehicles on them, street lights, and lighted buildings. When the tone of the engine finally dropped, it was at once a relief and a worry. He hoped against hope they were at their destination and not about to crash.

Suddenly he saw a red light slip past the window, then another and another. Landing lights. It had to be. The plane took a slight nose up attitude. Bump, they hit the ground, then another as the tail wheel hit. They were on the ground! The plane slowed and turned to the right. Breckon craned his neck to see where they were going, but saw nothing. There were no lights at all. After the turn, he thought he could make out a building in front of them. His hopes and fears were up, then down. Where were they? A strange hollow sound engulfed them, as it became totally black outside the plane. The plane jerked as it stopped. There was a brief pause and the engine stopped firing. A silence crept over him as the propeller wound to a stop. Only a faint rumbling continued, perhaps a large door closing. Then that too stopped. For a moment, Breckon sat alone in the dark. The absence of the noise, vibration, and continual jostling of the plane let a sense of peace settle on him. Relaxing, he momentarily forgot the pain.

A second later, unimaginably bright fluorescent lights blinked on. Breckon's muscles tensed, and the pain returned. Outside the window Breckon saw many men, one with a fire extinguisher, a few with weapons, others with wheel chocks, still others with medical equipment. There was even an ambulance in the hangar. The door handle twisted. Arab voices flooded the cabin. One man hurriedly climbed in. Breckon's mind raced considering the possibilities. Would he receive help or once again be a captive? Breckon watched in disbelief as the man rushed past him as if he didn't exist, flung open the cockpit door and began talking rapidly in Arabic. Ali answered, and there were shouts of joy and glee. The man was pumping Ali's hand, hugging him, and dragging him out of the cockpit. Breckon smiled as he realized this must be Ali's father. After they had disappeared out the small door, another man came in and spoke to Breckon.

"You Ed Breckon?" he asked in a soft inquiring tone.

"Yes, I am," Breckon replied.

The man looked at his bandaged head and side, and the crusted, dried blood on nearly all of his clothing. "Can you walk?"

"Yes, I think I can walk. But, I hurt a lot."

"I give you help," he said as he grabbed Breckon's upper left arm.

Breckon winced and said, "Not there, please, bullet fragments in that one." He got up and, stooping a little, shuffled down the inclined deck toward the door. As Breckon neared the door, another Arab reached in and picked up the AK-47. He flipped on the safety as he took it from the plane. Breckon sat down in the doorway and stepped gingerly onto the hangar floor. They brought a gurney next to him, but he said, "I want to walk around to the front of the plane."

Several of the men in the hangar were also looking at the plane, pointing and nodding to one another as they exchanged hushed comments. Breckon limped forward, favoring his right side. He stopped and stared at the large streak of blood on the lower wing. In the light, pieces of dried flesh could be seen on the leading edge. Breckon shuddered as the vision of the man tumbling in the sand stabbed through his mind.

Harris jumped out of the plane after Breckon and came up beside him. Breckon said, "Boy, we took a lot of bullets, I'm surprised none of us were hit. Look, the propeller blades were even hit. The engine shielded you guys in the cockpit. That's why the windshield was only hit high up. Looks like you won't get your damage deposit back, my friend."

Ali, who had walked to the front of the plane with his father, laughed at Breckon's comment. Ali said, "Ed, may I introduce my father."

"Very pleased to meet you, sir," Breckon said extending his hand

"I am, as well, pleased to meet you, Mr. Breckon." Looking at Harris, the sheik asked, "What is 'damage deposit'?"

Taryam chuckled as he spoke rapidly in Arabic with his father. The sheik's eyes twinkled as he turned to Harris. Starting in a solemn tone, he said, "Yes, Mr. Harris, you certainly will not get your damage deposit back. You received an airplane in good condition. Now look at it. It is full of holes. The propeller has dents in it, and it is heavily soiled. There are even bullets in the engine." By the time the sheik finished, he could hardly speak he was laughing so much. Breckon could see this was probably not his usual demeanor, but his delight at having Ali back was too much for him. In a sweep of his arms the sheik gathered Ali and Darin around the shoulders and squeezed them. "Brave warriors, you have done a great deed!"

Al-Taryam's delight was not only from having his son back, but he had his airplane back too. It was the main piece of physical evidence linking him to the raid on the site. In a short time, it would be erased from the face of the earth. After a pause he said, "And, Mr. Breckon, now we must see to your wounds."

They persuaded Breckon to lie down on the gurney and lifted him into the ambulance. The lights in the hangar went out, the door opened, and the ambulance sped off.

0150 hours, near Kuwait City

Chief Warrant Officer Jake Fergerson and his copilot wore night vision goggles. Warrant Officer Marlo Skradski said, "According to the GPS, we've arrived." They were unaware that this was the same place the AN-2 had landed less than an hour before.

When the wheels were on the ground, Skradski went to the rear and knelt by the open door with his pistol out. "Stay in your seats," he said to the blackness where Rebic, Kardell, and Mohed sat. "The GPS says this is the place."

A man approached the helicopter and stopped at the door as the rotor blades came to a stop. "We are expecting two guests, Tom Rebic and Craig Kardell. Might they be aboard?"

Turning to the dankness he said, "You guys wanna get out?"

Rebic said, "Sounds like this must be the place. Grab your stuff, Craig. You too Ashrof. Let's go."

Rebic said to Skradski, "Go back to the base at KKMC and check on the wounded. Then make contact with the rest. Stand down until I get back. Remember we're still working for the CIA, not the Army." Five minutes later, the Blackhawk was airborne and Rebic and Kardell were in the sheik's house.

Mohed was taken elsewhere to be cared for. His family situation could wait for resolution. The sheik, Rebic, and Kardell discussed the situation. Rebic wanted the news conference to be in the afternoon to coincide with 9:00 a.m. in Washington. Al-Taryam did not want the news conference at all but could not oppose it without opening up wider questions.

In the morning, the sheik would, through indirect sources, let it be known there would be a news conference at four in the afternoon in a hotel near the UN headquarters in Kuwait City. The information would imply it concerned recent military activities in western Iraq.

1205 hours, Kuwait City

Breckon awakened feeling stiffness in every muscle, but the intense pain of the night before was gone. He sat on the edge of the bed for several minutes, then hobbled to the john. He hardly recognized the figure looking back at him from the mirror. It looked like a rag doll, all sewn together. He had stitches in places he didn't know he had been wounded. Coming back from the bathroom, he saw a young Arab man standing by the door with his hand on the doorknob. "Please, I am a friend, I am here to help you. How you feel?"

Breckon was still woozy as he sat down on the edge of the bed. "I feel better than I did when I arrived. I'll say that. You seem frightened. Why is that?"

The man said solemnly, "They tell many things about you. You have powers that people do not understand. I am to say your friend Harris is here for you, and Sheik Al-Taryam likes to see you."

"By all means, I must thank him for all he's done."

The man immediately slipped out, and Breckon laid down again. A few minutes later Harris came in. "You look worse every time I see you. Did they get all the parts sewn back together?"

"Your kind remarks are always appreciated. Right now, I feel lucky to be alive, whereas last night I was afraid I wouldn't die. I don't want to go through that again. But, it's not done yet. How am I going to get out of here and back to Minneapolis?"

Harris sat in the chair beside the bed. Breckon took a sip of water from a glass with one of those bendy straws. "You had a CD on you that I managed to decode with the random numbers. It came out in readable condition, much to everyone's surprise. Not one bullet hole in it . . . . "

"And a good thing too," Ed broke in. "If there had been a hole in the CD, there'd be one in my butt too!"

"Anyway," Darin continued, "one of the guys here copied the video onto another CD. I was planning to catch a plane for New York to show it to my agent. He won't reveal the source. We're going to need some money to cover expenses."

There was a knock on the door, and the sheik came in. "Good day, Mr. Breckon. It is good to see you awake. You were wounded many places, though it seems you gave better than you received. We have learned you were pretty rough on your captors as you took your leave. They are calling you the Tiger's Fury. The people in the streets are talking of you. The story will spread fast."

Ed said, "That must explain the expression on the man who was here as I woke up." He paused a minute. "I worried that if I didn't get out to meet the plane, Darin and your son would wait too long and be captured or killed. I didn't want to kill all of those men . . . there was no other way. Everybody wanted me dead."

Harris was eager to make plans so he looked at the sheik. "We're trying to figure out how to get Ed back home. Even if he had a passport and ID, he shouldn't be using them here if he's on vacation in the western mountains of the United States."

Breckon broke in. "All the while I was in that hole, the only thing I could think of was to get a ride back on a U.S. military transport. The big question is, how do I get on one of those planes?"

Harris held up his finger. "This is a long shot, but could this work for a story? What if Ed was in Saudi Arabia working on something in, say, Riyadh? He was beaten up and robbed by some terrorist organization wanting to worsen relations between the U.S. and Saudi Arabia. Ed," he said nodding to Breckon, "you're certainly beaten up. He would then have to go to the U.S. embassy and tell the whole story, get a new passport, etc. It'd get in newspapers all over the world. Neither country wants that. Breckon, being cooperative, agrees to be flown back to the U.S. on an Air Force transport. Somebody gives him a few hundred dollars for incidentals and away he goes."

The sheik, deep in thought, weighed his options. He could make them all disappear but that would be tough, especially the UN guy and the tank commander. Too many people knew about the sheik's involvement. Then there was Gibbon. How many had he told? Breckon couldn't be turned loose. He'd go straight to the U.S. embassy in Kuwait with the story Harris had just told. Breckon would talk to save his life. He would reveal him, the sheik, as the power behind the rescue. It was in everybody's best interest to get Breckon back into his normal life as if he had never been here.

The sheik looked up. "There is someone I know in Saudi Arabia who can arrange a ride for Breckon back to the United States on a transport plane. A story something like you suggested, Mr. Harris, might be used."

As the sheik stood he said, "You had better rest, Mr. Breckon. There is a busy week ahead. And, you are by no means recovered. For now, Mr. Harris, come with me, and we will see to getting you on a plane for New York."

1555 hours, Kuwait City

A ballroom in the hotel had been quietly set aside for use during the late afternoon. When questioned, the hotel manager could not say who had reserved it. A nondescript city taxi pulled up half a block from the Sahara Hotel. Two unshaven men in dusty camouflage clothing carrying athletic bags got out and entered the hotel by the rear entrance. When they entered the ballroom, twenty-five people were milling around. Several TV cameras on tripods were attended by technicians. Electrical cables crisscrossed the floor.

Tom Rebic expected a larger turn-out, though he saw BBS, CNN, ABC, and several other international news organizations. At exactly 4:00 p.m. Kardell stepped up to the microphone and began to speak. "Representatives of the international media, welcome to this news briefing. Let me make introductions. This man is Captain Thomas Rebic of the U.S. Army, Armor Corps. I am Craig Kardell with the UN inspection team in Iraq. My specialty is chemical weapons. A few hours ago, we arrived from western Iraq. This briefing will cover events that occurred in that part of the country during the last couple of days.

"Late on the night of September 17th I was given the disturbing news that my wife in Arlington, Virginia was seriously ill. I immediately prepared to leave Iraq. Early the following morning I was driven to Dammam, Saudi Arabia where I could get a direct flight to New York. As we drove though Jubayl, the car stopped, and a man got in. He told me my wife was fine, but there was a mission of great importance that I was being asked to join. After due consideration, I agreed, and we were flown to a remote site in the Saudi Arabian desert. There I met Captain Rebic, who will tell you his part in this shortly. At this base, the man who met me in Jubayl showed us conclusive proof of a super-secret site in the western

Iraqi desert close to beginning production of chemical weapons of the most diabolical kind. Now Captain Rebic will tell you his part in this."

"Thank you, Craig," said Rebic as he stepped to the mike. "I thank all of you for coming today. About a month ago I was ordered to prepare for deployment to the Saudi Arabian desert. This isn't uncommon, as units from the U.S. Army rotate to this part of the world with the good graces of the local governments for training. This deployment was different. It was secret . . . . "

0905 hours Washington, D.C., the White House

The president had completed his Monday morning security meeting where most of the discussion had centered on the botched mission in southern Iraq. Both Defense and CIA had been caught blindsided by what had happened. If it hadn't been for the Saudi's unexpectedly grounding all U.S. aircraft, or even if the weather had cooperated so the KH satellites could have seen something, they would've had some idea of what happened. He was going to his reading room when Chet Daniels, his communications director, called.

"Mr. President, turn on CNN quickly. There's something about Iraq being fed from Kuwait City."

Opening a desk drawer, he pressed a button which caused a panel to lift on the front of a wooden cabinet across the room. It revealed a TV set. By the time the screen was fully visible, the picture had come in. He flipped to CNN with the remote.

Hotel in Kuwait City

" . . . My orders were to recondition at least six out of forty old M1 tanks left in storage several miles south of KKMC after the Gulf War. They were virtually scrap heaps. Due to the training, talent, extremely hard work of my men, and tons of spare parts, we were able to do exactly that. When you get good men working, it's hard to stop them. In the end, we got fifteen tanks in good condition.

"We were told the Army wanted to see how well the tanks would work after prolonged storage. That changed when I was introduced to a CIA officer. From that moment on, my mission became a black ops. We were ordered to deploy a small force to the west to an area southwest of a small Saudi Arabian town called Ar'Ar. There we trained intensely for two weeks. I met Craig and another man at our base near KKMC on the eighteenth where we were shown evidence of the WMD site. Then, with Kardell along, I deployed the remainder of my detachment to the base near Ar'Ar. On the afternoon of the nineteenth, I received my orders. The morning of the twentieth, we were to dash sixty-five miles into Iraq to an air base near the town of Nukhayb. Next to the airstrip was a hangar buried in the sand except for the entrance. Deep under the hangar was the secret site. We were to make a surprise attack on the site, capture documentation, and bring out samples of the weapons if there were any."

Captain Rebic continued, "At 0700 hours on the twentieth, after we crossed into Iraq, we were met by a battalion-size force of Iraqi armor. The mission had been compromised. There ensued an intense tank battle. In five minutes, my force destroyed more than twenty Iraqi tanks and as many support vehicles. One of my platoons of four tanks took the brunt of the fighting. They had come over a ridge and fell upon a reserve company of Iraqi armor. Much of the fighting was point blank. After the action, none of his tanks were fit for battle, but only two had to be towed from the battlefield. Two men were seriously injured when their magazine took a direct hit and exploded. None of my men were killed. I lost a total of eight tanks, none of which fell into enemy hands.

"After the battle, back in Saudi Arabia, we took stock. We still had seven tanks fit for battle and two Bradleys. An intense sandstorm had developed. We decided to move sixty miles to the northwest, traveling south of the border under cover of the storm and try our mission again if possible. At 1530 hours we penetrated Iraq's territory for the second time and arrived at the site shortly after sunset. This time there was no information leak, so we surprised them. While my tanks patrolled the area, I took one Bradley into the hangar. Kardell was in this Bradley with me. The two of us, with five additional men, went down what seemed like endless flights of stairs to the secret bunker. With two men, I entered a bay being readied to make chemical weapons with robotic equipment.

"There were two overhead robotic cranes and additional specialized metal forming equipment. The only occupants of this bunker were dead men. There had been a fight before we arrived. We have no idea who fought whom. All the dead men were Arabs. It appeared the cell was within a week of going into production. We retrieved two bags of documentation and certain other items. Most of these have been turned over to the UN. After our brief search, we left. Craig, now describe what you found."

Kardell stepped to the podium. "We had received information about where to find some of the weapons. We found several hundred, and selected representative samples to take with us. We also found many records in a file cabinet. We took as much as we could carry.

"Now I'll show you one of the weapons." Kardell reached into his bag and took out a can rolled in bubble wrap. Removing the protective covering, he held up a common aerosol can of antiseptic. "This can of antiseptic can be found in nearly any grocery or drugstore in America. But, if I were to press the button on top, the entire contents would empty. It contains enough sarin nerve gas to easily kill everyone in this ballroom." Murmurs went though the room.

A man called out, "How can you be sure it's safe, and how do you know what's in it?"

"There's no reason to be alarmed. The construction of these cans is as good or better that the original articles. They have to be good to prevent leakage which would reveal the shipments of these devices before they're put into use. In a minute we'll cover how we're sure what's in them.

"It doesn't take much imagination to figure out what something like this would be used for. They would surreptitiously be placed on store shelves. As deaths were reported, there would be a recall. But it's not that simple." Kardell pulled out other items, this time a can of lubricating oil and one of insecticide. "See, many different products. They also have other varieties. Here, a manual pump spray bottle, a soft drink, and a can of pork and beans. Let your imagination go wild. They did. That's why they had robotic equipment. It could handle small runs of different sizes and types of containers. All of the internal parts that release the gas are plastic, so x-raying wouldn't sort out the bad ones. In a week or two, the store shelves would be empty, with only a few thousand people dead."

There were no hands popping up nor questions being shouted. People were stunned. Things like this were only supposed to happen to countries like Iraq or Bosnia. The people of the Western countries had long ago given away their freedom to be safe. Safe from nature, safe from personal failure, and most of all, safe from terror. In one blast of reality, it hit home that a large part of their comfortable lives came packaged in cans and bottles. Each one also knew the governments to whom they had surrendered their freedom would be powerless to stop this terror, other than to impose a reign of terror themselves.

Rebic stepped up to the microphone. "There was aviation fuel leaking into the underground bunker. The fight in the equipment bay damaged some of the equipment resulting in intermittent electrical sparking. It was only a matter of time before the fumes from the aviation fuel and the sparks got together. As we were leaving the hangar in the Bradley, it lit. We suspect there's not much left of the site but charred equipment.

"Now to answer a question. The evidence we were shown on the eighteenth included a sample can that had been smuggled out from the site. We set up our standard army issue chemical detection sensors, and, in a very controlled test, hundreds of miles from any people, we 'pressed the button.' Sarin gas was detected in significant amounts. Our officer trained in NBC agents confirmed that the can had to be full of the agent to give such a large signature. In several other ways, we have verified that these cans and bottles we're showing you are of the same type. This is the real thing. Now we'll take a few questions in an orderly matter."

Hands went up.

"Yes, sir," Rebic said pointing.

"Hal Timton, *Reuters*. Who master-minded and ran this operation?"

Rebic answered. "The CIA in conjunction with the UN, I assume. I was operating under the CIA, and Kardell is with the UN, of course. I also want to say this. From the time I was given my final orders until we left the base near Ar'Ar, was twelve hours. My men had neither means, motive, nor opportunity to compromise the mission. This is borne out by the fact they all agreed to try the incursion a second time. That security leak came from someplace else."

"Yes, sir, on the right."

"Tim Randle, *UPI*. Did your mission have anything to do with the large Saudi Arabian air operation in the same vicinity yesterday? Word has it they shot down some Iraqi fighters and may have attacked some Iraqi armor."

Once again, Rebic answered. "I'm sorry. I've had my hands full for the last forty-eight hours. I don't know what you're talking about."

"But you must have seen aircraft."

"We saw no aircraft." Rebic was relieved he could honestly say he and his crew had not seen aircraft.

"Yes, over here."

"Frank Wallister, *Newsweek*. I direct this question to Mr. Kardell. Is it the policy of the UN to perform black ops as this obviously was? Isn't

the very nature of the UN to put a stop to such operations by the countries it polices?"

"I don't work for nor do I speak for the UN. I work for the U.S. Army
as a civilian in Virginia. I was ordered, not asked, to come here to be a
part of the UN WMD inspection team. I was ordered, not asked, to take
an oath of allegiance to the UN. I followed orders as they appeared to
be."

"Jack Chatton, *London Times*. Who smuggled out the sample, and
how did you know where to go when you got to the site. There must
have been someone inside. Was it CIA?"

Kardell and Rebic looked at each other. Kardell slowly returned to the
microphone. "If we appear hesitant to answer the question, it's because
neither of us knows the answer to it. There was someone on the inside.
We assumed it was a CIA operative. He was obviously a deep cover
agent."

A well-turned-out woman of thirty had been trying to get recognized
and was jumping up and down. Kardell pointed to her and said, "Yes
ma'am."

"Robin Lagenes-Bronson, *CNN*. Captain Rebic, you mentioned your
men a few times. Didn't you mean men *and* women? Did you misspeak
out of old habits?"

"No, ma'am, I did not misspeak. There are no women in my company. Not in the tank crews nor the maintenance platoon. In a rare stroke
of good sense, the Army let me choose my personnel. I was warned at
the beginning that this mission could turn ugly. I picked my men with
the thought of who would be best able to accomplish the mission. We
were in two intense battles and came out with only two wounded, something that wouldn't have happened with a mixed force."

From a seated position, Ms. Bronson shouted, "Are you saying that
women aren't brave?"

Captain Rebic knew he had struck a nerve but wasn't going to back
down. "No. With modern weapon systems, battle isn't so much about
courage as closely-knit, fraternal, crews who come to be part of the machines they use. Most crew members hardly see the enemy. The purpose
of these man-machine composites is to kill as many other people as fast
and efficiently as possible. Put sex, normal or abnormal, into that 'system,' and it won't reach peak performance. Anything less is deadly."

He could see from the woman's expression it was like trying to teach
algebra to a slow fourth grader. He continued, "In addition to that, the

conditions on this mission were horrible. To start with, everyone pitched in to get these tanks running in one-hundred-twenty degree heat. Replacing tracks on a sixty-five ton tank is hard work, especially when the metal is too hot to touch without gloves. Men sweated, men cursed, men stank, men bled. When we marched to the base near Ar'Ar, it was even worse. Before we had plenty of water. Now we had only enough to drink. Don't forget, the enemy we faced had no illusions. They run their armed forces like armed forces have always been run."

Bronson yelled defiantly, "You'll never get promoted after a terrible statement like that."

Rebic could feel himself getting riled up, but he hated the irrational attitude. "I don't plan on getting promoted. After this assignment's done, I'm getting out. Millions of your tax dollars have been spent training me, and it will all be lost. I hope you enjoy footing the bill. You and the lackeys who follow you around don't get it. That was not some garden party out there on the desert. They were doing everything in their power to kill us with three of them to one of us. If one man had failed for one second, some or most of us would be going home in body bags.

"Your attitude is driven by two things. First, you know categorically that you'll never be one of the women out there in the dirt and the stink with a bunch of men. And second, you really don't care how many soldiers die for your misguided cause. You just don't care! People like you believe technology has taken us to a point where fighting a battle is done by people sitting at computer monitors and clicking on the shoot button, all the time wearing camouflage fatigues and fingernail polish!"

Kardell glanced at Rebic and decided it was time to get out of Dodge. He took the mike and said, "That concludes our briefing. You'll be hearing more about this in the days to come. Thank you for attending." Grabbing their bags they headed for the back door.

As they walked, Rebic shook his head. "I guess I really put my foot in it at the end, didn't I? That woman is the epitome of the air-heads running this army."

Kardell smiled. "Well, I'd say you're not likely to make it big as a diplomat. A couple of weeks ago I would've thought someone saying something like that was nuts. After seeing what you did out there, what your men did, I know you're right. The problem is the press will make you out as a Neanderthal, and where that leaves us I'm not sure."

Rebic held out his hand to Kardell. "I hope I didn't make more trouble for you. If I don't see you again, it was a good mission. Thanks for your help and good luck." With that Rebic strode to the end of the block and waved to a taxi parked near the corner.

"Where to?" asked the driver.

"I'm not really sure," said Rebic.

The driver looked back at Rebic, "How about Sheik Al-Taryam's residence? He thought you might need a lift. He has made arrangements to get you back to your troops, if you will accept his hospitality."

"How can I refuse? He's helped so much already."

"He wants peace in this part of the world. War is not good."

The Oval Office

The president was in a purple rage. He stomped his finger on the intercom button so hard he almost broke it. "Get Packard in here now! I want that captain's head on a stick. I want Packard's head on a stick. In fact, get them all back, all from the eight o'clock meeting."

"What about the congressmen? They're here for their 9:15 meeting."

"Tell 'em whatever you want. The meeting's off!"

Chet Daniels had been standing by the president's desk for the last part of the press conference. "I've put out the word to the networks to kill the story, but that last part killed it all by itself."

The president looked somewhat relieved. "Did it go out as a live feed?"

"It appears it did. But, the podium did not have the UN symbol on it, and there was no lead in by someone the public recognized."

"Good. That's good. Put out the story, put it out internationally, that these men don't speak for the U.S. Army or the UN. They're unreliable, unbalanced, whatever we can get away with. Twist some arms if you have to, but bury it."

Chet was already on his way to the door. "We're already started. We'll pull out all the stops."

— 29 —

"Mr. President, the DCI and Secretary of Defense are here to see you," the president's secretary announced on the intercom.

"Yeah. Send 'em in." As they entered, he nodded to them to sit down and immediately opened. "What have you learned? You first, Jason."

For what seemed like the tenth time in the last twenty-four hours, Hughs was in front of his boss with inadequate answers. "We have verified many ways that the operative at the Iraqi site was not part of any American intelligence unit, though he was an American. And, he escaped. If he was killed after that, we don't know. We think he may have been on that biplane, which cannot be found. By back channels, we learned we're getting credit for the intelligence coup of the decade. We got a big fat 'well done' from Israel's Mossad."

Turning his eyes to Secretary of Defense Packard, the president asked, "Vince, what do you have?"

Vince Packard opened a folder and passed pictures to the president. "These are from the morning battle. You can see the carnage. Our men did what they were trained to do, and did it well. Their attack was well-coordinated and superbly led."

"You fools, I told you to be sure not to get some budding Rommel out there, didn't I? You remember that. You were sitting right there. How could you foul up so badly?"

Packard shook his head slowly. "You're absolutely right, sir. We got exactly what we asked for, a man who was good at maintenance and a screw-up at operations. The maintenance part is understandable. He got nearly three times as many tanks battle ready as anyone thought possible. The operations part is a different story. He got low ratings on performance tests because he was always using unconventional tactics. Of course, his maverick thinking was precisely what was needed in this situation. Through no fault of the messed up military bureaucracy, the perfect man was assigned to the job."

Packard now handed the president eight-by-ten color photos of the battle damage to the M1 tanks. He dwelled on them for some minutes shuffling them over and over. He seemed to be transfixed by what he saw. Pieces of the layered armor peeled back, ripped off, pounded in. A demolished engine, the missing magazine. Finally, the president lifted his eyes. "That's a brutal business."

Packard had to restrain himself. In a level voice, he replied, "You sent those men out there to get killed, sir." He hoped he had been able to keep the sarcasm out of the remark. "What did you think would happen?"

Handing the photos back, the president reverted to his normal self. "How do we handle this? We managed to kill the story, but I still hate those two guys for having that news conference in Kuwait. Wasn't that insubordinate? That captain knew he could get court-marshaled for that. And, what he said at the end was terrible."

Here Hughs interrupted. "That may be true, sir. But, we don't know how deeply that feeling runs in our armed forces. If we push this by a court-martial or other legal action we might lose a lot more good men. It's something we really don't want to know. I've had the commander and some of his men debriefed and they aren't saying much. They're scared of repercussions from us as well as from other quarters. As you said, the story seems to be well handled for now. We'll keep working away at the men. In time we'll learn more.

"Remember, attacking the air base was *their* idea. It made sense out of your whole operation. Even though the general public won't be aware of what happened, the intelligence agencies around the world are very much aware of it. And, don't forget, the tank crews know what happened, and we don't. That's their ticket to stay alive. They probably still have some of the stuff they took from the site. On top of that, they had some serious help. They probably don't even know how or why that was set up. I suggest you make a statement to the press supportive of the U.S. troops, and the UN. The UN will have teams there in the morning. They won't find much. What else is new?"

The president growled in a low voice. "It'll take some doing, but I'm intent on getting the UN inspectors out so I can bomb that place to rubble. What they intended to do to the American people can't go unanswered. I figure it'll take a couple of months to get the inspectors out. We'll pound 'em to dust in December."

0800 hours, Wednesday, September 23, New York

Harris managed to arrange his plane ticket so he landed in New York shortly after eight in the morning. His literary agent, Cliff Morgan, was even in his office. Harris told him as much as he thought he could, and they watched the first ten minutes of the CD video. Morgan then skipped around and viewed other sections.

"That's some incredible footage, Darin, but it's not worth much. The story's been killed."

Harris was short of sleep and could hardly believe what he heard. "So un-kill it. This is the real thing. Cliff!" Harris snapped in a hissing whisper, "I was there. All that stuff really happened. I saw two tanks destroyed a second before they would've killed me!"

Cliff put his forearms on his desk and looked Harris in the eye, trying to make up his mind about the man facing him. "Assuming I believe you, and I'm pretty sure I do, you still don't understand. When a story like this is killed, it's dead. You aren't aware of it, but this happens all the time."

Harris was stunned. "That's out-and-out censorship! You've just described a police state!"

"Call it what you want. That's what passes for reality in this world. As an example, do you remember the terrorist bombing of the World Trade Center on February 26, 1993?"

"Of course, the media covered that story in a hundred different ways."

"Yes, all ways but the important way. On October 28, 1993, the *New York Times* ran an article that was different. It told of an FBI agent who had gotten in as part of the terrorist group responsible for the bombing. It was his job to build the bomb. But, he was ordered by the FBI to make it so it wouldn't explode. Then, shortly before the fatal day, he was ordered to make is so it *would* explode. Well, he became concerned, so he taped his meetings with his handler both before and after the bombing. That was the story that appeared one time in the *New York Times*, front page, and then it disappeared. That story was killed just like this one. That's the way things work.

"I'll hang onto your CD. Maybe I'll be able to sell it later as background information as part of a special program on terrorism. We might get something from it."

Harris stood up, looking tired and discouraged. "What you're saying is all of what happened in Iraq really didn't happen."

"No. It happened all right. It's just that the pubic will never know about it. Understand that the vast majority of Americans aren't into heavy lifting when it comes to events beyond their immediate lives. They don't *want* to know. On the other side of the coin, the news managers have their biases. There are things they don't want to tell. The results are that the news you get has been sifted until it's pabulum."

As Harris turned to leave, he said, "Do what you can. I could sure use some money."

0630 hours September 26, Saturday, Lindbergh Airport, Minneapolis

Low-hanging clouds provided a steady patter of rain on the long, concrete runway as the wheels of the C-17 squeaked, making contact with the pavement. An early morning thunderstorm had just passed. Breckon was strapped into the comfortable seat in the crew area behind the cockpit. For the first time in weeks, he had been able to relax and feel safe. However, it had not erased the unsettled spot in the pit of his stomach.

The crew of the C-17 had not been told why he was on board. But, it didn't seem to affect them in their cordial treatment of him. The fact that he was there, and that they had orders to deliver him to a civilian airport was enough. Not many people in the world got such treatment.

The plane came to a stop at the Air Force Reserve station. Breckon thanked the crew for their hospitality and exited by the rear ramp. The sixty-six-degree, humid air gave him a chill. Being early yet for the morning rush of departures, the air traffic was light. The huge plane started to roll, the ramp still coming up. He watched as it taxied to the end of the runway and lumbered into the sky, the negative dihedral of its wings giving it a menacing look.

Breckon walked into the air-station and was met by a sergeant in an Air Force uniform. "That seventeen land here just to drop you off?"

"Yeah, expect so," Breckon said flatly. "Got a phone I could use for a local call?"

"Yeah, sure. Use that one on the desk over there."

Ed called Darin, who said he'd be around to pick him up in less than an hour. As Breckon waited, the Air Force guy tried to get information out of him, since C-17s only landed at Minneapolis International when the president came to town. Finally, Ed asked where he would be picked up. Since the rain had stopped, he waited in the parking lot.

When Darin's pickup came into view, Breckon saw that Cindy was with him. It made sense. She'd want to know what had happed and knew they wouldn't be able to talk about it at work. After he was in and they were on their way, Ed leaned back and closed his eyes. "I wonder if it's finally over? Thanks for the lift, ol' buddy. And, thanks for the help, Cindy. I don't know how you found where the container went, but it made the difference."

"I can't say you look good or bad," Cindy said with a giggle. "Because, I can't see you behind all that bushy stuff on your face."

Breckon playfully bumped his arm against her. "They practically had to use a sewing machine on me. It's amazing I'm alive . . . again."

"Seriously, how are you holding up?" Cindy asked. "Darin told me some of the stuff that happened."

"Guess I'm still numb. Other than that, not too well. Living for weeks thinking you're going to be dead any minute does something to the ol' brain. Then, getting out of there was so bloody. I still see the guy's eyes blinking after I chopped his head off." A shudder went through him. "Suppose I'll tell more as time goes on, but not now. By the way, how are things back at the booby hatch where we work?"

After the remark about the head, Cindy welcomed the change in subject. "Lots of trouble. George is really running scared. The CIA was there on Wednesday and had Plant 2 sealed. I think they're waiting to see if you show up as expected. Ratling is letting on as though you were afraid the gantry robots wouldn't work and cut out. I'm assuming those guys who attacked the site in the tanks found enough evidence to lead back to TAC. I told them the shipment was Ex-Works, so after it left our shipping dock the customer was responsible. That saves us a lot."

"What's on the news about the site?" asked Breckon.

"The story was stopped cold," Harris interjected. "It's off the radar screen, like nothing happened. Oh, they're reporting some military action out in the desert, all right. But the file footage on TV has nothing to do with the place." As he drove he related what his agent in New York had told him. Then he said, "When I get you home, you'll have to call the cops and tell them someone rummaged through your apartment. It took me quite a bit of time the way they putter around. Of course, they dig and pry at you trying to find out why it was your fault. After all, you must really be a jerk to have someone do that to you. Then you have to put your place back together. I did a pretty good job of tossing it."

"Yeah," Breckon said. "You'd better drop off Cindy at her place first. I'm awful tired."

When they were at Cindy's apartment, Ed said, "I'll walk you to the door. Inside the entry, they turned to each other. They fell into each other's arms and kissed long and hard. She was squeezing on some of his bruises that almost brought tears to his eyes, but it was worth it. Finally, they parted.

"I was so worried about you," she said. "I'm so glad to have you back, that I don't want to let you go. But, guess I have to. Darin will think you've been kidnapped again."

Ed smiled. "Under these conditions, that doesn't sound so bad."

0800 hours, Monday, September 28, Plymouth, Minnesota

Breckon made the rounds, carrying a cup of coffee, saying hello to everyone. There were mixed reactions to his appearance. When he got to Thomas, he said, "How, ya doing, Cindy. I went to Plant 2 this morning and saw the sheriff had sealed the doors. What happened? Was there a break in?"

"Hi yourself, stranger. Have a nice vacation?" She made a point to look at the bruises and scrapes on Breckon's face, neck, and arms. "Looks like one of those bears caught up with you after all. I told you, and I told you, but you wouldn't listen," she said giggling. "Seriously, it seems like some people are suspicious those gantry robots didn't go to Bulgaria as we were told. Maybe, they ended up in Iraq."

Several people gathered around as Thomas and Breckon talked. They bantered back and fourth a few minutes, and then he found a desk where the occupant was on vacation. As he started listening to his phone messages, he heard a familiar voice behind him. He cringed. He looked back, and Ratling was standing there with an evil look.

"Where have you been, buster! Deserting me like that. I thought you turned tail and ran because you knew those machines you designed would never work."

Breckon could feel his anger rising as he swiveled around. The man standing before him had ordered him taken to his certain death, and here he was accusing him of running out. "I've been on vacation, George," Breckon said in a voice loud enough so others were sure to hear. "You knew I was going on vacation. I had vacation coming. I turned in my vacation slips before I left. I made copies for my records as well. What's the big problem?"

Breckon was seated and Ratling was standing uncomfortably close to him as he glowered. "Well, the CIA's been grilling me. It seems the gantry robots were diverted to Iraq, and now they're after me for shipping them there in violation of the trade embargo to that country. You knew there might be problems, so you cut out."

"No! You're mad because I didn't go to the site for start-up. If they were at that place in Iraq that I saw on TV, I could have been killed. But, that doesn't seem to bother you. You were the only one who had contact with the customer, remember?" Breckon was getting mad, and he knew he had to stop talking before he said the wrong thing. He stalked off to the men's room to break off the conversation.

A little after ten o'clock, Breckon was called to the reception area and was introduced to two CIA officers, a big one, six-two and two hundred twenty pounds by the name of Burl Carson, and smaller one, five-seven or eight and one-fifty pounds called Mel Winger. After a short discussion, the three of them went to Plant 2. Having talked at length with Ratling, they wanted to interview Breckon alone as well as review the records. Breckon drove his truck. They followed.

The small agent broke the seal on the front door. Breckon used his key card to unlock it. In the lobby he turned off the alarm system and took them to the room were the project records were kept. It was a storeroom ten feet wide by twenty feet long. There were a dozen file cabinets along the wall and an eight-foot folding table with plastic cafeteria chairs around it.

"You see," Breckon began as he pulled out files, "I sent official submittals to a post office box in New York. If there were corrections needed, I received a typed but not signed letter describing what had to be changed. My documentation was never sent back with red marks on it. Then I'd make revisions and resubmit it."

"Were you ever introduced to, see, or even hear the name of, anyone on the receiving end of this communication?" asked Winger.

"No, I can't say I did," answered Breckon.

The two men examined the contents of the files Breckon had placed on the table. The small agent casually took an envelope out of his brief case and dropped an eight-by-ten glossy photo in front of Breckon. It was a picture of Najafi. Breckon instinctively reacted. These guys were good.

"You recognize that man, don't you," the small man shot at Breckon.

Breckon held up the picture and his mind raced. He stood up as he answered, "Yes, I certainly do. He works at the Palestine Deli in Northeast Minneapolis. At least I'm pretty sure that's him. I went in there and bought some dried dates before I left on vacation." As he studied the picture, he remembered it was one Harris had taken of Najafi that night at the plant. It looked as if these CIA guys actually tossed Harris's and his apartments again after Harris had left for Saudi Arabia.

"Wait a minute," Breckon said. "I was wrong. I don't want to sound insensitive, but those guys all look alike to me. I'm not sure if I ever saw this man, but I know this picture. You stole it from someone's apartment. He called when he got home and said someone had broken into his apartment. Hey, were you the rats who trashed his apartment . . . wait a minute. When I got home my apartment had been ransacked, too! You scum suckers! You broke into both of our apartments and totally trashed them . . . you slimy American Gestapo garbage!" Breckon could feel himself getting worked up, and he went to where the big guy was sitting. He pointed his finger at him, about to continue.

The man stood up and faced Breckon. In a quick sweep of his right hand, he grabbed Breckon's wrist like Shahid had done twenty times. Something snapped in Breckon. Instinctively Breckon positioned his feet and moved as he had done that last day of exercise out on the sand. Short step forward, punch to the abdomen, then slap the elbow out with his right hand and grab his opponents wrist and duck under the arm. The difference was, this man was not anticipating such a move. The big man flipped over and landed on the floor with a thump. Breckon did not loosen his grip on the man's wrist. The man cried out in pain. Breckon took a quick breath at the pain as he felt the stitches in his side being pulled.

The little man got up saying, "You can't do that. We're federal officers. That's a felony." He was reaching under his sport coat and pulling out a gun. The large man on the floor was trying to roll onto his side to lessen the tension on his shoulder. Breckon pushed down on his shoulder with his foot and the man howled in pain. With that he released the wrist and lunged at the small man swatting the gun from his hand as it cleared his jacket. He followed through with a left to the solar plexus putting the full weight of his advancing body into it. The small man fell backward and did not try to get up.

Breckon grabbed his hand, and lifted him up on a chair at one end of the table. He went through his pockets, and tossed his badge, wallet and cell phone on the opposite end of the table. He picked up the gun and laid it with the rest of the articles.

"Sit there and don't move," Breckon shouted at the small man. "If you make a try for it, I'll break you in half. I've seen you move, and I'm quicker." Breckon could hardly believe this was him talking. It was true, though, he had seen him go for his gun, and Breckon knew he was faster.

"You'll pay for this," the little man sneered back.

Breckon leaned near the man his eyes blazing. His nostrils were flared, and his upper lip quivered, at times revealing his clenched teeth. "You destroy my apartment, and then try to trick me with a picture you stole from my friend's apartment. You stinking pig!" Breckon was still writhing. He half sat on the edge of the table near the man, and flipped back the hair on the left side of his head revealing twenty stitches. "See that. A few days ago up on a mountain there was a disagreement over who owned the food, the bear or me. The bear's dead, and all I had was a knife!"

"Why is it always me!" the little man whispered.

"Unless you've forgotten," Breckon continued, "we're the only three people in this building. If I don't get the answers I want, there'll be no one to hear your screams!"

Breckon helped the big man up. He made him lay on the table. Standing behind his head, he made a quick blow to the shoulder joint. There was a sharp pop as the man cried out. "There, I've put your shoulder back," Breckon said. Breckon marveled that it had actually worked. Shahid had told him how to do it.

Breckon went through the large man's pockets too. He sat him on a chair next to the small man. The big man rubbed his right shoulder with his left hand. Breckon grabbed a yellow legal pad from the top of one of the file cabinets. He flipped pages until he came to a clean one and proceeded to write down the names and badge numbers. He took the driver's license out of each billfold and wrote down the addresses and license number of each man, glaring at the two men from time to time.

Then he slid the badges and wallets down the table to the men. "You know where I live, now I know where you live. That's fair." He took the bullets out of both guns, opened a file cabinet drawer behind him, and threw them in. He closed the drawer and pushed the button to lock it. Leaving the guns on the far end of the table, he took a chair opposite the two men. "Now, why did you trash my apartment?" he asked in a casual voice, looking at the small man.

"We didn't trash either apartment, they were trashed when we got there."

"Assuming for a minute I believe you, why were you there at all?"

The two men looked at each other for a minute. The little man shrugged. "Okay. What we think happened is this. Two men stole your identities when you and your buddy went on vacation. They used your e-mail boxes to send messages. Did you and Mr. Harris mention your vacation in e-mails?"

"Yes, as a matter of fact we did. Go on."

"E-mail isn't at all private if you didn't know. Some way they found two people who would for sure not use their identities for several weeks. They broke into your apartments looking for your passwords to your e-mail accounts, credit cards, and of course money or other valuables. They made it look like simple burglary. However, agencies of the U.S. government whose job it is to stop terrorism noted the use of your e-mail accounts for some very high profile illegal activities. Being with the local CIA, part of the Joint Terrorism Task Force, we were asked to make a routine check on the two of you. When we found you were on vacation, we went to your apartments. We had duly signed search warrants, a copy of which will be provided to both of you. The condition of your apartments fit with what was assumed to have happened.

"Then we found a very disturbing thing in Mr. Harris's apartment, the photo I showed you. Obviously, it was taken with a telephoto lens so it seemed you weren't close friends, but we did not know what relationship you had to him. By now you know or suspect that the machines you designed and built in this building showed up in Iraq. That man in the picture arranged the sale and shipment of them. I've leveled with you. Now tell us about the photo?"

Breckon thought a minute. "Well, okay. I never had any contact with the buyers of the gantry robots. Ratling always passed along changes and other correspondence from the customer to me. Of course, I was curious. One day a few months ago I overheard him on the phone setting up a meeting with the buyer for that evening here in the plant. Harris had a decent telephoto lens for his camera, so I called him. We staked out the place. That's when he took the picture. Do you know that guy?"

"He's only one of the most wanted international terrorists in the world. If you ever run into him, stay away. He's known to kill without the slightest provocation."

Breckon thought about how he almost killed the little vermin. If they only knew. "Is there anything else?" Neither man said anything. "Okay," Breckon said. "Now, who started that little piece of unpleasantness a few minutes ago?" Breckon said to the big man. "I admit I was angry. But, there was no call for you to grab me that way. You guys break into people's houses and apartments all the time, and don't give it a thought. You know it'll never happen to you. It's not a good feeling to know someone's been pawing through your life. People value their privacy."

"Well," the big man said, "I suppose I shouldn't have reacted that way."

"If you don't tell anyone, I won't. Deal?"

"Yeah, it's a deal," said the big man.

"And you," Breckon asked the little man.

"Yeah, I guess so."

"Fine, grab your guns, and let's go."

Breckon stopped in the entry to reset the alarm. As the two agents reached the door, the big man said, "You really kill a bear?"

Breckon gave a short chuckle that verged on a sneer, "Don't be ridiculous. I slipped and fell on the rocks coming down from the mountain."

The big man following the little man out the door stopped momentarily, turned, and said, "You're some piece of work, Breckon." As he turned to leave, Breckon heard him say to no one in particular, "You surely are."

— Epilog —

Ed Breckon made an impression on the CIA officers. They continued to have his name on the NSA watch list for some time, but they could not find anything to make a case against him. The new line of gantry robots began to sell well. Breckon thought he had come up with a novel algorithm to make the robots work synergistically. He had installed it in the programs at the site in Iraq the day before he made his escape but never had a chance to test it. Due to the brisk sales of the new machines, he never had two identical gantry robots in the plant at one time, so the theory went untested.

Breckon had a hard time getting his life back together. It often came to his mind what he had thought about Ali Taryam when he was on the Antonov AN-2, the poor little rich kid feeling bad about being alive. Breckon came to see what drove Ali to go on that insane rescue mission. Someone who had never experienced similar circumstances could not understand. Breckon not only owed his life to Darin and Ali, but he felt the need to atone for all the people who died so that he might live.

Darin Harris continued his art and photography. Small segments of the video he gave to his agent were used occasionally in the main stream media as "file footage."

George Ratling was grilled repeatedly by the CIA as they attempted to learn more about the customer of the gantry robots. They never stumbled onto the bribe money. However, those who paid the bribe were most unhappy with the outcome of the project. In February of the following year, George was found murdered in an alley in downtown Minneapolis. The crime was clearly an execution, and, as the homicide department had suspected from the start, it remained unsolved.

Keith Gibbon returned home, resolving never again to set foot in Saudi Arabia. Much to his surprise, none of the events he had orchestrated were connected to him, unless the spooks were deliberately trying not to alert him to the fact that they knew.

Ashrof Mohed waited patiently for six months for his family's fate to be decided. He was officially declared dead by the Iraqi government. Finally in March of 1999, his family got out of Iraq with the help of Sheik Al-Taryam. It was a shocking and joyous reunion when he was reunited with his wife and children. Under special U.S. laws that permit foreigners who expect to be killed in their homeland for aiding the U.S., they were allowed to immigrate.

After a couple of years had passed, Yousuf Hamoud began quietly making inquiries. He wanted to get back into the spy game. It continued to nag at him that someone had sold him out. This was galling because he had always been the seller.

Captain Thomas Rebic left the Army within a few months of returning to the United States. Civilian life was not good to him. He managed to support his family, but a large part of him remained in the Armor Corps.

Factual notes

The president of the United States gave the president of Iraq one of the objectives he sought. The UN inspectors were removed in the latter part of 1998. However, Iraq was intensely bombed in December 1998 in what was called Operation Desert Fox. It was never made clear why the U.S. President found that bombing so necessary. The UN inspectors did not return until late in 2002.

If the reader wishes to verify the October 28, 1993, story in the *New York Times* about the bombing of the World Trade Center, he is free to do so. Having learned of this, the author found the story in the microfilm archives in his local library.

The constellation of Iridium satellites continued to work flawlessly. This was no consolation to the investors who had poured nearly five billion dollars into the system, because the system failed financially. It completed beta testing and went into full operation in October 1998. By February 1999, it filed for protection under Chapter 11 of the bankruptcy laws. By April 1999 plans were in progress to deorbit the entire constellation of satellites and have them burn up over the Pacific Ocean while there was still money enough to do it safely. Negotiations with several buyers prolonged the system's life until at last it was sold for the value of the real estate on which the ground stations were located.

In the ten years it took to design, build, and orbit the constellation of sixty-six Iridium satellites, the tele-communications industry had changed. By the time the Iridium system was ready to go, the cell phone system had the mobile communications market cornered. The few cases where a true need existed for a direct-to-satellite phone did not come close to paying off the huge capital investment. Over the ensuing years, the system finally generated revenues in excess of 100 million dollars per year.

The teleplatforms in the C-17 Corrosion Control Facility at Altus Air Force Base do exist. The employees who work in that hangar know the differences between the actual teleplatforms and the one described in Chapter 1.

Forty underground bunkers as described were built in Iraq in the 1980s, as were many hardened aircraft hangars covered with sand. The location of an underground bunker under a hardened hangar is fictional as far as the author knows.

About The Author

Mr. Cody spent a number of years during the Reagan military build-up as a design engineer for various defense projects. This included avionics devices for aircraft programs and, of course, electronic modules for the M1 Abrams tank. Along the way, there were some years spent working on gantry robots.

With the fall of the "evil empire," the defense business slacked off, and the author began a new career in the bulk materials handling industry. This led to employment with a large international company that manufactured specialized machines and systems to handle and refine a variety of bulk materials including petro-chemicals. It was a good company, well organized, with a crack service department that supplied the supervisors for the installation and start-up of new plant and equipment.

Some of the projects were plant expansions in foreign countries. Occasionally, when the time came to begin installation of one of the author's projects, the entire staff of the service department was otherwise committed. In such situations his boss would call him into his office and say, "You go."

It wasn't kidnapping as such, but it was clear that if you wanted to keep your job, you went. Anyway, what could be so bad about that? You communicated with the customer's engineer at the site on a daily basis by e-mail, and followed up with frequent phone calls. He spoke with a heavy accent but seemed to be a decent sort.

You arrive late in the day and find your quaint little hotel is surrounded by a twelve-foot wall topped with razor wire. The gate to the compound is heavy steel. You are scuttled to the site the next morning in an unmarked van. When arriving at the plant, you notice the guards—lotsa guards—all carry automatic assault rifles. You are told that good jobs like that of a guard are hard to get, so they *will* shoot to kill. You are also told that if you lay down a screwdriver, it will disappear, and the water isn't safe to drink.

When it's finally time to leave, the screwdriver has indeed disappeared, and through the hot long days you were forced to drink the local water. To his considerable amazement, the author did not become ill from the local water. One out of two isn't bad.

www.ingramcontent.com/pod-product-compliance
Lightning Source LLC
Chambersburg PA
CBHW032138010726
47494CB00002B/268